Fury's Fate

Olympus Waking

Book One

Shaelynn Long

ALSO BY SHAELYNN LONG

The Changeling

wild thing

CONTENTS

Chapter 1	1
Chapter 2	5
Chapter 3	10
Chapter 4	14
Chapter 5	21
Chapter 6	27
Chapter 7	31
Chapter 8	37
Chapter 9	40
Chapter 10	45
Chapter 11	51
Chapter 12	57
Chapter 13	62
Chapter 14	69
Chapter 15	75
Chapter 16	80
Chapter 17	85
Chapter 18	89
Chapter 19	94
Chapter 20	100
Chapter 21	106
Chapter 22	113
Chapter 23	120
Chapter 24	127
Chapter 25	133
Chapter 26	138
Chapter 27	143
Chapter 28	149
Chapter 29	155
Chapter 30	161
Chapter 31	167
Chapter 32	172
Chapter 33	177

Chapter 34   182
Chapter 35   189
Chapter 36   194
Chapter 37   198
Chapter 38   202
Chapter 39   208
Chapter 40   213
Chapter 41   218
Chapter 42   222
Chapter 43   227
Chapter 44   231
Chapter 45   235
Chapter 46   240
Chapter 47   246
Chapter 48   250
Chapter 49   251
Chapter 50   256
Chapter 51   260
Chapter 52   268
Chapter 53   273
Chapter 54   278
Chapter 55   282
Chapter 56   288
Chapter 57   294
Chapter 58   300
Chapter 59   304
Acknowledgments   309
Excerpt from The Changeling: "The Witch in the
Woods"   312

About the Author   317

This one is for all the dreamers, the ones whose paths never seem like the logical ones to travel.
Dream and wander, my friends.

ONE

I shouldn't have met my sisters for that drink. Now, instead of utilizing one of my more useful talents, I was forced to walk the entire way with the pulsing nature of the city crowds only adding to my uneasiness. Heavy beats of dance remixes reached crescendos periodically as I passed doorways of popular clubs, even as I did my best to cringe away from the rhythmic, thumping sounds.

Shadows were always preferable, but I couldn't get to my destination without passing through the brightly lit downtown. Fluorescent streams of lights blinked in windows of various buildings, and faces blurred together as I hurried past lines of patrons waiting for entrance into various downtown hot spots. Pulling my long, dark hair forward to hide my features, I tucked myself deeper into the leather of my jacket. There were more than a few Creatures who frequented the area, and I didn't want them to see me. I wasn't in the mood for pleasantries, and I couldn't be bothered to break up whatever silly scuffles broke out, as they so often did, between the factions. I needed to focus.

When the hair at the back of my neck prickled, I moved a bit faster, though not so fast as to draw attention, human or otherwise. I shoved my hands into the pockets of my coat, wishing, not for the first time, that I could have pulled the wind around me and swirled away with it into the darkness.

A wrinkled flyer was thrust in front of me. MISSING, it read.

"Have you seen this girl?" a voice asked.

Raspy with overuse and full of desperate sorrow, that voice tugged at me. I granted the flyer another look. Underneath the offering of a reward, a grainy, black and white photograph stared up at me. The young woman didn't look familiar.

I shook my head, an apology on my lips, but as I pushed the flyer away, I made the mistake of looking up. The woman before me was middle-aged with dark skin, deep set dark eyes, and an orange scarf covering her hair. If her voice held sorrow, it was nothing to the deep well of sadness settled into her features.

"Please," she begged. "Have you seen her?"

Even though I looked back down at the photograph, I already knew I didn't recognize the girl. I almost wished I did. She was beautiful. Striking, really. Dark, upturned eyes with a fringe of dark lashes. A riot of dark curls around her head like a halo. The bright smile she wore would make anyone feel more at ease, even if their heart was as cold as mine.

"It's my daughter," the woman continued. "She's been missing for a month."

I didn't say the things others might: that perhaps she'd run away or that the mother really should be talking to the police. I'd lived too long. I also didn't tell her the likely truth—her daughter was probably dead.

The human world is just as dark as that of the Creatures and just as filled with misery and unfairness.

"I'm sorry," I said. "She doesn't look familiar."

"If you see her, please—" the woman's voice broke. "Please help her come back to me."

"Of course."

"Please," the woman said again as she grabbed my arm.

"Ma'am," I started, but a young man came toward us and put his arm around the woman's shoulders before I could say anything more.

"Ma, she said she hasn't seen her."

His eyes met mine, and they were full of weariness and apology.

He'd already given up hope. He was out here with his mother so she wouldn't be alone.

"I'm sorry," I said to him.

He nodded and led his mother away from me. I heard her line of questioning start again before I was even a few steps away from where we'd been standing.

Another human life cut short, and its loss probably felt by many. The truth of the situation was grim.

Telephone poles, cork boards, and alleyways all over this city were peppered with flyers just like the one she'd tried to hand me. They almost always contained similarly grainy, black-and-white photos of young women who hadn't returned to their loved ones. Most, if not all, never would.

I was certain that at least some of those posters held images of women stolen by fairies or wolven. Undoubtedly, vampires played a role, but the humans could be just as capable of turning on one another as the factions were. I allowed that bleakness to settle over me like a second skin. I needed the cold, the distance.

As I continued into the night, I heard the couple in front of me bicker over the mundane task of cleaning their apartment. It was all I could do not to roll my eyes. Keeping my head low and my eyes focused on the cement, I let the sidewalk lead me away from all of it.

Once I exited the park, leaving behind the fountain turned off for a winter that would soon arrive, I turned down a quiet side street. At last, I was fully cloaked in the familiar stillness of night.

I glimpsed the red brick of the house I'd been instructed to look for —the Gregory Estate. Thick, black bars of imposing iron stood at least twelve feet high, serious about keeping people out. That gate, however, couldn't do anything to stop me. I looked around before pulling at the slight autumn breeze until it whipped around me in a frenzy. I allowed it to envelop me, and together we twisted and turned until I stood on the other side.

The wind released me from its embrace and continued through the darkness, dying out into a gentle whisper before it even reached the far line of trees along the edge of the property.

Stealthily, I moved forward through the shadowy yard. I knew

Roland Gregory employed witches in the past, which meant any number of traps could be awaiting something inhuman like me. My last few targets hadn't been so complicated, nor had they been as evil.

Anticipation coursed through me.

I broke a lock on the glass doors leading inside from the large patio where I crouched. Once inside, I was greeted by a large, dark room with tall ceilings. It may have been a ballroom at some point. In its current state, the space was home to overstuffed sofas and a rather large entertainment center. The important part was the room lay empty.

I had expected a dark, smoky scent of magic. There was nothing. I thought through the possibilities of what I might find on the opposite end of the house, but none were dangerous enough to deter me. Perhaps Roland was truly that confident in his abilities.

Stupid, arrogant vampire.

I entered a cloth-draped room with a large, antique four-poster bed in the center, trussed up in rich fabrics of sapphires, golds, and creams. It was sumptuous and lovely, but I wasn't there for the scenery. I was there for him.

Roland was feeding.

Deep set, darker-than-emerald eyes flicked upward to look at me, his pale face arranged in nothing close to surprise. He knew this day would come. Roland rose slowly from the young woman beneath him on the bed. Her long, red curls were strewn about wildly, as if she'd put up a fight. She probably had.

It was why I was here.

Roland's illegal hunting had gone too far and had been happening for too long. Roland and I stared at one another, both understanding the situation in a way that the girl could not. I regretted she was present, but there was nothing I could do. There could be no more chances for him.

TWO

The bodies piling up in Detroit were a problem. Humans were asking too many questions. Spectacularly vicious crimes were splashed across their screens. They were an imaginative species, the humans, and their imaginations were rapidly removing the cloak we'd hidden ourselves under.

Too many people had disappeared or been turned against their will for The Twelve to ignore what was happening. As one of the three Furies, I was to send Roland's spirit to Tartarus, one of the Hell realms —a place for the spirits of Creatures who had been deemed unworthy of Earth.

We did not feel regret, nor did we feel pity. It was not our way. We were created to exist as an arm of Justice, and so we did.

I felt nothing as I stared at Roland. It was not a cold nothingness like what I often felt; this nothingness cleared my mind and readied it for what it might see when I reached out to the vampire. For true judgment, I needed the clarity. Seconds later, after I'd sifted through his mind, I knew what was necessary. There was no bringing Roland back from the edge. He'd made his decision and plunged himself into the madness that too often consumed those of his kind. The victims this vampire had strewn about throughout the years were too clearly seen as

I peered inside. In his memories, I heard their cries, saw their tears, and felt their fear as he attacked without mercy.

With a cruel smile I knew had spread, showing off the length of my incisors, I moved.

Almost instantly, I was behind Roland, pulling him from the bed and away from the young woman. I pushed him to his knees. Though I was deadly, I hardly looked it, and I welcomed the surprise he felt at my strength.

The Creature populations knew we existed, but many did not recognize the faces we wore until it was too late.

For thousands of years, through thousands of lifetimes, that had been my duty as the Alekto, alongside my sisters, the Megaera and the Tisiphone. In this era, we were known as Olivia, Leslie, and Gabrielle Beckett—a trio of assassins, to put it simply—to be guided and guarded by the also-immortal Guardian, Evangeline. We, the Furies, gleefully delivered justice. Our Guardian kept us safe and gave us a point of contact should we need to speak with the Steward, or, if all Hell broke loose, The Twelve.

We attempted to disguise ourselves anew in each century. The Twelve quietly called us forth from the depths so long ago that I had no memory of when or where it all began. We were molded into what was required.

So it was, and so it must be.

I felt Roland try to turn and look at me. He quickly reassessed his assumptions, and I smiled maliciously. I was a living nightmare, a horror story told to newborn vampires in hopes of curbing the bloodthirst that haunted them. Roland was likely convincing himself I was nothing more than a rogue vampire looking to claim riches and territory. The underestimation was a common mistake—one I almost relished. It made my job that much easier.

There was no need to ready myself for what duty called on me to do. In that dark part of my being, I celebrated. I nestled into the cold, dark abyss of my soul and welcomed the familiarity.

I knelt, the blade at my back already in hand and firm against Roland's throat. He smelled of fear. I knew it was the girl's blood in his veins that made him smell that way, and I hated him even more for it. Not all Creatures were monsters, even if the humans might categorize them that way. Roland, however, was the very worst sort of Creature.

I wouldn't feed from him, despite my need. His memories would become my own if I were to consume any part of him, and I wanted no trophy, no remembrance of this.

Roland groaned, trying to twist around and touch me, to see my face, but I was too quick. I already had both of his wrists wrapped in a silver Hephaestian chain. He couldn't move unless I allowed it.

The vampire pressed his back against the front of my body, desire pouring from him in sickening waves. The blade of my knife, glowing beautifully in the soft lamplight of the bedroom, dug harder into his pale skin.

"It cannot be," he whispered.

"And yet, here I am. Justice."

Roland's skin smoldered and smoked as my blessed, silver blade began its work. I pushed the weapon even harder into his neck. He screamed in response.

"I've done nothing wrong!" he protested.

"I think your young victim would disagree, Roland," I said, lifting both of our faces to look at the young woman who lay motionless on the bed before us.

She would be the last thing he saw as his body died. I would make sure of it. I wanted the imprint of her, his last victim, on his brain as it turned to ash. I pulled the knife across, just an inch, as Roland continued to speak.

"She was willing."

"You reek of her fear," I ground out.

He laughed, uncaring in his depravity.

"She's just a stupid human," he spat. "They should have bowed to us centuries ago. Instead, we are forced to coddle them, allowing their ignorance of us to stretch on into eternity."

"You know the Laws."

"The Laws need remaking."

"That is neither your call nor mine," I growled.

"The humans don't deserve protection. The only way to make them useful is to turn them, and this one begged for it." A cruel smile stretched his mouth wide. "She pleaded with me to make her mine."

I had heard enough.

"I see her memories, Roland, and I smell the lie on your breath."

Visions of what Roland did to her assaulted me as soon as I had neared the bed. Her mind tried to force the memories outward to rid herself of the nightmare. Their horror pressed in on me. I knew he had forced the poor girl to beg for her life. He toyed with her, dangled her humanity in front of her face as an impossible dream. She'd done whatever he'd asked.

Through her eyes I saw the wicked smile that crept across his angelic features, heard the mental argument she had with herself as she recalled his handsome gentility when he'd met her earlier in the evening. The memory threatened to choke and gag me. I slammed a thick barrier down between my own thoughts and those of Roland's victim. I had no patience for the game, not anymore. I wanted nothing more than to finish the assignment.

I took a deep, cleansing breath to steady myself. My judgment was clear.

"Losing your touch?" Roland laughed wildly.

He would not reach me with his barbed words. I shoved my anger deep within me where it belonged. The words of the ancient ritual rolled from my tongue and floated on the air between us.

"Roland Gregory, you have broken the laws of your brethren and so you must pay your debt in full. I, the Alekto of the Furies, release your spirit to Tartarus, where you will be judged for your rebellion and disregard. The truth of your nature will be revealed. In Tartarus, so it shall be."

I pulled the blade across Roland's throat and stepped back to watch his body crumple onto the expensive, antique rug. The poisonous blessings embedded within the blade moved through his veins, burning him from the inside out. In moments, he was nothing more than ash . The smoky, gray wisps of his spirit were soon moving through time and space toward their eternal damnation.

My gaze moved to the woman on the bed. I stepped over the pile of ashes without a thought. The human's eyes of deep chocolate brown drew me in as they searched my face. It was as if she tried to memorize my features. As if she would choose to take the memory of them with her into the afterlife.

One of her freckled, delicate hands lifted a fraction of an inch, but it collapsed back onto the satin coverlet. A memory of another frail, fragile human hand reaching for me so, so long ago scraped its sharp nails against my mind.

THREE

Long fingers reached across a thin, well-worn patchwork quilt. Another hand—mine, surely, with those short, blunt nails and callouses upon the palms—reached forward, holding tightly. The pulse beneath my fingertips was faint. Sorrow and panic built, sharp and clanging in a way I thought might shatter me apart.

But I could not see the face of the one whose hand I held. Features blurred and misted, never locking into place long enough for me to identify anything familiar. The waves of feelings threatened to drown me in their roiling depths.

The intensity had to equate to love. What else could be that strong? Tears pricked my eyes just a moment before cascading down my face. A broken sob tore from my chest as I bowed over the hand I still clutched. It was if I thought I could hold the soul within that breaking, weakening body by sheer force of will.

"Don't cry for me, love," a voice rasped from the body on the bed.

"You cannot leave me," I cried.

I heard the well of sadness as she replied. "I would not choose it, but I do not think the choice is mine."

"What if it could be?" I whispered.

It was forbidden, but I could facilitate such a thing. I could save her. I knew it. I could keep her with me for always.

"That is not," she began before a fit of coughs wracked her weak and dying body. "That is not... our story."

She thought I spoke only out of grief, a crazed sense of righteousness that I could change this path. But I could. She did not know it yet, but I could change it all.

"I will rewrite it, then."

The abrupt surety was fierce, eradicating my tears and sorrow. I had a choice. I would choose to save this woman. I would save my love, even if it meant we could not be together, for I would surely be snuffed out by the gods for betraying my power this way. She was strong enough to go on without me. I did not have that same strength. Without her, I would waste away into a shell, praying for Gaia to take me from this plane of existence. I might as well choose my death.

Her hand freed itself from my own and raised ever so slowly to cup my face, but it never quite reached me. Weakly, it fell. I had taken such care to keep her away from the world of Creatures. With such a soul as hers that burned so brightly with life and humanity, I could not introduce her to the world of darkness and violence. Not when she was such a beautiful dreamer. But it was so obviously my only choice.

I remembered the way her hands had moved, so achingly gentle, over my flesh. That was before, when I could feel her strength even through those soft fingertips. She'd gripped me to her with such fierceness as she murmured visions of a life together in my ear. Those hands had held my own as I shared secrets and fears. Those hands meant safety and kindness and adoration.

I could not stand their weakness. I could not imagine a world where that hand never again found mine. I would not allow it. And it was within my power to stop even Charon from taking her, if only I had the courage to take that step.

I leaned over her body, scenting the illness rotting her humanity from the inside. We may not have that future together as we had dreamed, but at least she would have a future. I could not see it taken from her if I had the power to stop it. I whispered my plan.

"You cannot," she tried to say with a strength she didn't have.

Her eyes--I could see them now—were dulling as the life leached from him. I recalled their deep emerald color from times past. I would not forget them again.

"Who will stop me?"

"You know we must," voices said from behind me.

Those voices echoed with a power that resonated within me. It ricocheted and bit into me with its sharp edges. A power could only be held by my sisters. For the first time, I resented that power we shared. With it all, I could save him.

I glanced over my thin shoulder to see my sisters standing there, witchblades at the ready. Rage filled their features, hardening them into nothing resembling human faces. Their otherworldly eyes held pure violence, their jaws held tight, and their muscles strained to hold their bodies taut. They would hunt me if I went through with this decision. It was there—all over the faces of women I loved and stood by.

If I did this, they would view it as a dereliction of duty. It was a clear misuse of our powers. But they could not understand what I faced. I had always known I would lose her, but to do it decades before the years wizened her mind and body was a twist of fate too cruel for even me to appreciate.

"Betrayer," hissed the sister closest to me.

I stood, my own limbs falling into their familiar, predatory stance. I would have to kill them to save her. So kill them I would.

But a whisper of breath had my head whipping around and body lurching forward. The figure on the bed exhaled one final time. The eyes began to cloud in the absence of the soul that must surely have already escaped the prison of that body.

I cried out.

Huddled on Roland's lavish rug, screaming, I fell out of the brutal and terrible memory. I too easily recalled the woman from the street and her pleas for help finding her lost daughter. I tried to shake the thoughts away, but they wouldn't budge. They hovered between me and the young woman, whose shallow breathing clawed through my rationality and knowledge of what I was called to do in this type of situation.

I could not save that woman's daughter, not without completely abandoning my duties. I had not been able to save the one I loved so long ago. But I could save this human. I could make that choice. *Was I ready to do that?*

She, too, was someone's daughter, perhaps someone's sister. I couldn't bring myself to just walk away, despite having done so for the centuries since that ill-fated day. Something about the woman on the street had pierced through the hard shell I'd built up over years of mindlessly fulfilling my duty. Her sorrow, maybe. Perhaps a being could only handle so much, and Gaia knew I had seen more than my share of misery.

I should have been on my way to Tartarus, following Roland's soul, so I could report to Demetrius. The sound of the girl's fluttering heart, rapid and unsteady, made my decision for me.

Damn the consequences for involving my sisters and Guardian. This human did not deserve to have her life so brutally taken from her. I promised myself she would live. I would make sure of it, even if I knew her life would not make up for all the ones I couldn't save—the ones The Twelve would continue to prevent me from saving.

Damn the laws.

Damn The Twelve.

Damn it all.

I wiped the blade of my dagger on the already blood-soaked bedspread and slid it back into its sheath. Decades of habit demanded I at least attempt to clean my weapon. I didn't want to take anything scented with Roland if I didn't have to. The bloodstains on my clothing would be enough to deal with. Later, I could run the blade through flame until it was cleansed. The sheath would have to be replaced.

I scooped the woman up. Her head lolled back at an unnerving angle. I did not spare a glance to where Roland's body had been. It was no longer my concern. Demetrius would receive my report when I was able to flash to the other realm. Roland already burned in Tarturus.

This time, justice would include the saving of an innocent.

I wind-walked out of the manor with the young woman in my arms, in full knowledge it might already be too late.

FOUR

The large, old, brick home I shared with my sisters and Evangeline was as tomblike as usual. Most of the rooms, too many in number for us to possibly enjoy, stood empty and cold. The quiet, rhythmic clicking of Evangeline's knitting needles echoed. Silence continued in the wake of my sudden appearance in the previously undisturbed sitting room. Evangeline showed no outward sign of surprise, though, and pointed to the sofa as she sent out an alert to my sisters, using the amulets we wore at our necks. With that task completed, Evangeline set her knitting needles neatly into the basket beside her chair.

My sisters whipped into the room, Leslie with her inhuman speed and Gabrielle within inky shadows that clung to her.

"What's so important?" Leslie demanded playfully. "I was chasing a rogue wolf through San Francisco, and I'd hate to think what she might get up to if I don't...."

Leslie didn't finish. Her eyes had finally found the woman—the very human woman—on our sofa. Gabrielle stood stiff, shadows scattering. No one moved. For a moment, we all stared at one another across the space.

But there was no time to worry about what I had done.

"What in Gaia's name were you thinking?" Gabrielle finally breathed, her eyes moving rapidly from the body to where I stood sentry.

Being in the house for long periods of time made the Megaera twitchy and anxious. My sister's shadows once again roiled around her body, the only outward sign of anything amiss. I had not expected to see her this evening. I wondered where she had been called in from.

"I don't think she was," murmured Leslie.

The very air around Leslie buzzed with movement and excitement. Pale, almost white waves of her hair hung to her waist, where her own blessed blade fit snugly in its sheath. When at home, we did not hide who or what we were. It was only outside of this sanctuary we were expected to appear less than. It grated on us, but Leslie, our Tisiphone, seemed to feel it most.

I was beginning to understand those frustrations, after these long centuries.

I didn't bother to correct Leslie, to tell her that I had, in fact, thought about what I was doing. I had made the choice in full awareness of what it might mean.

"We should put it out of its misery," Gabrielle said flatly.

The cold blade of my knife was at her throat before she finished speaking. Her shadows encircled my wrist, giving me the sense that I would have my own blade turned against myself if I pressed any harder against their mistress.

"A healer. Now," I demanded anyway.

"You've lost your mind," she seethed.

But Leslie quietly agreed to contact a healer, so I sheathed the knife and stalked back over to where the human lay. Gabrielle gave me a look of pure, dark rage before she left, but Leslie was kind enough to toss a concerned glance in my direction before she made her exit to contact the witch. I was left with nothing to do but sit and wait for the woman to wake.

I had never handled waiting well. I paced back and forth, detesting the silence and how it amplified the human's heartbeat in my head.

"She may yet live, but the body weakens," Evangeline said as she looked to me from the young woman's side.

I sighed with frustration and sank into one of the black velvet chairs across from the sofa. The girl laid there, her skin too pale and her breaths too uneven. Once vibrant red curls lay dull, as if the life had already been leached from them. Her heart fluttered softly, the tie between the soul and the body weakening. I watched her carefully, my concern an enigma even to myself.

I tried to believe in whatever it was that allowed good things to happen, despite not being well-versed at it. I had once known the things people prayed to, and I had no interest in assistance from any of them. Evangeline, though, had spoken my fears out loud: the young woman might not wake.

It would, of course, simplify matters, because there would be no need to wipe her memories of us, this house, or even Roland. Despite knowing all I had done, it would still complicate everything.

Something inside me unclenched with every heartbeat from the body on the sofa.

"You're certain there was nothing in Roland's manor that could tell us who she is?" Evangeline asked, her thin, dark brows furrowed together in the way they did when she was truly concerned by something.

"Nothing I could sense," I said. "Perhaps Demetrius could rifle through Roland's memories."

Evangeline's dark eyes narrowed. She was not pleased.

"Of course," she responded, her voice cutting. "I'm quite sure the Steward has nothing better to do with his time than rifle through one naughty little vampire's mind to find a human's memory, Alekto."

I flinched as though she'd slapped me. Her use of our titles was never good. I refused to let the embarrassment color my cheeks. I struggled for a semblance of the control that usually came so easily to me.

"Pardon my foolishness. I can return to the manor and see what I find," I said in a low voice.

I rose from the chair and bowed my head slightly in deference to my ancient leader.

"No."

A burning thread, something akin to outrage, wove its way through my mind.

Gaia, I was tired.

"If the child wakes, she'll know who she is and where she belongs. We'll return her after she has woken and provided us with such information. We shall not waste our time," continued Evangeline.

We were to protect the humans, were we not? And yet, this somewhat callous attitude toward victims of the supernatural had always been there. Evangeline had little patience for their weaknesses, especially when it turned them into targets for those like Roland.

Silently, I watched as Evangeline perched on the arm of the sofa, next to where the woman lay. My Guardian's eyes were focused back on the woman's unconscious features, taking in the light movements of breathing and of the life we all felt.

Though I was still hungry, I felt no stirring beneath my skin yearning for her blood. I knew it would reek of her garish memories. The scent of fear, tangy and cloying like rotting citrus, still clung to her.

Once the girl woke, we would play on her gratitude for our heroic efforts and return her to life with only hazy memories of what she would believe had happened. It was always easier—for them, anyway. I would remember this night for years to come. I would be left to live with the recollections of the young woman's fight for survival.

"Yasmina is on her way," Leslie said as she bounded into the room.

Gabrielle entered, too, slinking in behind Leslie. I was surprised at her return. Her gaze between the young woman on the sofa and me felt heavy, weighted in distrust.

"I will meet Yasmina," Evangeline said, referring to the healer. "The three of you may go. Return to your duties."

I was immediately anxious at the idea of abandoning Roland's victim. Human matters did not typically interest me beyond making sure my supernatural brothers and sisters did not go beyond the Laws The Twelve set into place centuries ago.

How strange that I felt some sort of protectiveness over the woman, the human.

Leslie paused at the doorway and looked back at me.

"Would you choose to stay?" she inquired.

"I would."

Silence.

"Very well," Evangeline finally said.

I knew she was not happy, but as a Guardian, it was her role to guide and recommend. She would not placate us, but neither would she hide the truth of her feelings.

Without another word, Gabrielle and Leslie made their way behind the sofa to show their support for my decision. Evangeline assessed the situation, nodded, and left the room.

"Demetrius will not be pleased," Leslie said quietly.

"I know."

"Liv..."

I knew she wanted to know why I had intervened, why I cared, but I had no answers. I held my head in my hands. Leslie sighed heavily and moved to kneel in front of me on the Turkish rug. She gently removed my hands from my face. Her eyes, so unnaturally blue—the eyes we all had—stared back at me. Instead of the admonishment I feared, I saw only concern.

"She was just so fragile," I admitted.

Leslie nodded. "They are quite so," she murmured, glancing back at the girl. "But you could have alerted the authorities, yes?"

"I don't think even the humans' advanced technologies could save her. I felt I had to choose between bringing her here and knowingly allowing her to die."

The girl on the sofa moaned softly, her breath hitching on the exhaled sound. I stared, without blinking, until her chest rose again.

Leslie stared at her hands clasped together in her lap, when I looked at her. My hands clenched the velvet arms of the chair I sat in, nails leaving indentations in the delicate cloth. I grasped at the anger and wrapped its familiarity around me like a blanket.

"Do we or do we not service Justice, my sister?" I asked just above a whisper, allowing the depth of my rage and sorrow flood the words.

"We service Justice at the behest of The Twelve," Leslie amended, her eyes finally meeting mine.

"We do not carry out our justice in any way we see fit!" Gabrielle cried, finally deigning to speak.

I immediately wished she had not.

"So she deserved to die because an immortal Creature crushed her will and made her a victim?" I asked.

"I care not for her at all," Gabrielle said.

I stood in defense of a woman I did not know, daring the Megaera to speak of it further.

"I will not—" I interrupted, but Gabrielle held up her hand, and I ceased speaking.

"I care for you a great deal, however," she continued.

"I know that."

"We should not keep secrets."

The words sat there between us all for a moment. The sentiment was soft and pretty, and however much I may have wanted to agree with it, it held too much naïveté. We had lived too long. Gabrielle's head lowered with a sigh.

"This has angered our Guardian. Demetrius will be furious, too. I am certain of it," she said, finally.

"I can handle Demetrius."

"You forget your place," Gabrielle snarled from across the living area.

"No, sister, I believe you have forgotten yours. I am the Alekto of the Furies, am I not?"

I spoke of our trio as it had been spoken of for eons. Though three sisters we were, varied in our gifts and resplendent with talents beyond any human ken, the center of any group was always the anchor. It was there I stood.

The Twelve had declared my position upon the day of our creation, and so it had remained for the centuries of our existence. Unchanged. Unchallenged. We were Furies.

Violence rose within me quickly. I barely had a moment to leash it before the door to the room opened and Evangeline entered with Yasmina.

The mood in the room shifted. Gabrielle's shadows immediately slithered away. My sister schooled her features into nonchalance, and I smoothed my own face into something so opposite of the emotions roiling inside. The temperature of the room even rose a little from the thick chill between my sister and I.

Leslie took the opportunity to blink out—probably back to the wolves she'd been after when Evangeline called her in. I wondered if she would take the opportunity to stay away, knowing what I'd brought home. She may return, just to see the chaos I'd wrought.

For now, at least, we were not visibly at odds. It was for the best. It would not do for anyone to see us that way, at each other's throats and bickering like schoolchildren. No, our disagreements were secretive and dark, so much in opposition to the deep well of trust we had once held between us. The centuries had worn away at our bond, but no one outside this house knew that. It had to be that way.

FIVE

That next evening, I strode into Tully's, a local bar that mostly drew in a clientele of Creatures. Leslie, having returned at dawn covered in werewolf blood, had joined me and Gabrielle as we'd left the house, the previous evening's spat seemingly forgotten. It appeared, then, we were having a sisterly outing.

I sensed a few humans inside, and the grimace on Gabrielle's face said she did, as well. Though the Laws dictated our natures must be kept secret from the human population, the fact of the matter was that many Creatures required some form of human contact to survive. Vampires needed to feed, so they were allowed to keep feeders on hand if there was a signed contract. A copy of the contract was required to be filed with the local Magistrate, a sharp-nosed little demon named Declan. The Magistrates—one per city—worked directly with Demetrius.

Demons like Declan needed the energy humans had in spades. Positive energies like lust or humor were fine, but so were the more negative energies like jealousy or spite. The demons enjoyed spreading the myth that the negative energies were stronger and thus far better sustenance for their kind—the truth was they just had more fun with those.

Demons tended to congregate in larger cities in much bigger groups, but their infighting was something terrible.

Atlanteans, more popularly known as merfolk, kept to coastal areas and towns when not in their hidden city. They fed on humans but held to those who traversed the seas where disappearances were a bit easier to cover up. We rarely had cause to drop in on their territories.

Witches were the exception to almost everything. They did not require anyone or anything. Some chose more natural magicks while others chose the darker or lighter versions. The Magistrate only interfered with witches if their practices garnered human attention: a psychic too right too often or a celebrity who shot to stardom seemingly overnight. Otherwise, even The Twelve preferred to leave the witches to their own business.

Inside Tully's, I sensed a handful of vampires, three demons, and two witches. No fae, but that wasn't a surprise. The fae kept themselves to more rural areas of the earthen realm, as their aversion to metal made city dwelling quite difficult. They were like demons in that they could feed from the humans. Unlike demons, however, fae didn't have to. What they really needed was the vegetation grown by the humans. Fae didn't reproduce well, either—the human myths were dead-on with that theory—so they often needed human assistance to continue their familial lines.

Leslie led us to a table on the far side of the bar where a curvy waitress with blue hair came to take our orders. I asked for whiskey, while Leslie and Gabrielle both ordered beer. The crimson pleather seats beneath us were a bit cracked and worn, but being at Tully's wasn't about comfort. Visiting Tully's was about getting information.

"He's cute," said Leslie, her voice low as she leaned across the table toward Gabrielle.

"The dark-haired one by the stage?" Gabrielle asked.

I watched her eyes drink him in, her mouth quirking in the closest thing she ever got to a smile. Leslie smiled—a real smile. I shook my head at their ridiculousness.

"He's a demon," I said.

Leslie grinned in response. "Exactly."

I groaned.

"Demons are exciting," Gabrielle said in a low voice.

After the centuries of lives we had lived, one would think they would've gotten such things out of their systems. But Leslie laughed, and Gabrielle got up from her seat next to me to slink over to the tall, dark, and handsome demon by the stage. His yellow-green eyes noticed her immediately, a wide grin spreading. I wasn't even sure they'd said three words to one another before they headed out the side door.

"So much for sisterly bonding," I sighed.

"Oh, come on, Liv. You know Gabrielle. We're lucky she even came."

She was right. She usually was. The waitress returned with our drinks. Leslie pulled Gabrielle's over to her.

"Mine," she crowed.

I hmph-ed my disinterest into the glass before I took a long swallow. The burning sensation left on my tongue and down my throat was warm and delicious.

"So... about last night," Leslie started.

I wiped at the slightest of smudges on the table with my thumb, wishing she'd chosen any other avenue of conversation.

"Leslie, I don't—" I began.

"I know you don't want to talk about it," she interrupted. "But what is going on with you? Last night was weird, for sure, but if we're being totally honest, you've been off for a while."

I sat back and considered what she said about last night being the tipping point. That's what it felt like to me as I stared at the woman's dying body in Roland's bed, recalling the moment I had forced myself to stop caring about the humans. It was the moment that had changed everything, when I had, like Gabrielle, started to cling to duty in the way I could not cling to another person.

Suddenly, it had been too much. Too much death, too much evil, too much suffering. Needless tragedy.

Was I getting tired? Many of the longer-lived Creatures suffered spells of madness. I had never feared such a thing, but perhaps I ought to have.

The low tones of a conversation nearby took me out of my musings. A few words spoken in hushes caught my attention, "missing" and "murdered" being two of them. I raised a finger to my lips and looked meaningfully at Leslie. There was a booth behind ours.

I tried to remember who I'd seen sitting there. If memory served me correctly, it was a large demon with blonde hair and orange eyes across from another demon, only slightly smaller with brown hair and dark eyes.

"And then Eowyn comes in all angry-like, says that Vinny and Big Dan fished Liam's body outta the river."

"What was he doin' in the river?"

"I don't know. That's the thing. We reported it to the Magistrate and all, but it just don't make no sense."

"I don't know, Ernie. Dead demons aren't really a shocker, you know? We're a violent group, eh?" The other voice said with a deep laugh.

"Except Liam said that this chick he'd been seein' wasn't quite right, you know?"

"So, she bumped him off. Big whoop."

"Nah, Mick. This *is* a big whoop. The biggest of whoops."

"Yer a dumbass, Ernie."

"I ain't no dumbass, Mick. Yer just not seein' the big picture. Somebody's out there takin' out demons."

"Yer a dumbass and yer crazy."

"I ain't crazy. Just you wait. First Benjamin, then Kiara, and now Liam? Things ain't addin' up."

"You failed math, ya chump," Mick said.

I heard the unmistakable sound of a fist hitting cheekbone, and then the bar was in an uproar. The fight spilled out of the booth and onto the scuffed, stained wood floors of the bar. Tully herself came from around the bar, bat in hand, and I took that as the sign to get out of there as fast as we could. It was best for us not to stick around while it got sorted out. Leslie looked back only once as we made our exit, but the desire for violence glinted in her bright eyes for some time afterward.

———

"Alekto, report to Demetrius," Evangeline ordered as soon as I entered the house behind Leslie. "Tisiphone, come into my office."

With one hand on the blessed amulet I wore, I flashed into Bellanca, the realm from which The Twelve ruled. No one wanted to spend more time in Tartarus than they had to.

I found Demetrius in one of the caverns he used as an office. He was seated at an old desk that was carved, I had been told, from trees on Atlantis, before the city had fallen into the sea. Elbows rested upon the surface, clad in black, heavy robes. Demetrius' interlaced fingers were folded upon his abdomen, relaxed, but that didn't mean anything.

He allowed me to stand in the doorway for a long moment without acknowledgment. That's how I knew he was displeased. I stood my ground, though, with feet firmly planted, and glanced around the office as if unconcerned. It wasn't entirely an act. The dark anger I carried with me was almost always begging to be set free, and I knew Demetrius would be a decent opponent. He had played such a role at various times throughout the centuries, both in training sessions and outside of them. This was not our first row, and it wouldn't be our last.

"You abandoned protocol, Alekto," Demetrius said, finally.

His dark, fathomless eyes met mine. The strong, ebony features of his face were pulled taut. Weaker beings would cower.

I was no weak being, and I cowered before no one.

"I saved a soul," I countered, staring him down as I moved toward the desk.

"You *may* have saved a soul," he argued.

For a moment, we stayed there with eyes locked. Neither of us blinked, and neither of us made a sound.

"What is this truly about?" Demetrius asked.

"I had a choice to make, Steward, and I made it."

Were he less formal I may have earned an eye roll. His grunt of displeasure, though, was familiar, and something about it soothed me just a bit. With a sigh, I explained myself.

"I realized there was a chance to save the human. We would have had to clean up the mess, regardless."

"Is it alive?" he asked.

"The human? Yes, *she* is alive," I said.

"And its memory wiped?"

"*Her* memory will be wiped and Evangeline will have her delivered home as soon as she is conscious and stable."

"Should I plan on a repeat performance of this derivation from your work?"

I felt that flicker of rage that was always with me flare to life.

"If the situation requires it, perhaps you should."

"And do you require a reiteration of your duties?"

"My duty is to Justice," I spat out.

Demetrius' face contorted as he said, "Your duty is to The Twelve and the justice they have decided upon."

"I was not aware duty precluded me from saving a soul whenever possible."

Demetrius sighed heavily.

"I suppose all is well enough," he acquiesced.

I smiled coldly.

Demetrius looked for a moment as if he would speak further but then must have thought better of it, because the only thing he did was wave me away.

"You are dismissed."

I turned and exited before my anger bubbled up and out. I wanted fresh blood, and Bellanca was not the place to find it.

I gripped my amulet once more and flashed back to the Earthen realm, the hunger gnawing at my insides.

I could pretend for a while that it was only hunger.

SIX

I stood beneath the warm glow of the kitchen light that hung over the sink, sipping a goblet of blood. I stared out the window into the darkness of the new moon and took in the shadows that covered the lawn and gardens. Slow, careful mouthfuls soothed away my wretchedness. I was still angry. I suppose I never truly wanted to let it go —not all the way. The rage was who I was. It was what I was built for. Leslie and Gabrielle were the same. Separate Leslie from her vengeance or Gabrielle from the dark shadows, and they'd cease to be themselves.

The tension in my shoulders loosened a bit, though. I took long deep breaths, trying to focus on the coolness of the air as it entered my nasal passages and how my lungs slowly filled and expanded. Barely audible exhalations followed. Settling into my body wasn't something I was good at.

For so long, my body had been a tool used for duty. It was the thing that housed the heart that had betrayed me, falling for a human I would never have enough time with. It had even done the unthinkable, that heart. It broke. Maybe it even shattered. Since then, I'd silenced that traitorous organ and I'd pushed this body to its limits, as if I was unconsciously seeking out a way to destroy them both.

Perhaps I was. Perhaps I always had been.

Out of the corner of my eye, Leslie sat on the railing of the porch. The pale waves of her hair caught the light from the lamp she'd lit. She was a picture of utter stillness, the total opposite of everything inside my mind and body. I moved to the kitchen door as if I could go to her and absorb some of that peace.

Company didn't necessarily sound like something I wanted, but neither did loneliness. My mind was being far too honest with itself. Perhaps my sister could offer me a distraction.

I stepped out onto the wooden planks of our porch and collapsed into the cushions of a wicker chair.

"Better?" Leslie asked, balancing carefully on the porch railing, long arms outstretched to her sides for balance.

I watched her for a moment, each step quick but sure. Something about it echoed the way she seemed to go through her days. I admired her for it. Maybe I hated her for it, too.

"Yes," I finally answered.

It was somewhat true, at least. The blood had nourished me in the way I needed it to. I could pretend that was all my sister meant. Her quick glance in my direction, however, told me she wasn't buying it.

What had I done? Why had I bothered with the human at all?

For lifetimes, I had only cared about my duty. Nothing else, not even my sisters. I received my orders, and I dispatched Creatures to Tartarus. That's how it worked. That's how it was supposed to work.

Leslie reached the end of the railing and swiftly turned, her hair flying in a bright curtain behind her. The sky, just visible above the trees in our back garden, was slowly losing its grip on the darkness. The rest of the world would soon begin rising. I slowly took another mouthful from the goblet, closed my eyes, and leaned back into the cushions of the chair. The darkness enveloped me, and I sighed into its familiar depths.

"The two of you have been so edgy with one another lately," my sister murmured.

"Gabrielle and I have always had that kind of relationship."

Leslie's laugh, a soft sound, carried through the night.

"That I know. I was speaking, however, of you and our Steward." I took a mouthful of blood to avoid responding right away. "I know that the two of you have never really gotten along. But things are different. You aren't just angry in... in—" Leslie seemed at a loss for words.

"In the way that only we can be angry?"

My sister laughed. "Yes. But now? You're pulling at your chains."

"I am not," I protested.

Leslie's gaze snapped to meet my own.

"I would not speak of it if it were not the truth," she said in that dark voice she'd used earlier.

Her eyes blazed electric blue, but I met them, anyway.

"The Steward oversteps himself," I muttered.

"At times," Leslie acquiesced. "But he is trying to fulfill his duty, same as us."

"And just what are his duties? Traipsing around after us, telling us exactly how to exact justice, as if we have not been at this for eons? As if we were not created for this purpose?"

"Your deviance last night impacted more than just Demetrius," Leslie said quietly.

And there it was. The admonishment.

"I made a choice," I ground out.

"But you are not alone."

"I believe we said the same to you about Vallerie," I snapped. The words hung between us for a long moment before I finally exhaled a heavy breath. "Forgive me," I said.

I meant it.

"Always."

I hoped she meant it, too.

I tossed back the contents of the glass and rose from the chair, somehow past exhaustion and into something else that muddied my brain and weighted down my limbs. I moved to the door sluggishly, goblet clutched in hand.

"Goodnight," Leslie called.

"Goodnight," I said, but a glance over my shoulder told me she'd already blinked out, off to wherever she was currently hiding from our Guardian.

I rinsed my goblet and placed it beside the sink in our small kitchen before heading upstairs to the beautiful silence of my bedroom.

I kicked off my heavy black boots and socks, tossed my leather jacket onto an oversized chair near the window, and stripped off my tight black jeans and the long-sleeved black shirt I'd worn out earlier in the evening. I didn't even stop to note if they landed in the basket near the closet.

All that was on my mind was showering so I could climb into my palatial bed, unwilling to take more than I had to with me into that particular sanctuary. I scrubbed my hair, rinsed it, and then pulled a coconut scented body scrub from the stone shelf in the shower and got to work.

Once I was as clean as the soap could get me, I turned off the water and stepped out onto the thick bathmat just outside. I dried myself quickly. Wet hair hung to the middle of my back, straight as a pin. I didn't have the energy to dry it, but if I didn't, there would be a mess of snarls on my head to deal with when I woke. I grumbled under my breath as I dug through the vanity drawers for my hairdryer and plugged it in.

I stared at my face in the mirror as my mind twisted over thoughts I'd tried to push away during my shower.

For so long I had done my duty as expected. I had not wanted more than the existence I was assigned to. I had not craved anything else. My sisters and I kept the world of Creatures in check, which allowed us to have the kind of freedoms we did. Why did that suddenly feel constrictive? Why, suddenly, was it not enough for me? Why did the chains of my duties feel heavier than before?

The questions ran through my mind, and I could not come up with a single answer. I clicked off the hairdryer, leaving it on the edge of the vanity as I turned away and went into my bedroom.

The thick rugs strewn about the dark wood floors felt plush and soft beneath my bare feet. I feared sleep would not come, thanks to the memories of Roland's young victim, but I crawled into bed, anyway. If I had to face those nightmares, I would do so in satin sheets.

SEVEN

W hen I woke, my mood was not much improved, thanks to the host of nightmares and ghosts that haunted me while I slept. Once dressed, I went into the kitchen, opened the refrigerator, and pulled out one of the packets of blood Evangeline had delivered each week from one of the donation centers.

I wasn't sure what the specifics were of the deal—she seemed to make a new one in every city, ranging from us being a very elite medical center or a top-secret lab—but I appreciated that I didn't have to go looking for a blood source like I had in times past.

Blood was best when warm, so I made sure it was the perfect temperature using the microwave—another truly wonderful human invention. I could certainly appreciate that cleverness while also detesting the way it combined with their curiosity. That combination, while it led to innovation had also, at times, resulted in deadly consequences. For a moment, I wondered if it was that curiosity had led our still-healing human woman to what would have been her death. I wondered if, as she'd stared into Roland's eyes, she'd seen something too mystifying to ignore, like a moth to a flame.

Trying to push the girl from my thoughts, I poured the blood into one of the many goblets from the kitchen cabinets. Evangeline said that even though we were Creatures, we were still ladies, and so we must act with class and dignity. Gabrielle usually rolled her eyes at that, but I kind of liked the goblets. I'd certainly had blood from worse vessels.

When I was barely halfway finished with my breakfast, Evangeline appeared in the parlor. I'd been lounging there with Leslie, who'd inexplicably returned to the house and was midway through a long diatribe about the heinous crime that was the return of the low-rise jean. We both sat up at attention.

"Evangeline?" Leslie asked.

The look on my Guardian's face was austere, but something in her eyes was off. Her regular stoicism was absent. Something had thrown her. And while something in me was intrigued to discover just what might affect a Guardian in that way, another part of me wanted no part of it. I placed my goblet on the side table next to me and leaned forward, bracing my forearms on my denim-clad knees.

Evangeline called for Gabrielle.

Our Guardian's voice sounded like it typically did, but with just a hint of worry or perhaps concern. Maybe it was panic? Whatever it was, it was not a familiar tone, and I didn't like it. I felt the urge to move, to react.

This is not good.

"Here," Gabrielle said, strolling through the archway.

Where I was slender, possibly even slight in stature, Gabrielle was all curves. Her dark hair, more brown where mine was a true black, was piled on top of her head in a fashion that I could never be bothered with.

Gabrielle took the cushion on the sofa next to Leslie. I remained in my chair. Evangeline paced for a minute, cleared her throat, and took a seat in the armchair next to mine.

"Demons were killed tonight. A den of them," Evangeline said quietly.

"What?" Gabrielle asked, sounding shocked.

I just sat there. Leslie's growl echoed in my ears.

"A den of demons near the Elmwood Cemetery were completely wiped out."

It was easy to assume we were being sent after the ones who'd performed such a heinous act. That was our norm. But if that were the case, our amulets would have simply shown the names. There would be no need for Evangeline to relay the message.

I don't like this at all.

Evangeline removed her phone from her pocket and unlocked it. The photos she showed us were of a once-lovely home surrounded by pine trees. The house was a shell—completely blackened with soot and ash, a dark and foreboding scene. Our Guardian's reaction made sense.

"The house was set on fire?" I asked.

"It was. Arson seems to be secondary to what actually took place. It was covering up the murders."

"Wait," said Gabrielle.

She gestured for Evangeline to hand over the phone. Gabrielle stared at the screen, her fingers tightening on the phone with each swipe. Her jaw clenched.

"I was there last night," she finally said as she handed the phone back to Evangeline.

"What?" I asked.

"Wait—you were?" Leslie asked, turning to look at her.

"That demon—the one I left the bar with? That is... was... his house."

Evangeline, who never liked to hear of our escapades, busied herself with settling into an armchair. Leslie and I glanced to one another and then back to our sister.

Gabrielle, features devoid of emotion, shrugged.

"How many?" Leslie asked.

A witchblade was already out and twirling in her hand as she took in the information.

"At least eight."

"There were twice as many there last night. There was a party. The fire must have happened much later," Gabrielle said.

"How were they murdered?" I asked Evangeline.

"Throats slit."

"With?"

"An athame of some kind, it seems. Possibly a witchblade."

I could not look at Gabrielle as I thought about the witchblades we all carried. I couldn't help glancing to the one in Leslie's hands.

Could she have done such a thing? Could Gabrielle?

The thought seemed ludicrous. Such deviance from our duty would have been shocking.

Witchblades weren't terribly uncommon, after all. But they were expensive, which naturally limited the pool of potential owners. The fact they were made of Hephaestian steel, blessed by a witch, and then named under a full moon meant only a select few could get their hands on one. Witchblades made rounds, at times, through the underground markets, however. It could have been just a coincidence. But I'd never really believed in coincidences.

———

Later, Leslie and I patrolled the neighborhood. Since we had no one to hunt, we took to the city streets, neighborhoods, and parks to keep ourselves moving and busy.

The evening was quiet, however, and that came with its own sense of unease. We had meandered down paths familiar to us, but I also led us down and around the art academy. It was so brightly lit at all hours of the day and night that it would have been uncommon—and idiotic— for anyone or anything to illegally hunt there.

"Should I be concerned that you've stuck around here for so long? It's unusual," I said to my sister as we rounded yet another city block.

"Should I be concerned that you're saving humans?"

"Not really the same thing."

"Puts us in positions we're not typically in, though."

I stopped and looked at her.

"Leslie, why are you here? You never stick around for this long between jobs. Why aren't you in London or Istanbul or, I don't know, Tokyo?"

"I'm tired of Tokyo."

"You've only been there a few months."

"Still."

We started walking again. It was clear that Leslie didn't want to elaborate on her reasoning for staying in Detroit. Leslie traveled from city to city, and though we suspected Gabrielle had her own private hideaway somewhere, none of us were certain where it was. We'd narrowed it to Australia, but I thought she was in Melbourne, and Leslie insisted it was Sydney.

"If Detroit wasn't suddenly so interesting," Leslie mused as we walked along the path that led from the sidewalk to our house, "maybe I wouldn't want to stick around."

She winked at me and skipped off into the house. A happy Leslie was odd, indeed. I preferred her angst.

Evangeline returned home just after Leslie and me. Almost as soon as she appeared, the amulet hanging from my neck grew warm. Glancing down, I watched the names of those who required dispatching scroll through the mist inside the black stone. My sisters, both of whom were in the parlor with me, did not seem bothered by it. Something about the number of names I saw grated on me. My nerves felt prickly, as if I needed to tear out of my skin.

And I could have, I suppose, though I was uncertain if there was a true death for someone—or something—like me. I had never tested the boundaries of my immortality. I had never had a desire to.

Is that what I felt? Desire? Something new and haunting beckoned to me from the dark abyss as I sat, sipping another glass of fresh blood.

"Are they responsible for the fire?" I asked.

"No," Evangeline said.

If these Creatures, the ones in our amulets, were not the ones responsible, that meant there were others—so many others—violating our laws.

"The Creatures are getting out of hand," I said quietly, though my words sounded much louder in the silence of the room.

Evangeline's near-black eyes lifted to meet mine. Confusion filled Leslie's eyes while Gabrielle's face flashed angrily before landing on her more typical mask of boredom.

Why is Gabrielle here?

"There is nothing about this we cannot handle, Alekto," Gabrielle continued in her clear, quietly condescending way, crossing her arms over her chest.

With her use of my title instead of my name, she had put us on a precipice. A hair's breadth from battle. Anger smoldered within me, hot and dark. Rage was there, too easily grasped and wielded.

Ah, yes. This was why we'd stopped residing together.

"I was not calling our ability into question," I said softly.

The taste of blood turned bitter in my mouth, and I deposited my mostly empty goblet down on a side table. I moved to exit the room, the heels of my boots thudding loudly on the marble floor. I neared the hallway that would lead me out into the night. Vengeance waited. But my sister spoke again.

"What are you questioning?" Gabrielle demanded.

Her words might as well have been a battle cry. I would not be cowed. Pivoting quickly, I squared my shoulders.

"The number of creatures who no longer wish to be held to the Laws has increased tenfold. The Twelve are meeting more often than I can remember in centuries past. I grow concerned about what it could mean," I replied, matter-of-factly.

Gabrielle's eyes narrowed. "Those who do not wish to be held to the Law will still face Justice. Their numbers do not matter, sister."

"I am simply noting that the unrest in our world has grown."

"Well, then, let us be on our way so that Justice prevails," Gabrielle said.

She pushed past me, gait smooth and posture unbothered. It was likely she truly wasn't. Gabrielle was the one who took our duty the most seriously, held to it the tightest.

I wondered how far she would go if she thought I was in danger of shirking that duty.

I wondered how firmly she would grasp a knife if it needed to be plunged into my back.

EIGHT

Only Evangeline was in the house the following evening when I woke. She was at her desk reading through what looked like an overwhelming pile of missives composed upon various types of paper. Some Creatures adapted to modernity better than others. Evangeline's communications could range anywhere from paper-thin vellum, to a leaf, to animal hide. Leslie told me a messenger had once sent a pinecone—code written out on each of the tiny spines.

"The human has been healed and taken home," Evangeline said as I entered the room.

"She was unconscious this morning," I remarked, trying desperately to hide the war of panic and concern that burst to life within my chest.

"And now she has been healed and taken home," Evangeline replied, looking up from her papers.

I would not ask who the human was or where she had been taken., but I had to clench my jaw to ensure it. Instead of inquiring further, I took a seat in one of the upholstered, rust red chairs across from her desk. They were far nicer looking than they were comfortable, with the reclaimed wood backings hard and unyielding.

Rather like Evangeline.

"Any updates on the demon murders?" I inquired, attempting nonchalance.

Evangeline's eyes lowered as she shook her head.

"Unfortunately, no. Yasmina was brought in when there was hope that one of the demons might survive, but he did not last the night."

"And the humans?"

"What of them?" Evangeline asked in surprise.

"A house fire is bound to be more difficult to cover up. There's no way a neighbor didn't call 911."

"Oh, there were firemen called. We had our hands full wiping memories. Absolute chaos."

"And what of the demon, Liam? He was pulled from the river recently?" I asked.

"How did you know about that?"

"A couple of demons were talking about it in Tully's the other night." Evangeline did not answer me. "Is someone targeting demons?" I asked, tired of the long, stretching silence.

"I—" Evangeline began. "We don't know."

"What do you mean you don't know? Who knows then?"

"We're not sure what's going on. Demetrius is confused, which annoys him to no end, as I'm sure you know. There are increased deaths in the demon community, to be sure, but with the general unrest it seems most likely that various factions are warring with one another."

"But fires? Drownings?"

Those were not the ways demons killed one another. They weren't violent enough.

"The demon from the river didn't drown. He was stabbed in the chest with a witchblade. Demetrius managed to keep that from the general population."

"So the working theory is that a demon is running around with a witchblade killing other demons?"

It sounded even more ridiculous out loud than in my head. Evangeline cleared her throat primly. She patted her already smooth, chin-length, black hair.

"Olivia, there is no working theory. There is an increase in Creature killings, but that is all we know."

"Mmhmm," I murmured.

"Alekto," she said. "It would not do any of us any good if we were to make assumptions about what is happening. We must operate on fact. One fact is there have been more Creature killings than typically seen, as of late. Another fact is that a few of those killings have been done with a witchblade. A final fact is that most Creatures are upset with the Laws and the governance of The Twelve."

I didn't respond. I didn't really have a chance to.

Evangeline looked pointedly at my amulet as it warmed and show-cased its names.

"I suppose there is one more fact," she said.

"Yes?"

"You will escort, to Tartarus, the souls whose names appear in your amulet, as is your duty."

I didn't like that it sounded like a reminder. I knew my duty. I knew my role. But then I remembered the strange coincidence of Gabrielle and the demon from the bar.

"Yes, Guardian."

"You are dismissed," Evangeline said with a nod.

I rose from the chair and left her office, more disconcerted than I had been when I'd walked in.

NINE

I looked again at my amulet and the names of the damned inside it as soon as I was outside in the blessed darkness of night. The list continued to grow. In other times, I had gone weeks or months without a single name. Lately, it was surprising if I went more than a few days. Something was happening, and I didn't like that I didn't know what it was.

I pulled the familiar leather of my jacket tighter around me. A dagger was at my back, as always, but it could sometimes be hard to get to. I debated returning to the house for a secondary dagger—a smaller one I could tuck into my boot—but it wasn't worth it. I had small knives at my wrists already, held there by vambraces that had been made for me long, long ago. There were compartments in the thick soles of my boots, as well, with knives hidden inside.

I glanced at the swirling darkness inside the amulet again. Two wolven, a solitary fae, three vampires, and a demon. I would start with the vampires. Perhaps I'd be able to see something in their minds before releasing their souls.

It was fruitless to hope they might just tell me.

In the name of Justice or not, no Creature trusted another who held a knife to their throat. I unceasingly held that knife.

I couldn't be both a nightmare and a savior, and I'd been the nightmare for too long.

The brisk night air heeded my call, and I vanished from where I stood, stepping out of the whirlwind and onto the lawn of a dilapidated manor somewhere outside of Milwaukee. It looked as if it stood in perpetual honor of All Hallows Eve. What may have once been red brick was now covered in grime, soot, and a myriad of other things that looked as dark as charcoal.

The house was a cliche at best and a neighborhood eyesore at worst.

I strode up the crumbling brick stairs and through the front door that hung off its hinges. My senses piqued at the Creatures within, and I headed for them near the back of the structure. They were in a room where dust motes that floated through the air, moth-eaten brown velvet curtains hung in front of boarded up windows, and the thick smell of rot clung to everything.

Two heads—a dusty blonde and the other blue-black as midnight—lifted to look at me as I leapt over a shabby, velveteen sofa, landing mere feet from them. Neither moved, blood dripping from their fangs, falling beneath them and onto the body below.

Knife wounds covered a pale torso, and there was no thump of a heartbeat. The vampires had made shallow cuts and drank from them, toying with the human before it died. It was just a body now, and I could not spare it another glance.

I wholly embraced my duty, reaching out with my mind to feel their anger and frustration. They had been promised a rich, glorious vampiric existence. Instead, they were left in these decrepit dwellings and ignored by the one who turned them.

There wasn't enough blood. There was never enough blood.

I shook my head to clear those thoughts away as they threatened to overtake my own.

"You have broken the laws of your brethren and so you must pay your debt in full," I began.

One of the vampires—the dark-haired male—lunged at me over the body, but I anticipated it, stepping to one side, dropping a knife from my wrist into my hand, and grabbing him by the throat. I pushed him against the decaying wall, bits of plaster falling from above to coat us both.

He tried to speak. My grip on his throat tightened. I liked the fragility of it beneath my fingertips.

"I, Alekto of the Furies, release your spirit to be guided to Tartarus, where it will be judged for your rebellion and disregard. The truth of your nature shall be revealed." I slid the thin blade across his throat and watched the blood rivulets fall. "In Tartarus so it shall be," I finished.

I let go and turned back to the woman, Juniper de Fiori, and found her still crouched over the body, her face slack. It was probably shock.

"Y-you—" she started.

"I am Justice," I said softly as I made my way to her side. "You have broken the laws of your brethren, Juniper, and so you must pay your debt in full."

She began to whimper and move away, but I grasped her tiny wrist in my hand. Again, the delicacy of the bones under my palm garnered my attention.

"I, Alekto, release your spirit to be guided to Tartarus, where it will be judged for your rebellion and disregard. The truth of your nature shall be revealed."

My voice was so low it was almost a whisper, but I knew the vampire heard every word I said. I still held, in the hand that was not gripping the delicate wrist, the knife I had used to release the soul of the male. I held it to her throat, gave the Creature a chance to ready herself, and then I slid the blade across.

"In Tartarus so it shall be," I said to no one.

———

The wolves who faced me were young, barely more than children. I supposed they were young adults by modern standards.

Their youth bothered me.

Exhaustion weighed down my limbs, and it felt more difficult than ever to draw the blade from its sheath along my spine. My anger toward their Alpha grew. I knew him. He was Surrey-bred, just one in a long line of wolven. He should have known better than to allow his pack to become embroiled in whatever schemes were quickly overtaking our world. It was impossible that such young wolves could have gotten themselves into so much trouble—so why was I there and not hunting the ones truly responsible? The grip of my right hand was firm against the blade's handle as I took a step forward.

"We didn't understand!" one of the wolves cried, his voice breaking as tears fell from his eyes. They were so full of regret that I found them hard to look into.

His sorrow was palpable, the taste of it acrid on my tongue.

"We're so sorry," the other wolf whispered.

Escorting souls had never felt remotely unjust before. But these wolven—they were practically children.

Children who made a mistake.

They were not like Roland Gregory, a Creature who gleefully abandoned our Laws and desired to take over the human realm. These creatures had wanted something different—a different way of interpreting the Laws or perhaps even being governed, to be sure—but that was not the kind of justice my sisters and I were sent to deal out. In that moment, I did not feel like Justice. I felt like a weapon being wielded, and I desperately wanted no part of it.

For perhaps the first time in my long, long life, I wanted to attend a hearing. I could not, of course. It just wasn't done. But I found myself wanting to know if there was a different kind of justice for these wolves other than to spend eternity in Hell.

I swallowed my frustration, past the lump in my throat. I didn't want to do it, but I had to. I clung to the sense of duty that had only recently been so grasp. I swallowed again.

"Amira Gavreaux and Ewan Crawford," I began, ignoring the soft whimpers that drifted toward my ears. "You have broken the laws of your brethren and so you must pay your debt in full. I, Alekto of the Furies, release your spirits to be guided to Tartarus, where they will be judged for rebellion and disregard. The truths of your natures shall be revealed. In Tartarus so it shall be."

My blade sliced through the throats of the wolven easily. They didn't even try to escape. As their bodies fell to the blood-soaked earth in the quiet woods on the edge of the city, I knelt and closed my eyes.

I was so very, very tired.

TEN

I gathered myself, releasing the remaining souls on my list while the moon was still a sliver in the sky. With my amulet in hand, I flashed into Bellanca and found my sisters already there. Gabrielle's shadows moved about her, wrapping her body in their darkness. Leslie was wiping blood from her switchblade, the picture of dark vengeance. I gave them the briefest of nods when they turned and saw me.

"Demetrius called me in," I explained, though neither had inquired about my presence.

"He's in a good mood," Gabrielle said.

"My presence should fix that," I quipped.

That earned me smiles from both my sisters. As unsettled as I'd been for the last few days, I needed that small bit of comfort.

"I can walk part of the way with you," Leslie said. "I need some new weapons."

Her hobbies tended to begin and end with weaponry.

"What kind of weapon are you seeking?" I asked Leslie.

"A sword."

"Why a sword?" I asked, amused.

"Why not a sword?" Leslie countered, a mischievous smile playing about her lips.

"You can't exactly carry one around," I argued. "A bit conspicuous, don't you think?"

I had visions of Leslie wandering about, sword on hip, utterly terrifying the humans.

"I'm not learning it to tote it about, Liv. I'm just learning to use it. I found a fae warrior willing to teach me, and after eons of daggers, athames, sticks, and archery, I'm a bit... bored."

"You did dagger work with the demons! Athames with the witches! Leslie, you did archery with the fae!" I cried.

"Exactly!" she exclaimed. "I've trained with the best. So now I want to learn something new." Even Gabrielle had to laugh in astonishment at our sister, but both her laughter and my own died off as Demetrius' assistant came toward us from down the long stone hallway.

"Ah, Alekto. You are present," called Allura.

Always with the formal titles.

"I am," I replied, inclining my head toward her.

Beside me, Leslie tilted her own head in deference. Allura stood tall, briefly inclining her head in deference to the three of us. This, too, soothed my rough edges a bit—for the moment. I was sure Demetrius would have my hackles back up in no time.

"Well met, Tisiphone," Allura said to my sister.

"Greetings."

"Megaera."

"Well met," Gabrielle replied.

"Come now, Alekto. Demetrius awaits."

Without bothering to see if I would follow, Allura turned, her dark layers of cloaks and long braids of various colors whirling about. The weight of the black stone floors and hallways bore down on me as I followed. I wanted nothing more than to be back in the human realm. The chill of Bellanca had nothing to do with temperature. It was the weight of it—the heaviness upon one's soul. Tartarus was worse, of course, but that was a hell realm. Bellanca was a different sort of plane all together. Tartarus' weight was harsh and cutting, whereas Bellanca stayed with a soul for some time, like a quiet reminder of our duties and the laws that bound us to them.

I hated both the weight and the reminder.

"Come now," Allura called, hastening me along.

"I hear we are fulfilling our duties again," Demetrius said with a smile as we entered his office.

"I was not aware I had duties that had gone unfulfilled," I replied.

Allura turned away and left without so much as a glance toward me. Demetrius opened his mouth to speak, but we were interrupted.

"Alekto," said a voice from behind me.

Sunee.

She was a witch and represented that species of Creature as part of The Twelve.

"Sunee," I said, bowing immediately.

With my head lowered I clearly saw the blood splattered on my clothing and boots. Not even black could hide blood, but it usually did a better job.

"Well met. Follow me."

The witch turned and began walking.

"Ah, Sunee," Demetrius began. "Forgive me, but I require Alekto's report from last night's assignments."

Sunee turned back, raising an eyebrow.

"Steward, I require the Alekto. She will be available after we have spoken and may certainly give you her report at that time. I do not believe her report will change the status of the soul in Tartarus," she tittered.

Demetrius hadn't even opened his mouth to reply before Sunee turned back around and began walking. I wasn't sure how this might pan out later once Demetrius had stewed over this little power play, but I knew without question where my duties lay.

I gave Demetrius a cheeky little wave on my way out of his office.

I followed Sunee through a stone arch, across another cavern, and through a secondary arch. One set of steps later, and the witch opened a heavy wooden door. A beautifully decorated living space awaited us. The scent of citrus welcomed me in, as spicy and tangy as the magic that clung to Sunee.

"Welcome, Alekto, into my home."

I had never once, in all my centuries, been invited into the home of one of The Twelve. Almost all of them spent most of their time elsewhere, even if they had quarters here.

"Thank you," I said.

I ducked my head in respect quickly before walking past her and into the large, but cozy, domed room. Plants were stuffed into almost every corner. The varying shades of green did a lot, though, to brighten up the otherwise drab walls. Witches often surrounded themselves with herbs and whatnot, so the plant life was not much of a surprise. Long ago, I had a dalliance with a witch, and I remembered how the scent of lavender always clung to her hair.

Pillows in an array of rainbow shades were on couches, chairs, and in piles on the rug-covered floor. Sunee waved me over to a sofa as she took a seat in an armchair.

"You have noticed the unrest," Sunee began as I took my seat.

"I have," I agreed.

"Our people are unhappy with the way they are being ruled."

I opened my mouth to protest, but she waved away the words before I could even form them.

"No, no. Let us not tell one another untruths in this place, Alekto. Our people are unhappy with the way things have been. I am not like my fellow council members. I will not put my head in the sand and ignore that the world we have inhabited for so long—perhaps too long —has radically changed. The Creatures want something different."

"What do you require of me?" I asked, genuine curiosity bubbling within.

Sunee laughed.

"Ah, Alekto. The eons have not been kind to you or your sisters, I'm afraid. Always wielded as weapons."

"We deliver Justice," I said slowly as confusion planted roots in my thoughts.

"I don't disagree. What I disagree with is not using you and your sisters to the fullest of your skill sets."

I didn't say anything. I didn't even know what I could say.

"You and your sisters could so easily integrate yourselves into the world of Creatures. You're not known to any of them. I would like to ask you, specifically, to gather some information on what it is exactly the Creatures want."

I was uneasy to say the least, though I could not deny something deep within me cried out for an opportunity such as this. Something new, something unlike the decades that had gone on and on, one after the other.

"Leslie and Gabrielle?" I asked.

"There may come a day when we need your sisters to be involved, but for now, I would like to ask that only you play this role. We simply don't know what we're dealing with yet."

"I understand. I will do as you've asked."

"Olivia," Sunee said. I knew I must look surprised. None of the The Twelve ever used our human names. "Olivia," she said again. "I have no doubt that you will do as I have asked. What I truly wish to understand is if you *want* to do as I have asked."

I thought for a moment. I didn't know how much to trust Sunee, despite my instinct to open up to her and tell her all I had felt over the previous months.

"I wish to find out why the lists of those to be judged and sent to Tartarus keep growing," I admitted.

There was enough truth in that.

Sunee smiled gently.

"Then please find out why our people are so unhappy. The witches, as you know, have not yet been implicated, and I am hesitant to involve them until I am forced to. You know how the distrust is between the species. That's a fire that certainly does not need stoking."

I nodded in agreement.

"You may have luck with the wolven or the demons," Sunee mused.

"Might I try the vampires?" I asked.

An idea was taking shape. Infiltrating a very specific vampire nest would be the first step.

"Certainly," she said. "Report back when you're able."

I stood and bowed once more before turning to leave.

"Oh, and Olivia?" Sunee called.

"Yes?"

"Do not breathe a word of this to Demetrius."

I smiled. "As you wish."

"Our Steward, while certainly capable of fulfilling his duties, tends to... overreach. Let us prevent him from making that mistake here. The Twelve are handling this situation."

I took my leave.

ELEVEN

W hen I found Leslie, she was still deep in discussion with
the blacksmith. I flashed back to the human realm, alone.

Dawn had passed and I had not slept, but my mind was
sorting through all that happened in Bellanca. It seemed best to burn off
as much of the rebellious, wandering energy as I could, but I felt the
sticky presence of blood in at least one of my boots. Crimson half-
moons were underneath my fingernails, begging to be scrubbed away.

A quick, tepid shower was what I needed. Sometimes, I could revel
in a hot bath after souls had been escorted, but I couldn't stomach it
today. The very idea of relaxation curled my hands into claws. I heard
the ripping before I realized I had torn the towel I held to shreds.

I left the scraps on the bathroom floor, eager to be away. I pulled
soft black leggings and a forest green tee-shirt from the closet. The cuffs
of the leather jacket I had worn were blood-soaked, but I grabbed a
similar one before pulling on another pair of thick-heeled boots—this
pair without the weapons in the soles—and was out of my room as fast
as I could be.

Evangeline was tucked away in her office. I could hear the quiet taps
on her keyboard. It was unlikely that anyone would require my services
so soon, so I left without a word.

The park was close, and the natural surroundings were often a place of calm and serenity while remaining in the city. I moved in that direction and enjoyed the feel of a crisp, fall breeze. The sidewalks were busier than I'd like, but it was daytime, after all, and the humans in this midwestern state knew enough to enjoy the outdoors while they could. It would soon enough be bitterly, horribly cold. Still, the rush hour foot traffic—humans on their way to work and all—scraped against my already frayed nerves as I tried to keep my distance and failed.

At least most of the scents were relatively pleasant in this part of the city in the morning: buttery smells of baked goods, hints of cinnamon and cloves, and freshly brewed coffee.

I buried my gloveless hands into the pockets of my jacket and made my way to a grove of trees near the southern edge of the park. I usually found a bench closer to the pond on the eastern side, but I didn't like to become a Creature of habit. Habits were troublesome, especially when noted by others. I tried to vary up my routes and haunts as often as I could. I found a seat near some pines and sat down.

The chill of the metal beneath my legging-clad legs seeped through quickly, but I didn't move. The laughter of children in the playground reached my ears. A memory wove its way through my mind, and I relaxed enough to follow the smoky tendrils of it until a clearer picture formed.

I was walking through a garden. My dress—no, a blue chiton—moved around my feet as I walked. The faint voices in the distance seemed to grow louder, and I moved faster.

"Mitera!" One of those voices called.

Mother.

I ran then, holding my chiton up in one hand to free my legs. I came through a clearing of olive trees and stood in knee-high grasses. I could smell the salt of the sea nearby as waves crashed upon the golden sands.

"Mitera!" the same, little voice called.

I looked over and saw a young child, no more than four, with long, black curls. She knelt on the sun-soaked earth beside a freshly dug hole. I moved to kneel beside her, noticing a doll with brown yarn for hair. The doll, clearly beloved by the little one, lay at the bottom of the hole.

I lay down beside the hole and reached down to grab Safiya.

Safiya. That had been the doll's name.

The small child beside me, doll firmly in her grasp, threw her arms around me.

"Agapo se," she said in my ear.

"Agapo se," I replied.

I love you.

My mind cleared of the memory. It was not the first time I had experienced a sort of vision, but they had almost always been old memories. This didn't feel familiar at all. I had never had children. Creatures could most certainly reproduce, but we were something else, something other. We had been created to be what we were. We had no family outside of the three of us. I told myself it could not be my memory.

If not my memory, what had that been?

I knew of some Creatures who could implant or share visions, but I had certainly never experienced it. I glanced around, searching for someone who might be unknowingly sending me these psychic waves, but then I shook my head in annoyance at myself. The child had spoken Greek. It seemed unlikely that anyone around me would have that memory. The clothing in the vision had been far from modern, as well.

Then I saw Allison, Roland's victim, walking through the park. Her red curls were piled on her head in a style she probably didn't even realize was Grecian. I remembered a long, long time ago when my sisters and I styled our hair similarly, readying ourselves for gatherings where we had been summoned to fulfill our duties. The Greeks still told stories of us, though none ever grasped the truth of our nature. Things were simpler.

I had enjoyed being feared.

I was lost in thought, remembering countless victims. I felt the glide of a knife through skin in a manner so similar that all my victims—*no, not victims*—blurred together.

I did not have victims. I had those accused of crimes. I had those traitorous to the Realm. Never victims.

"It's you."

Allison stood in front of me. She was breathing hard, staring into my eyes. I couldn't help but stare into hers. I watched as the memory of the night I saved her played through her mind. Everything was too vivid, too graphic. The scent of her own blood filled her nostrils, her body weakened from the loss of so much of it. She could still feel the sharp prick of fangs at her neck, wrists, thighs, and breasts. She had been unable to move, unable to fight, and it took too long for her mind to finally separate, putting a barrier between her physical and psychic memories.

Her scent changed as the images whirled through her brain. I hated the way her fear made her smell—musty and sickly sweet, like old perfume.

I shook my head to clear it again.

"You were the one who saved me that night," she whispered as she took a seat beside me.

I rose from the bench as quickly as would be humanly possible, still conscious of my otherworldly speed. But I still rose so quickly that Allison fell to one side. My arm shot out to steady her before I could even think, and I moved too fast.

I smiled politely, forced warmth into a smile so she wouldn't continue to badger me.

"I think you're mistaken. You must have me confused with someone else."

"No, I don't think I do."

Her eyes were clear and certain.

"What's your name?" she asked.

"Olivia."

It was out of my mouth before I could stop it, even though I knew how careless and silly it was. A part of me was fascinated that she remembered me. A part of me, that seemed to be growing steadily, loved that she recognized me, saw me as a hero. For so long I had played a villain, a scary story, a weapon.

Still, I should not have told her my name.

"Olivia, I'm Allison, though I think you already know that," she said.

"I'm sorry, Allison, I really think you're mistaken."

"I saw you yesterday outside my art school."

"I don't think—" I began.

"Please don't," she interrupted. "Don't insult me. I remember everything about that night. Evangeline, your sisters, the woman—a healer? Yasmina? Please. I just want to talk to you for a moment."

I looked away from her. "You really shouldn't remember any of that night, nor any of us," I said.

"But I do."

Her head was cocked to the side, one eyebrow raised, as she looked at me. Perhaps we missed something about her. I had followed Evangeline's orders—for the most part, anyway. I knew nothing of her, nothing about her background, aside from her name and the downtown college she attended. I'd only been able to glean so much information from Yasmina without her growing suspicious.

"You may be right," I conceded.

Allison smiled. She gestured off to the east.

"My parents own a cafe a few blocks away. Could we get a cup of coffee?"

Thoughts whirred as I attempted to piece it all together. I knew I should leave, but instead, I thought I might play along for the afternoon and then notify Evangeline of the situation. Yes, I could see how this went.

I fell into step beside Allison and walked toward her parents' cafe.

"I'm surprised you're alone," Allison remarked.

She seemed shy now that she knew who I was. I couldn't blame her. Sure her memory of me was tangled up in the horrors of that night. My moment of heroism, if it could even be called that, did not erase my association to a world she never should have seen.

"Oh?"

"The three of you seemed close."

I was amused by that. I gave up trying to hide the smile that fought to spread across my features. My sisters and I had been together for so long. In many ways, we revolved around one another.

"You remember them? I didn't think you were conscious."

"Your voices drifted in and out, but I heard the arguments. Only people who love each other fight like that."

I wasn't entirely certain about that. I had seen, too often, the knife edge difference between love and hate.

"Do you have sisters?" I asked.

She shook her head and spoke, but I didn't hear any of what she said. My mind was wrapped around the wonder of why I was asking her about her life. Why did I care if she had siblings? Why was I following her to a cafe? I couldn't seem to help myself, though. I was drawn to Allison, drawn to the fact that she somehow blocked the memory charm Evangeline used on her.

TWELVE

"Alex!" Allison called out as soon we walked in the door of Little Bird Bakery, a sky-blue storefront I'd walked by a few times but never entered.

The cafe was bright and warm, smelling of honey. It wasn't terribly busy, but I felt the discomfort at being around so many humans. It wasn't something I often did—visit cafes and restaurants. In centuries past, I sometimes went with my sisters or Evangeline, but as cities grew more crowded and our lives continued, it became more comfortable to separate ourselves, to remain distanced and aloof.

Why was I here? Why was I doing this?

Allison waved at a man, maybe a year or two older than herself, with dark brown curls that just touched his shoulders. He wore black-rimmed glasses, and he was tall—much taller than Allison, who was quite close to my own height.

"Alli!" he called out.

She waved him over. He finished up with the customer he was waiting on and managed to get through the crowd huddled in front of the counter to make his way over to us.

I hated that I noticed he was attractive. Clearly I'd been spending too much time with Gabrielle.

"Where have you been?" he whispered furiously.

He took Allison's elbow and led her toward a booth in the back corner. I followed, not sure what else to do.

"You didn't come home last night," he continued.

I didn't understand. Was this a boyfriend? A friend? A coworker? I was having difficulty parsing through his words to sense whether his anger was something to be concerned about.

"I stayed at Jen's," she said.

"You should have been resting at home."

"I'm sorry I didn't call, and I'm sorry I'm late for my shift."

Alex blew out an exasperated breath.

"I ran into Olivia in the park, and I guess I lost track of time," Allison continued.

"After what happened the other night, you swore you'd be more careful."

He turned to look at me, and I was not prepared for the protectiveness I saw in his dark brown eyes. It was a loyalty I rarely saw amongst the humans.

"Olivia, this is my *very* overprotective brother, Alex," Allison explained, waving one hand in his direction.

"Allison!" an older man called from behind the counter.

"That's my dad," Allison explained.

Alex stood to let Allison out of the booth. She remained next to our table just long enough to say she'd be back in a few minutes. I watched as she wove her way through the crowd. She was greeted with smiles and warmth, and when she walked behind the counter her father pressed a kiss to her cheek. She took the apron he held out to her and quickly tied it on.

"So," Alex began. "How do you know my sister?"

I tried to come up with something that would sound remotely plausible. I thought back to the bits of conversation that floated through the air toward me the other night .

"I, um, met her at Tully's a few nights ago," I said with a smile that was much brighter than the situation called for. "We were having drinks and just kind of started talking."

Alex laughed, but he seemed even more on edge. "She'll talk to just about anybody, I suppose," he replied.

His eyes slid over to where Allison was still talking with their father. I quirked an eyebrow at him. He grimaced.

"Sorry—I'm just... being overprotective, I guess. She didn't come home the other night, and when she did, she was really vague about where she'd been. It just isn't like her."

So Allison hadn't told this brother of hers about us. That was something. And it was definitely something in her favor.

"I'm sorry," Alex said, reaching out and placing his hand on my arm. "I didn't mean to sound so..."

"Overprotective?"

He laughed. He had a nice laugh.

"Yeah," he said.

"I think it's nice," I replied.

Why had I said that?

Conversing with humans was not something I did regularly—or even at all—and I felt very out of my depth. My words earned me another smile from Alex, though, and this one was warm and kind.

"Alex, Pops wants you," Allison said, returning to the booth.

Alex rose and gave me another smile.

"I'll see you around..." he said, pausing as he raised an eyebrow in question.

"Olivia," I said.

"I'll see you around, Olivia."

Alex walked back over to the bakery counter, and I turned my attention to the redhead in front of me.

"Allison," I began.

She stopped me with a wave of her hand.

"I have a lot of questions."

"I don't know how many answers I can give you," I replied honestly.

"Well, let's start with the answers you can."

———

Even after we'd talked for more than an hour, something told me this was just the first round of questions. I was both concerned and excited by the prospect. We had started with the easier things, like what had happened that seemingly fateful night and why I took her from Roland's.

"Are you a vampire, too?" Allison finally asked.

"No," I said, with a shake of my head.

"But you're not human."

She said it so matter-of-factly. It wasn't even a question.

"No," I admitted.

She stared at me for a long moment. Consternation was clear. Her eyes tightened and her brow furrowed. I took pity on her.

"Have you ever heard of a Fury?" I asked.

Allison's forehead wrinkled further as she considered the question.

"Yes, actually," she mused, her left index finger tapping the center of her bottom lip. "I did a course on Greek art a few semesters ago, and I think we looked at a painting or two."

I shuddered as I thought of how my sisters and I might have been depicted. It was either too real or too far from the truth. Neither idea was remotely flattering.

"So you're saying you're a Fury," Allison continued.

"Yes."

"And your sisters?"

"Furies."

"So many of you."

"Just three. You also met my Guardian and one of our healers. Both witches."

"If there are vampires and Furies and witches, what else are there? Fairies?"

"Fae, yes. They're not the small sprites, though, that seem to be popular. They're... more angular, I suppose, in their features. Vicious. Violent. Very in tune with the earth."

"Vampires, Furies, witches, fae."

I was already so deep in this. I sighed. "And demons, wolven, and atlanteans."

"Atlanteans..."

"Similar to what humans call mermaids?"

"And they live in Atlantis?" she asked, grinning.

"Some."

Her grin faded a bit. I watched Allison's face transform into something much more focused, much more intent. I let the silence linger as she took time to process it all.

Something wasn't sitting right with me. She was too calm. She acted like she was surprised, but it didn't echo in her eyes. I looked for the tightening of her mouth which might indicate tension or stress. I looked at her hands, fingers loose around the mug of tea in front of her.

Nothing about her body language said she was truly bothered by what had happened to her. I reached out, caressing the edges of her mind with long fingers of my power, but her mind was quiet, blank, like she was shielded. But most humans didn't have the awareness to do such a thing.

My instincts screamed at me. Trusting her went against everything I knew, and I was so angry with myself for thinking this was a good idea.

"Listen, Allison, I really need to go," I said.

Her eyes met mine. My skin crawled.

"I'd like to talk again," she said.

It rang true. My instincts had been telling me that something about this was off, but I still didn't say no immediately. The words rushed up my throat and onto my tongue, but I couldn't seem to part my lips and speak them out loud.

"I can try," I finally said.

"Take my number," she said.

She grabbed a pen from her apron and a napkin from the end of the table. She scrawled some numbers on the napkin and thrust it at me.

"I'd really appreciate it if we could talk," she said meaningfully.

Without agreeing, I got out of the booth and left Little Bird Bakery as quickly as I could.

THIRTEEN

Back at the house, I poked my head in the doorway of the guest room Leslie claimed as her own. She lay across a periwinkle comforter atop a massive bed. Per usual, the folk music my sister loved blasted from a record player.

"Where have you been?" she asked as she looked up from the book she was reading.

I wanted to tell my sister the truth. But I couldn't. Not yet. Perhaps not ever.

And I wanted to wrap my head around the conversation with Allison, anyway, before I dared speak of it.

"I just went for a walk," I said nonchalantly.

"Are Evangeline and Gabrielle still furiously whisper-fighting downstairs?"

"Yup."

"Any idea what it's about?"

"Nope."

"Don't want to worry about it?"

"Not really."

"It's weird having all of us... around."

"Yeah. It's... been a long time."

I felt Leslie's eyes on me.

"Feel like sparring?" she asked.

Though getting put on my ass by my sister in a sword fight or a round with sticks was probably not the best move I could make with my head all over the place, I couldn't think of a reason to say no. The physical activity sounded promising for helping me work toward clarity.

I met Leslie in the basement a few minutes later, after I'd changed into workout gear and another pair of boots.

Leslie tossed me a stick—her favorite sparring weapon as of late—and turned to grab her own from the rack.

"No swords?" I teased.

"Not until Claire has my new one ready."

"Should I be looking for a flashy new sword, as well?"

"If you want," Leslie shrugged. "But it won't help you win."

She laughed as I used one end of the stick to swat her rear end.

We settled ourselves into place on the mat, each in a corner, and I used a few minutes to stretch my arms and legs. When I was finished, I looked up at my sister and gave her the all-clear nod.

"All's fair?" she asked.

"All's fair," I replied.

With a grin, Leslie stalked across the mat, whipping the stick around her waist as she moved toward me. I held my position and waited.

My sister was fierce, but was also impatient. She whipped through the space in a blur, heading toward what I recognized as an attack. Sure enough, in just a moment, our sticks met one another in the air with a loud crack. I held my position once more as Leslie burst into frenzied movements.

I was able to advance a bit but soon retreated under a barrage of furious, direct attacks. Finally, seeing an opening, I went low and slid my leg underneath Leslie. I wasn't quick enough, though, and she jumped in a typical show of perfect timing. I cursed softly and rose before she could put my ass on the mat. Minutes passed, and I broke through her advances to regain some of my lost ground.

Back and forth we went, sweating and audibly swearing before long.

Increasingly inventive curses and the cracking sounds our sticks made as they met filled the room. My breath came in pants, and it was harder and harder to find entry points.

Thirty minutes went by before we put our sticks up, retreated to our corners, and hydrated. Leslie glanced in my direction, and I saw the challenge in her eyes. I was sweaty and fatigued. I should call it. But I couldn't.

We returned to the mat, and it was another forty minutes before we called it quits. We lay on our backs, panting, sticks abandoned on the mat beside us.

"I could totally pin you right now," Leslie said.

"Yeah, yeah," I grunted.

I felt Leslie's gaze on me.

"Did you work through whatever it was?"

"I think so," I replied, tasting the lie on my tongue.

More silence.

"Let's hit the showers."

Her trust in my word cut me, and I was solemn as I followed her. We put our sticks back on their rack—Evangeline would have our heads if we didn't properly store the weapons.

Unfortunately, it also gave me time to take quick stock of the blades we kept in storage, and two witchblades were missing.

———

I was too restless to get any sleep, and by that evening, I couldn't stand my own secrets. Nothing I did pushed the noise from my head. I tried reading, playing the piano, angrily throwing paint at a canvas, running on the treadmill downstairs, and even baking muffins. Evangeline entered the kitchen and raised her eyebrows at the pile of bowls I'd stacked in the sink and the several dozen muffins organized in neat rows on cooling racks.

"Is there something I should know, Olivia?" she asked.

I shook my head, which earned me a slow blink.

"Be sure to add more flour and eggs to the grocery list," she said as she turned and left the room.

I took that as my cue to end my baking.

Thankfully, both of my sisters were still in residence and willing to accompany me to one of the downtown clubs.

"You want... to go out?" Gabrielle asked.

I knew they would be surprised—I was the least likely of all of us to go out for an evening—but I needed the pulsing bass to replace the litany of thoughts pounding through my mind.

"Yes," I said flatly.

"There's supposed to be this awesome DJ at The Tunnel tonight," Leslie suggested, lifting an eyebrow.

"That sounds perfect."

Gabrielle gave me a once-over, her bright eyes narrowed.

"I don't know what this is about, and I guess I don't really care. I was planning to go out anyway," she finally said.

Leslie was more than happy to put me in a short black dress of hers. I agreed as long as I could wear my own boots. The combination made me smile. The dress ended high enough on my thigh it made even my short legs look longer. I probably stunted my height a bit by adding the platform boots with moons and stars cut out of the 4-inch soles, but they were different enough from my everyday combat boots that I felt separate from who I normally had to be.

I typically kept my makeup simple, but that, too, my sisters handled for the night. Gabrielle performed some sort of cosmetic witchcraft with an eyeshadow palette and fake lashes. I liked the result. What she'd done to my features had given me a sort of fae-like sharpness in my cheekbones and jawline with the lashes and smoky eyeshadow making my eyes look supernaturally large.

But if I didn't look like myself, perhaps I wouldn't feel like myself.

I didn't really want to feel at all.

———

The pulsing bass from the DJ booth pounded in my bones and in my brain, effectively keeping my secrets at bay. I drank it in. Gabrielle and Leslie found their own amusements almost immediately. Leslie wrapped herself around a gorgeous blonde fae girl in a tight gold dress, and they looked to be settling in to dance all night. Gabrielle found her pleasure at the bottom of a few drinks from the bar and then a series of dance partners, none of whom could keep up with her manic energy.

I saw one of the wolven stride up to Gabrielle, though, and I knew I probably wouldn't see her for much longer. I was content to dance for a while, enjoying the sheer volume of the music and the way it left no room in my mind for anything else. I was halfway through a glass of vodka when I saw Allison's brother across the bar. He noticed me, as well, and raised his beer to me with a nod. Before I thought about it too much, I hopped off my barstool and made my way over to where he sat.

"Allison's brother, we meet again," I said, smiling.

"How are you this evening, Allison's friend?" he asked, smiling back.

He had a very nice smile, broad and white. His dark curls were pulled back and away from his face. Without the glasses I'd seen him in before, I could clearly see his sculpted cheekbones and beautiful, mahogany eyes.

"I'm quite well, thank you," I replied.

The seat next to his was empty and I climbed up—a feat, I'll admit, in my very short dress and very tall boots.

"Not to sound cliche, but do you come here often?" he asked.

He had to lower his head to be heard, and I liked the way his voice felt against my ear. It was deep and maybe even had a bit of a sultry edge.

"Not really, no. I'm not much of a club person," I admitted. "What about you?"

"My friend is the bartender," he said, waving at the handsome man pouring drinks for the crowd. "So I'm not here often, but I do drop by every once in a while. Allison likes it here."

"Is she here?" I asked, looking around.

"Not tonight," he said.

I made a face and his brow furrowed.

"Are you sorry?" he asked. "That she isn't here?"

"I'm not sure yet," I admitted.

That earned me another very nice smile.

"I'll be sure to tell her that I saw you," he said, leaning down again. His eyes stayed on mine, and I almost shivered.

"Thank you," I said softly.

"Dance with me?" he asked.

I nodded yes, but I wondered what I was doing as we made our way through the crowd and onto the busy dance floor. I was playing a game I wasn't sure I was prepared for. I didn't usually toy with humans. They were too breakable.

But nothing about Alex felt breakable as his arms came around and held me. I felt his strength as he spun me away from him only to pull me back. I barely noticed when the final notes of one song built into the early notes of another.

My arms were around his neck and his thigh between my own, our hips moving in luscious ways. Gabrielle stared at us from across the bar, her surprise clear. But it was when I saw Leslie's eyes also staring at me that I realized just how stupidly I was behaving.

I pulled back from Alex, but he misunderstood and leaned down, as if he thought I was going to say something. For a moment, I forgot my sisters were watching, and I stared at his full lips, parted ever so slightly. His dark eyes blazed, and for just that one second, I almost forgot he was human. But I didn't, and he was. He was a human: breakable with a finite amount of time on this Earth. I had only been with a human a single time, and I remembered too clearly how that ended. I didn't want to relive that. I didn't want to feel the need to check my own strength in the way Creatures had to with lesser beings. I couldn't cross that line. Not again.

I felt wretched. I felt monstrous. I felt out of place.

"I have to go," I said abruptly.

"I'll walk you home," he offered, immediately leading me off the dance floor.

"No—I don't think that's a good idea."

"Let me call you a ride, at least," he said.

"I'm fine, really."

I smiled at him, trying to show him a normalcy I didn't feel. I wasn't just a girl leaving a boy in a nightclub because it was time for her to go home. I was a Fury: ancient, violent, and bound by duty.

I had to walk away from this human who could never know who or what I was.

The secrets I'd managed to keep at bay were back and pounding in my skull like the bass had been just a short time before. I left the bar and barely made it around the corner before I pulled the wind around me and traveled like the ancient being I was.

FOURTEEN

I wasn't ready to go home. I didn't know how much longer my sisters would stay at the club, and I didn't feel like explaining who Alex was or why I'd spent so much time in his company. It was best, I figured, to make a stop somewhere to settle my mind.

I stepped out of the wind and into the alley beside Tully's. As usual, it held a few dumpsters with graffiti decorating their metal sides, broken-down wooden pallets assembled into some kind of makeshift shelter, and pieces of trash that skittered along the pavement as my wind died away. It was also bereft of both humankind and Creatures, which was exactly what I wanted.

I straightened my hair and tugged down the hem of my dress. I wished I had a coat to pull around me. I'd dressed more for form than function.

I still wasn't sure if I wanted to sink into the shadows or find a pleasant distraction, but at Tully's, both were at my disposal. The dark and dirty dive bar was just what I needed.

I strode in, settling an unwelcoming grimace across my features and blatantly ignoring the appreciative glances from various Creatures around the room. I climbed onto a barstool for the second time that night.

"Whiskey, neat," I told the bartender.

"Sure thing, doll."

I inhaled, taking stock of the room. By scent alone, I knew the bartender was a feeder, or at least had been in recent weeks. There were too many different smells on him, and the faint marks of fangs were just barely visible at the neckline of his shirt and near his wrist. Both were common places for vampires to feed from. The marks were a bit faded, though, and I wondered if he was on his way out. Not that he'd know. Vampires were a callous bunch.

It was why my sisters and I let the general Creature populations think that's what we were. It didn't invite questions or curiosity. It instilled avoidance, whether born out of fear or a lack of desire to play in the power games.

A muskiness wound itself into my nostrils, and I knew there were most definitely wolves nearby. In the back corner a couple of demons were wrapped around one another, dark scents mingling with the spiciness of sex. An old jukebox played a strange medley of music from all different eras, drowning out its low hum of electricity, but the sounds helped push the thoughts from my mind.

Ian—I'd read his little black name tag—placed the glass down in front of me with a sexy sort of grin that told me he was used to attention. I smiled but didn't do anything else to encourage him. If I had wanted a human, Alex would have been far more along the lines of what I desired—maybe exactly what I desired.

No. I can't go there.

I slowly turned around on the barstool to glance around.

The corner of the bar where the scuffed and worn leather booths were installed seemed inviting tonight, but clearly there was at least one part of me too amped up to simply sit in those shadows and observe.

Perhaps, I could find both a distraction and someone to help me with my little task from Sunee.

Vampire, it is.

Though the bartender was certainly cute, he wasn't going to get me into a nest to help me figure out what Roland had been up to. If I wanted entry and information, I needed someone else. I perused the clientele over the rim of my glass.

In the corner opposite of the booths, a slender demon girl swayed to the music coming from the jukebox. Several pairs of eyes drank in the sight of her, all smooth skin and tantalizing movement. Her blonde hair hung down in her back in waves that swung in the same rhythmic way as her hips. Though part of me wanted nothing more than to saunter over and slide my own body against hers, she didn't have what I needed. Well, not everything I needed, anyway.

A smile found its way to my lips as I continued my observations of Tully's patrons. My eyes met the otherworldly topaz ones of a fae male. Those eyes had been taking in the sight of the demon girl until they'd wandered in my direction. On another night, I would have been interested in seeing just how long I could keep those eyes focused on me. Not tonight. I didn't want to need anything, least of all sex.

But if I combined sex with my task from Sunee, I could keep lying to myself that I was fine being alone.

I kept my gaze moving, moving, moving. Only a vampire would do for me this evening—a vampire who could aid me in gaining entry to a very specific nest.

There.

My eyes landed on a well-built, dark-haired thirty-something near the pool table. Well, he'd been in his thirties when he'd turned, anyway. He met my eyes and lifted his drink. I let another slow, wide grin spread across my features, lifting my drink in salute, meeting those hazel eyes of his with my own blue ones. I rested my lowered drink on my bare thigh and let my eyes drift over him for a few more seconds before forcing my gaze to wander.

I slowly spun back around on my stool, but I had no more than set my glass back down on the bar when there was movement to my left.

"Hello, darling," the voice said, rich and British.

"Good evening, Fabian."

———

"It's good to see you," Fabian said.

He took the stool next to mine, and Ian placed another glass of whiskey on the bar in front of us. Fabian's fingers wrapped around it.

"What are you doing here?" I asked, genuinely curious.

It had been some time since Fabian and I were in the same city.

"My Sire asked to see me," he said.

"Raoul?"

"Yes. He called us in to find information about... well, I'm sure you know."

The Creature uprisings. The unexplained deaths. The general uneasiness that had spread amongst our kind.

"I've heard some things."

"I'm sure you have, darling. You always seem to be in on the gossip," he said with a grin.

I watched as he took a long drink, barely noticing Ian refilling my empty glass. Something about the rich honey of Fabian's voice tugged at something deep within me. The familiar warmth of arousal I usually felt around him began to pulse, especially as he pressed a soft kiss to my cheek. My body clearly remembered other kisses he'd pressed to far less innocent parts.

"It really is good to see you," Fabian said quietly, somewhere near my ear.

I needed to redirect this conversation, at least for a moment or two. Ending up in bed with Fabian wasn't a bad thing—in fact, I'd known that's where I'd wanted to end my night as soon as I'd seen him across the bar—but business came first.

"You may not feel that way when I tell you what I'm in search of," I admitted to him.

He was as good a candidate as any other vampire for getting me what I wanted. Perhaps better. Fabian was old. The older vampires were able to trade in secrets the baby vamps could only dream about. Theirs was a culture where age truly did matter.

He grimaced. "I should know by now that you don't make social calls."

"Oh, that's not entirely true. I was at your last birthday."

I smiled at the memory. I brought him a very old bottle of whiskey, and we had spent the evening drinking it in various stages of undress.

"You were at my birthday ten years ago," he said, leaning his head toward mine and smirking.

"Has it been that long?" I mused, feigning nonchalance.

Fabian rolled his eyes and turned back to his glass.

"Well, if I remember correctly, it was still a very social call," I murmured in a low voice.

That earned me a smile, and like Alex's, it was a very nice one. It was also fanged. My insides burned at the sight of those fangs.

"That it was, love."

"And I never said this couldn't be partly social," I said. "But I need something first, and I'm pretty certain you can get it for me."

"As ever, madam, I am your humble servant," Fabian replied.

A warm, genuine laugh erupted out of me. Fabian might play at being grumpy, but the truth was he'd been one of the best friends I'd ever had. Admittedly, he was also one of the only friends I'd ever had, and sometimes the line of friendship got more than a little blurry. Still, he was there when I needed him—like when I was seeking information —and didn't complain too much that my social calls were, as he'd noted, few and far between.

We were immortal, and so what was time? What we had was what we had—and we didn't try to make anything more of it. My life was complicated, and Gaia knew Fabian had seen enough.

"What exactly is this favor you'd ask of me?" he inquired.

"I need to know who the closest associates of Roland Gregory are."

Fabian's eyes grew large, and he let loose a long breath.

"You know Gregory's gone, don't you?" Fabian asked.

I nodded, even though I knew Fabian wasn't really asking. I also knew that Fabian suspected I wasn't quite who I said I was, but regardless of whatever knowledge he'd been able to amass about me over the last century or two, he still believed I was a vampire. A nomad to be sure, as I was rarely in the same city for more than twenty or thirty years. I also changed my name often enough that he'd dispensed with even attempting to remember it. Still, though, that behavior wasn't too odd for a Creature. Few of us were called the names we'd been given at birth. Fabian had never seemed to care much, anyway.

"Word has it he was finally punished for being such a bad little vampire," Fabian said, lowering his head to mine conspiratorially.

I shrugged.

"Well, I don't much give a shit about the prick, anyway," Fabian said with a gallant sort of shrug. "I can easily drum up some names for you."

"Perfect," I said with a smile.

"Now, love, what do you say we get out of here?"

I tossed back the rest of my drink and met his gaze.

"Lead the way."

FIFTEEN

Fabian drove us to a mid-century brick home in a lovely little neighborhood full of similar houses with beautiful lawns. I wondered how long he'd been so nearby. He hadn't mentioned it. I hadn't asked.

With the vampires, they often had access to unimaginable wealth, which meant buying property in a city they may have only just arrived in was nothing at all. I knew of a vampire once who'd purchased and abandoned homes all over the country, never caring enough about a place to worry about selling it when they moved on.

Fabian's home, though, looked cared for. The grass—still green despite winter being so near—was flush to the edges of the property and edged with the kind of neatly trimmed hedges I thought only existed in the home and garden magazines Evangeline liked to look through. We walked up a stone-lined path, hand in hand.

The entrance of the home before us was arched and made of a dark stone like the path we walked upon. Somehow, though, the entire place looked warm and inviting. It suited my friend.

"This is certainly one of the nicer places you've lived," I teased, leaning my shoulder against his as we stood on the porch.

Fabian smirked. "It doesn't take much to be nicer than that awful flat I had in London."

Raoul, Fabian's Sire, had him hiding there to do reconnaissance on another vampire nest, so the priority was not comfort. The flat had been an incredibly small studio in one of the less-pleasant parts of the city. The toilet was hidden behind a grimy curtain left from a previous tenant. A squeaky iron bed frame was on the opposite side of the room.

"I seem to recall some very, very good times were had in that flat," I said, meeting his smile with my own.

"And as fondly as I also recall those memories, I am positive you will enjoy this place a lot more."

With that, Fabian swung the door open and gestured me inside. I expected to find a clean and modern interior, but the sense of my friend that I found lingering in the space was a surprise. This house was different than other places we'd spent time in.

I followed Fabian's broad shoulders into a foyer of dark paneling and black and white art prints of various locations. Upon further inspection, I realized I recognized the images. They were places Fabian had lived.

I hadn't known he was quite so sentimental.

I couldn't help but watch him more carefully as he tossed his keys on a small table and sauntered through another archway. I needed to maintain some distance, but it was going to be difficult with Fabian. He'd long been a source of comfort. He was a safe place to land when I needed it. He was the only friend I allowed myself outside of my sisters.

Maybe I don't want to keep that kind of distance anymore.

"More whiskey?" Fabian asked over his shoulder.

"Please," I said, taking in the surroundings.

Despite the very traditional brick outside of the home and the foyer, the inside was an industrial dream. Rich, warm-toned woods accented with wrought iron and steel combined in something that felt stately with just a hint of warmth amongst what was so contemporary in its design. Caramel leather couches in an L-shape around a fireplace looked deliciously comfortable. I made my way over.

"Here you go, darling," Fabian said, holding out a crystal glass of amber liquid that even a human would have been able to scent was expensive. Its aroma, dark and smoky, wafted from the glass I held.

I'd often equated that smell with Fabian. It was hard to remember if whiskey had been my favorite drink before we'd met or if that was due to him. My own sentimentality surprised me, but Fabian sometimes had that effect on me. For such a rugged countenance, the vampire was all warmth and softness.

Fabian switched on the fireplace, sitting beside me. He sat sideways so that he could look at me, those deep-set hazel eyes watching me carefully for a long moment. I wanted to believe he was just drinking in the sight of me in the same way he consumed the expensive liquor, but we knew each other too well. Lines of concern etched themselves between his thick, dark brows.

"Why Gregory?" he asked quietly.

I took a slow sip of the drink in my hand.

"Something is happening," I said, finally. "Something in our world that I don't yet understand."

Fabian grunted and shook his head. "A general bit of unhappiness, that. Happens every few centuries."

"Not like this," I said without thinking.

I saw Fabian's eyes widen just a little. I knew he filed that little bit of information away in that too-intelligent mind of his.

"It's more than what I've seen in the past," I offered carefully.

Fabian nodded, but the attempt I'd made to cover up my little slip of the tongue clearly wasn't that convincing. I wasn't even certain if I wanted it to be. A distinct and growing part of me wanted to lay everything at his feet.

But I am not a princess needing a prince to save her. I am a Fury, and I cannot involve anyone. Not even Fabian.

"So what brings you here?" I asked in an obvious attempt to change topics. "The last time I saw you we were in Seattle."

We'd kissed in the rain.

"And that's where I've been, mostly. I spent some time in Vancouver, too. Some friends had mentioned they'd seen you there, as well."

They'd had to have been relatively young vampires to have recognized me. My sisters and I had changed our identities around seventy-five years prior. I'd met Fabian, though, just after we had moved from Reykjavík, where I'd had a blonde pixie cut and my name had been Eva. Fabian, to his credit, took it all in stride.

Of course, it wasn't that strange for vampires to move about, and that was what I pretended to be.

I'm so fucking sick of pretending.

I took a drink of the whiskey and tried to refocus on the information I needed.

"Rumor has it that Gregory wasn't the only naughty little vampire," I continued. "I'm hoping that figuring out who his nest-mates were might clarify some things."

"Some things," Fabian said, clearly amused.

He took a long, slow drink. I watched his throat bob, and it made me want to forget all about the intel I had asked for.

"Things," I said in a low voice.

Fabian's eyes slid slowly over me, and I decided I didn't care about Roland Gregory's nest-mates any longer.

"But those things aren't exactly what I had in mind when I said I'd come home with you," I said.

Fabian's eyes watched me carefully.

Was that disappointment? Had he hoped I would say more?

I tossed the thoughts from my mind as quickly as they arrived. Leaning forward, I set my empty tumbler down on a stone coaster on the low coffee table near the sofa. I took the crystal glass from Fabian's hand and placed it on another coaster. Pivoting quickly, I threw my right leg across Fabian so that I was seated across his lap. My dress, already scandalously high on my thighs, rolled up to my hips. His warm smile told me that he was caring a lot less about my interest in Gregory than he had been a few moments ago.

"And what things, love, did you have in mind?" he asked.

His index finger traced a line upward from my knee, stopping just short of the dress' hemline. I sighed into the warmth that spread through my belly and put my arms on either side of Fabian's head. He leaned back so his eyes could still stare into mine, heat searing through me.

"The same kinds of things I have in mind every time we see each other, *love*," I murmured.

I pressed my lips to his, and he eagerly met my tongue with his own when I opened for him. There was no more talk of Gregory or Creatures or anything at all really for the next several hours.

Sixteen

I woke up to the feel of Fabian's body behind mine, and I stretched, groaning as my muscles pulled and ached in delicious ways. I languished in the feeling for a moment before nestling back into his warmth, wiggling backwards until my body fit completely against the length of his. There was a grunt before a strong arm wrapped around my middle and tugged me even closer.

"Too early, darling," Fabian said softly.

At least part of him disagreed that it was too early, and that part of him was making its presence known along my backside. I wiggled a bit more, earning a huff of laughter. I couldn't help but smile.

"It's just an hour or so from sunset, and at least one part of you isn't tired," I teased.

I rolled over to face him, ready and eager to pounce upon him and lose myself in the sex that was sure to follow as the sun sank below the skyline. Fabian, though, settled me against him. His eyes met mine.

"Are you ready to talk about what was on your mind last night?" he asked.

Though Fabian might not have known exactly what I was, it didn't mean he didn't know me well. For whatever pleasure we found together in bed, a friendship existed at the core of the decades we'd known one another. This was the perfect example. He'd known I was distracting myself by distracting him, and since he didn't want to push and certainly didn't mind the sex, he put aside the knowledge and let me take what I needed. But, as always, he was here for me to talk to if I wanted that.

I relinquished a heavy sigh and buried my face between his neck and shoulder, placing soft kisses across the skin there. Though the marks my teeth had left were fading quickly with his supernatural healing, it warmed me a bit to see them there.

Mine, I thought, even though I knew better. He couldn't be mine. That wasn't how things could be between us.

"There's a human," I began.

I pulled back just in time to see Fabian's eyes widen in surprise, but he didn't comment. It made it a bit easier to loosen up and let the rest of the story go.

"She... might not be entirely human, actually," I mused.

I sat up on one elbow.

"Have you ever heard of a human whose mind couldn't be wiped?" I asked him.

Fabian's eyes widened for a moment before his features settled into thoughtfulness.

"She fought off a memory alteration?" Fabian asked. "From a witch?"

"Mmm," I began, furrowing my brow as I tried to figure out the way to describe what had happened. "It's more like it just didn't work on her. Like a shield, but it was one of the best I've seen."

Fabian rearranged the pillows behind him so he could sit up. He looked contemplative, and I was comfortable letting silence linger. He mindlessly ran a hand through his already mussed hair, and the short dark strands stood up in all different directions.

"I can't say I have," he finally said, scratching at the stubble on his chin.

"Me, either. It's perplexing."

"I would think."

The silence built again.

"This human," Fabian started. "You suspect she might be a half-Creature?"

"Or something like that, yes."

I couldn't think of another explanation. Fabian's confusion should have concerned me, but I was comforted by it a little bit. Maybe we were dealing with something new.

Fabian scratched at his stubble again. I snuggled up, laying against his side, leaning my head upon his shoulder. He held me there for a while, as both of our minds puzzled over what I'd told him.

"She knows what you are, then?" Fabian asked.

"Yes," I said.

"That's dangerous."

He was right, even if he didn't realize the depth of the danger. I wondered if it would hurt him if he understood Allison knew who and what I really was, when he, a Creature I'd shared so much with, didn't know much at all. I looked up into Fabian's hazel eyes. I saw only concern. Guilt pooled in my stomach, roiling and burning. I put my head back down and lazily drew circles on his abdomen with my index finger, trying valiantly to distract myself.

"I know," I finally said softly.

"And you don't want a contract?" he asked.

He had worded the question carefully, acknowledging that whatever I was may not require a contract with a human. It was so at odds with his devil-may-care attitude that he used to traipse about the world, but it told me that somewhere deep within the vampire was a soul who bothered to take care of others. I mattered to him. The guilt pitched again in my stomach.

Perhaps whatever Fabian had surmised I might be was scary enough to deter him from questioning further. I wasn't sure what I preferred—his love or his fear.

Of course you know.

"I don't," I said out loud.

I wasn't sure who I was answering, myself or Fabian.

"You're playing a very, very tricky game."

He had no real idea of the depths of this game I played—of the game I'd been playing since whenever I had been brought forth as a

Fury. But I heard the concern in the warm honey of his voice, and I took a moment to relish in the soft kiss he pressed to my forehead. And just as the doubts began to enter my mind—about Allison, about her memories of the night with Roland, and about the danger I'd put Fabian into by sharing this much with him—Fabian spoke.

"Your secret is safe with me."

―――――――

Buoyed by the faith Fabian had in my judgment, I texted Allison. I didn't even bother to dress before I made plans to catch up with her over coffee at her family's cafe. With that done, I forced myself to leave the warmth of Fabian and his bed.

"You know I don't tell you this lightly," began Fabian, hands behind his head and watching me walk across the room. "But—be careful, yeah?"

I turned to look at him, saw the seriousness in those eyes of his. I nodded before gathering the various pieces of my clothing strewn about the house.

I heard Fabian rustling about behind me. I noticed he didn't bother to find the clothing he'd worn the night before. That warm pull deep in my belly flared to life as I recalled tearing at his shirt with my nails. I was fairly certain it was in tatters somewhere in the kitchen.

"Here you are," Fabian said, handing me the bra I was still searching for.

"Where was it?" I asked as I pulled it on.

"Back of the sofa."

He was dressed more casually than he had been last night. Worn denim and a dark tee-shirt hugged his muscular frame, suiting him much more than the button-up and trousers. It allowed the dangerous edge that hung about him to breathe a bit, if such a thing could happen.

I liked that edge.

I tore my gaze away from him, my teeth leaving indentations in my bottom lip. Fabian laughed softly, knowing exactly where my mind had wandered.

"I have to go," I said.

"So you said," he replied, grinning wickedly.

Staying here, returning to bed with Fabian? It sounded so much better—for just a moment.

If I hurried, though, I could wind-walk home and make it to the bakery in fresh clothing. The talk with Fabian had given me some strength to find out more about the girl. My arms full of clothes, I went into the small bathroom near the kitchen.

Though I hadn't spent long at Tully's, the dress I'd been wearing had the familiar stale alcohol scent of a bar, and my nose wrinkled as I finally tugged it on over a lacy black underwear set. As I splashed water on my face, I noticed there were remnants of last night's makeup. I'd have to take care of that, too, before I went to the cafe.

Fabian returned to lean against the doorway, a steaming cup of tea in his hand. The scene we created was domestic and cozy. There was no denying that when Fabian stood before me, I could ignore the griminess. The softness in his gaze set me alight again. It took everything in me not to rip my clothes back off and push him back toward the master bedroom and into the spacious rain shower I'd spied earlier.

"Thank you for last night," I said, rising up on my toes to kiss his cheek before making my way to his front door.

"Anytime, darling."

"I have to go," I said, yet again.

"We never have enough time together," Fabian said.

"I'll be seeing you," I told him.

I opened the oak-paneled door and stepped outside. I only barely heard his murmured response.

"I know better than to ask when."

SEVENTEEN

The words on the laminated menu blurred together. I didn't know why I even bothered to look at it. None of it was going to satiate my kind of hunger. I closed it just as someone said my name.

I looked up into warm brown eyes.

"Hi," Alex said.

The shirt he wore was tighter against his skin than last night's had been. It clung in ways that indicated the kind of strength that was underneath the clothing.

Gaia above, stop undressing the man with your eyes.

"H-hi," I stammered.

"Not expecting me?"

Nothing about his tone made me think I'd stared at him for longer than was polite, but my face grew warm, anyway.

"I was supposed to meet Allison here," I said, reaching for my phone and looking at the time. "Oh, I guess she was supposed to be here already."

Alex grinned.

"Yeah, she just called me. Her class went late. She asked me to let you know."

"Well, I guess I'll just see her some other time," I said as I stood and grabbed my bag from the wooden chair beside me.

"No," Alex said.

He reached out a hand to stop me, fingertips brushing my left hand, which was still on the table.

Electricity burst through me, setting me on edge. I pulled back to examine those long fingers.

But it was just a hand.

I recalled Allison's ability to break through the mind wipe Yasmina had performed, and again I wondered if there was something happening I just couldn't sense.

I'd felt that same electricity last night when we touched, but I told myself it was nothing—just the alcohol, the state of my nerves. I hadn't been in a mood to investigate, and I still wasn't.

The weight of my secrets was stifling.

Alex's eyes watched me. It irritated me that I couldn't get a read on him. It made me feel less than what I was, which was completely illogical. Senseless.

Yet I felt something deep within me that argued against logic—and perhaps my sanity—because I felt things with the two of them that weren't strictly human. It was truly bothersome.

"Let me bring you a cup of coffee," Alex offered.

"I should really be going, if Allison's not going to make it."

Alex's eyes met mine. One eyebrow raised.

I put my bag back down on the seat with a sigh. "Tea would be great."

"Any particular kind?"

I leaned back in the chair. "Surprise me."

Alex smiled and walked back to the kitchen.

Not for the first time, I wondered what I was doing. Why did these humans matter to me in the least? I tried to convince myself that discovering how Allison was able to recover her memories despite our intervention was about keeping my world's secrets. I tried my damnedest to believe that lie.

So many lies.

"Here you go," Alex said, setting down a white ceramic mug of Earl Grey in front of me.

Tendrils of steam wafted upward, the bergamot aroma comforting and wonderful. Though I didn't need the human food or drink to survive, I can eat and drink without issue. Some of the truly great art that humans had been able to create was in their culinary exploits, and it's an area of humanity I indulged in frequently. What the food didn't do, though, was fill me in the way that blood could.

My melancholy thoughts scattered as Alex placed down a second cup of tea and took the chair opposite. I quirked an eyebrow.

"I hope you don't mind if I keep you company," he said.

He rolled up the sleeves of his navy blue henley, revealing black lines of ink on his tanned, muscled forearms.

"I suppose that would be okay," I murmured, raising the mug to my lips.

"Careful—it's hot," Alex said.

The warning seemed... cute? The heat of the tea, though, was nothing for me.

"Thank you," I said, "but it's fine."

He glanced down at his own steaming mug, furrowing his brows. When he looked back up at me, he pushed his glasses up on his nose. It appeared more habit than need, something he did, perhaps, when he was nervous.

It was at odds with the lean strength of him exuding that quiet sort of confidence.

"About last night—" he began.

"I'm sorry—" I said at the same time.

We both stopped and smiled awkwardly. Alex ran a hand through his hair, raking through the waves haphazardly. It triggered thoughts of Fabian, but I pushed them back.

"I'm sorry," I began again.

"For what?" Alex asked.

"Just for rushing out last night. I suddenly realized what time it was, and I had an early morning."

"Really? Allison said you're a night owl."

"She talked to you about me?" I asked, concern growing like a pit in my gut.

"A bit."

An angry voice rose above the soft music playing in the cafe and tore my attention from the man before me. I looked around to find the source, sitting just a few tables away. A middle-aged man engaged in an argument with a waitress. I was up and moving before I even realized what I was doing.

"You're done here," I said to the man.

"Bitch, nobody asked—"

I grabbed the man by his shirt collar and pulled him to a standing position. "I said you're done."

I let a little bit of the otherworldliness show in my eyes, knowing they flashed an unholy shade of blue. The man gulped. I let go of him, and he fled without a word.

"Are you okay?" I asked the waitress.

"Y-yeah," she stammered. "Thanks."

I nodded brusquely and walked back over to the table I'd been sitting at with Alex, whose eyes were wide and staring at me incredulously.

"What?" I snapped.

"What was that?" he asked.

"I don't like bullies."

"Uh huh."

His brown eyes watched me carefully, but he didn't look scared. Nothing about his body language told me he was afraid of me. If anything, he looked intrigued.

That was unnerving.

"Listen, just tell Allison that she can call me or whatever. We can catch up some other time."

I grabbed my bag and exited the cafe as quickly as I could, but I felt Alex's eyes on me until I was through the door and past the large storefront windows.

EIGHTEEN

I t was fully dark outside the bright warmth of the bakery, though the neon lights of the city did not allow for that blessed darkness to surround me, even as I desperately wished it would. I made my way down the bustling, crowded sidewalks of downtown. It was a weeknight, but that didn't matter. Not here. The clothing I saw or the gaiety in the crowds sometimes differed depending on the time of day, but the sheer number of people never felt like it changed.

This city, like so many others, was a busy hive of noises and smells. The number of orange barrels in and alongside the roadways had been drastically reduced, signaling to the denizens—human and Creature— that winter was truly on its way and construction projects had to cease. The acrid smell of hot asphalt had long since faded. There was new graffiti, its scent sharp and pungent, installed on the side of an abandoned coffee shop, bright against the dirty bricks.

I wished for more appealing autumnal scents of cinnamon and freshly brewed coffee, but alas, the smells around me were a bit less warm and welcoming. The chilly breeze that whipped down and across the sidewalks was a biting blade of winter snow and ice. Cigarette smoke, penetrating and gritty, wafted through my nostrils.

As I made my way through a back alley that would get me out of the crowd, the stale and bitter smell of old urine struck me. I wanted to gag. Quickly pulling at the wind, desperate for escape, I whirled away.

Just as the gray sky lit up and thunder crashed loudly, I stepped into Tully's. A strange time of year for a storm like that. Anxiety sank its claws deep into my gut. There was a part of me that hoped I would find Fabian inside the bar, but there was another part of me that knew I if I saw him I would tell him what happened at the cafe, and he was already concerned—rightfully so—over the situation with Allison.

It turned out my wishes didn't matter. My roving eyes told me that Fabian wasn't present.

And, unfortunately, there was still a situation for me to deal with, because while it wasn't my friend-and-sometimes-lover inside the noisy bar, there were other Creatures that drew my attention.

"Olivia!" cried three voices in unison.

Dressed head-to-toe in haute goth fashion, the Fates moved to stand in front of me. Platform boots pushed their already tall frames to significant proportions, keeping the attention of the patrons who'd heard them call out to me. It was hard not to stare at the three of them, beautiful as they were with their golden skin, upturned eyes, and delicate, pointed faces. They reminded me a bit of the fae.

"Chloe, Lexi, Atlanta—it's been so long," I mused, kissing each one of them on both cheeks.

"How long has it been?" Lexi drawled.

Not long enough.

Her attention wasn't really on me, though. Ian, the bartender from the other night, was sporting fresh puncture wounds on his neck, and Lexi—called Lachesis in the earliest days of my existence—was drinking him in like she had just come in from the desert. I recalled thinking he was on his way out of popularity with whomever held his contract.

Clearly, I'd been wrong.

"*Ugh*, Lex—keep it in your pants," Atlanta said, rolling her eyes.

"He's yummy," Lexi murmured.

The three of them were ancient and yet were like horny teenagers almost each and every time I saw them. Since I didn't know where they were outside of the earthen realm, maybe that really was the case. Perhaps they craved attention like I did blood. I had no idea. What I knew was there was never a small issue that brought them to me. It was always something big—like the plunging of Atlantis into the sea or the Salem witch trials. They also wouldn't involve me in fates that were not tied to the world of Creatures, so there was little doubt in my mind why they were here now.

This can't be good.

"I'm guessing this is about the murders," I said in a low voice to Atlanta, leaning a bit across the space between us so that my voice wouldn't have to carry far.

"You got it, sister," Atlanta said. "Let's grab a booth and chat, yeah?"

Atlanta slipped her lace-clad arm through mine and began moving. Chloe ended up having to grab Lexi by the hand and drag her with us, since she was still making eyes at Ian, who was clearly very intrigued by Lexi's assets—the ones her corset pushed sky-high. We ended up back in the same booth I'd been in the other night with Leslie. No sign of the fight that had taken place, though.

The furniture at Tully's was sturdy. I suppose she knew her clientele.

Atlanta perched next to me, draping her long frame in a way that was somehow elegant amidst the grunge. The other sisters sat across from us in nearly identical positions: elbows on table, hands folded, and jaws held tight. Lexi's eyes darted around the room, ensuring our solitude, before anyone spoke.

"All right, Livvy-baby. We've got a sitch," Lexi said, finally pulling her gaze to mine.

I almost wished she hadn't. Her Fates' eyes were eerie—eerier than mine, and that's saying something. The irises white and pupils pale gold, they were so clearly otherworldly. Power radiated from the three of them in waves like rich old women sometimes drenched themselves in very floral perfumes. Their movements often mimicked one another, as well, which meant it was like watching three versions of the same being. Off-putting, to say the least.

"And the sitch is big—I mean, huge," Chloe said.

Then she winked.

"Please don't quote *Pretty Woman* at me," I begged.

The Fates have a thing for old romantic comedies, and their memories were incredibly vast. It was, sometimes, comical to see what they'd recall from a film.

But I wasn't interested in playing games. Not tonight. My rapidly fraying nerves couldn't handle it.

"Party pooper," Chloe pouted.

"No one says that anymore," Atlanta said, nudging her with her shoulder.

"How do you know?" Chloe fired back.

"I watch reality tv."

This is devolving quickly.

"Ladies?" I asked, in an attempt to draw their attention back to me.

All three pairs of eyes met mine.

I don't like that.

"Why are you here?" I inquired.

All three of them leaned low, and their black hair pooled together on the scuffed and worn tabletop. I leaned forward, too, understanding that whatever they were about to say was, in fact, big—I mean, huge—and it was probably going to make me very, very unhappy. My amulet, though, remained cool against my throat, which meant no decisions had been made yet.

Perhaps there was still time to course correct whatever was going on.

"We need you," Chloe said.

"You have to stop this Creature nonsense," Lexi continued.

"Because the Old Ones are waking up," Atlanta finished.

"Or being woken up," they said together.

The Old Ones are waking up.

They didn't have to tell me any more. The Old Ones were the old gods, the ones who had formed The Twelve. They were the ones who originally sat upon the twelve golden thrones of Olympus. They were vengeful and righteous, jealous and maddening, cruel and deceitful. There was very little they loved, and they hated even less. It was often their general ambivalence that was the thing to fear. There was very little gray area with beings like that—and their rigid thinking meant death and war, among other terrible things. If they woke from their centuries-long slumber, it was the end of everything I knew. They were my Creators, but I had no love for them. I certainly did not trust them.

"How do you know?" I couldn't help asking.

Their eyes glowed with that eerie light again, and I immediately regretted the question, despite craving more information.

"We can feel it," Atlanta said stiffly.

"We are starting to hear their thoughts," Lexi said, emotion creeping into her voice in a way I had rarely heard.

It took so much to rock them, these deities. Their memories were vast, and their sense of time so unlike anyone else's. If they were shaken by this, I had every right to feel the fear shooting through my body.

"And this is connected to the uprisings and riots and murders," I managed to say as my thoughts continued to whirl, forming dark patterns.

I didn't phrase it as a question. I didn't mean it as one.

"We cannot see all the threads. Not yet," Chloe admitted.

Oh, Gaia. I wish I didn't know that.

A long silence hung between the four of us.

"If the Old Ones wake, we don't have to tell you the havoc they'll wreak," Atlanta said, her eyes serious.

No, you don't have to tell me.

"You are old, but you have not forgotten," Lexi added.

"If the Old Ones wake, Fury, your existence—and that of your sisters'—will never be the same," whispered Lexi.

Her eyes were distant, and I knew this was more than a warning. This was a Seeing.

"What do I do?" I asked.

But I knew even before they said it that they didn't have the answers.

NINETEEN

The girls' eyes were still glowing when I made my apologies and left, needing to escape the pounding rhythm of the words they'd said. The walk home was full of darkness and shadows clinging to me like old friends, but their comfort, so often easily reached, couldn't be pulled around me as I ambled forward. I couldn't even bother to skirt around the pools of lamplight. I just walked.

The nighttime scratching and snarling of an animal rooting around in one of the many alleyways momentarily shook me from the litany in my mind.

The Old Ones are waking up.
The Old Ones are waking up.
The Old Ones are waking up.

I had not needed The Fates to tell me if the Old Ones woke up that my life as I knew it would cease to exist. Though my memory fogged at certain points, given just how long I had been alive, I could recall what my life had been like during the reign of the gods. Zeus' wrath and vengeance. Athena's hunting—and not just of Creatures. Poseidon's rage and despair. Hades' jealousy. Artemis' hunt on the loose, cavorting through the wilds and later the more civilized areas with wild screams and abandon.

When the humans' belief in them waned, so did their powers, and at some point, they stopped leaving Olympus or their respective lairs. From what we understood, many of them simply went to sleep and did not wake up.

I sometimes wondered if that was the root of the human's tale of Sleeping Beauty—the fair and powerful taken down by an unknown darkness, left to sleep for eternity. But there was no beauty in the tale.

Only doom and destruction and despair would surround us and fill our lives if the Old Ones awakened. The Twelve were not perfect. They were far from it. But The Twelve were at least Creatures themselves, ruling other Creatures. The Old Ones were not Creatures. They had never been human. Any humanity they had was long abandoned, laid to waste at the feet of easier emotions like rage or hatred.

They mostly despised us, as well, but they still used us to do their bidding.

We don't have to tell you the havoc they'll wreak.

The havoc they'll wreak.

The havoc.

I paused at the gate of the walkway to our brick home. I took in the soft lights glowing from the windows, ivy wrapped around the eastern turret, and even the beauty of the surrounding homes. I didn't know how to tell Evangeline about what The Fates had told me. I wasn't even sure I could. For all I knew, as soon as I opened my mouth, the words would dry up on my tongue like dust I would then choke on. It wouldn't be the first time the girls put a gag order on someone.

And beyond what limitations The Fates may have placed upon me, I wasn't even sure if I wanted to share what had been said. So much was in turmoil, in the gray shades of doubt. Evangeline and Gabrielle's secretive murmurings, the overheard discussion at Tully's between the two demons, Gabrielle's strange coincidence regarding the house of murdered Creatures, and the unforgettable warning from The Fates.

You are old, but you have not forgotten.

Not only were the Old Ones waking up, but The Fates hinted that someone in this realm could be the cause of it. I had no idea how anyone, Creature or otherwise, could go about waking up a god, but if The Fates had mentioned it, it was worth more than mere consideration.

Who would benefit from such a thing?

But the horrible, honest, truth was that most Creatures would easily benefit from the Old Ones regaining their thrones. It would bring back the days of all-out war between the various factions, but there were some Creatures who missed that, who craved it. There were some, like the fae, who might see it as their only option. The fae required nature, and any fool could see what was happening to this planet. If the fae could gain the ear of a god, they could find themselves in their own earth realm version of the Elysian Fields.

I probed harder into my mind and searched for any connection point that could lead me to a possible answer. Yes, the fae would benefit. The demons would, too. With all the chaos and destruction that would follow in the wake of the gods' return, they would rejoice in their own wicked ways. The witches could benefit from that kind of power being awoken, but they were already powerful, and even the gods steered clear of them.

I wondered if Leslie might have a sense about the vampires. Her mind worked in more calculated ways than mine ever had. She was a warrior at heart--a true seeker of vengeance. Her soul screamed for it. Until I could infiltrate the group of vampires that had been Roland Gregory's nest, she was the best option I had.

But I couldn't talk to Leslie. I couldn't talk to Gabrielle or Evangeline. Even Fabian could not be trusted with information like this. At the very least, it could put him at risk, and I refused to be the cause of it. He'd done enough, agreeing to gather the names of the vampires who had been close to Gregory. I had no one else.

For the first time, it struck me that I could not trust my family. We had our squabbles and our disagreements and often allowed distance between ourselves, but still—they were the only family I knew. They were all I had. If I could not trust them with this, I was well and truly alone.

The emptiness rocked me, nearly taking me to my knees. I held tightly to the wrought iron fence, not caring as the metal cut into my hands. I laughed at the thought. What was blood to me when I wasn't even certain it was my own? I had been feeding from others for so long I couldn't remember what it was like to feel my own blood coursing through my veins.

Maybe I was just a human-shaped husk for a soul more monstrous than any other I'd ever seen. Who else could look at the only family and friends they'd ever known and suspect them of such heinous acts as waking the Old Gods for pleasure and power?

If I had known it would be a true sort of death, I may have taken a witchblade to my own throat in that moment. But I didn't know, so I clung to the gate in despair, and it was a long time before I moved.

————

I crept silently to my bedroom and closed the door behind me. I slid to the floor, my head dropping into my hands. It was too much. I could sense Gabrielle and Evangeline in the rooms around my own. I ached to speak to them. I wanted to lay this burden at Evangeline's feet and beg her for guidance as I never had before. Her position was more protocol than anything else—but she'd been our confidante and the one who made us into who we were. The first few times we'd had to change identities and locations had been rough, and her aid during those times had been a blessing. But someone like me did not deserve blessings. It was no wonder I had been cursed with the information.

The Fates' information never came cheap.

It was 1559. January. At that time, we resided in Europe, as the corona-tion of England's latest queen, Elizabeth I, was sure to result in celebrations that the more sinister Creatures might take advantage of. Though we had always been careful not to involve ourselves in the world of Creatures, Evan-geline had become more lenient over the last century. Gabrielle, Leslie, and I—known then by other names more apt for the time—took full advantage. Gabrielle, secretive as always, changed partners so quickly that none of us could even learn their names. I was not even certain she had learned them. This was fine with Evangeline. It was safer if we did not form attachments. It was Leslie who proved more troublesome. I was entirely too focused on our duties. I was Justice, after all, and we had no way of knowing whose name might appear in our amulets next. I had to be stone, so I was.

Leslie had become involved with a witch, Vallerie Whitley. Vallerie was inhumanly beautiful, though, and this earned her the attention of the villagers. She and her mother, Rebeckah, both tried to steer clear of any obvious wrongdoings, but eventually became a bit too well known for their tinctures, potions, and spells. Vallerie's long blonde curls and sapphire eyes, too, became the infatuation of a young man, Hugh, and he pursued her with earnestness.

The Fates appeared to Evangeline, warned her of Vallerie's destiny. We were warned to maintain our distance or risk our own sentencing in Tartarus. But Leslie did not heed the warning. She made plans with Vallerie to run away together, to outrun what awaited the witch. We did not anticipate she would make so drastic a move, and so we did not realize when she snuck from our home and into the woods.

Hugh followed Vallerie to the secret meeting with Leslie at dusk, returning with tales of their frantic kisses and secret plans. The jealousy and embarrassment Hugh felt at being looked over—and for a woman, at that—led him to call for Vallerie's head. The village did not listen, but only because they chose to burn her at the stake instead.

A witch.

A whore of a witch.

A demon whore of a witch.

We heard Hugh's tales as soon as they were spun from his lips, and we wind-walked to Leslie . We ripped her from Vallerie's arms and shielded her. Vallerie was dragged from the darkened woods by the angry mob of villagers while Gabrielle held Leslie.

"We can save her," Leslie pleaded.

She was on her knees at Evangeline's feet, clutching the brown skirts to her face, dampening them with her tears. Evangeline's face remained hard, though it didn't quite reach her eyes, which were sad in a way I had never seen before.

"We could have intervened, saved her from this wretchedness," Leslie sobbed.

"The Fates have spoken," Evangeline said and pulled her skirts from Leslie's grasp.

"Please, sister," she begged, turning her cries toward me.

I was stone.

This was why we had always remained separate from the humans and Creatures alike. This was why we could not involve ourselves with anything but our duties. Leslie rose to her feet and made a move as if she would run to the village square where the smoke from the flames beneath Vallerie's feet had already twisted into the sky. Before anyone else could, I grabbed my sister and pressed a witchblade to her throat.

"This is no business of ours," I growled.

Gabrielle's witchblade was also out. We had spent the last evenings hunched in chairs at the hearth, worrying about this very moment. I had not believed Leslie would sink so far, but Gabrielle anticipated it.

"She thinks she loves her," she said softly.

"Love," I scoffed. "A game. A dream, at best."

"But a dream all the same," Gabrielle said sadly.

"Not for us, Megaera. Not for us."

I murmured that mantra to Leslie as she knelt once more on the forest floor with my knife still held to her throat.

"Do it," she pleaded, her blue eyes bright with fury and pain.

"You would choose death?" Gabrielle asked.

"If Vallerie is dead, then I beg you to give me death, as well."

When the torturous memory ended, tears fell from my eyes—those same eyes that had looked at my sister with such contempt and disdain. I undressed and slid between my sheets, but sleep did not come quickly. I was afraid of what else my memory might show me, afraid of what other past sins I might have to face.

TWENTY

I finally fell asleep, but it was a fitful, wretched sort. I tossed and turned, kicked my sheets and blankets off only to pull them back again, clicked on the ceiling fan and then turned it off, played soft music, played angry music—nothing worked. And when I did fall asleep for more than what felt like a few moments, I was plagued with images and hazy memories I couldn't even be certain were memories at all.

The Fates were before me, but I knew them by their original names. Clotho held high a thin, shining, golden string as Atropos wielded a pair of golden scissors. Lachesis' eyes were opaque white and illuminated from within.

I knew they were Seeing. I felt it in the pit of my stomach.

"No!" I cried, stretching my hands out before me.

"You have committed the gravest of sins," Lachesis said in a strange, airy voice.

"You have betrayed your family," Atropos added.

"You have killed one whom you should hold dearest," Clotho said.

"You may not have wielded the weapon," Atropos spoke.

"But you are responsible just the same," murmured Clotho.

"The punishment will endure for the rest of time," cried Lachesis with eyes that shone brighter than anything I had ever seen before.

Instead of cutting the string, the golden thread held by Clotho burst into flame as I watched. Horror filled me, cold and aching.

I woke with that cold and aching horror still in the pit of my stomach. I didn't recognize that memory, but the horror of it filled me, nonetheless. I threw the blankets off my body but didn't move from my bed. Somewhere in the back of my mind I was reminded of the odd things I'd seen in the park the day I met Allison. They had to be memories to affect me so deeply, but I had not heard of such a thing. I had never had such a gift in my arsenal. Gabrielle did, to some extent, but when I knew so little and trusted even less, I could not bear to ask her.

Could this be my past? Could I have been....?

It hit me. This existence and the mystery about my creation. I thought I had just been pulled from the ether to work at the behest of The Twelve, but there could be more to it. What if this immortality was a punishment for something I did during a human life? The only punishment I was aware of that had been dealt with in such a manner involved the murder of family members—matricide or filicide.

Had I been a mother at one time? Had I killed my child? What had I done? Why were these memories coming to me now?

The memories hadn't shown themselves to me until after I had met Allison, which made me wonder if the two things could be connected. With the Fates also showing up, it seemed less and less likely that it could be a coincidence. I sighed heavily, throwing myself back onto the pile of pillows behind me. Even if the Fates were involved, they wouldn't tell me anything. I couldn't think of anyone who would.

I scrubbed my face with my hands until stars filled my vision. Nothing could shake the images of what I'd seen from my mind.

I wasn't going to sleep, that was certain, even though it was only early afternoon. I needed at least a few more hours.

A shower, fresh clothes, and some blood aided me in feeling somewhat back to normal, but I found myself pacing the hallways of the house.

"Olivia?" Evangeline called from her office.

"Yes?" I asked in a timid way that was so unlike me.

She poked her head out, long hair swinging like a curtain.

"Are you all right?"

"Of course," I snapped.

Evangeline's eyes searched mine.

"I'm going out," I said, unable to withstand the concern.

I grabbed a jacket and headed out the door. If I couldn't escape the memories and questions, at least I could get out of this house. It felt like the walls were closing in on me.

———

"Darling, I adore you, and I am so very pleased to see you again so soon, but it's too fucking early," said Fabian.

The door was open, but he stood well within the shadows. A crimson silk robe hung open over matching pants that left little to the imagination, but I felt no stirring within. I wasn't even sure how I had ended up here except that I'd begun walking and found myself staring at his front door. I'd knocked before I could talk myself out of it.

"Come inside," he said.

I heard his footsteps retreat, and I moved through the open door to follow him, closing it gently behind me. The sound still echoed. The house was dimly shrouded, and I could just make out Fabian's outline as he walked up the first few steps to the second floor.

"Don't just stand there. Come along," he said.

I followed him up the staircase and into his room. The bed earned a glance, but I knew I would just be distracting myself. Fabian deserved better. I threw myself into the overstuffed chair near the window and let my legs dangle over the sides. I stared up at the ceiling for a moment, hoping for some kind of clarity.

I turned my head and watched Fabian lift the books from his nightstand. He grabbed a piece of paper—torn from an envelope, by the looks of it—from his nightstand. He took the seat next to mine and extended his arm.

"The names you asked for," he said.

I sat up, staring at the paper, before I leaned forward to take it.

"Thank you," I said. "I'm not actually here for that, but thank you."

It was Fabian's turn to look surprised. It was painful, that surprise.

It told me he was used to me using him—for information, for distraction, for the sex that was the distraction. Guilt pitted in my stomach.

"Did I somehow earn a purely social visit?" he inquired with a smirk.

It surprised even me when I managed to laugh.

"I suppose you have. Gaia knows you've put in the time," I said sardonically.

"That I have," he said with a wry, knowing sort of smile.

That smile had certainly earned Fabian a tumble a time or two. I wished things felt so carefree and easy. I played with the hem of my shirt as Fabian moved to the edge of the bed to be closer to me.

"Talk to me," he said gently.

Oh, Gaia, if only I could.

I tried to smile at him, but I knew it didn't reach my eyes.

"I shouldn't," I admitted.

"Is it worrying you?" Fabian asked, his brow furrowed.

"Is what worrying me?"

"The mind-wipe that didn't work."

"Oh," I said. "Maybe a little."

"You should Turn her."

I felt horrified at the suggestion. "It wouldn't be fair."

"Fair," Fabian laughed. "Such an odd ideal for a Creature."

I smiled. It was true. I looked down at the list of names in my hand again. It wouldn't be dark yet for several hours, which meant the scrap of paper was pretty useless until then. I liked to hunt in the dark.

I looked at Fabian, and a smile that started off soft and kind slowly spread across his face. It grew to something more familiar, something that tugged deep within me.

"Come to bed, darling," he said in a low voice. "You can play your spy games later."

I hesitated.

"Just a cuddle, love. You look like you could use it."

The unexpected wave of emotion nearly toppled me, and tears pricked my eyes. More than a lover, I needed a friend, and it spoke volumes to me that Fabian knew me well enough—against all odds, despite my disappearing acts, and my desperate need for secrecy—to notice. Fabian's eyes took it all in. The smile disappeared. He held out a hand to me. I took it, crawled into bed, and sank into the warm comfort of friendship.

———————

I left Fabian's, but I'd barely closed the heavy door behind me before I pulled the slip of paper out of my pocket.

Blythe Baker
Istvan Narkovic
Sabri Elam
Laura Ashe

A small nest, all things considered. But it was likely Fabian had only been able to discreetly gather these few names. It was certainly better than what information I'd had before, which was absolutely nothing. Though I was a skilled huntress, I'd never had to play games of espionage. This was something new, and I tried to tamp down my feelings of excitement at the challenge.

I pulled the wind around me and flew across the city to land in the backyard of the Gregory Estate. Roland had been alone that night with Allison, but signs pointed to at least a few of the nest mates residing there, as well. It wasn't surprising. Most vampires, especially those in nests, chose to live in a single home. A commune of sorts. In the early centuries, vampires had entire villages to themselves, but that lifestyle was difficult to maintain in the more modern eras.

I watched the house carefully, crouched in a line of bushes near the back fence of the gated lot. Much of the back of the house was glass, overlooking the spacious backyard. A few of the windows had curtains blocking the inside of the house from my gaze, but as far as I could tell, there was little to no movement inside the manor.

A sudden, blinding light pierced my eyes, and I ducked down into my forearms for cover. When my eyes had adjusted, I slowly looked up and out over the lawn once again. Automatic lights, surely on a timer of some kind. Of course. Roland's disappearance must have sent the nest into a frenzy of panic. Safety measures and precautions had clearly been implemented, much to my dismay. There was no way for me to get across the lawn. Even wind-walking would trigger any kind of motion detector, and I was willing to bet there was one.

I leapt over the fence of the estate and crept through a neighboring backyard. I needed a second plan—and fast—but there was nothing to be done for the moment. I wind-walked home, mind ablaze with possibilities of how best to approach Gregory's former nest.

TWENTY-ONE

A few nights later and just past sunset, I had every intention of infiltrating the estate again. I continued to gaze at the wrought iron gates for a while, letting my mind go quiet before I needed to waltz in there with a breezy sort of confidence. Without it, they would try to kill me. They wouldn't succeed, but it would mean starting completely over with a new nest. The vampires might be too nervous by then to let anyone unfamiliar inside, even with the right names and supposed Sire.

Fuck. Just do it.

As I went to pull the wind around me to bypass the closed entrance, I felt the tell-tale warmth at my throat, stopping me immediately. With an exasperated sigh, I drew the necklace out from underneath my shirt.

"Duty calls," I whispered to no one.

Two names. Again, more than usual. It tugged at me in a way that was hard to ignore, especially as I could find only a bitterly cold wind to ride in on. It pushed me onto a quiet, tree-lined road.

The outline of a small house that was difficult to see through the overgrown bushes and pines in the nearby yard. I listened. No birdsong, no rustling, no movement could be detected. The thought tendrils I sent out told me nothing.

It was unfamiliar territory, and it was unnerving. Even in the dead of winter when the snow deadened the forest soundscapes, my ears could detect the burrowing of animals into their shelters, the desperate pecking of a bird needing sustenance. We were barely into November and there was no snow upon the ground to silence anything. It was far too quiet.

Shivers crawled up my spine. I dropped a knife from my wrist sheath into my hand before I crept up the path and peered through a broken window along the northern side of the house. From there, I saw a body, twisted at an angle that told me someone or something had been here already.

Damn it.

The broken window held no telltale fibers, but it was the cleanliness of the sill that unnerved me. The silence told me there was no immediate danger, so I made my way inside the structure.

Two bodies.

Two wolven with their hearts ripped from their chests.

None of the wounds indicated the use of witchblades, which was a relief. It was the only thing that settled me amongst the blood and sinew of the scene. I had never gotten to a location and found a body instead of a living soul. I couldn't help but wonder if this could be connected to the rash of Creature murders that had been occurring.

It seemed unlikely to be a pack brawl. The wolves were careful about their rankings and where the battles for them took place. And when the packs fought for territory with the others, there were no bodies.

What would leave the body behind?

Could it be a coincidence? Or could whomever was murdering Creatures be targeting deviants? While that would simplify things in one regard, it would certainly complicate others. Never before had Creatures attempted to police themselves—not between the species, anyway. That had always been our duty, and even though the Creatures did not know specifically who we were, they knew enough of our existence.

I could report to Demetrius. I could lay this in his lap and never think about it again. It wasn't my problem, was it? The Twelve wanted to rule, so they could deal with this gods-damned mess.

But if I did that, Sunee might have my head. She wanted me to find out what was going on, and she didn't want to me to alert Demetrius. It should probably worry me that The Twelve were working around their own Steward—not a showing of confidence, certainly—but I wasn't sure I could let myself go down that road. How long could I allow my conscience to tug at these fraying threads before it was too much?

I would sit helplessly and watch the world burn if The Twelve decided that's what needed to happen.

Wouldn't I?

Once, I could have unequivocally said I would. I had changed, though. Something had changed within me in some uncomfortable and unexpected way. My eyes had been opened.

I also had another soul to dispatch. Only one of the bodies I'd found matched the soul I'd been assigned, which meant the second wolf had not yet been targeted by The Twelve as a deviant. There went my theory.

Never had my work been so mysterious.

Still frowning, I grabbed at the chill of the wind once more.

———

"In Tartarus so shall it be," I said softly.

I pulled my blade across the throat of the male vampire who'd had the misfortune of belonging to a name in my amulet and stepped back, allowing the body to fall to my feet. It immediately turned to dust. He had once been a nest mate of Roland's—the only connection I'd found so far between the list I'd gotten from Fabian and the names I was assigned. Though I'd tried to glean information from this assignment, I had not been successful.

I stood and looked down at my amulet once more. Nothing.

I sighed in relief.

"Olivia?"

I hissed and whirled around to find Alex in the doorway of the room where I'd found the vampire. He stood in all black, dagger in hand, and in a defensive position. Without realizing it, my body had lowered into a crouch, put itself on the edge of violence.

For a moment, we simply stared at one another. Alex's blade

gleamed in the firelight. My witchblade glowed all on its own. Alex stared.

"Olivia," Alex began. "Your eyes."

"You shouldn't be here," I said to him.

I knew my eyes were blazing their unnatural blue—they always did when I escorted a soul.

"You're not human," he said, his voice resonant with an edge of surprise.

It wasn't a question, but I shook my head, anyway. We both stood from our crouched positions and took tentative steps toward one another, but we stayed at least an arm's length away. Trust was clearly a commodity for us, and neither of us was willing to extend it.

"You shouldn't be here," I repeated.

"I shouldn't be here?" He scoffed. "What in the seven hells are you doing here? And what are you?"

"I can't tell you that, Alex."

"Are you a Creature?" he asked.

"I can't tell you that, either."

"You're going to need to tell me something," he said.

"Alex—" I began.

But I didn't know what to say.

"You should be running," were the words I eventually chose.

"And yet I'm not," he said as he twirled his dagger in his hand.

"What are you?" I asked.

"Fiagai."

It was a name I'd not heard in more than fifty years, but it meant danger. I had many questions. I doubted Alex would give me answers without receiving any himself.

"You know the name," he said in a low voice, moving closer.

He was too close now. He could strike out with his blade. I would have to kill him. I didn't want to. I nodded in response and kept my eyes roving over him, alert to any sign he might strike.

"How do you know that name?" he asked.

I didn't answer.

"What are you, Olivia?"

Again, I didn't answer.

"You killed one of your own," he said, looking pointedly at the body behind me.

"I am Creature and... not Creature," I said.

"If you are a Creature, we are enemies," he said.

I nodded in understanding. I had encountered Fiagai before.

"I don't want to hunt you," he said.

But it was his duty. Fiagai were an Ancient Celtic group of hunters whose sole purpose was to eradicate Creatures in the human realm. They weren't immortal, but they did live longer than was typical, and they were faster and stronger than average humans, as well. They were evolution's response to an influx of beings not meant for this realm.

The Fiagai believed their duty was sacred.

I understood duty.

"I am no enemy of the Fiagai, Alex, but if you are trying to ascertain if I am human, I must assure you that I am not."

His intake of breath was sharp.

"I am not your enemy," I repeated.

Alex took a step backward from me and ran a hand through his unbound hair. He was breathing hard as he stared at me, brown eyes ablaze with confusion and frustration and adrenaline.

"Nothing in my blood burns for me to take this blade and strike you down," he said softly.

"We are not enemies, Alex."

"Tell me what you are," he pressed.

I wanted to. Gaia knew I wanted to. But despite not being enemies, Fiagai and my kind were not friends, either.

"Tell me this," he demanded. "Are you hunting my sister?"

I gasped. "No!" I cried.

He breathed a sigh of relief. "Then what is she to you?" he asked softly.

"A human soul that didn't deserve to meet its end," I replied. "I shouldn't have saved her. I wasn't supposed to, but she was there and so helpless..."

I trailed off. There was absolute shock in the widening of his eyes and a tightness around his mouth that told me something was amiss.

"Olivia, what are you talking about?" he demanded.

I realized my mistake then. For all their talk of closeness, Allison hadn't told Alex anything about how we met or what had happened that night.

Curse it all.

"The night I met your sister," I said, "she almost died at the hands of a vampire."

Alex let loose a string of violent curses.

"I took her to my home, found a healer, and hoped against hope she'd live," I continued.

"And she knows this?" he asked.

"She does," I admitted. "A memory wipe was attempted, but it didn't take."

"And yet she lives," he said in disbelief.

"No one knows it didn't work," I said in a low, quiet voice. "I tried to stay away from your sister—she would have been safe as long as she stayed quiet about all that she saw. But she remembered me."

We stared at one another again. He took a step toward me, but I immediately stepped back. It was then he seemed to realize he was still wielding his knife. He raised his hands in a peaceful signal and then slid the dagger into a sheath along his thigh. I could see at least three more weapons he could probably have in his hands in milliseconds, but I appreciated the gesture nonetheless. I slid my witchblade into the sheath on the inside of my boot. I looked back to Alex, met his eyes, and saw the question before he even asked it.

"Why?" he asked aloud.

"I don't know," I said with a shrug. "If the memory wipe didn't work, I knew that the order would be given to turn her immortal. It just didn't seem right."

"Because it isn't!" he said. "She's human. She's not even Fiagai."

I had assumed this, knowing the Fiagai line typically only took the eldest children.

"That's why I didn't report it."

"Thank you," he said, closing his eyes.

I reached out and touched his shoulder. I understood that kind of love, that kind of loyalty, and I could practically taste his relief. The connection to his brethren glowed like an ember in his eyes when Alex spoke of it. I bet his soul shone just as brightly. And I felt myself drawn, against all odds, to what I learned of him.

"Tell me what you are," he said softly.

"I can't," I said.

"You saved my sister and for that I owe you a debt. You are safe from me, Olivia, but please—please just tell me what it is I'm not understanding here."

"You are sworn to the Fiagai?" I asked.

He nodded. "Since I was sixteen."

"And you were hunting this Creature?" I asked, gesturing behind me toward the pile of dust that had been a vampire only a short time ago.

Another nod.

"Why?" I asked.

"If you know of the Fiagai, you know our duty," Alex said.

I did, and it was the only reason I said the rest.

"For the world of Creatures," I said, "I am Justice."

His eyes widened, and it told me that my existence had become more than a story for Creatures. News of us and what we did had spread beyond. "You're a Fury," he breathed.

"Come sit," I said, gesturing at a small sofa near the fireplace at the opposite end of the room.

I supposed I didn't want to be any nearer to what had just been a vampire any more than I had to. I didn't typically stick around once I'd fulfilled my duty—I should have been on my way to Tartarus. But we both sat, and I felt that same electrified feeling I had when we'd touched the other day. I moved a bit to one side so that our legs weren't quite so close together.

"My name in this time is Olivia," I began, "and I am the Alekto."

TWENTY-TWO

I gave Alex only the necessary details, but even those were probably too much. I was, after all, a myth. The Fiagai I had come across never made it back to their brethren to confirm our existence. They had tales, as the other bands of human hunters did, but we had always remained firmly in story form. Now I was standing in front of a human hunter, bred only to kill Creatures, and thought about all the others like him I'd dispatched over the years.

I hoped I would not have to make that choice with Alex. I told myself it was because of the pain it would cause Allison, and not at all having to do with the warmth in his brown eyes or the interesting way the waves of his hair fell over the sculpted planes of his face. I would not admit his beauty.

"This Creature," I said, "was my latest assignment. I sent his soul to Tartarus where he will be judged."

"By whom?"

I shook my head. I had already said far too much. More would be unwise.

"I think that's enough information for tonight," I said.

Alex didn't look happy, but he did not press me for answers. We sat there for a moment, side by side in our respective silences, and those few moments allowed me to piece together other events of the evening. I recalled the two bodies where I had only expected to find one. I thought about how those bodies had been left. I thought about what I knew of Fiagai, and the pieces began to fit together into a much clearer picture than anything my imagination had started to create.

"Alex, are you responsible for the deaths of two wolven tonight?"

"Why?" he asked, voice sharp.

That tone was answer enough, but I continued.

"Because I was to escort a wolven soul tonight, but when I arrived, both in the residence were dead. Hearts ripped from their chests."

Alex's head lowered. His broad shoulders, too, narrowed, like he attempted to close in on himself.

"It's my duty," he said.

I understood. Far too well, perhaps. It seemed I was not the only one with a duty that, at times, weighed heavily.

"Alex, you have to know that there's a system in place for Creatures who don't respect the laws," I started.

His eyes, a fiery golden brown, darted to mine.

"And how well is that system working?" He demanded as he shot to his feet. "We know there's infighting. We know about the demands to enslave us and return to what it was like before the laws."

"That's a small group—" I started.

"That's bullshit, and you know it."

He began to pace. I sighed out of exasperation—at myself for humoring this, at him for speaking of things too true for my liking, and at the world of Creatures in general and the predicament my role in all of it put me in.

"We're doing what we can," I said.

"It's not good enough."

"I know."

I reached out my hand and grabbed his, forcing him to end his pacing. I met his eyes again and was immediately sorry I did. His anger, so hot and righteous and right there under his skin, radiated from him. I knew what it was like to feel rage like that. I had never wished it upon anyone, and I certainly didn't wish it upon Alex.

That anger, though, felt like a beacon for my own. The pulsing, molten rage underneath his skin beat a rhythm that echoed within me. My own rage wanted to boil up and out of me, burning its way out of the humanlike skin I wore until I was nothing but white-hot fury.

Fury.

I stood up, still meeting his eyes, and looked down at our still-joined hands. Something old, something familiar was there in that joining, in the touch of my palm to his. Something rooted my skin to his, and that same something pushed away the pulsing fury that I could so readily wield.

Alex's eyes were wide. He felt it, too.

A low growl escaped before his mouth crashed into mine. The kiss deepened and I slid my tongue against his. We couldn't get close enough. I was burning from the inside but couldn't stay away from the flames. As quickly as his mouth had covered my own, Alex pulled away. He did not go far, though. Our foreheads pressed together, and the sound of Alex's breathing, fast-paced and hard, echoed around us.

"What are we doing?" he groaned.

He was right to question it. I knew I should have, but I felt quiet. For so long, I'd been something that pulsed and raced and raged. But in Alex's arms, I felt peaceful.

Quiet calm had never appealed to me, but I was soothed in every place his skin touched mine.

I stood on my toes to press another kiss to Alex's lips, achingly slow and gentle. He kissed me back, and it was a long moment, maybe hours, before I could pull my lips from his.

———

"I have to go," I said softly to Alex, who lay on his side next to me on the sofa.

"Same," he said, but his lips lowered to mine in what might have been our hundredth or thousandth kiss.

I wanted more. My skin already craved the soft and gentle touches of his fingertips. I grew cold at the thought of untangling my limbs from his and moving away from the delicious warmth that I would forever associate with him.

It was more than what I had known before with others. It piqued my curiosity. How could it not? But there was concern. How could I feel so much in so little time?

I could not take more of him. I wouldn't. I rolled off the couch and reassembled the weapons we'd removed, sliding knives into their respective sheaths along my spine, wrists, thighs, and ankles. I put my boots on and watched Alex out of the corner of my eye do his own reassembly of weaponry and clothing.

"It feels strange to think of you as Olivia now," he said suddenly, looking up at me. "You are so much more than that, I suppose."

I smiled. It had taken me a long time to get used to the ever-growing list of names I'd had and used over the centuries.

"It's my name," I shrugged. "Or one of them, at least."

"Tell me."

He moved closer, and I did not move out of his path.

"I have been Arabella, Natalya, Farohildis, Hadriana, Lysandra..." I listed.

He laughed.

"Oh, I can keep going," I said with a grin.

"I'm certain of it. You've lived a lot of lives."

"Just the one, really. It's been a very long, complicated existence."

I was hit with a pang of sadness then. My life—seeming so meaningless—stretched out behind and before me.

"And Alekto?" he prompted, which shook me out of my melancholy thoughts.

"What?"

"Your name. Alekto. Where did that fit?"

"The name I was given. It's only a title now."

"Ah... so that part of the myth is accurate, at least."

"That part?" I asked.

"Well, your shape is human. I don't see feathers or talons or anything so obviously supernatural."

I had heard those rumors—that we were fierce, birdlike creatures. I had no talons. I was packaged into a feminine, seemingly innocent shape.

"Most Creatures have a human shape," I pointed out.

"Ah, yes, but they have other shapes. Do you?"

"I... I don't know. Not that I'm aware of. My sister could probably tear someone apart with her bare hands, but there's no shifting of any kind," I jested.

"Perhaps I'll just call you Fury."

The smile that had spread across my features fell into a frown.

"Or not?"

I cleared my throat.

"Fury is the name I am called when I am on duty—when I am sending souls to Tartarus," I said quietly. "It's like Alekto—only used when I'm..." I trailed off.

Alex nodded slowly.

"Then, Olivia Beckett, I don't know how, but I would very much like to see you again," he said as he came closer.

His cupped my face in his hands and kissed me one more time. I could not allow myself to sink into his warm embrace, even if I wanted to. The desperation that both concerned and vexed me.

"Goodbye, Alex Drivas," I said.

I made no promises. I had none to offer. My life was not my own, nor was his. We were bound to our duties, and the reality of that was rapidly sinking in.

With that thought in mind, I stepped back, grabbed my amulet, and flashed out of the human realm. I did it without thinking and certainly without, at first, the realization there was no one in this realm apart from my sisters and Evangeline who had ever been able to see me do that. And I certainly didn't, in that moment, probe into why I had felt so comfortable showing Alex what no other human on earth had ever seen.

———

I wind-walk straight into my bedroom, scattering my weapons across the floorboards in a manner that would infuriate Leslie and probably Evangeline, as well. I pulled the clothes from my body and set them into an old canvas bag I'd once used to transport weapons. They would have to be burned. I'd never get Alex's scent out of them. The last thing I needed was Evangeline or one of my sisters catching a whiff of him on my clothing. Thankfully, his scent did not betray his otherness in the way so many scents did. Gabrielle had lost an entire wardrobe once, forced to burn everything to rid herself of a wolven's scent when their tryst ended. Evangeline had been furious—both at the tryst and at the loss of the clothing during a time when material was harder to come by.

Once the bag was stowed deep in the recesses of my closet, I went into the bathroom to shower. I rinsed my body head to toe underneath near-scalding water and remembered what it had been like to have Alex's hands roaming over the same skin. I shampooed my long hair four times, ensuring that it would retain only the scent of coconut and not the scent of Alex running long, powerful fingers through the loose strands.

Why was he haunting me this way?

I'd become more yielding as the centuries wore on. I'd softened from the stoniness Leslie saw that long-ago night in the woods as she heard her lover's screams and smelled the foul bitterness of burnt flesh in the autumn air. I'd taken lovers. And while there was a sense of comfort to be found in their arms, I had never lost my senses in the way I had when I was wrapped up in Alex.

I scrubbed at my skin with a sea salt mixture, as if I could remove the top layer and, thus, Alex's memory all together. But while it left my body soft and scented, I remembered all too well the electric fire that had raced through me as Alex kissed each of my fingertips, the inside of my wrist, up my forearm and bicep, over my shoulder, and ended at my neck. I felt the soft flick of his tongue just above my collarbone as it wrested from me a soft moan. The gentle tug at my hair pulled another sound from deep within me. I'd bitten into his shoulder to silence myself. He'd laughed in a low tone, but the contraction of his muscles against the very sensitive part of me as he lay between my thighs only incited the flames between us to grow higher and hotter.

I hadn't noted the passage of time. I forgot my surroundings. I was truly lost in the man surrounding me. I couldn't afford it, that level of distraction. But I would have paid dearly for one more hour or even one more kiss.

I didn't know how I could move forward without him or with him.

It wasn't safe—not in any sense of the word. Any time I spent with him was a risk, and I was no gambler.

As frustration burned in every thought that raced through my brain, I turned the handles of the shower and stood beneath the ice-cold spray.

Let me be stone.

TWENTY-THREE

I raised my hand, poised to knock on the heavy office door that was already propped open, but Demetrius waved me in before I could. *Odd.*

I walked into the darkened room and took a seat in one of the stiff leather armchairs in front of the desk. Surrounded by the warm golden sheen of candlelight, Demetrius looked fierce and otherworldly. This was a domain that was his and his alone. I was sure he thought he painted a picture of stoic wisdom with his hair neat and silvered at the temples and as he stared at me over steepled fingers. He sat back in his chair, the picture of serenity.

I would not give him the satisfaction of speaking first. The silence swelled between us as we played our strange game. We both had eternity. There was no reason to rush.

I removed a knife from my wrist and used it to clean underneath my fingernails, sure it would grate on him. My nonchalance coupled with a lack of desire to pay obeisance usually did.

"Well, you don't look injured in any way," he finally stated.

"Did you expect me to be?"

"I no longer know what to expect from you."

I smiled. I couldn't help it.

"My souls are in Tartarus," I supplied.

"Yes, but I expected your report hours ago. Where have you been?"

"I was delayed, obviously."

Again, silence filled the room before Demetrius finally gestured impatiently for me to continue.

"The vampire was easy enough. There were signs of other vampires living there, but the miscreant was alone for the evening. The wolven, however, proved a complicated assignment. Someone had been there before me."

"Someone," Demetrius stated.

"There was a fight of some kind. The wolves were licking their wounds when I arrived," I lied.

"Ah," he said. "Pack politics, I'm sure."

He waved it away, and I let him. There was no reason to involve Alex or the Fiagai. Demetrius didn't need to know that the killing had been different than the others. What could he do about it? It was clear from the things Sunee said that he was being kept out of their discussions. In this, at least, I knew my place.

"You are dismissed," Demetrius said.

In the blink of an eye, I slipped through the office door and was through various tunnels and up the staircase.

I rapped on the door and waited impatiently for an invitation. Though we had come to an agreement, I still hesitated to barge into the private quarters of belonging to a member of The Twelve.

My right foot tapped out a rhythm as I exhaled loudly, waiting. A few moments passed, my right foot still tapping, but then the door opened.

"Come in," said Sunee.

She turned back inside. I took one step and then another, again surprised by the riot of colors present in the otherwise darkened space. Sunee sat on one of the sofas, near the same spot we'd spoken last time, and she lifted a steaming cup to her lips. I moved closer.

"I apologize for disturbing you, Sunee," I said.

I dropped low into a bow.

"Come, come—no apologies, and certainly no bowing," Sunee said, waving away my words and my bow with one heavily ringed hand that glinted gold in the lamplight.

"Something's happened, hasn't it?" she asked.

I took a seat on the sofa opposite Sunee's, and she immediately offered tea with a nod of her head toward the teapot. I declined, so we sat in silence as she sipped from her cup.

Now that I was there, I wasn't quite sure how to begin.

"The Fiagai are active again," I said finally. Sunee nodded. "You knew?" I probably shouldn't have asked, but I did.

"We only recently confirmed their activity in the same area you're located in. They've been more active in other parts of the world, but that's almost always been the case."

I nodded thoughtfully, as if this made total sense. It didn't.

"Wait... we?" I asked.

Sunee paused, as if she hadn't meant to say "we" at all.

"I have been working with some of the other members of the council—those who are of a similar mind—to get a clearer sense of what is happening in the earth realm with the Creatures."

I didn't say anything.

Sunee tilted her head to one side, as if listening to something. Just moments later, as Sunee reached for the pot of tea, two atlantean members of The Twelve strode through the door. I immediately rose to my feet so I could bow and greet them.

With the pleasantries out of the way, the atlanteans arranged themselves in the chairs furthest from the fireplace to my left. Atara, who sat closest to me, was tall, her muscles taut beneath golden skin. Her long blonde hair, some pieces in waves and others in tight braids, was tipped with aqua in a style I had seen on humans, though it was natural for the atlantean. Her pantsuit, which included an artfully draped white silk jacket, glimmered with iridescent jewels near her neck. She was beautiful but intimidating, and I had never handled being intimidated well. I sat up straighter and squared my shoulders. I was sure she noticed the change, but I didn't care.

"We are suspicious," began Atara in her melodic voice.

"Very suspicious," interjected Ramiel, the opposite of Atara in almost every way imaginable.

Atara placed a gentle hand on Ramiel's well-muscled forearm to soothe him. The male atlantean did not look soothed, however, and I was glad for the comfort of my witchblades against my back, strapped to my calf, and hidden inside my boots.

"You have recently come into contact with a human woman, yes?" Atara asked.

I didn't want to lie, but I didn't want to say anything that could incriminate me, so I didn't speak. I met her ocean blue eyes with my own.

I didn't nod. I didn't blink. I didn't move.

"We already know about Allison," Sunee said gently.

I willed myself to stay still, avoiding looking Sunee in the face. My hands wanted to roam over my weapons, finding comfort there, but I would not move.

"We know about the brother, as well," grunted Ramiel. "The Fiagai."

Again, it was only the power of my will that kept me seated and silent.

"What about them?" I finally asked quietly.

"I don't know how to put this," Atara said to Sunee, gesturing helplessly.

"Olivia, the Allison and Alex you have recently met are the reincarnated souls of your long-ago husband and daughter," Sunee said.

I stared at her. I stared so long that my eyes burned. Blood could have poured from them for all I cared. I was certain there already had to be a crimson pool of it beneath me. Sunee's words had ripped my heart from my chest.

I don't recall when I moved from my seat. No one spoke a word to me. The silence felt heavy, smelling like potpourri and its heavy rose scent. I waited for the ground to shake beneath me. I waited for lightning to strike me down. I waited for another memory, jogged loose by the words that had just been said to rock me to my core. Nothing happened.

I paced over the fringe of the various rugs strewn about Sunee's cool stone floors. No memory seared itself into my brain. No earthquake arrived. No quiet bliss of death for me. *Never death for me.*

"Olivia," Sunee said gently.

"That's not really my name," I stated flatly.

I know my eyes must have flashed with the glory of my anger. The rage, hot and heavy in my stomach, threatened to burst out with every word I forced from my tongue.

"No," Ramiel acknowledged in his gruff voice.

I wanted to return to pacing, but I stood my ground. Shoulders squared, feet apart, I wanted to fight—the need for it thrummed through my veins.

"You were, long ago, named Alekto. Later, as you now realize, that became your title. I'm sure it was a joke to the Old Ones—a humorous name they could give you that you would never realize was your own."

I stared.

"Or they were simply lazy," Atara laughed.

"Who was I?" I ground out.

"You were the eldest daughter of an important family. You and a young boy named Iason were childhood friends. In adulthood, that friendship blossomed. Soon after your wedding, you became pregnant, and you gave birth to a daughter, whom you named Eleni. When Eleni was five years old, you returned to your home after a day at the marketplace to find her and your husband murdered."

I said nothing.

"You were so angry," Sunee said quietly.

I stared. I begged my mind to show me their faces, to force any of this make sense, but there was no memory to cling to. I only had these words to tell me my own history. I hated it. I hated them.

"Your anger grew and grew until it burned too hot for your human body. From what we understand, you turned into a Fury, vowing to avenge their souls," said Sunee, who had risen from the sofa and come nearer to me.

"But I didn't just avenge their souls, did I?" I asked.

"No," said Atara.

Her head shook back and forth slowly.

"When their murderers were dead, you vowed that you would hunt down every murderer, every miscreant, every evildoer until the end of time," Sunee shared.

"But the gods couldn't allow that—it undermined their own system of justice," Atara explained.

"So you were given a title and a duty. You have held your title and performed that duty admirably ever since," said Sunee.

"I'm so proud," I spat out.

No one said anything for a while. I stood there, turning their words over and over in my mind.

"My sisters?" I asked in a whisper.

"Similar stories, though they are not truly kin to you, if that's what you're asking," Atara supplied.

"Why now? Why are their souls here now?"

They knew of whom I spoke.

"You are drawn to Alex, Olivia, because of who he was to you once," Sunee said. "We think his soul—and with it, Allison's—were pulled from the afterlife as a way to distract you."

"Worked out quite well, hasn't it?" I asked. No one said anything. "Who could have done this?"

Ramiel, Atara, and Sunee all looked at one another. I hated the implication the silence brought with it. That anger that had burned within me so brightly that it had once torn away every shred of my humanity threatened, once again, to overtake me. I didn't want to leash it. "You think a council member did this?" I cried.

"Or someone close to the council, yes," Sunee responded meaningfully.

I knew what they insinuated. And as insufferable as Demetrius could be, I had a difficult time imagining him at the center of such obvious insurrection.

"Why?" I bit out.

"Demetrius has been advocating for a seat on the council for some time."

"He wants to be, what, the thirteenth? There are twelve seats. They're filled."

"He thinks he should replace someone on the council."

"What does distracting me have to do with it?"

"If you are distracted it will demonstrate a stronger hand is needed to guide the Furies, and that the hand should belong to someone intimately aware of The Twelve and their..." Sunee trailed off.

"Tools? Weapons?" I offered snidely.

"For lack of a better word, yes. He also needs you and your sisters distracted so that you won't connect him back to any of the strange occurrences."

"Do you suspect him of the uprisings, as well?" I asked.

"We're not sure. Someone is whispering in the ears of Creatures, but we are not certain yet if it is Demetrius or somehow an unhappy coincidence."

I thought back to what Fabian reminded me of—Creatures pulled at their bindings every so often.

I did not know if I preferred that to a betrayal.

"What of a second?" I asked.

"A second?" inquired Ramiel.

"Yes, a second," I repeated. "Someone doing his work in the earth realm so that his hands remain clean."

"An option we had not considered," Ramiel mused.

"For centuries, I was told that my duty was to hunt down every deviant Creature. I know intrigue, and I know duplicity."

"That you do," mused Ramiel. "Your vengeance has served us well."

He stroked his smooth, dark face. His eyes were almost black, yet alight with the excitement of bringing down a foe. My own violent nature recognized his. I needed to get out of this room, and out of this realm, before I did something we would all regret.

"I need to return to the earthen realm," I said to the three council members.

Sunee glanced at the others before she slightly inclined her head toward me in acquiescence.

"I will await further orders," I continued.

"I do not need to caution you about the delicacy of this situation."

"I understand."

I bowed slightly before leaving Sunee's quarters.

TWENTY-FOUR

I couldn't face Evangeline or my sisters.

What did they know? What could they know?

My body was at war with itself, both wanting Alex and fearing him. It didn't feel right to hide away at Fabian's, now knowing what I did about Alex and Allison. Losing myself in the way I often did with him felt wrong in the wake of all I had learned.

I went home long enough to pack a bag and leave a note that I was on business for The Twelve. It was enough information to avoid having anyone search for me while also preventing too many questions.

The words of Ramiel, Atara, and Sunee ran on a loop through my mind. When I could no longer stand it, I researched, analyzed, and hunted down every scrap of information I could on Roland Gregory and the vampires he had taken under his wing. With everything else so out of control, I latched on to that purpose. I could infiltrate that nest, gleaning information about whom or what was instigating the uprisings.

I needed an outlet for my anger. If I could channel it, I might make some progress on finding out who had dared bring my husband and child into this realm.

And then it was time. The cold wind whipped around me, tearing my hair from its braid and sending tendrils flying around my face. I stared at the Gregory Estate. I didn't want to be there, but I didn't truly wish to be anywhere at all.

I wanted time and answers to the questions building in my mind, neither of which I was likely to receive.

My eyes roamed over the impressive brick facade, well-groomed yard, and iron gate. I let my rage fill me until I hated all of it, until I wanted nothing more than to wind-walk into the manor and hunt each and every vampire down. I could have relished in the feel of their blood pouring over my hand as I sliced my witchblade across their throats and rejoiced in the knowledge that I had prevented another senseless murder.

Memories tore at me with sharp claws.

"No, no, no, no," I whispered as I knelt in a pool of growing crimson.

My chiton, a pale pink, was already soaked at the knees. I barely noticed the slow path it took upward as the material took in more and more of the life-force from the body in front of me.

"No, no, no, no, no," my whispers turned to cries and then to screams.

Another body nearby. Also faceless.

More blood. So much blood.

Screams shredded my throat. There was so much sorrow and so much anger, and it was all embedded in my soul. I would feel this forever. I would hate this forever. I would rage like this forever.

I stood in absolute stillness, clenching my jaw against the waves of emotion. I refused to be shaken by the memory. Instead, I opened the gate and strode up the path to the house. There was a familial nature amongst vampires, and I was set to take advantage of all of it.

I grabbed the ouroboros door knocker and made enough noise to wake the dead. The door slowly creaked open and the pale, white face of a male vampire showed.

"Hello?" he asked.

I smiled warmly, making sure that my fangs showed.

"Hi. Is Roland around?"

The sorrow in his eyes made me feel nothing.

"I'm sorry, but Roland is gone. We haven't seen or heard from him."

"Oh," I said sadly, making sure to frown in a puzzled sort of way.

"He's sort of the only person I know here, and I need a place to crash. His old nest-mate, Fiona, said this was where I could find him."

I gestured to the duffel bag that hung near my hip. The vampire, who I supposed was Istvan Narkovic, looked torn. He opened the door a bit wider and gestured me in.

"You can talk to Blythe and Sabri—maybe they know someone."

"Thank you so much!" I said.

I followed him through the entryway and into one of the formal parlor areas. An Indian woman lay prone on one of the dark teal sofas, propped up by a mound of fluffy white cushions. Another woman, pale as Istvan, sat primly in one of the chairs near the fireplace on the far wall. Both looked over as I walked in.

"Blythe, Sabri, this is... oh, I'm sorry. I didn't catch your name," Istvan said. "I'm Istvan."

His cheeks blushed pink as he offered me a hand, and I took it with another smile I made sure reached my eyes.

"I'm Lydia," I said brightly.

"Who is your Sire?" asked Sabri.

Looking me over thoughtfully, she sat up.

"Fiona? Roland's old nest-mate?" I said, letting my voice lilt up as if I was nervous, unsure.

Blythe snorted.

"You mean Roland's old fuck buddy."

Istvan gasped while I allowed a blush to heat my cheeks.

"Well, there's no doubt we're talking about the same Fiona," I giggled.

That earned me a wry smile from Blythe. Sabri still looked me over skeptically.

"Where are you from?" Sabri asked.

"Quebec. I got in a little bit of trouble up there, so Fi thought I should come down here and lay low at Roland's for a bit."

"What kind of trouble?" Blythe asked.

She gestured at me to take a seat, so I took one in the sofa opposite of Sabri's.

"Me and some of my nest mates partied a little too hard a few nights ago, and the humans we were hanging out with went from entertainment to *entertainment*, if you know what I mean."

"Hmm," replied Sabri.

"We didn't do it on purpose, really, but they're just so fucking fragile, yeah? And come on—absolutely no instincts whatsoever. They're sheep," I laughed.

The laughter around me was warm and congenial.

"Well, Lydia, we're happy to let you stay here. Gaia knows there are enough bedrooms in this place," Blythe offered.

"Really? Even just a night would be so awesome," I gushed. "Just somewhere safe until I can find some lodgings of my own."

"Play your cards right," Istvan said as he sat next to me, "and you won't have to."

He grinned and put his hand in the crook of my elbow conspiratorially. Sabri rolled her eyes.

"Sure, yeah. Stay or whatever. Just don't *entertain* here, okay? We're laying low," she said in a dark voice.

"Of course, of course. I wouldn't *dream* of bringing trouble to your doorstep."

"Ooh, Lydia, I'm so glad you're here!" Blythe cried. "Sabri is obviously a total bitch, but Istvan and I have been dying to have a little fun."

"Oh, my god, Blythe. You're already fucking dead," Sabri snapped.

She was up and out the door before I could even blink. Istvan and Blythe stared after her, but they didn't seem that surprised. Apparently, this was normal behavior.

I could work with that.

"Ignore her," said Istvan.

I could work with that, too.

"She's taking Roland's disappearance really hard," said Blythe quietly, who'd come to sit on the other side of me.

We heard a scream and a crash.

Blythe rolled her eyes.

"Like Istvan said, just ignore her."

"Let's go find you a room!" suggested Istvan.

I allowed myself to be led out of the parlor and up the staircase.

Istvan and Blythe helped me select a room. Though Istvan tried to not-so-subtly drop hints that he'd like to go out for the evening, Blythe insisted I needed rest and relaxation. In fact, she pulled a myriad of toiletries from the bathroom cabinet, lined them up on the counter, and pushed a fluffy white towel into my arms.

"You need a quiet night," she insisted. "We can do a crazy night out tomorrow."

"But I wanted to—" Istvan whined.

"You can finish that sentence later, Istvan. Tonight, Lydia deserves some pampering."

With that, she tugged at Istvan's arm until he exited the bathroom. Blythe shut the door behind them with one more bright smile tossed in my direction, leaving me alone. I hung the towel on the rack—heated, of course—near the tub. I slid the strap of my bag off my shoulder and let the whole thing fall to the floor.

Irritation and impatience had my hands curling into fists.

I wanted blood and vengeance, not a damn bubble bath. But I couldn't exactly start slitting throats—at least, not until I got some answers about what Roland had been up to. As much as I didn't want to stay in this house, I knew it was likely one of the three vampires would check on me during the evening, so it was best that I stayed put, embodying Lydia.

Lydia would want pampering, silly nitwit that she was.

I started the bath water and kicked my boots into a corner. I hung my jacket on a hook on the back of the door and undressed. When I was in nothing but underwear, I inspected the various oils and things Blythe had put on the countertop.

Selecting bubble bath with a citrus scent and swirling a few capfuls into the running water, I enjoyed the pleasantness as it wafted through the steam. I divested myself of my black bra and panties and lowered myself into the water.

Any desire to cling to my rage left almost immediately. The tub was deep and luxurious, with bubbles foaming gloriously. Once the tub was at its limit, I turned the tap off, lay back, and let the water soothe me.

I lay there, breathing in the scent of citrus, until the bath turned lukewarm and was no longer enjoyable. I considered emptying it just enough to run more hot water, letting my troubled mind quiet, but I was hungry and needed to find a blood stash. I was a bit concerned, given that the rest of the Creatures in this house were Roland's nestmates, that they might take blood only from the vein, and I couldn't afford to blow my cover. I pulled the stopper on the tub, removed the towel from its rack, and wrapped the warmth around my damp skin.

When I was dry, I changed into fresh clothing from the duffel. I hadn't brought anything too out of the ordinary. I pulled on an oversized black sweater, gray leggings, and some thick, woolen socks. I quickly rebraided my hair, made sure the rest of me looked presentable, and went in search of nourishment.

TWENTY-FIVE

T hankfully, Istvan was in one of the less formal rooms near the rear of the manor on the first floor. The space had a dark scent —like amber, perhaps—I couldn't place. Roland hadn't smelled of it when we'd met that fateful night. None of the nest-mates I'd encountered smelled that way, either. Another mystery to add to my ever-growing list. The room, however, I recognized from the night I broke in, noting the glass doors had been fixed.

A wraparound couch of dark navy sported several pillows in varying shades of blue with a thick knitted blanket in cream hanging from the end of one side. Tasteful art—whirls of mustard, crimson, and ivory—decorated the two walls that didn't house floor-to-ceiling windows or the repaired glass doors. A huge television hung on the wall opposite the sofa. I almost sat down next to Istvan, sensing he was the easiest to get to know and thus would be the easiest to break. However, there was my hunger to deal with, and I could play my spy games much better on a full stomach.

When I inquired about potential food sources, Istvan paused his show and kindly showed me to the stash of blood bags in the kitchen's stainless-steel refrigerator. He even pulled a mug down from one of the many stark-white cupboards and handed it to me.

"Microwave is over there," he said.

He'd pointed to the rectangle of stainless steel on another set of white cupboards. The marble top had light swirls of gray and gold, but they were pale, almost colorless. It was a beautiful space, and it was so much more modern than I had expected, given the very traditional, brick, formal exterior of the house.

"Roland just had the kitchen remodeled last year," Istvan said, noting my curiosity.

"It's beautiful."

"He had plans to redo the rest of the house, too, but with him gone, Sabri's in charge of the purse strings, and she's a bit more... fiscally responsible," he said with a wry smile.

"Why Sabri?"

"She's been with Roland the longest. She's not his oldest, obviously. Couldn't be, not by a long shot—you know how vamps are. He collected her a couple of centuries or so ago out of a pretty bad situation, and she's been his right-hand girl ever since."

"That bad situation have anything to do with her bad attitude?"

"Nah. That's due to more recent events."

"They weren't..." I trailed off.

"Lovers?!" Istvan exclaimed. "Hell, no. Sabri doesn't swing that way. She just hated what he'd gotten mixed up in. Feels some type of misplaced guilt, I'd guess."

Istvan's eyes widened as he realized what he said.

"I take it whatever it was he was mixed up in wasn't exactly *legal*," I said with the last word as a whisper.

"Not even close, sister," he whispered back.

"Vamps will be vamps," I crooned.

Istvan laughed. He was fun. I decided to let him off the hook for a moment. No use in pushing him, and I really was hungry.

"None for you?" I asked, gesturing to my mug.

"I'm already a few bags deep. When you're done in here, we can watch TV."

Left alone in the kitchen to warm the blood, I sipped at it slowly and took in the view. This had been one of the rooms I peered into when I'd been looking over the place. It was clear now why I had never seen any movement. I took a few more moments to look around and see if there was anything suspicious, but it was just a kitchen. There looked to be a formal dining space through the archway, and that room also looked out over the backyard, but I didn't want to be caught poking around anywhere.

I finished my drink and rinsed the mug before putting it into the dishwasher. It was important that I was a good houseguest until I had the information I needed.

With that done, I found my way back to the spacious room where Istvan sprawled on the couch and talked back to the television. I had never consumed much television. Leslie was the only one in our house who really had modern interests. I listened to music, sometimes composing it on the grand piano in the sunroom, or trained. Gabrielle painted, I knew, but she often did it away from the house, and we rarely saw any of the artwork she produced. Leslie suspected that she rented studio space downtown, but we had never bothered to confirm it.

"What are you watching?" I asked.

"My housewives."

"Your... housewives?" I asked, confused.

He looked aghast and patted the cushion next to him.

"Come sit, honey. You've got a lot to catch up on."

And that is how I spent a night learning about every single season of every single city of the *Real Housewives* from a 19th century Hungarian vampire.

———

And, though it had been a nice distraction, not even Istvan's elaborate, detailed backstories of his favorite program kept my mind from wandering. We watched so many episodes. I could almost keep all the cities and their respective casts straight. Istvan beamed with pride.

When he finally went to bed, I went back upstairs to the lavender suite that I'd been given for my stay. It was beautiful, though so different from my own room at home. It was soft, feminine, and light. It fit Lydia —who I'd created her to be. Talking to Istvan had made it difficult to remember who I was. Being Lydia was both more difficult and easier. I could sink into her joy and peace of mind. She had little else to concern her now that she had a place to crash. My mind, however, raced with all that had happened. Exhausted, I crawled into bed fully dressed and stared at the ceiling.

My husband. My daughter.

I had been a wife, a mother. Those roles had been ones I'd chosen for myself, born out of a desire for a family and all that came with it. The life I had built with Iason and Eleni must have been filled with so much love and joy for the loss of it to affect me the way that it had. To know I had been the one to find them murdered in cold blood was almost too much to bear. The horror of it burned through me with such heat that it tore me from my humanity. I had been left with this—this existence of sorts. The once-steady ground of my purpose was like quicksand beneath me.

It pulled at me, leeching away my strength and tugging me down into the depths of emotions I'd had little cause to feel over the centuries of my existence. The utter devastation left me so bitterly cold, but not numb enough to take away the pain all together.

If I had never met Alex and Allison, would I have ever known about my past? Before the last few weeks, I had never dreamed of a human life. I had assumed that, different from the Fates or the Gorgons or the Gray Sisters, I had been created to be a Fury. I had thought I was only ever a Fury and nothing more, nothing less.

My own sorrow and anger and vengeance had reduced me to this. Of course, I knew there were those who believed I was more than I had been. My humanity had burned away and given me what most might view as a glorious existence. I had once believed it to be a true and righteous existence.

But everything I thought I knew was left in ever-deepening shadows of doubt. It was easier to think that my existence as a Fury—near solitary and wholly focused on duty—was limited in ways my human life had not been.

For the first time I could recall in my existence as a Fury, I cried. Tears traced hot paths down my cheeks as I laid on the bed in the fetal position. I crossed my arms over the empty womb that had once grown a child. I knew that child had been the product of a love that I had somehow known so deeply. I allowed that love to dissipate in the wake of anger and fury. How could I have forgotten them? How had my vengeance become the thing that I embraced and not my loved ones— not even their memories? How could I have grown so cold within the heat of my rage and fury? Had it been my fate all along?

I grieved for the life I had and never remembered. I mourned my husband and daughter and the knowledge that their souls' peace had been disturbed for whatever machinations were in motion. And I lamented the loss of the clarity I'd once had about who I was.

TWENTY-SIX

I left a note stuck to the refrigerator in the manor's pristine kitchen. It was late afternoon and just before sunset, and it was the perfect time for me to slip out. No one was awake. I knew Sabri didn't care if I ever returned, so I didn't bother addressing her at all, but I wanted Blythe and Istvan to know that I'd gone "exploring."

The truth was last night's grief still ached within me. A hollowness settled deep inside. I simply was not up to facing anyone and pretending, especially the carefree, bubbly Lydia with her funny quips that left Istvan in fits of giggles.

Wandering around the city's streets, breathing in the crispness of new snow and listening to the muffled crunch of flakes beneath my boots, was a good distraction. Freshly fallen snow has a way of making the world seem cleaner than it is. There's a sense of hope and wonder that falls with each flake. I was feeling too wretched for that and either scowled or bared my teeth at anyone who came too close to me.

I should have gone home to escape the crowds, those who would not be chased from the city by such little snowfall, but I didn't. To see the faces of those I believed were my only family and not utter a word of what had been told to me felt as if the secret had been branded upon my skin.

How could I withhold such a thing?

Why had I agreed to keep it secret?

It was my secret, wasn't it?

I had been lured into secrets only to realize the ones who had kept those secrets watched me, interacted with me, and perhaps even cared for me. I knew better, and yet I had blindly trusted a system I knew was broken. Nothing the Old Ones had created could be truly good. But I allowed myself slip to slip into the leashed existence. To be confined.

I still seethed at the idea of anyone daring to confine me, knowing what I knew about my past, and I found myself standing in front of Little Bird Bakery. I was so deep in thought that it took me a moment to register where I was.

"Olivia?" a female voice called.

I looked up and saw Allison waving from the bakery's open door. Seeing her with all my secrets so close to the surface I could taste them on my tongue was disconcerting. The halo of red curls around her head brought tears to my eyes, but I blinked them back. She waved at me, her smile bright and cheerful—the opposite of my despair and violence.

"Come in!" she called.

My daughter.

I had a chance to learn my daughter's soul. Even if I couldn't tell her, I would know, and maybe it would be enough. I sighed, squared my shoulders, and plastered a smile to my face.

"Hey!" I said.

Homey, winter scents of cranberry and orange surrounded me as soon as I entered the bakery. Sure enough, Alex was carrying a tray of cranberry and orange muffins through the kitchen doors. I caught his eye and smiled, but it felt like the whole world stopped turning.

My husband. The soul in that man knew my own.

Mine. Mine. Mine.

I broke out of my reverie too aware that I'd been staring possessively at him. There was a sudden sharpness in Alex's eyes that told me he'd noted the possessiveness. The predator's smile that spread across his face told me he didn't mind it. He gestured toward a booth in the back.

"What was that all about?" Allison asked as she followed me to where Alex had gestured.

I whipped my head around and found I couldn't quite meet her gaze. Heat rose to my face.

"Nothing," I muttered.

"Mmhmm," she said. "Come on."

I slid into the booth with Allison directly across from me and looked her over as if I would find something new about her. I tried to memorize her features, noting the soft sprinkle of freckles across her nose. Did my Eleni have those same freckles? How much of my daughter was inside Allison? Alex soon appeared with two steaming mugs of what smelled like chai.

"I know you like tea, and it's cold outside," he said and placed the mug in front of me.

"Thank you," I said.

He stared at my mouth as I said the words. An internal war waged across his face. I didn't know if the angel or devil on his shoulder won, but his warm lips pressed to mine, and I melted into the kiss.

"Hi," I said softly as he pulled back.

"Hi," he said just as softly.

"Give me a second. I just need to tell Pops I'm taking my break."

Alex's dark jeans were tight against his well-muscled backside, and I enjoyed the view as he made his way back across the shop. When I turned my head, I found Allison staring at me, her eyes wide.

"Nothing, huh?" she laughed.

I sputtered, sighed, and began to speak, but she waved my words away.

"No, no—you don't have to explain. It's none of my business, and you don't really seem like the 'girl talk' type," she said with a grin.

"And he's your brother."

Father.

"He's my brother, yeah," she laughed. "But..."

I knew what she wanted to know.

"He doesn't know what I am," I lied.

Allison looked thoughtful for a moment. "Does your kind typically, you know, get with humans?" she asked.

Not unless their souls are their reincarnated loved ones come to haunt their present existence, no.

"No," I said succinctly.

"Won't this raise questions?"

"Possibly."

Because it's supposed to raise questions. You, my daughter, are a distraction, and so is your father. You are a dream. You are a nightmare. But you are mine.

"Is he in danger?"

"No more than he usually is."

Allison assumed, as I'd intended, I was speaking of the regular dangers humans were in, living in a world of Creatures they didn't know existed. I raised the mug to my lips and took a sip. I'd no more than set the mug back down when Alex slid into the booth beside me. He wrapped his long fingers around his mug of tea that had been waiting beside mine.

"How are you?" he asked quietly.

Broken. Reassembled. Hollowed out. Amazed. Worried. Thrilled.

"I've been better," I admitted.

I couldn't admit to the riot of emotions within me. Not here. Maybe not anywhere. Thankfully, Alex didn't press for details.

"Things are getting weirder," he agreed.

He had no idea.

Allison sighed loudly from the other side of the booth. We both turned to look at her.

"I've changed my mind. This is totally my business," she said. "How did this happen?"

Neither of us said anything. Allison groaned. "Fine. Keep your secrets. But I'm not about to sit here and watch you two make googly eyes at one another."

She got up and wound her way through the bakery toward the kitchen. I wondered if Eleni had ever grown tired of watching me kiss Iason. *Had we been so in love? Had we felt electricity, these strikes of lightning?* I looked over at Alex, and he stopped my roaming thoughts with his lips. Like I had that first night we'd kissed, I felt a soul-deep thrill pulse through me. One of Alex's hands found their way to my waist beneath my coat, but the other gently cupped the back of my head, tilting it so he could slide his tongue between my lips.

"Alex," I murmured as I pulled away. *Iason.* He was breathing hard and wide-eyed. "I don't think we want to do this here."

He laughed softly. "No, we don't. I just missed you."

That he admitted it without reservation struck a chord within me. There was no hesitation in his words. I pressed a kiss to his lips, trying to keep things chaste, but needing to feel him, to tell him in the only way I could what those few words meant to me.

I missed you, too. I think I've been missing you for centuries.

I sat back against the booth's leather. Alex put one arm around my shoulders and pressed his lips to my forehead.

"This really takes the idea of a complicated relationship to a whole other level, huh?" he asked.

I managed to swallow my tea before I spit it out.

"That's an understatement, I think," I agreed.

His laugh sent chills through my body. I loved the sound. He leaned over and spoke softly into my ear.

"I felt that."

The warmth of his breath sent another shiver skittering down my spine in the most delicious way. I met his eyes with my own.

"Are all of you like this?" he asked.

His eyes roved over my face, and the mix of emotions I saw in them almost undid me.

"Like what?" I asked, trying to keep my voice even.

"So... electric." I didn't say anything, but the expression on my face gave me away.

"So you feel it, too," he mused. "And it's definitely... normal."

Nothing about this was normal. I wanted to scream the words at him, wanted to pull his face to mine and whisper all my secrets. I wanted to unburden myself at his feet.

"You are entirely too perceptive," I said instead.

"If I wasn't, I'd be dead."

I couldn't think of it. I didn't remember the blood or the memory that tugged at me whenever I looked at him.

"Can we get out of here?" I asked.

TWENTY-SEVEN

Alex only had a few minutes before he needed to return and help Allison close the bakery. We ended up taking a short walk around the block to get away from all the eyes in the cafe. He held my hand, and I found my mind wandering down mental roads that led to melancholy. The busy sidewalks were filled with humans that had no idea things like us walked amongst them. *I am a monstrous thing*.

I couldn't help feeling it. The rage and violence that tore at me earlier had not disappeared. It never would. I knew that. I was a creature born of my own making. I should stay far away from both Alex and Allison. I did not deserve them.

Something like me does not deserve a happy ending.

But I wanted one. As I held Alex's warm hand in my own, I knew both he and his sister could so easily become everything to me, and I didn't know what that meant.

Frankly, I didn't know what it could mean.

"Stay with me tonight," Alex said, breaking me from my thoughts.

"What?" I asked.

He grinned—that beautiful grin—and pulled me around a corner into an alleyway. Faster than I even knew he could move, he had me pressed up against a brick wall of what I thought was a restaurant.

"Stay with me tonight," he repeated.

He didn't wait for an answer. His mouth met mine in a searing kiss. I parted my lips to invite his tongue in, and he obliged. As the kiss continued, I found myself wrapping his brown curls around my fingers as I tried to pull him closer. *Closer. Always closer.*

Mine.

A slight tug on his hair wrested a moan from him that loosened something deep within me. I wanted him in a way that I couldn't remember wanting anyone. I released his hair. My hands traveled under his shirt and over the muscles of his stomach. My fingernails trailed lightly over the skin before digging in as the pressure of his kiss increased. I wanted to rake my nails down his back. I wanted to see my marks upon his skin.

"Liv," he panted, pulling his mouth from mine.

He did not mind the mixture of pain and pleasure. That was clear. I felt it as he pressed me harder against the wall, his kisses traveling from my mouth to my earlobe, which he bit gently, and made it my turn to moan quietly. He tugged the collar of my jacket aside with a finger, licked the spot where my neck met my collarbone, and laughed softly as I ground my hips into his as a response.

"Oi!" someone yelled.

Our heads whipped around to see a bald man holding a bag of trash. He must have just stepped outside the restaurant. I hadn't registered the sound of the heavy door. I should have been concerned by that. I should have, perhaps, been mortified. Instead, I laughed. I buried my face in Alex's chest and laughed.

"Take it somewhere else, yeah?" the man called, waving us back toward the street.

Alex stepped back, grabbed my hand, and led me back to the sidewalk. We were still laughing when we returned to the bakery, even though I had no interest in letting him go back inside.

"You never said you'd meet me tonight," he reminded me as he wrapped me in his arms under the awning.

"Yes," I said quietly.

"Yes?" he asked, but he was already smiling down at me.

"Yes," I said. "I'll meet you tonight."

He took my phone from my coat pocket and tapped away at it for a minute.

"I put my address and number in there. I'm done here around 8. Meet me at 9?"

"I will see you at 9." I stood on my toes, pressed a chaste kiss to his lips, and then made my way back down the sidewalk.

Thunder cracked, and lightning lit up the sky.

———

"Olivia and Alex sitting in a tree," cooed a soft female voice.

Damn it all to Tartarus.

"K-I-S-S-I—"

"Shut up, Lexi," Atlanta said. "Come on, little Fury, we need to chat."

I didn't really have a choice but to go with them. I let Lexi take me by the arm and lead me to a diner the next block over. We made a conspicuous group as we walked together, but we were also intimidating enough that no one bothered any of us. Once again, the girls were head-to-toe goth chic, with Lexi bordering on pastel goth a bit more than the other two. As we had on the street, we looked even more out of the place inside the restaurant, but it was a quiet place to talk. Most of the diners inside were homeless seeking a cheap cup of warmth. No one glanced at us more than once. This was a part of the city where people were careful to mind their own business. The waitress, who smelled of stale cigarette smoke and the bitterness of coffee, brought us menus and then disappeared into the kitchen. Chloe immediately tossed her menu on the table behind us and then faced me.

"We know what you were told," she began.

"The Twelve know so much and yet so little," Lexi said in a singsong voice.

"We told you where to focus," Atlanta said pointedly.

"Ladies, I have not forgotten what you said. Far from it. It's been forefront in my mind."

"Are you sure?" Lexi asked, winking. "It seems like you had something—or someone—else on the brain. I don't blame you. He's delicious."

"Mine," I snapped.

Even Atlanta—unshakeable, stoic Atlanta—looked surprised at my vehement response.

"No one is moving in on your man, bitch. Calm down," Chloe said, rolling her eyes.

"Everyone calm down," Atlanta broke in. "Your boy toy isn't our focal point here. We're here to remind you of where the big problem lies."

"The Old Ones. I'm working on it."

"It's gotten more complicated," she admitted.

"More complicated?" I asked.

I was impressed I kept my voice at a civil level of volume.

"There are lies within the truth and truth within the lies," Atlanta said, as if any of it made sense.

"Right. Of course."

"Pay attention," she snapped.

The Fates losing their tempers? This cannot be good.

"If I could tell you more, I would," Atlanta said.

Her tone seemed apologetic.

"I'm being told a lot of things by a lot of people," I said.

"We know," Chloe said with an eye roll.

"The future keeps shifting," Lexi added dreamily.

I pressed my hands to my face. Conversation ceased as the waitress appeared with coffees we hadn't asked for. She left the table again, not in a hurry, but she didn't even ask us if we wanted food. I could have used the distraction.

"Why are you even here?" I groaned. "None of this is helping. Sunee is telling me things; Evangeline is telling me *nothing*. I'm angry and confused and so fucking frustrated that I almost wish my amulet would do its glowy thing right now so I could have a way to channel it all."

Lexi wrapped her arms around me and pressed a kiss to the side of my head.

"I am sorry, little Fury. You are at the center of something you do not yet understand."

"I don't want to be at the center of anything!"

"Then you should not have saved the girl."

I stared at Lexi.

"What?" I whispered.

"Lexi," Atlanta warned.

"It's in the past," Lexi snapped in a way that I'd never heard before. "It cannot be altered, cannot be changed."

"Still," Atlanta said.

"I know the rules," Lexi intoned.

No one spoke for several moments. It gave me too much time to think about what Lexi had said. My decision to save Allison had shifted things—and in a monumental way.

"You were meant to save her," Lexi said quietly.

"So, I made the right decision but it changed everything. Awesome."

"Stop looking backward," Chloe said.

"Oh, I'm sorry," I bit out. "Is my existential crisis *bothering* you? My world as I know it is falling apart. My husband and daughter have brought back from the dead. My sisters are keeping secrets. The Creatures are fighting each other in ways we have never seen."

No one said anything, so I kept going.

"I *hate* my role in a way I never imagined. I am sick of the fighting and the gods-damned secretiveness and the laws that don't make any sense. The Old Ones died eons ago and yet we are living our lives in the ways they dictated? Why?"

"Things are unfolding, Fury. Things long forgotten and too long hidden away," Atlanta replied.

I groaned. They could be so *fucking* unhelpful.

"Fates have been decided," Chloe said in that eerie, singsong way. "Your fate as a Fury, and your fury's fate."

The fucking riddles.

"You are going to want to trust the ones you love," Chloe said.

"And love the ones you trust," Lexi added.

"But love and trust may not be worth the price you'll pay for them," Atlanta concluded.

"I hate your riddles," I groaned.

"A point of no return is coming," continued Atlanta, as if I'd not said a word.

"And power is the prize," cooed Lexi.

"Find a way to move ahead with neither your heart or eyes," ended Chloe with her eyes burning bright.

"Now you're rhyming. This is fantastic," I muttered.

I understood the significance of the Seeing, though. The fact they had Seen something for me twice in so brief a time was worrisome. Or it might have been, anyway, if what they had Seen wasn't so horrible. Their words burned into my mind and repeated themselves. The pit in my stomach, gone when I'd been with Alex, returned.

"No one said it would be easy to have it all," Chloe said sadly.

"In fact, no one said you could have it all," Atlanta clarified.

I sighed because I knew she was right.

TWENTY-EIGHT

I returned to the Gregory Estate and used the key Istvan swiped for me to open the massive front door. As I walked inside, my mind full of everything the Fates had told me just the hour before, Sabri was coming down the staircase. She wore knee-high boots with a chunky heel, but the padding under the rug was so thick she barely made a sound.

"I suppose those idiots gave you a key?" she asked.

"Yeah," I said sheepishly.

She rolled her eyes and continued down the staircase. When she reached the bottom, I'd expected her to exit the front door. She looked like she was on a mission. But Sabri turned and started down the hallway toward the kitchen.

"Come on," she called over her shoulder.

I shrugged and followed.

When we got into the kitchen, she reached inside the refrigerator for a couple of blood bags, grabbed some mugs from a cupboard, and started to transfer the contents of the bags into the mugs. There were two mugs and two bags, so I assumed one was for me. I was patient enough to stick around and find out. Sabri's willingness to speak with me piqued my curiosity.

"I'm sorry if it upsets you that I'm here," I said.

She pinned me with a look.

"It's not you," she said finally.

She turned to place a mug in the microwave. She closed the door, pressed a few buttons, and the mug with its contents began spinning around in slow, methodical circles that were strangely soothing.

"Is this about Roland?" I asked.

"It seems like everything is about Roland," she sighed.

"How so?"

I cocked my head, watching her remove the mug when the microwave beeped, and replacing it with a second mug. She placed the warm mug in front of me, a slight bit of steam wafting upward. I nodded my head in thanks and waited for her to reply.

"Roland is... was... is?" she said and sighed heavily. "Shit, I don't know how to reference him. Roland was...enigmatic. He drew people to him in a way that was hard to ignore. He could be funny and charming. Incredibly witty. It'd been that way as long as I can remember."

"... but?" I asked.

I heard the hesitation to continue in her voice, but I felt like she might be handing me the very information I needed.

"But," she said, "there's a certain amount of risk in that, isn't there?"

"I suppose."

"A charismatic vampire can draw lots of attention. Great for hunting," she acknowledged.

I appreciated her candor. We both knew there were vampires out there who hunted, even if it was against the laws.

"Also great for contracting with a human, if you're not the hunting type," she said.

"Or if you choose to follow the Laws," I added in a murmur.

She smirked. So did I.

"That, too."

Sabri removed her mug from the microwave and returned to where she'd been standing at the island. I was seated across from her and watched as she blew carefully, sending her own wafts of steam floating. The spicy scent of the blood washed over me. I raised my mug to my lips and waited for her to continue. I didn't want to persuade her or dissuade her. I simply hoped she wanted to talk more than she didn't.

"But sometimes that same charisma can bring things to you that you're not prepared for," she finally said quietly.

"And you think that's what happened to Roland?" I asked.

"I think there are things much scarier than vampires who go bump in the night, and I'm not talking about any of the known Creatures. I've known fae and demons and witches and all of the rest of them during my time on this earth. None of them are even close to what was drawn to Roland a few months ago."

"Sabri, what are you saying?"

"I'm saying that something—because I don't have a name for whatever it was—came to Roland and started him down a path that eventually led to his demise. I don't know what that demise was, though I obviously suspect The Twelve are involved. How could they not be? Roland had been illegally hunting for years. In the last months he was here, he was careless. More than careless."

"Cocky?"

"Unbelievably so," she whispered. "In a way I'd never seen. And I've seen Roland through a lot of shit."

It almost felt like she was talking to herself more than she was to me.

"Istvan mentioned the two of you were close," I prompted.

"Istvan is a child," she scoffed, "but he's right about me and Roland. Even at his worst—stupidly stubborn and proud—I couldn't leave him on his own. I tried to protect him from this thing, this *being*, but it said all the things Roland wanted to hear."

"What do you mean 'it'?" I asked.

I was beyond intrigued. The suspicion was that someone or something was whispering in the ears of Creatures, but to have it confirmed was beyond what I'd even hoped for. And by Sabri? This was gold. I took another drink from my mug and leaned toward her conspiratorially.

Sabri looked torn. She so clearly wanted to get this off her chest, but she obviously felt some loyalty toward Roland, even though she rightly assumed that he was not coming back.

"Sabri, what's happening here? Does Fi need to know?" I asked.

I suspected the idea of bringing Fiona into this would push her. In what direction, I couldn't be sure, but I was willing to take the risk.

"No," she said. "There's no reason to involve anyone else."

"Because Roland is gone?"

"Because Roland was its foothold here. Roland was the way to make inroads into the vamp community. Without him, I don't know if there's anyone left to trust."

"Sabri, what is here? What was it that pushed Roland to be so careless?"

"I don't have a name," Sabri replied softly. "We never learned its name. All I know is that this thing—this Creature of the likes no one has ever seen—is whispering into the ears of the various factions that the Old Ones are awakening, which means the time of the Creatures is nigh."

"The time of the Creatures is nigh," I stated.

I kept my tone disbelieving, but inside I was practically screaming. This was more information than we'd been able to get from anyone so far, and it was all leading back to a single source. This really seemed to indicate the situation we were experiencing was more than just Creatures pulling at their leads—this was Creatures trying to rise in power and being eerily close to success.

"I know how stupid it sounds, Lydia."

I sighed. I knew that this was likely my only chance to get any kind of real information on what was going on.

"It doesn't sound stupid, Sabri, so much as it sounds just flat-out odd. What kind of thing could pull this kind of attention?" I asked.

"All I know is that Roland thought it was a myth."

I waited, sipped at the blood.

"I don't know what to think it is. Because it's not human and it's not Creature. It's this mythical being of some kind. Incredibly secretive, and it never looks the same when it appears. Instead, it shows up with a previously agreed-upon passcode of some kind."

"So this thing sets up meetings with a passcode."

"Less rules, more killing, control of humans—it's handing them their dreams, Lydia. And Roland fell for it."

She raised her eyes to meet mine, and I was surprised to see the gleam of tears shining in them. She really had been close to Roland. The guilt was a sharp pang again.

"I assume you tried to talk him out of it?"

Sabri began pacing in front of the island I was seated at.

"Of course!" she cried. "I begged and pleaded. I tried emotions, I tried logic. But he was like an addict—he got a taste of its power and what life could be like for us in a world controlled by Creatures."

"But the Old Ones? They've been long asleep, Sabri. Even he had to realize that."

"Oh, he was suspicious, to be sure. At first, anyway. But he was slowly convinced, especially when other nests accepted the premise."

She looked sad again instead of angry, but she continued speaking.

"All I know is he went to some meeting—I don't know what made this one different—but whatever happened, it completely changed him. He was merciless afterward in a way I've never seen."

Tears coursed down Sabri's face.

"He scared you," I said.

She nodded.

"You have to understand, Lydia. Roland saved me. I would have been stoned to death for refusing the arranged marriage my parents had contracted for me. He took me away from there. He gave me a life where I could do as I pleased."

"And then he abandoned you."

"More than that, he abandoned our ways. There are laws. Are they perfect? No. But they are there to secure our way of life. I don't want to be a monster. I didn't think Roland wanted to be one, either, but he just... he embraced it so fully," she ended on a sob.

I found myself out of my chair and holding her before I gave it a thought. She cried into my shoulder, her dark hair hanging like a black silk curtain. She cried so hard she shook, the sheer force of the tremors making me believe in the truth of what she said.

When Sabri finally wiped her eyes and stepped away from me, she looked exhausted. I left her near the island to warm up another mug for her to take to bed. The poor thing had been carrying the guilt for what happened to Roland. That much was obvious. She thought she should have been able to stop him, but she couldn't. I wasn't convinced anyone could have. It seemed like Roland heard what he wanted to, especially after years of feeling stifled by the laws. I worried other factions neared the same point of no return.

"Come on," I said softly to her.

I led her by the arm up the stairs and into a bedroom I'd figured out was hers. It was so bright and unlike the rest of the house. Swaths of gold, crimson, and aquamarine fabric hung from the walls, with more of it draped around the posters of the bed. I tucked Sabri into the crimson sheets and pulled a coverlet over her. I put the warm mug on the nightstand.

"Thank you for telling me what you did," I told her.

"I don't know why I told you," she said sleepily, hunching down into the piles of pillows against the headboard.

"Because you're tired. You have been carrying a burden felt all alone." She didn't respond. "And deep down you have to know that none of what happened was your fault," I replied.

I leaned over and brushed her hair from her face. Her dark, almost black, eyes blinked up at me.

"You're not really Lydia, are you," she said, asking the question but not really phrasing it that way.

I didn't answer.

"Do I need to fear you?" she asked as her eyes fell closed.

"No. You have nothing to fear from me."

And she didn't. The truth was that Sabri, Istvan, and Blythe had done nothing to warrant any kind of judgment from me, as far as I could tell. I left the sleeping vampire in her bed, went to the room I had been staying in, packed my things, left a note for the occupants of the house that I'd gone home, and walked out the front door.

TWENTY-NINE

Before I could think of returning to my actual home, I needed to tell Sunee, Ramiel, and Atara what I had found. I held tight to my amulet and vanished into the air to reappear in the other realm. I wasn't particularly in the mood to see anyone—not even my sisters or Evangeline—but I didn't want it to be said that I'd withheld information from The Twelve. I had made a promise.

"Come in," called Sunee when I knocked on her door.

She and Atara stood just inside, as if Atara had only just arrived or was getting ready to leave.

"Sunee, Atara," I said, making the proper bows in their respective directions.

Old habits die hard.

"Alekto," said Atara in that musical tone. "You have news, I assume."

I nodded, and Sunee ushered both Atara and I into the same sitting room we had met in before. There was no tea this time, so I suspected Sunee had not been expecting either of us, and that meant Atara had only just arrived before I had. It was either that, or Sunee was not interested in having Atara stay for long. Ramiel's absence from this meeting was noted and filed away in my mind.

All the Fates had said was too fresh in my mind to forget. I didn't love or trust any of The Twelve, but I would be careful, thoughtful.

"Roland was pinpointed by someone or something and basically primed as a lynchpin of the plan, I think."

"Who did this?" Atara breathed.

"I don't know. There were no names. The only thing I could get was this was basically a kind of living myth. The 'myth' met Roland and leaders of other factions in secret. Always wearing a different face, always using a different passcode. Whatever this plan is, it's been in place for a while. There aren't loopholes to exploit, and the trail has gone cold."

"You've done well, Alekto," Sunee assured me.

"I know."

I didn't need their assurances. I didn't want them. I didn't think I wanted anything.

"What was the bait?" Atara asked.

I explained to her all that Sabri had shared with me. I explained the Old Ones were known to be the prize, especially their lax views on using humans in whatever manner was wished.

"Someone wants to wake them on purpose. They want them to rule."

"Is it about exchanging us for them, I wonder?" Atara asked.

"It's about power," I said. "Power to do what they want, and I think they're willing to throw their lot in with the Old Ones. It's been too long since they ruled. No one remembers what it was like."

"Chaos," Atara murmured with a gleam in her eye.

"Yes, but I think we also need to consider that it could just be about change. They're not getting what they want, so they'll take change at any cost."

Sunee nodded gravely.

"Alekto, you must know that we're doing our best, but the Laws are the Laws for a reason."

"Yes, once upon a time. But humans have evolved, Creatures have evolved. The Laws have remained stagnant."

It's no wonder there are riots.

I got up to pace as I had during my last conversation with Sunee and Atara. I knew Atara's cerulean eyes watched me as my boots treaded heavily on the rugs. Sunee watched me, as well, but her expression was far more neutral than Atara's. Atara looked worried. Sunee didn't. And I didn't like it.

I found myself desperately wishing for Leslie or even Gabrielle. I knew things were tense, at best, between Leslie and I, but her tactical mind was far better for pulling this apart and seeing where the threads led. Gabrielle, too, would be valuable, even if only to ask who needed beheading. I missed my sisters. *They're not your sisters.*

But they were my sisters. We had all transformed into what we were because our vengeance burned through us in the same way. If I could just focus on that, the blood didn't matter. The blood had never mattered. I never assumed we were truly sisters; I'd believed our sisterhood was in our creation. And it was, just in a slightly different way than I'd thought.

"Alekto, we must discover who is meeting with the factions," Sunee stated.

I stopped pacing and looked at her. My jaw clenched as I thought about how to respond.

"I will try," I finally said after a pause. "But this Creature has hidden their tracks well."

"You are a hunter," she said.

"I am Justice," I clarified.

"You are what we need you to be."

"I am as I was created."

It was a standoff as we stared at one another.

"I will do my best to find out who or what it is at the root of this, but when this is all finished," I said. "I expect changes to be made that reflect the concerns of the Creatures."

"You overstep," murmured Atara.

It was a warning, but a much gentler one than expected. Probably gentler than I deserved.

"I am Justice," I said.

I turned on my heel and left Sunee's quarters. I had somewhere to be.

———

I stood outside the door of Alex's apartment. I raised my hand to knock but lowered it again. If I went inside, I knew what would happen. I'd felt too much with Alex to believe anything else was possible. My head hung low as I stared down at my boots, marveling over all that had happened in the last few weeks. My existence had been just something that was for so long. I didn't think about it. I didn't concern myself with things outside my control. But things were changing. I was changing.

My husband is behind that door.

I raised my hand and firmly rapped on the door.

"I wondered how long you'd wage this war with yourself," Alex said as he opened the door.

I smiled and ducked my head, warmth spreading across my face.

"It's okay," he said softly as he gestured for me to enter.

"There are things I should tell you," I began.

I turned so Alex could slide my jacket from my shoulders. I unwrapped the scarf from around my throat and handed it off. He hung both on a rack near the door, took my hand, and led me to the dark gray sofa in front of the large windows overlooking the city.

"More secrets," he surmised.

His voice was deep and honey-toned, and his scent, like warm spices I couldn't quite identify, was all around me as we sat facing one another.

"I don't want to have secrets," I admitted softly. "I have so many, and I have had them for so long. I don't want to have them with you."

He took my chin in his hand and raised my face so that our eyes met. His brown eyes with their flecks of burnt umber and gold, fringed with dark lashes, drew me in.

"Then let's not have any," he whispered.

His lips met mine in a kiss that made me want to toss aside all the thoughts in my head and just focus on the fire and flames I felt building between us. I could so easily sink into that warmth.

I pulled away, putting my hand on his chest.

"Alex, I know you," I said.

He smiled. "I feel like I know you, too."

"No, Alex," I said, shaking my head. "You don't understand."

"Then help me."

There was such earnestness in that face of his. I leaned over and kissed him briefly.

"There's no easy way to tell you this," I started.

Once I began to tell him what Sunee and Atara had told me—about our past, the one I never remembered—I couldn't stop. The words were a flood flowing from my tongue and crashing over the both of us. As the words dripped, Alex took my hands in his, and I saw the shine of tears in his eyes. It was so clear to me in that moment that I loved him.

It made no sense. There was nothing logical about what was happening, and so much of my life had forced me to focus on the tangible, the logical, and where my duty lay. I wanted this for myself, with a soul-deep yearning I was quickly learning to embrace.

"And you believe them?" Alex asked quietly when I finished.

"I do," I admitted.

"We were married," he whispered.

A tear rolled down his face.

"I'm sorry," I said.

"For what?" he asked.

There was nothing but surprise on his face.

"For being so caught up in my vengeance that I forgot you. I forgot Eleni. I'm so sorry."

I broke down crying. It wasn't the mournful grief of the crying I'd done alone as I grappled with all I had learned, but it was the heartache finally rising to the surface.

"I'm sorry we were brought here," Alex said.

"No!" I cried.

"I'm sorry that we were brought here only as a distraction and not as a reward for your strength and your goodness and your beauty," he clarified.

He kissed my forehead, my cheeks, my closed eyes.

"I am not good," I said.

"You are far better than you realize."

"I am a monster."

"Then we are both monsters."

I stared at him. I couldn't disagree with him without admitting that

I was not so monstrous, not so terrible as I believed. But I wholeheart-edly believed in my wickedness.

Alex took in the tightness in my jaw. The frustration I felt as I grap-pled with my thoughts must have been obvious. But he didn't say anything. He didn't try to dissuade me. Perhaps Alex, too, felt guilt over the things his existence had wrought.

He took my hand and led me into his bedroom. I stood in front of the massive bed and pulled him to me, letting him experience the strength I had to offer—that I would use to protect us from whatever was coming. I relished in the way he matched my kisses, in the way his hands gripped me to him in the same way I knew my own hands were pulling him closer.

I tore the shirt from his body and tossed my own nearby. Warmth radiated from him. It felt like he could burn me alive. I relished in it.

Alex trailed soft kisses from my cheeks to my ears and down my throat. More kisses across my collarbone, along the edges of my bra, and then down my sides.

"Off," he murmured as he tugged at my jeans.

"Off," I agreed, tugging at his.

I did not worry about what was happening in our world. I allowed myself to be consumed by something other than my duty, and I knew I could never go back to the way I had been. Each kiss tore away at the walls I had built, and each moan Alex wrested from me was a release from the sorrows I carried. It did not occur to me until later that the second warning I had received from the Fates may have been to prevent that very thing, and by the time I considered it, I was too far gone.

THIRTY

A buzzing woke me, and it took a several minutes for me to realize where I was. My eyes opened to a broad, freckled back. I wanted to snuggle back into it and ignore the world and the gods-damned vibration. But I pulled myself from the bed, blearily stumbled through the room, and eventually located the vibrating cell phone in the pocket of Alex's discarded jeans.

"Alex," I murmured.

He was fast asleep on his stomach, right arm stretched across the mattress toward the space I had vacated just moments before. I hoped maybe the phone call wasn't important, but the screen flashed "Dad," and I figured I should wake him. I crawled back into the bed and tapped his arm.

"Alex," I said in a louder voice, moving closer to the bed.

"Yeah?" he said.

He raised his head and looked me. I was met with the full force of his smile, and if I'd been wearing anything, I would have removed it immediately. As it was, I was back to wishing we could ignore the call and spend the next few hours together in bed. Unfortunately, the cell phone was still buzzing in my hand.

"Good morning," he said.

"Good morning."

I handed the phone to him, and he made a move to toss it on his nightstand.

"It's your dad," I told him as I crawled back into the pile of sheets and blankets.

He quickly swiped across the screen.

"Pops?"

As he spoke, he rose from the bed and paced around the room. I enjoyed the view as he gathered clean boxer briefs from a drawer and the jeans I'd left on the floor after pulling the phone from the pocket. Alex didn't make a move to put any of the clothing on, though. Instead, he sat down on the edge of the bed with a sigh, clothing clutched in one hand.

"Let me know when she gets there, okay? Yeah. Love you, too,"

He hung up the phone and sighed again.

"What's going on?" I asked.

He looked over his shoulder at me, anxiety obvious across his gorgeous face.

"Allison's late for her shift at the bakery."

"Maybe she stayed out a little too late?" I asked hopefully.

"She didn't go home last night, either. And the last time that happened..." he trailed off.

He didn't have to finish. The last time Allison had disappeared, she'd been taken by Roland Gregory and bled to within an inch of her life. I had a hard time believing she'd fall for vampire lures again, though, especially when she knew the dangers.

I said as much to Alex, forgetting that I hadn't yet told him that his sister knew of our world.

"Wait... you told her?! About Creatures?!" he exclaimed.

I looked pointedly at him. "Knowing what I know now, I'm surprised I had to. You're Fiagai. I assume your father is, as well."

"Yes. But children who aren't slated for the brotherhood aren't informed. It's part of how we keep the secret."

"What does she think you do at night?" I asked.

A brief grin.

"She thinks I have a *very* eclectic nightlife," he said.

He tossed the phone and the clothes to the floor and turned to crawl toward me. The sight of him made my mouth water, and I unabashedly drew him closer once he was within reach. I ran my hands through the soft curls of his hair.

"I wonder if you had long hair as Iason," I asked quietly.

"It's a bit of a rebellious thing now, I'm afraid," he chuckled.

"What?" I asked, intrigued.

"Fiagai are to keep their hair short. Tradition and all that."

"Shorter hair is harder to grab in battle," I mused.

He kissed me.

"Exactly," he said. "But you keep your hair long."

"I do."

He ran his hands through the inky strands, watching as they shone blue in the sunlight streaming in the window.

"No such rules for you, then, I guess?" He asked.

"Oh, there are plenty of rules, but just not that particular one."

"I assume this is breaking a rule," he murmured, nuzzling my neck.

Shivers ran down my spine.

"You're sort of a gray area," I admitted.

"A gray area, huh?"

I couldn't help but think of Leslie and what she had gone through with Vallerie. We had all learned our lesson. It was far easier to enjoy dalliances than anything long-term. Casual sex was fine. Alex kissed along my jaw with an open mouth, licking the skin there. More shivers ran through me, but they had more to do with the memories coursing through me rather than his romantic ministrations.

"I am choosing not to ask for clarification on relationships with once-husbands-now-sort-of-enemies," I said, trying to remain light-hearted.

Alex's breath was warm against my skin.

"So you are also a bit of a rebel," he said quietly.

"Not until lately. You're a bad influence."

"I might be," he laughed. "But we've waited literal centuries for this, even if we didn't know it."

And once those words were out of his lips, I was done talking. He was right. I had waited centuries to be in his arms again, and I would not waste this. Not for the tragedies that had already occurred and not even for my duty. I bared my neck. He recognized it for the submission that it was. That predatory gleam that I'd seen in his eyes at least once before was instantly there, and I lost myself completely to him.

———————

Alex's regular shift at the cafe began after lunch. I walked him to work. He lived only a few blocks from the cafe, so it wasn't that far out of my way if I was going to begin hunting afterward, and I wasn't ready to leave him yet. Hand in hand, we walked down sidewalks busy with lunch hour foot traffic, busy patrons going in and out of the area restaurants or stopping in front of food trucks. My stomach growled, and it was loud enough that Alex heard it.

"We can grab you something," he said. "Either at one of the trucks or at the cafe."

He saw the hesitation on my face, and our pace slowed. I could see him replaying memories and trying to come to some sort of conclusion. For the first time, I felt fear when I wondered how he might handle my need for blood. It was one of the undeniable Creature traits I had. Harder to ignore than some of my others.

"You can eat food," he surmised.

"I can."

I watched his face, careful to guard my own expression. I pushed away the memory from just a few hours ago of my submission to him.

"But you don't have to," he continued.

"No," I said slowly.

"Which means you must survive on something else..." he trailed off.

I knew he had already added it up and was just delaying saying the words out loud. As if ripping a bandage off a wound, I let the words out.

"I need blood for survival," I said. "All the long-lived Creatures do."

We kept walking. Neither of us said a word. I didn't sense disappointment, and I didn't smell any fear. But he was Fiagai. In terms of controlling emotions, he was probably trained just as well as I.

"We get it from blood donation sites or from human donors with contracts. It's as above board as we can get it," I said, hating that I was explaining this.

I hated the way my voice held the strain of embarrassment. It was defensive—colored with emotions I didn't want to show. We reached the cafe, its bright blue exterior shining in the sun. I glanced through the big windows at the front. I didn't see Allison. And though my worry for her was genuine, I knew I was using it as a distraction from what Alex might say. He released a sigh from deep within and blinked up at the sky.

"I should have realized," he said.

"Why would you? I doubt you've encountered others like me," I said, with a staccato of a laugh that sounded too sharp.

"No, but it's like you said—all the long-lived races have that same need."

He looked matter of fact. And I felt the question—the need for confirmation that everything was okay—rise within me. I kept the words in my mouth and refused to speak them.

"I get it, Liv. It's fine."

But Alex's jaw clenched as he said it.

"Fine?" I asked.

It was a challenge. *Hate me. Fear me.*

"I mean, it's a little disappointing that I won't be cooking dinner for you," he said with a smile. "I'm a damn good cook."

The relief flooded through me, and I welcomed it and hated it at the same time.

"I can eat food, Alex," I laughed. "In fact, I like food. I just don't need it."

He pressed his mouth to mine and smiled as he pulled away.

"Can I make you dinner tonight, then?"

I knew I should say no. Sunee and Atara wanted answers. But I agreed and squeezed his hand as he moved backward toward the bakery door. He gave me one more devastatingly beautiful smile before he entered the building, and I turned away. So many things rioted within me. Embarrassment that I had felt so ashamed of what it took for me to survive, hatred for the vulnerability I wanted to show but had shackled, frustration that I both knew and did not know Alex, and worry that I might already be too dependent upon his existence in my life.

THIRTY-ONE

I wanted something to occupy my mind. Patrolling would do that, and I would feel less guilty about spending another night with Alex. I wasn't sure if checking out any of the known Creature dwellings was worth my time, but with so little information about the thing that was talking to the factions, it was all I could do. I started at a house just outside Chicago I knew belonged to some demons. They'd caused trouble a few years back, but never enough to get caught.

But even if there was illegal activity going on, I couldn't stop it. I wasn't supposed to interfere. The only way I was to escort souls to Tartarus was when the names appeared in my amulet.

I crept around the edge of the house, knowing full well I shouldn't be there—not without a direct order from The Twelve. But my suspicions had been accurate. There were demons inside. If they'd been behaving like good little demons should, I told myself I would leave. And I would have. I did not want to deliver justice to Creatures who deserved nothing more than better treatment and freedom to live their lives as they'd been born to do.

But that wasn't the kind of Creature I heard inside. I peeked around the corner and stared in horror through a small window. A college-aged human male who was hanging upside down and bleeding from shallow cuts, toyed with by a female demon. Horror filled me, soon followed by the anger I worked so hard to keep at bay. I recounted all the times I'd known about Creatures who ignored the laws. Each time, it had been maddening, but I was told to channel that sense of righteousness into working for the system.

But our system was so broken. We knew it was, and I wanted so badly to be done with it. I saw what was happening in front of me, heard the cries, and decided it was time I finally embraced my gods-given duty: Justice. I didn't need a committee or a council or politics.

I recalled the submission to Alex, then, and I could see it in much clearer light. It had been so out of character, and yet it had felt right. What if I submitted again, but this time to my own will?

If I was the escort to Tartarus, then that's what I would do. But I would escort of my own volition.

I am Justice.

I didn't bother with the door.

"Am I late for playtime?" I drawled as I wind-walked inside.

The demon stared at me, her deep violet eyes unblinking and wide. She moved for the knife she had set aside after using it to carve shallow slices into the male's abdomen, arms, and thighs, but I was faster than she was. It was in my hand and out of reach before she'd taken two steps.

I tucked the knife into an empty sheath along my thigh. I stepped in front of her and gazed into her features. She was awfully good-looking. I wound my fingers around her pretty throat and drew my witchblade from the sheath along my spine.

"You're misbehaving, little demon."

"Wh-Who are you?" she asked.

The human man twisted in the blood-soaked ropes he was still tied up in.

"I am Justice. Who are you?"

I tilted my head as I waited for her answer. I felt her throat work underneath my fingers.

"Who are you, little demon?" I prodded.

"Naomi Graine."

"You have broken the laws of your brethren, Naomi Graine."

I squeezed her throat a little harder and brought the witchblade up to rest against the very bottom of her jaw.

"You must pay your debt in full."

The demon squirmed.

"Ah, ah, ah. Observe the ritual, demon," I said quietly. "You are out of options."

She stopped squirming and stared at me, wide-eyed. I laughed darkly, the sound bubbling up and out of my throat.

"I, the Alekto of the Furies, release your spirit to be guided to Tartarus, where you will be judged for your rebellion and disregard. The truth of your nature will be revealed. In Tartarus so it shall be."

As I had so many, many times before, I sliced with my witchblade and watched as her life force pulsed out onto the floor. I closed my eyes and exhaled. I had made a choice. It was done. And for the first time in a very long time, I truly felt like Justice.

———

I cut the human down from where he hung and waited until he could stay conscious enough to call for help. I left him with the friend who arrived, wrapping his bleeding form into a blanket they found discarded in the corner of the room. I did not care that he had seen my face and heard my voice and could very well identify me.

I knew there would be questions—so many questions—when souls began to arrive in Tartarus with no record of an escort. That was Demetrius' problem. If he truly was at the center of the riots and discord, he deserved it. If he wasn't, he would figure it out.

I rode the vengeance and ignored the rest.

Where to go next? I recalled conversations with Istvan and Blythe about places they'd often gone to party with Roland. Those would be ideal places to start, I was sure. A few houses came to mind, especially one that belonged to a particular vampire whose name had continued to surface: Laura Ashe. She had been part of Roland's nest but had moved out just before his demise. Istvan thought it was a tactical move to get another house of vampires within Roland's circle of power. Since I had nothing else in mind, it seemed as good a place as any to try.

I found the house on the edge of the city near a golf course. It was a dark brick home with blindingly white trim and perfectly manicured lawn. As I stood behind trees at the fence line, the red front door opened, and something walked out. It was human-shaped or wore a humanlike skin, but no scent wafted toward me on the cool breeze. It didn't make footprints in the light dusting of snow on the ground. I didn't recognize the bright red hair and tall, lithe body that made its way toward the front gate.

Whatever the thing was, it was not even attempting to blend in. No jacket, no hat, no scarf, no gloves—and it was cold by human standards. My eyes followed the Creature as it continued through the gate and down the street. There were trees nearby, and my gut instinct was that the Creature would head toward those and transport herself in some way. I kept my distance, a bit concerned that the scent of my shampoo might carry on the wind. But my eyes were on her as the red hair melted into brown, the stature shrank and became curvier and much more familiar. It took me longer than it should have to realize that I was staring at my sister, Gabrielle.

It was too much of a coincidence. I remembered Sabri's words.

"All I know is that Roland thought it was a myth."

My sister most certainly was a myth, was she not?

She was secretive and violent and capable of all that it had been said the Creature was. But though we had many talents, shapeshifting was not one of them. If Gabrielle really was working at the behest of Demetrius, altering her appearance might be as simple as getting a witch to assemble an amulet of some kind or brew a potion. I no longer knew what my sister might be capable of.

I followed Gabrielle, who did not wind-walk as I expected her to, but traveled through the trees until she came to the base of a large pine. My sister looked around before she altered her appearance. This time, her skin changed to burnished gold, the hair lengthened considerably, and her frame appeared to grow several inches. When the transformation was complete, she placed her palm on the tree. I couldn't hear from where I hid, but she must have muttered some kind of phrase because the tree split apart and opened to reveal a staircase lowered into the ground. As soon as her dark head was below ground, the tree closed once more.

I wanted there to be some kind of explanation. I wanted there to be a logical reason, but Sunee's words ran through my mind.

"My sisters?" I asked in a whisper.

"Similar stories, though they are not truly kin to you, if that's what you're asking," Atara supplied.

Vengeance bound us, made us the same. That vengeance, then, could have so easily been turned to work against The Twelve. If Gabrielle thought The Twelve were actively working against justice, I knew in my soul she would turn. Her sense of our duty was the strongest next to mine. And hadn't I just turned against The Twelve in my own way? It all made so much sense. Too much sense.

Soon enough, my thoughts were interrupted by the vibration of the cell phone in my pocket. Fabian's name was on the screen. Immediately, I was on guard. Fabian rarely called me.

"Hello?" I answered.

THIRTY-TWO

"D arling?" Fabian said into my ear.

"What's going on?" I asked.

"I need you to come by. There's something I need to tell you."

That didn't seem particularly auspicious. I couldn't help but grimace.

"I'll be there soon," I said.

I ended the call and pulled the wind around me, right there amongst the trees. I didn't want to wait for whatever was going on. I'd had enough of surprises. A few moments later, I strode up the walkway to Fabian's house.

He opened the door before I raised my hand to knock.

"What's happened?" I asked.

A hundred scenarios ran through my mind. I knew the vampires were gathering, asking their various forms of spies to investigate Roland's "disappearance." I didn't know how many Creatures—vampire or otherwise—knew about who Roland had been meeting with. More eyes on the situation weren't going to be helpful for my own investigation, especially if those eyes were capable ones like Fabian's.

Fabian didn't say a word, however. Instead, he gestured for me to come in. I stepped inside, the smell of a particular type of death hitting me immediately. The musty smell of new vampire filled my nostrils. I felt my eyes blaze brighter, and all my senses went into high alert. I crept forward slowly until I turned the corner and saw the source of the smell.

My daughter.

I turned and my eyes found Fabian's. His hazel eyes were sad but not remorseful.

"What have you done?" I whispered.

Without waiting for an explanation, I raced to Allison's side. I knelt there. I brushed her curls back from her face and took her left hand in mine. I lowered my head over our fingers, nearly touching them with my forehead. I had never prayed. I had never needed to. I knew what listened to those prayers and the kind of double-edged assistance they might offer something like me. But in that moment, I hoped someone was listening, and I didn't care of it was the Fates or the Gray Sisters or even the awakening Old Ones.

"You wouldn't do what was necessary," Fabian said tightly.

He didn't come closer. I didn't want to look at him, but I made myself do it. His features were taut and his mouth downturned, but the rest of his body was primed for the fight he assumed would come. I stayed where I was, kneeling at Allison's side, and held tightly to her cold hand.

"How dare you," I whispered. "I was saving her from this, Fabian. Saving her from this life."

Fabian sighed loudly.

"And I'm saving you," he said.

I was on my feet before I even realized it. I nearly shredded the front of his tee-shirt with my nails, I gripped him so tightly in my anger.

"I didn't ask you to save me," I spat in his face.

"And you never would."

He barely reacted to my vitriol, and that only further set me alight.

"I don't need saving," I ground out. "I never have."

I whirled away from him to stare at the wall as if a solution would come to me. There was no solution. Allison would rise a Creature, and the only way to prevent that from happening was a true death. I knew I couldn't do that.

"I'm going to respectfully disagree," Fabian finally answered into the heavy silence.

"I saved her. I fucking saved her!" I cried out, whirling again to face him. "I pulled her out of Roland's estate and took her home and made sure that she saw daylight. I didn't do that so she could end up like this."

The moment the words were out of my mouth, I regretted them. I had just given Fabian everything he needed to put the pieces together. He already knew I was something other than a typical Creature. Knowing I was at Roland's? That was the final piece of the puzzle, if Fabian was as smart as I thought he was.

I watched as the realization dawned across his handsome features. His eyes softened, and his mouth fell into another frown. There was a time when I would have wanted to kiss that frown away. Instead, it was taking all my energy not to rip his head from his shoulders.

"It all makes sense now," he replied.

"Fabian, don't. Don't say what I think you're going to say," I warned him.

But Fabian just scoffed. He pointed at Allison lying so utterly still.

"What are you going to do? She knows your secrets—and I'm suspecting she knows a lot more of them than I ever dreamed—and you allowed her to live. Fucking hell, you did more than allow it--you made sure she survived!"

Fabian scrubbed at his face with his hands. It was something he only did when he was truly worked up. I'd only seen it a handful of times.

"It is in your best interest to stop talking," I suggested.

My voice was toneless, emotionless.

"What are you going to do, love? Send me to Tartarus?"

"I don't want to."

But there it was. He had followed the breadcrumbs, some dropped decades earlier. He knew my identity. That he stayed was a testament to his bravery. That bravery stood a good chance of getting him killed.

"Then don't do it. I would bet that girl—that child—knows everything you are, and she breathes."

"No, she doesn't. You made sure of that."

We both stared at Allison's cold, unmoving body for a long moment. Fabian broke the silence with a sigh and brought his hands up to rest on his hips. He looked at me and then looked away, staring at the walls as if he would find the solution there that I couldn't. But the only thing that held a solution was me—but that solution was dependent upon a decision, and it was a decision I didn't want to make. I waited until he came to that conclusion and raised his eyes to meet mine.

"Fabian," I began. "There is more at play here than you even know. Our house of cards is coming down around us."

"Enlighten me."

And, Gaia help me, I wanted to. I wanted to tell him everything. I had always trusted him—trusted him possibly more than anyone until I met Allison and her brother. *Alex.*

"Fabian, you need to pack your shit and get out of Detroit, out of Michigan, probably out of the country."

"I'm not going anywhere, love."

"Fuck, Fabian. This isn't a joke."

"I'm not laughing."

I snarled, and Fabian stepped back.

"I am not your enemy, darling. I never have been, and I didn't do this to hurt you. Her existence was a risk that you seemed to be able to live with, but I couldn't. I couldn't live with it, okay?"

He ended with a growl that, had I been any other kind of being, would have terrified me. I merely shrugged at him.

"It wasn't your call to make."

"Friends, darling, don't let their friends twist in the wind like that. You are headed down a bad path."

"We're all headed down one."

Fabian cocked his head to one side.

"The Old Ones are waking up, Fabian. There's some mythical fucking *something* whispering to the various Factions, encouraging war, which is only forcing the Old Ones to wake up even sooner. The Fiagai are back in action in the U.S., you've just turned my fucking daughter into a vampire, and her brother, who is my reincarnated husband, is absolutely going to lose his shit when he finds out what you've done. So, pack up, get out of this city, and start praying to whatever or whomever might keep you alive."

Fabian stared.

"I was apparently human once," I said with another shrug.

"Holy shit."

"Yeah. It's been an interesting few weeks."

"She's your daughter?" he asked, gesturing at Allison.

"Reincarnated, yes."

"And you're married?"

"I was. He died. She died. I became—well, I became what I am—and they were reincarnated to basically haunt me so that I won't figure out who's behind the waking of the Old Ones."

"This is a lot."

I stared at him.

"Oh, is it? It's a lot for you, huh? Try living it."

I stalked back to Allison's side and watched for any sign of her waking.

"You're sure you did it right?" I asked.

"Wait a minute now, love. You're pissed that I turned her, but now you want to make sure I did it correctly."

I glared.

"I know how to turn a human," he sighed.

"You better hope so," I warned. "Because if she doesn't wake up, I'll..."

"You'll what, darling?"

"I'll escort you to Tartarus and make sure you never leave."

THIRTY-THREE

S ince Fabian didn't appear intelligent enough to heed my
warning, I was surprised when he was at least intelligent enough
to leave me alone and wait for Allison to wake. I sat next to her
and murmured tales from my life. I gave her the memories I'd begun to
unravel. I told her of my sisters. I even shared the vague recollections I
had of what things had been like when the Old Ones roamed the earth
and ruled the world of Creatures. I had no idea if she could hear me in
her unconscious state, but if there was any chance that I could help her
feel less alone, I would do what it took.

"She won't wake for several hours, you know," Fabian said from
behind me.

I heard him coming down the stairs and had already ceased my
storytelling. I wasn't feeling generous and would not give him anything
more than what I already had. It was a strange sensation, not trusting
Fabian. I didn't like it. It made me angrier.

"We need to move her," I said.

"What? Are you mad? She's perfectly safe here."

"Not if her brother comes looking. We need neutral ground."

"I suppose the brother is one of those Fiagai fucks," Fabian mused.

"I wouldn't phrase it that way in front of him."

"Fucking Hell."

"If you'd bothered to talk to me about your concerns rather than just running off half-cocked to save the fucking day that didn't need fucking saving, we wouldn't be in this gods-forsaken mess."

Fabian didn't reply, which was the smartest thing he could do.

We sat in silence, both staring at Allison. The sun continued its path downward, and that set me on edge.

"Where would she be safest?" Fabian finally asked, again showing some sense.

"My house."

Fabian didn't reply, but I could tell he didn't love the idea.

"It's the most neutral ground we're going to find, and if this turns ugly, I need backup. I have that in my sisters and Guardian."

I watched Fabian process the information, which involved running his fingers over his bearded chin.

"I don't need your permission," I said quietly. "I could wind-walk you to the middle of the desert, or I could flash you into one of the Hell realms."

Fabian snorted and rolled his eyes.

"Or I could just kill you."

I think we both hoped I was joking.

"Allison," I said to her softly, "I'm going to take you to my home. You'll be safe there."

I grasped Allison's hand in my left one.

"Fabian," I said as I looked up at him. "Do yourself a favor and get out of the country. I won't be able to stop Alex or the rest of the Fiagai from hunting you."

Fabian's face tightened, but he nodded.

"Open a window," I demanded.

"Why?"

"Just do it."

The winter wind whipped through the house as I grasped Allison's hands. I pulled the wind around us in the way I had so many times before. We whirled and landed in the backyard of my house. I didn't care that it was still daylight and any one of our neighbors could have seen me suddenly flash into the yard with a seemingly dead woman in my arms.

I carried Allison to the same parlor where I had taken her the first night I met her. Seeing her body there again broke something in me. I felt hot and desperate, my skin growing clammy as reality hit me like a freight train.

"Evangeline," I cried.

Panic colored my voice. The Guardian burst through the archway of the parlor. I knew she scented the difference in Allison the moment her nostrils flared. I nodded briefly at her.

"What happened?"

"It's a long story. Right now, you need to know that she is not part of the brotherhood directly, but she is Fiagai through her bloodline."

"She was. They won't protect her now," Evangeline said.

She softly brushed Allison's curls away from her face the same way I had when I first saw her. Frustration stirred within me that Evangeline's protective nature stretched to this woman because she had been made into a Creature, whereas before she could have been tossed to wolven for all anyone in this house cared. I tried to suppress the frustration and focus on the problems at hand. There were too many for me to allow my own issues to take front and center.

"Her brother," I began, then paused to swallow thickly. "Her brother is going to demand retribution."

"I'll secure the house."

"I'll head him off, but if she wakes earlier than expected, I will be called."

I did not leave room for questions or doubt. Evangeline nodded and assured me that everything would be taken care of.

———

I wind-walked to the bakery to meet Alex, blowing into the nearby alleyway. I walked toward the front of the happy blue exterior and thought through a myriad of variations of how things might go and what I might say. There was no sugar-coating this or approaching it gently. The news I had to share could send Alex on a downward spiral. What was worse was that I hadn't had time to shower. The mix of scents on my body was sure to exacerbate the situation—and quickly. But I had no other choice. It wasn't fair for me to leave him to trail her scent alone, and I knew that if I didn't show up to the bakery and deal with this head-on that he would begin hunting by himself.

When Alex stepped out of the bakery, he pulled the door closed behind him gently, but he kept his eyes on me the entire time. There was a smile on his face that began to wilt almost immediately. I watched as the light in his eyes flickered and died out. Pupils dilated. A growl built deep in his throat, deep and animalistic. It brought the delicacy of the situation to the forefront. He was literally bred to hunt Creatures, and for better or worse, that was part of tonight's equation.

"Why do you smell like new vampire?" he ground out.

"Alex," I began, but unbidden tears filled my eyes.

"No," he snarled. "No, no, no!"

"Alex," I said again.

The tears ran down my face.

Alex turned and punched the bakery's facade. The wood held, but barely. I grabbed his bleeding hand and held it between my own.

"I'm so sorry," I whispered.

The maelstrom of emotions in Alex's eyes almost took my breath away. I think he tried to fight his instincts, but there are limits to strength, even for someone as gifted as Alex. The blow that he had been dealt would have overwhelmed anyone. At least, that's what I told myself as I stood there and watched him wage an internal war.

"Let me take you to her," I said.

"I can't," he whispered with a shake of his head.

I put my hands on his arms and felt the tension in his muscles. I knew he was holding himself back. I knew the level of effort he was putting in to suppress his nature. It could give at any moment.

"Try."

I said that one word, and Alex lowered his forehead to mine. We stood there, foreheads touching, both breathing in and out as evenly as we could. I kept my fingers curled around his biceps, wanting the solace of physical touch, but perhaps I was also afraid of what he might do if I wasn't ready to physically restrain him.

"I don't know if I can," he finally said.

"Just try," I repeated.

I got one nod.

I grasped his hands and mine and pulled at the wind.

THIRTY-FOUR

We stood in front of the house, hand-in-hand. I remembered my own battle I'd had to fight when I knew what my duty dictated and felt my instincts pulling me in another direction. Unfortunately, for Alex, both his duty and instincts were pulling him in the same direction, and it was likely only his heart preventing him from acting.

I did not bother to ask Alex if he was ready. No amount of preparation could ready him for facing his sister whose existence made her a sworn enemy. I simply stepped forward and watched carefully to see if he would follow. He did.

I led him into the parlor.

"You're awake!" I cried when I saw Allison.

She was sitting up and staring around with wide eyes. Her fangs had descended, I noted. Evangeline rushed in from the kitchen, goblet in hand, and placed it in Allison's hand. Her pupils dilated as the smell reached her now-sensitive nose, and she drank greedily.

Alex watched with abject horror.

"Alex," I said in a warning voice.

He snarled.

"This is neutral territory," Evangeline intoned in her otherworldly Guardian voice.

She placed herself between the siblings, her thin figure belying the strength I knew was there.

"I will honor the code," Alex said in a low voice.

Evangeline nodded, but she did not remove herself from between them. Allison finished the goblet, and I noted Gabrielle slinking in and hurriedly handing her another one. I wasn't certain Allison was in a place yet to register the presence of her brother. New vampires were quite singularly focused once awakened.

"Who turned her?" Alex demanded.

"Does it matter?" I asked.

"It was an illegal turning," he pointed out.

I watched Allison carefully. Her hair had taken on a brighter coppery hue than she had as a human, and her eyes were a brilliant mahogany with flecks of gold that hadn't been nearly as noticeable before. It was the way of the vampires, though, to be altered in their new existence. I continued watching as Allison licked her lips and handed her second empty goblet to Gabrielle. She was offered a third and shook her head, but Gabrielle insisted, and Allison held the glass delicately in her slender, pale fingers.

"Olivia," Allison said softly.

I went to her immediately and took her hand once I'd placed myself at her side. She looked down at our clasped hands and then her eyes met mine.

"What am I?" she asked.

"You're a filthy fucking vampire!" Alex yelled.

Allison's eyes widened. She looked from me to her brother and back again. I nodded slowly and squeezed her hand gently.

"You were turned," I said softly.

I heard Alex muttering curses under his breath, and the floor practically shook as he paced about the small room.

"So I am a Creature," Allison replied.

"You are."

"Do you have to kill me?" she asked.

Tears filled her eyes. I quickly shook my head.

"No, Allison. There are Laws you must follow, and we will make sure you are made aware of them. You are safe as long as you adhere to those."

She sagged in relief, and I was reminded of just how young she was. Evangeline knelt in front of Allison and took the hand I wasn't holding.

"We will teach you the ways of the Creatures, child," Evangeline assured her. "Though I am quite curious as to why you are already so familiar with Creatures."

I bowed my head.

"She tried not to tell me," Allison said quietly. "I pressed the issue."

"What?" Gabrielle said.

I'd forgotten she was in the room. She stood near the doorway. I watched her try to sort out the information.

"The memory charm—it didn't work," I explained.

"But you kept this from us?" she asked.

I wanted to rage. I wanted to scream and yell that there was so much she was keeping from us. She didn't have the right to feel anything about this. But I couldn't. I didn't know enough yet, and I felt bound by the promises I made to Sunee, Atara, and Ramiel. The war of the Creatures was bigger than secrets between sisters. *Wasn't it?*

"I can't do this," Alex said suddenly.

My head whipped around to look at him. He stood, feet apart and arms in battle stance. I couldn't see a weapon on him, but that didn't mean anything. A Fiagai would never be unarmed.

"Alex, you must try," I pleaded.

"I have been! But everything in me is telling me she has to die," he grunted.

I noticed it then, the trembling in his muscles. I hadn't realized what being so near a vampire might do to him. As I fought my instincts, I wanted Alex to do the same, regardless of the fairness of that wish.

"If he cannot control his nature, he will have to leave," Evangeline said.

Tears filled Allison's eyes.

"I don't understand," she whispered.

Her eyes were large and pleading in her heart-shaped face. She stared at her brother as if sheer will could keep him there. It was then I knew I had made a mistake in bringing him there. It would have been better for her to never have understood the gulf that was now between her and the only family she had ever known. I had been selfish to prioritize our long-ago connection. It didn't matter that she had been my daughter. She was someone else's now, and I, in the few hours of her new existence, had shattered any hopes of her having a relationship with those she had known before.

"Alex, we have to explain this to her. If you need to go, then go," I said.

My voice was clear and even and gave no indication of the riot of emotions I experienced. I watched him take in my words and nod once. His muscles remained tight. He would stay as long as he was able to. I loved him for that.

"I don't know the lineage," I admitted to him.

One more nod.

"Allison," he began. Alex stopped speaking. His throat worked, and I wished I could help. But this wasn't my story. "I am part of a brother-hood called the Fiagai. Pops, too. And Grandma Drivas, and her mother before her. The brotherhood takes the oldest children. There is no choice, no option. I don't even know if it occurs to anyone to fight it."

Allison's eyes widened, but she listened.

"This makes us enemies?" she asked.

I squeezed her hand as Alex murmured an agreement.

"Oh," she whispered.

"It's an ancient Celtic tradition," Evangeline explained. "He is fighting his instincts, but the Fiagai are strong—stronger than typical humans. They are bred to be so."

"How? Why?" Allison asked.

Alex waved a hand at Evangeline to continue.

"It is thought that they were created to protect humans from Crea-tures so long ago that the origins are mostly myth now. There are similar groups of enhanced humans in other places around the world, as well. The Fiagai is just one example."

"I am doing everything I can, Alli," Alex said, voice thick with emotion.

"I didn't ask for this," Allison replied.

"I know you didn't, but I can't help my nature, either," Alex said to her.

"It is, quite literally, in his blood to kill Creatures. The Fiagai see them as the enemy to the human race," Evangeline said quietly.

I gripped Allison's hand in my own as it became clearer to me I would have to choose, at least for some time, between her and her brother. The love I felt for both of them was shocking, especially in consideration of the brief time I had known them.

But it wasn't brief, was it? And though I was his lover, I was her mother, regardless of whether I gave birth to her in this lifetime.

"I can't stay here," Alex ground out. "I can't fight this much longer."

"Allison will remain here with us. We will teach her the laws and keep her safe. For so long as she is within these walls, you will not hunt her," Evangeline said.

She rose to her feet and stared Alex down. I saw something akin to relief in his eyes as she said that, as if the pressure on him lessened a bit.

"Alex, don't do this," I said. "You can fight this. I did."

"That's not fair, Liv. You are literal magic."

"And you aren't?" I demanded.

I squeezed Allison's hand before I rose out of my seat. Gabrielle quickly took my place, and though I didn't love that, dealing with Alex was the more pressing matter at hand.

"You are stronger than this," I said.

Alex shook his head sadly.

"I am not."

"Fight this, damn it!" I cried.

"I can't!" he roared.

He pivoted immediately and made for the door. I followed him out of the house and onto the front path. I felt Evangeline's presence near me, but I couldn't fault her for being protective. She was my Guardian, after all.

"Alekto," she said to me.

"He can do this," I said in a low voice.

"You are asking him to do the impossible, and we are lucky we have gotten this far without bloodshed. Let the Fiagai go."

"I can't!"

"You must."

Evangeline put her hand on my arm and tried to pull me back into the house. I stared at Alex, looked into the deep brown eyes I had spent the morning drowning in.

"If it is discovered that I allowed her to live, my life is forfeit," Alex said.

"She is under laws of sanctuary," Evangeline reminded him.

"And for that I am grateful, but everything in me says that I have betrayed her. It would be better for her to have an honorable death than this parasitic existence."

"Parasitic existence?" I said.

Alex's face fell as he realized what the words meant for someone like me.

"Is that what you think of me?" I asked.

"It is his nature," Evangeline said.

"Nature can be fought," I muttered.

"You think I am a parasite? A blight upon humanity?" I asked Alex.

I saw the truth on his face before he could say words that would indicate the opposite.

"I see," I said.

"Olivia, it is in my blood to hate Creatures and the ways they feed."

"So why not take my life?"

"He could certainly try, but it is doubtful he would succeed," Evangeline laughed dryly.

"Nothing in my blood asks for yours," Alex said.

He had said this before, but I hated that we were doomed to stand at such odds.

"Thank you, Guardian, for granting sanctuary. By law, I must tell my father what has happened. It would be best for her to remain in sanctuary for some time," Alex said to Evangeline.

I stared at the ground and squeezed my eyes closed. I couldn't believe what he was saying.

"As a daughter and sister of Fiagai, it is likely the brotherhood will come out in force to rectify such a tragedy."

"Get out of my sight," I whispered.

"What?" Alex said on a gasp.

"Get out. Go do your duty. I hope it keeps you warm at night and grants you peaceful dreams."

I turned on a heel and went into the house. I heard Evangeline mutter a few words, but I was careful not to listen in. I strode back into the parlor, Evangeline at my back, and returned to Allison's side. Gabrielle was sitting with her, and they were talking softly. Though I was unsure of my sister, I appreciated her willingness to step in and care for this new Creature. Again, though, I was struck by how different she was with Allison now that she was a vampire when she had been so utterly dismissive of her—and her life, even—when she was simply a human.

"He's gone," Allison said softly.

I nodded, and her eyes welled up.

"I'm so sorry. This is my fault," I told her.

"How?" Gabrielle asked.

I found myself in our small parlor with my daughter, my sister, and my Guardian at my side as I told them, in great detail, all that had happened up until Allison's turning. There was shock and surprise, but ultimately, both Gabrielle and Evangeline felt Fabian had done the right thing. For this one evening, I supposed I could admit that Fabian had been willing to sacrifice our long-time friendship in order to protect me and that it was, quite possibly, one of the most beautiful thing I had ever witnessed for a Creature. My anger could wait.

THIRTY-FIVE

When my story concluded, Evangeline went and got another goblet of blood for Allison. I was grateful when she returned with one for me, as well. With all of the wind-walking, I'd used more strength than I'd realized. We sat in solitude for quite some time, sipping our goblets. I held tightly to Allison's left hand. The reasoning for why I was able to spend time with her openly was sad, indeed, but as it was the reality we were faced with, I embraced it.

"I think I would like to meet Fabian," Allison murmured quietly.

"I would like that, as well," I replied.

"Do we know where he is?" Gabrielle asked.

She was in the black velvet armchair, seated sideways and drinking from her own goblet. Her legs, clad in the tightest of black jeans, hung over the armrest. Evangeline, with her typical perfect posture, sat regally in the matching chair. Both faced the sofa where Allison and I lounged. I knew Evangeline didn't like my booted feet on the table, but she didn't say anything. That's how I knew it had truly been quite a day for all of us.

"I told him to run," I admitted.

I knew I should not feel guilt over what had transpired and why it was so necessary for Fabian to run, but I did, anyway. The guilt hung low in my belly, aching. I had felt so much guilt over the last months. Feeling it over Fabian was unexpected. He had the best of intentions, and he would spend the remainder of his life looking over his shoulder. Fiagai, much like the other bands of hunters across the realm, were hard to pick out from a crowd. It was likely Fabian's end was near. Of course, he had not known that Allison's family were of the brotherhood, but something told me it wouldn't have mattered.

"Could we not offer him sanctuary?" Gabrielle asked.

"We cannot," Evangeline said.

I understood. It hurt and I hated it, but Fabian had turned Allison without a contract in place and without it being approved by The Twelve. To harbor someone like Fabian would be to make enemies of the entire council, and we could not afford that. Not now. Not when everything was already in chaos. Probably not ever.

"I can check in on him, if you'd like," Gabrielle offered.

I smiled at her, trying to ignore the confusing memory of her and her many disguises out of my head. I hoped the smile looked genuine. It was sweet of her to offer her assistance. A very sisterly gesture, certainly.

What was she up to?

"I'm afraid it would only draw attention to him," I said. "The Fiagai will be on alert by now, and they'll be looking for any of us to make a move."

"Surely you didn't tell Alex who turned her?" Gabrielle asked, horrified.

I shook my head.

"Of course I didn't. And I won't. But I can't ask Allison to do the same, and whether or not anyone tells the Fiagai anything, they are hunters. They will track him. By now they'll have started moving in concentric circles around the city from her last known location."

"They won't get anything from me," Allison muttered. "They can all go to Hell."

"Oh, sweet child," Evangeline said. "I know this is difficult for you."

I squeezed Allison's fingers and felt much more at ease when she squeezed mine in return. If nothing else, she knew I would be at her side, even if I had not yet been able to tell her about what Sunee told me. The poor girl had enough of her life changed. She certainly didn't need to find out any time soon that she was my reincarnated daughter.

"I'm so sorry, Allison. I feel like it's all my fault," I said.

"No!" she cried. "You saved my life."

"Barely!"

"Even this existence—this one I don't totally understand yet—is better than death. I know that. And I would have died at Roland's if you hadn't saved me."

"But I'm the reason you're here! Fabian turned you because it would keep me safe."

"If I had known you were that unsafe, perhaps I would have asked to be turned, anyway."

Her face crumpled, and I reached out and pulled her to me. Her anger had so quickly turned into grief.

"I would have said no. It wouldn't have mattered," I said.

"Does he really h-hate m-m-me?" Allison stammered through her tears as she pulled back to look at me.

I knew she was referencing her brother. They'd been so close. He'd protected her, fretted over her. No doubt he was as sick over this as she was.

"He doesn't want to," I said quietly.

"So he d-does?"

"It's in his blood, I'm afraid. Fighting it is impossible."

Even as I said the words, I hated myself for them.

"But you did!" Allison said, meeting my eyes with her own and effectively calling me out on my own lie. "You said it yourself. You were supposed to let me die, and you didn't. You fought your instincts and your duty."

"It's not quite the same," I said.

"Isn't it? You had a duty, and you chose me instead. My own brother can't do the same?"

No one spoke. Not one of us knew what to say. Evangeline moved from her chair to Allison's other side and began rubbing the vampire's back in small, soothing circles.

"Olivia's duty is ingrained in her, yes, but the Fiagai... it is quite different, I'm afraid."

"I am still the same person!" Allison sobbed.

Though it broke my heart to hear her sobs and see her tears, it was a necessary step forward in her existence as a vampire. Leaving her life behind and saying goodbye to her loved ones today certainly expedited the process, but she would have had to do it sometime, anyway, as everyone she ever knew grew old and passed on.

"This is not your fault," Gabrielle crooned.

She put her goblet down on the table and came around the small coffee table. Evangeline removed herself and returned to her armchair as Gabrielle wrapped herself around Allison. We sandwiched the girl between us, both holding on tightly as the sobs wracked her body. I looked up at my sister and softly smiled at her, truly grateful for her presence.

"It feels like my fault," Allison muttered.

"No, no, no," I said, smoothing her curls with my hand. "This is not your fault. You survived. You are a survivor. And you will have an entirely new family of Creatures once it is safe for you to go out."

"Won't the Fiagai hunt me down?"

She pulled back far enough to meet my eyes.

"I don't know," I admitted.

"We'll take whatever precautions are necessary," Evangeline interrupted.

"Precautions for what?" asked Leslie as she entered the room.

Her nostrils flared as she took in the scent, and her eyes narrowed as she saw Gabrielle and I wrapped around Allison. She sat down hard in the chair Gabrielle had vacated and looked at each of us each.

"What is this?" she asked quietly.

Her tone was even, emotionless. I genuinely feared what was coming. Evangeline must have had similar concerns. She positioned herself on the edge of her chair.

"Allison was turned last night," our Guardian said.

"Oh?" Leslie replied.

"She is of a line of Fiagai," Evangeline continued. "We are offering her sanctuary."

"How interesting."

Allison had turned to watch Leslie, but her eyes found mine. Her brow furrowed.

"And how long will we be babysitting for?" Leslie asked.

"Tisiphone," Evangeline warned.

"What? I didn't know we were running some sort of halfway house for Creatures."

"These are special circumstances."

"Mmm. I see. I recall, though, that we do not historically involve ourselves in these types of situations, no matter how *special*."

Vallerie. Of course this had brought up those memories.

"This is a situation unlike any we have ever faced," Evangeline said after a moment of silence.

"I suppose that depends on your perspective."

"If it's that bothersome to you, feel free to go back to gallivanting around the globe," I snapped.

"Perhaps I shall," Leslie sniffed.

"You have no obligation to be here," Gabrielle added.

Leslie stood and left the room without a word.

I looked back and forth between Gabrielle and Evangeline. Evangeline shook her head to warn me away from saying anything in front of Allison, and Gabrielle just shrugged. Maybe later I would feel calm enough to check in on Leslie. Though I understood she was upset, it wasn't like her to react so emotionally. Nothing bothered her.

Not usually, anyway.

Perhaps I didn't know either of my sisters the way I'd thought I did.

THIRTY-SIX

O nce Allison was settled in for the evening with Evangeline standing guard to prevent any bloodlust-driven mishaps, I finally allowed myself to admit there were other things that needed to be taken care of. Allison was as safe as she could be, and the only way to make her safer was to deal with everything else.

But everything else was complicated—in a way that made a newborn vampire seem like the easiest thing to handle. I watched Evangeline gently tuck a blanket around the vampire who'd been so human such a short time ago.

I couldn't keep ignoring my duty. The demon I'd sent to Tartarus without her name presenting itself to me in my spelled amulet was likely something Demetrius was going to eventually hunt me down for. I was surprised I hadn't received a summons from him already. It was possible that Evangeline intervened. It was something I knew I should have inquired about, but it had been a long day with much to consider and much to deal with.

There would be hell—perhaps literally—to pay for what I'd done with the demon. It wouldn't matter to anyone that I'd likely saved a human life. That demon hadn't yet racked up enough bodies on whatever tally sheet The Twelve seemed to be keeping. The spree she was on didn't warrant attention. It didn't warrant a solution, at least not in the eyes of the council.

I didn't regret it. I couldn't. I had been in the right to protect a human—a species naturally weaker than demons, vampires, atlanteans, and certainly the fae. I had sworn an oath. I knew my role. I knew my duty.

I was tired of games and secrets. I was tired of waiting around for someone to point my witchblade in whatever direction they wanted.

I was a weapon.

I closed my eyes, grabbed my amulet, and opened my eyes when I was firmly inside the other realm. Allura awaited my arrival, which made me wonder if my theory about Evangeline was accurate. Without a word, she turned on a heel and walked, and I followed her down the hallways to Demetrius' office. He stood behind his desk, palms flat upon its dark surface, and his brow furrowed as he examined the documents spread before him. I glanced over enough to know there were more uprisings to examine and names of Creatures that my sister and I would likely see in our amulets in a few days' time. It depended on how quickly The Twelve moved, and frankly, they moved like the long-lived Creatures they were. They were never in a rush, so everything continued to move painstakingly slowly.

"Steward," I said as a way of greeting him.

He slowly raised his head to look at me. His dark eyes were flinty, full of frustration and maybe some disappointment. But I was no child to be admonished, and I raised myself to my full height. Everything I was projecting dared him to question me.

Fucking try it.

"What were you thinking, Alekto?" he asked.

His voice was far gentler than I'd expected it to be. It was soft and deep. There was no rage. I wanted rage. Rage made people make mistakes.

Instead, the Steward sounded more like an exasperated parent than someone whose plans were being ruined. I kept my facial expression hard.

"I am Justice," I stated plainly.

There was a slow nod, and then Demetrius sank into his chair. He stared up at me. I noticed lines around his eyes that I didn't remember seeing before. Dark circles framed those eyes, as well. He looked exhausted.

"We have a process—" he began. I opened my mouth to interrupt, but Demetrius put up his hand. "Please allow me to finish," he said.

I sat in one of the chairs before the desk, hands near my weapons. If Demetrius was at the center of the uprising, he might be provoked into unexpected action. I didn't want to, but I would slit his throat if it meant walking out of here in one piece.

"We have a process, Alekto, and you and your sisters are very much a part of that. I respect your diligence and your desire for justice to be served, but to go out, as a vigilante of sorts—it just creates the kind of chaos that The Twelve are seeking to nullify. This kind of chaos is making things worse."

"The process is broken," I stated.

"The process is not perfect," he admitted. "Any one of The Twelve could concede that, I hope. But this is not the way to get things done."

"The way to get things done is not to wait around until the bodies pile up to whatever number seems unacceptable to Creatures who are, frankly, old as shit and no longer in touch with human matters." Demetrius stared at me. "I was quite literally built for this, Demetrius. *We* were built for this. We were given a duty. I cannot speak for the Megaera and the Tisiphone, but I can no longer sit back and wait for orders when I know the kinds of injustices that are being committed day in and day out in the human realm. I won't."

"Then you are no better than the Creatures who pull at their bindings."

"My own bindings have become restraints, and no doubt many of the Creatures feel the same."

Demetrius placed his palms down on the top of the desk, as if he needed a moment to clear his head. I didn't much care what he needed.

"You are better than this. Your sisters are better than this. I beg you to adhere to the established rules, Alekto. To do this any other way incites chaos, and we have enough of that, do we not?"

I let his words linger in the air. So far, Demetrius seemed only concerned in the way a Steward should be. He had not indicated anything else was amiss, like his plans to join the council himself.

"The Old Ones are waking," I said.

His eyes widened. He sat forward in his seat, hands gripping the armrests of his chair.

"How do you know of that?" he asked.

"Does it matter?" I responded.

"I suppose not. Who else knows?"

"I don't know. But if the Old Ones are waking, all your pretty processes will evaporate into the air. What then, Demetrius?"

"Until it happens, we must hold tight to the laws."

"The laws? The laws are archaic. I cannot hold tight to this broken way of living, and you shouldn't want me to."

"Not this again!" Demetrius said exasperatedly.

He shot to his feet. Here was the anger I'd hoped for, the emotional reaction that might let something slip.

"Your duty is to The Twelve, Alekto. I have said it many times already, and I will continue to remind you of that fact. Without The Twelve, you are exactly like those souls you escort to Tartarus. You must await instructions from The Twelve."

"You're wrong. I was created for this and given this duty by the very Old Ones we all fear. Perhaps it makes me bloodthirsty. Perhaps it makes me vengeful. But my sisters and I are some of the only ones who can claim a gods-given right to do what we do."

I rose out of my chair slowly and deliberately. I was nothing but calm confidence as I stared across the space at the Steward, whose chest was still heaved. A glimmer of satisfaction burned within me at that.

"The Twelve have their roles, Steward, but we have ours." He sputtered, but I held up my hand. "Do not be so foolish as to assume those roles are equal," I said flatly.

Without another word, I strode out of his office.

THIRTY-SEVEN

I headed straight for Sunee's living quarters. I had managed to hold tightly to my calm facade so long as I was in Demetrius' presence, but I unleashed my true feelings as soon as I was away. The flames of my fury licked at my insides, begging to be stoked. My fingers itched to grab around a blade, my body burned with the need to move, to fight, to do *something*.

Gaia, I was not made for these secret-keeping, political games.

The walk wasn't long enough to cool my temper, unfortunately, and Sunee silently took in my dark expression as she opened the door and admitted me into her home. She said nothing. The silence continued to build as I stalked through the living quarters. I heard soft footsteps in my wake, and I could smell the soft scent of lavender that often wafted around the witch.

"Demetrius is most displeased," Sunee remarked.

She took her customary position on the sofa and poured a cup of tea. There was no reason for me to respond to the statement, as it was so patently true. I remained quiet. Quiet seemed best, given my mood. I made my way to the sofa where I usually sat and took the offered cup of tea.

"Oolong," was all she said.

I nodded and sipped. It was warm, and the spicy floral notes of it wafted upward into my nose. Sunee made no move to speak, and we simply sat there in the silence, sipping tea. My cup was half-empty before a scone was offered, and I took it. Scents of lemon and lavender floated around me as I took my first bite.

"This is lovely," I bit out, the words at odds with my tone.

"Thank you. I bake when I am upset."

"We have that in common."

That earned me a genuine look of surprise.

"Shall I send you some recipes?" she asked.

"Evangeline might appreciate that. She's quite tired of muffins."

The grin that had been threatening to spread across Sunee's face finally shone through. I tentatively smiled back.

"I am concerned about your provocation of the Steward," she said gently.

I took another bite of my scone. Any reason I had for doing what I did sounded childish as I contemplated it here in the witch's quarters. Odd, since I had felt so righteous before. I delicately sniffed at the air again, concerned that there might be the scent of a spell that I had not picked up on, but all I could confirm were the heavenly smells of the tea and the scone.

"I don't wish to speak of it," I said.

Sunee blinked, but if she was surprised at the dismissal in my tone, she didn't let it show.

"I met with Atara and Ramiel earlier. They are interested in what you may have discovered."

I had almost been able to put it from my mind—the memory of watching my sister's disguise melt from her as she left that Creature's residence. I could see it all too clearly. Her dark hair had become more and more visible and the features softer and more familiar until they were those of someone I trusted. Worse, they were the features of someone I loved. The sting of betrayal was still sharp.

"Something happened," Sunee said as she leaned forward.

I nodded.

"I don't want to pry, child, but it is imperative that we know what we are working with."

Her gentle voice was almost as soothing as the tea still in my hand. I took another bite of the scone, chewed it as I thought through the words I might say out loud, took another drink of tea, and then set both on the table in front of me. I intertwined my fingers together and looked straight at Sunee.

"I have no evidence other than this: I saw the Megaera leaving a Creature's home in an unrecognizable disguise. When that disguise was removed, I was able to confirm her identity. I pursued until she donned yet another unrecognizable disguise, spoke a spell into a tree, and descended into the earth. I can only assume it was a fae dwelling of some sort."

"To be sure," Sunee mused.

The silence fell around us once more.

"This must be difficult for you," Sunee said quietly.

"It is. I do not remember an existence without her, and thus she has had my trust. To think of her betrayal..." I broke off.

Sunee nodded in understanding.

"It is a difficult thing to consider that those we love the most might not share in those feelings, and worst yet, that they may have the potential to do unspeakable damage to us because of it."

"If she truly has been involved in the uprisings and with some sort of mutiny, it is beyond anything I thought her capable of," I replied.

"Ramiel has been able to gather some intelligence that it is Demetrius who has been working against us," Sunee said.

"Is that why I have gone unpunished?" I asked.

"Atara and I intervened on your behalf. It is in your nature, after all, to crave this sense of justness—and we do think that some movement could be made to let the rest of the council see that."

"Truly?" I murmured, unwilling to let my interest show in my tone.

"Yes, " she said. "You were created by the gods for this kind of work. Though the gods are absent from our world, it does not mean that all that they did was done in evil or rooted in treachery. In many ways, the Old Ones saw what the world needed. No one can argue that."

I probably could have, but I wisely kept my thoughts to myself. It wasn't Sunee's fault she didn't have my memories, my experiences with those who had once ruled.

"Is there a chance, then, that my sisters and I might someday return to our gods-given work? That we could mete out justice the way it was intended?" I asked.

Sunee smiled.

"It may take some time, but Atara and I do believe we could get a majority of The Twelve on our side."

"What about the Steward?"

The smile fell from the witch's face.

"If we can prove it is Demetrius at the heart of the uprisings, it would be easier, to be sure, to ask the rest of The Twelve to consider the removal of the position all together."

The Twelve without a Steward. How strange.

"What of the Guardians?" I inquired.

"They could report straight to the council. There's no reason to have the middleman, so to speak. The Twelve could stand to move a bit more... efficiently, we'll say," she said with a conspiratorial tone.

"It may be likely that he will implicate a member of The Twelve and try to take their seat," Sunee continued.

"What? Whose?"

"He is a witch, child. His powers are bound by the stewardship, and he has no coven to speak of, but he is still a Creature."

"Does Veradis suspect anything?" I asked, mentioning the male witch on the council.

"No. He's a stubborn mule. Even if he was challenged directly, he believes too solidly in his own power," Sunee muttered.

It aligned with my own knowledge of Demetrius. He wasn't unpleasant, per se, but his confidence was a bit off-putting. Sunee listed a few more names of council members who might be willing to align themselves. It was clear we needed more evidence, and it meant finding out exactly what Gabrielle was up to.

THIRTY-EIGHT

y dreams that day were a blur of memories. Some moments I remembered as I had once lived them, but there were also several that had obviously slipped my mind over the centuries. Others were hazier, more like the strange visions I'd had of those I assumed to be my family. The Fates made appearances, as well, blending in and out of with their odd rhyming and murmurings about secrets and trust. To say it was a poor night's sleep was putting it lightly, but it wasn't really a surprise. The situation with Alex and Allison was bound to have caused some memories to resurface. I wished fervently that I could make sense of more of the things I saw in my dreamscape. It felt like I needed to put the various pieces together, but I wasn't entirely certain what kind of picture was meant to be formed. I rolled out of bed and shuffled down the hallway to the room Evangeline had put Allison in. The door was open, so I made my way to the kitchen, which was also empty. I eventually found Evangeline in the living room with Allison. Evangeline sat doing needlepoint of all things while Allison held a book.

You can take a woman out of the century she was born in, but you can't make her change. My Guardian was proof enough of that.

Fucking needlepoint. I shuddered. What a horribly *quiet* activity.

"How are you feeling today?" I asked Allison.

She tilted her head toward the goblet of blood in her hand.

"I'm on my second one of these, so I'm feeling a lot better than I was when I woke up."

She tossed me a smile, though, and it warmed me to see it.

"I've told her the hunger pangs will wane over time," Evangeline said, giving Allison a soft smile.

"They will," I agree. "Drink as much as you need, though. We all do."

Allison smiled and took another drink.

"No issues overnight?" I asked.

"None. I slept like the dead."

I groaned and tossed a throw pillow from the nearest chair at her, but Allison swatted it away with the book in her hand.

"Olivia, the blood," Evangeline warned.

I rolled my eyes and plopped into the chair next to the sofa. I inspected the cover of Allison's book more closely as I recognized it as one of ours from our library.

"Dante?" I asked incredulously.

Allison grinned.

"Seemed prudent," she laughed.

I rolled my eyes at her, too.

"Evangeline also said she'd make some space upstairs for me to work on some art, and I think Dante might be a good inspiration," Allison said.

"It's good for her to return to things she loves, as often as she can. It will help with the hunger," Evangeline explained.

I nodded. Evangeline knew more than any of us about the new beginnings of vampires. Because we typically stayed away from most Creatures, we didn't often cross paths with their traditions and practices. I was glad to have Evangeline here for Allison. I wanted the best for her.

"As long as you paint me something," I replied with a grin.

"I promise."

I gave her another smile and looked back over at my Guardian who was stitching neatly and humming softly to herself. I quietly excused myself to get my own goblet of blood from the kitchen. I wondered if

Leslie and Gabrielle were still sleeping.

"Have you seen the others?" I asked Evangeline when I returned.

"Leslie was up and about before all of us. She's downstairs training."

Of course she was.

"Gabrielle is still upstairs sleeping. She was helping me earlier, so she needed a bit of rest."

"Evangeline is being polite. Gabrielle pulled an early shift of guard duty for me," Allison said.

Interesting.

Evangeline opened her mouth to speak, but Allison waved the words away before they could even come out.

"It doesn't bother me, truly. It's best we're careful. I know that."

Evangeline gave another doting smile to Allison before turning her attention to me.

"Olivia, would you mind speaking with Leslie? I'm concerned."

I nodded tightly. I wanted to go to her and find out what had triggered her the previous evening. It was a chaotic time as we dealt with the uprisings and the increased traffic to Tartarus, but Leslie usually handled those kinds of additional responsibilities with a lighthearted ease that neither Gabrielle nor I had ever been capable of.

I made sure Allison was well-situated before I went downstairs into the training room. When I turned the corner and saw her, I knew that whatever she'd felt the night before wasn't quite out of her system. Sweat dripped from Leslie's brow and into her eyes. She wiped at it angrily as she whirled her fighting sticks around her body. She didn't bother to hide her otherness. She was a blur of chaotic motion.

"I suppose the Guardian sent you down?" she asked, whirling to a stop in front of me.

She said it like a challenge, and I felt my temper rise within me. I didn't want to fight with her, so I did my best to tamp it down, but there was a small part of me that wanted to put her on her ass for what she'd said about Allison the night before.

For what she'd said about my daughter.

"What's going on, Leslie?" I asked.

This was a different tactic. I wasn't one to talk about feelings, and I was never the one to inquire about whether anyone or everyone was okay. I wasn't built like that and whatever softness I'd maybe had as a human was long gone by my early days as a Fury. I wanted to tread carefully, though. It may have been due to the recent recollection of memories about my sister's loss of her lover or perhaps even the warnings from The Fates. Whatever it was, I felt compelled to be as delicate as I could with my sister.

Leslie, though, narrowed her eyes at me, as if wondering at the game I was playing. I let my feelings show in my expression, though, and saw her face soften a bit.

"You know you can talk to me," I said.

Leslie tossed the sticks to the side and sat down hard on the mat. She put her head in her hands.

"I'm sorry I was such a bitch," she breathed.

I sat down next to her and shot her a smile.

"I've been a bitch for centuries, Les. You don't have to apologize," I said jokingly.

That wrung a small smile from her features, at least.

"I just... found out some stuff the other day that really has me on edge. I took it out on Allison. I know it's not an excuse. It just felt like one more thing being tossed onto a burning pile of garbage."

"I know what you mean. Allison calls it a 'dumpster fire.'"

Our eyes met, and the need to tell her about what I'd seen of Gabrielle burned inside me. I didn't want to keep secrets. The knowledge that Leslie had never kept anything from me, either, weighed on me heavily. I remembered the warning: *Find a way to move ahead with neither your heart nor eyes.* I knew what I was feeling was in my heart, but I saw my sad and downtrodden sister before me. I didn't know how to escape that heaviness.

"I don't know about that," Leslie finally laughed.

I cocked an eyebrow.

"Spill," I demanded.

"Ugh, I shouldn't."

"But you will."

"Fuck it. Yeah, I will. Gabrielle's being real shady, and I might have, sort of followed her?"

"You trailed her?" I asked.

"Yeah, but you totally would have, too, if you'd seen how weird she was being!"

"I did, actually. I've got my own concerns about our sister."

"I think she's working with one of The Twelve. At the very least, she's been disappearing to the hell realms far more often than she ever has before, and that in and of itself is strange."

My heart sank. I'd feared this, and it was almost exactly as I'd pictured. I hadn't realized Gabrielle was traveling to the other realm more often, but it made sense given how often she disappeared. It made too much sense.

"I've been working with Sunee," I admitted.

Leslie's eyes grew round.

"What?" she gasped. "Why?"

"There are suspicions about the uprisings and the riots. A few of the council members have started asking questions, and because we can move through the earth realm without anyone really noticing, I was asked to investigate."

"Whoa," she said in a heavy breath.

We sat there in silence, both of us assembling this new information into what we had already known.

"How long have you been working with her?" Leslie asked.

"Not long. No one else knows, obviously. I don't even think Evangeline has any idea. I think there are a lot of suspicions about Demetrius, so maybe that's why they haven't involved anyone."

"Demetrius?!" Leslie cried.

"Shh!" I said. "Yes. From what I understand, he's been quite vocal about interest in a council seat."

"But he's the Steward."

"Maybe he wants more power?" I asked, knowing that's what Sunee suspected.

"When I followed Gabrielle, she was meeting with various Creatures. It was strange," Leslie said.

"Was she disguised?" I asked.

"Yes!"

"I saw her, too. I watched her remove one disguise and don another. Spells, you think?"

"Has to be. I tried to see if she was wearing any extra jewelry that might hold them, but I haven't noticed anything."

"Hmm... she could have had something inked," I suggested.

It was a drastic move, having a spell inked into skin. Only the most powerful Creatures could do it, but it was an easy way to be sure the spells needed were at hand. Jewelry could be ripped off or removed, whereas the only way to remove spelled skin was to slice through the design or remove the entire piece of skin with the tattoo.

"Ugh, that one demon. Remember him? Horace? Henry?"

"Hagar," I corrected.

A few centuries before, Hagar had skinned his victims—all witches —and sewed their inked skin to his own to grant him their powers. He had indeed grown powerful, but once my sisters and I had been sent to escort him to Tartarus, there was nowhere for him to run. In the end, after we'd wind-walked all over the country chasing him, Leslie had been able to fire arrows into the few visible tattoos. It had given us the seconds we needed to release his soul.

"Do you think the disguises are of real people?" Leslie asked.

"I have no idea. I certainly didn't recognize either of the ones I saw her in."

And as we sat there picking apart the various details of what we knew about our sister, I recalled that the Fates had warned me against trusting those I love... while also telling me to love the ones I trust. I hoped I hadn't made a mistake.

THIRTY-NINE

The next few days were blessedly quiet. Allison settled into her new existence. Evangeline hovered around her in a way I had certainly never seen from the Guardian before. Gabrielle returned to her normal pattern of disappearing and reappearing whenever she felt like, and Leslie and I tried to trail her, though we were often unsuccessful. Once Gabrielle wind-walked, it was difficult to tell where she had gone. I couldn't pull at the same wind and end up in the same place. I needed to know where to direct the wind so I could travel with it. Gabrielle wasn't exactly sharing a travel itinerary.

I spent a lot of my time running through drills with Leslie so that we could talk through our suspicions. I was also careful to make time for Allison. I didn't want her to feel more alone than we knew she was.

Evangeline had been able to gather from her own sources that the Fiagai were out in force. So far, they hadn't called in any of their brethren. No outsiders. It meant the number of hunters we were dealing with was fairly small, even for a larger city, but the Fiagai had survived centuries because of their careful training and almost superhuman strength. A number of Creature murders had The Twelve in an uproar. I hadn't heard anything from Ramiel, Atara, or Sunee since I'd left Bellanca after having tea in Sunee's apartment.

Ramiel wanted the heads of the Fiagai on spikes, but from what Evangeline heard, Sunee had intervened. The Fiagai, for all their talents, were human. Humans deserved protection. We hadn't been able to keep the knowledge of Allison quiet for long, and Sunee used that information to further support her own stance. The Fiagai were within their rights to demand recompense for one of their own being turned. The family of Fiagai were supposed to be untouchable. From what we heard, at least one Fiagai had been taken out on the council's orders while Ramiel and Sunee had raged at one another in the halls of Bellanca.

Now there was a cease-fire, at least on the Creature side of things. The Twelve couldn't control what the Fiagai did, though one of the council members floated the idea of contacting whomever was in charge to call a truce.

Last I knew, none of us were allowed to intervene. I told myself it didn't matter whether anyone did or not. I didn't care. But Allison cared. She cared so much that I often fell asleep and woke up to the sound of her quietly sobbing.

I hadn't yet been able to check in on Fabian. I'd hoped to find a way to see if his home stood empty, but with the sheer number of Fiagai in the city, it felt like I would bring trouble right to Fabian's front door. I didn't know what kind of loyalty Alex might feel toward me. I didn't know how many of my secrets he might still be keeping. I couldn't take the chance that Alex had told his brothers everything and that they would use that knowledge to track my movements.

And if Fabian was as foolish as I worried he was, I would lead them right to him in an attempt to glean information. I worried for my friend and wished, not for the first time, that we had been able to offer him sanctuary as we had Allison. My sense of justice was torn. Were bad things done for the right reasons truly bad? I didn't know, and that rocked me more than anything else—even Allison's turning.

The grayness of things that had once been so easily seen as black and white was certainly worrisome. I wondered if I would ever be the same. At least part of me hoped I wouldn't. Life was infinitely more complicated than it had ever been, but I felt more alive than I had in eons. At times, I could almost forget that war was brewing.

And we couldn't fight that war on two sides, trying to figure out who was terrorizing our people from the inside and dealing with the hunters. Chaos reigned, and it felt like the end of days was inevitable. The Old Ones would surely awaken. The fear that everything I just brought into my life would dissipate in the wake of it all should have emboldened me.

It did not.

I tucked myself away into the home I shared with my Guardian and Allison. My sisters visited more than they had in at least ten years. I trained when Leslie dragged me downstairs, but I began taking those moments as opportunities to train our new vampire. I was like a proud mother. I *was* a proud mother.

Allison's newfound speed and strength were impressive, though Allison certainly didn't have the drive to become any kind of weapons or combat expert. She was much happier upstairs in her studio, where she had made good on her word to paint me something. Inspiration was taken from Dante, as promised, and I'd received a dark but inviting painting of the Acheron. To look at it pulled at me in a way that felt familiar, but I wasn't sure why. Nonetheless, it received its proper placement on my bedroom wall where I could stare at it before I went to sleep each night.

I couldn't stand the waiting. After nights of dreams full of blood and vengeance, I woke needing—with a desperation I'd rarely known—to know if Fabian was all right. I used the wind to travel and stepped out in the backyard where I hoped against hope that no Fiagai were waiting. I felt alone, but I was nervous about sending out any psychic tendrils to make sure. From what I could sense, the house was empty, anyway. I grabbed at the wind and left.

———

I stood in Tully's with a whiskey in my hand. It was a bit early in the evening to be drinking, but I didn't care. I wasn't the only one. The bar was full and noisy. I took my whiskey and escaped to a corner.

Fabian's house was empty. It could mean he was safe. It could also mean he was dead. I hadn't dared to check. I hadn't wanted to leave a scent. I wrapped my fingers around the cool glass of amber liquid and said a silent prayer to Gaia, hoping none of the Old Ones had risen close enough to consciousness to hear my pleas.

"Liv," a voice said quietly as a body pressed into my wide.

A haggard-looking Fabian peered out at me from underneath the wide hood of a jacket.

"What are you doing here?" I whispered loudly at him.

"I'm leaving, don't worry. I just... wanted to see you. You know, in case..." he trailed off.

I shuddered. I didn't want to lose Fabian, but I was at a loss of how to protect him. We didn't keep any safe houses, like the vampires sometimes did.

"You need to get to someone who can keep you safe. And find a witch. You need to mask your scent. Permanently, if possible."

"Word has spread that the Fiagai are looking for me. No one will take me in."

Fabian tried to say it lightly, like it was just an inconvenience, but I saw the weight of his predicament in the way he carried himself. His shoulders sloped downward, as if even during our conversation he was trying to hide away.

"You should have left already," I muttered.

"Come with me."

I stared at him.

There was no way that I could leave. I had a duty. *But wasn't I sick and tired of my duty? Wasn't I exhausted of the weight on my shoulders?* I could potentially keep Fabian safe. My own scent didn't register as an enemy to the Fiagai. If Alex had kept my secrets, there was no link, no connection to me and the supernatural.

I didn't want to think about how closely we would have to stay for my scent to mask Fabian's, but there was certainly a part of me that would not have minded. My mind—and, if I was being honest, my heart —traveled back to Alex. I thought about his soft, dark curls and those eyes I could so easily lose myself in.

"I can't," I whispered, my voice breaking.

The dimmest bit of light that had been in Fabian's eyes flickered out.

"Please," he whispered. "Liv, I—"

"I can't," I said, my throat thick with unshed tears. "Please don't say anything else. I can't leave her."

"Or him."

"I can't go with you. That's my answer," I whispered brokenly.

I got out of crowded, noisy bar as quickly as I could.

FORTY

Leslie and I spent an evening in the training room sans Allison, who begged off so she could finish a painting for Evangeline. We were halfway through our second round with the daggers when we heard footsteps racing along the floor above us. My sister and I took one glance at each other and raced upstairs. Evangeline stood at the door, hands in fists at her sides. I pushed her gently aside so that I could look through the peephole.

Alex stood on the pathway, and he carried a brown leather bag in one hand. He looked every bit the warrior he was, eyes ablaze with fury and his stance ready for battle. That lanky body of his belied the strength I knew was there. I had not realized how much it might hurt me to see him like that, but it did. It tore at something inside me.

I opened the door. Alex's eyes widened, but they remained fixed and furious.

"You do not have business here, hunter," I said.

I could not say his name.

"I disagree," he said, holding the bag out to me.

I stared at the bag. I didn't want to take it. Everything in me screamed not to. There was only one possible reason that Alex could have for showing up.

Allison stepped to my side, and Alex's brown eyes moved to his sister. I'm sure he noticed the changes. It would have been impossible for someone like him not to. Her scent had changed from something light and floral, like peonies, to a spicier, darker scent akin to night blooming jasmine. Skin that had once been ivory had taken on a creamier hue, and not a blemish was in sight. The lashes around her bright eyes had darkened and thickened. Everything about her was more inviting. All the better for the predator she had become. I didn't want to recognize the look of disgust on Alex's face, but I did.

"Say what you need to say, and then remove yourself from this place of sanctuary," I said flatly.

He is not Iason. He has not been Iason in centuries.

Alex upended the bag, and dust floated out on the crisp, midnight air. A pile grew on the snow beneath his feet. A heavy ring bounced and landed, and my heart ripped.

I fell to my knees.

Fabian.

I stared at the ashes of my former lover and friend. There was no doubt about it. It was as I had feared. That ring had been on Fabian's finger for as long as I had known him. He'd told me once that it was his family crest. The dark silver of it glinted in the moonlight. A soft keening rose around me. I did not realize it was coming from within me. Not at first.

"Is that...?" Gabrielle said.

I hadn't registered her presence at all. She hadn't been there, and then suddenly she was. And she was staring down at Alex with something close to murder in her eyes.

"You would show that monster despair?" Alex asked.

"You know not of what you speak, hunter," Gabrielle growled.

"This beast turned my sister—without remorse and without consent! How dare you?!" Alex said. "I tore his body limb from limb and waited for it to turn to ash."

I fell forward, face in my hands as sobs wracked my body. I had known it was an outcome. I had realized it was probably inevitable. But the pain of it was something far more than I had ever considered it might be.

And it's all your fault.

"What's going on?" Allison asked.

Gabrielle put her arms around my daughter and murmured soft, quiet things to her, and then I felt Evangeline lead Allison away from the scene. My sister tried to bring me to my feet, and I let her. She reached forward and snatched the ring from the pile of snow and ash.

I held my hand out, and she placed it within my palm. It felt heavy, and probably heavier because his death pulled at me in the way it did. In the way it had to. *Oh, Fabian.*

Alex stared at me through all of it, unmoving and breathing heavily.

"The Creature who turned my sister—you knew him?" he finally asked, tone incredulous.

"Oh, she knew him," Gabrielle said.

Alex's eyes filled with horror. He knew what she meant.

"Congratulations. She saved your sister's life, and you just repaid her by killing her lover."

Alex's horrified eyes searched my own, and as much as I wanted to look away from him, I couldn't. Gabrielle didn't know what Alex was to me—both Allison and I had felt that was best kept a secret for now—but she might have said what she did, anyway. It didn't matter. The words were out there, and I was not a liar. The truth had just been laid bare, and I would accept whatever happened afterwards.

"Olivia," Alex said.

His tone was flat, empty. The horror that filled those brown eyes had melted away, and he was looking at me as if he did not know me at all.

"Megaera, go check on Allison for me, will you? She's had a shock."

Gabrielle did not pause, though I could see she wanted to. Regardless of what had just happened, I was the leader of the Furies. I was the center. If I gave an order, it was to be followed. I had not meant to pull rank, but centuries of being looked to for guidance and action made it so easy.

I sagged against the doorframe. Fabian's ring was clutched in my hand, and I knew I would clutch my grief around me just as tightly. I just needed Alex to go. I didn't even want to look at him.

"She has no reason to lie, so I am going to accept what your sister has said was the truth."

"As you should," I exhaled.

"How long ago?" he asked.

"What?"

"How long ago did you sleep with him?"

That flatness of his tone had burned into white hot anger.

"Just after I saved Allison. Before I met you that night at the club."

"You loved that... that monster?"

"Yes," I said simply.

"How? He took my sister!" Alex raged.

"He did. And he was also my friend. And, yes, sometimes he was my lover. Fabian was..." I trailed off. "He had a good soul."

"You dare talk to me about his soul."

"Your righteousness is misplaced, Alex. He turned your sister. He did it to save me."

"Save you? From what?" He snapped.

"From myself," I laughed sadly. "Saving your sister and knowingly letting her retain her human nature after I confirmed the memory charm didn't work are two strikes against me. If anyone had discovered the truth, I would likely be sent to Tartarus."

Ah, that made him pause.

"How did he know about Allison?" he growled.

"I did not give him her name. He must have figured it out somehow. He was concerned only for my safety. He didn't know—not about who she is to me, who you are to me."

"Like it would have made a difference."

"It likely would have. You have no cause to understand it, but Fabian has been a true friend, and he only did what he did for the sake of my safety."

"I am not sorry."

I stared up at him. I had unknowingly moved closer to him as he spoke. The desire to touch him, to be near him, was nowhere to be found. I saw only his mask of arrogance, of hatred. I saw in him the same things I saw in the faces of Creatures I sent to Tartarus. I had no patience for it.

"You say that you killed him for your sister," I started.

"I killed a Creature who performed an illegal turning."

"But this was personal, wasn't it? This Creature turned your sister into a vampire."

"And he has paid the price."

"But what price will you pay, Alex? You have allowed your vengeance and your duty to coincide. You have avenged a sister you will not even try to maintain a relationship with—and she was turned against her will. You are not who I thought you were."

"I could say the same to you," Alex spat.

"Then I suggest we part ways now. Do not come here again, hunter. I will not guarantee your safety."

I whirled around, strode into my home, and slammed the door. I would hold tightly to this anger for as long as I could, knowing that the weight of my grief would press down upon me soon enough. And when it did, I would mourn only my longtime friend. Alex deserved nothing.

FORTY-ONE

I wore the ring with Fabian's crest on it around my neck on a silver chain. It hung there, like an albatross, just below my amulet. What his last moments must have been like were too easily pictured for someone like me. I'd certainly sent enough souls to Tartarus to be able to reason out what the end was like for a vampire. Had he felt it—the escape of his soul or the crumbling of his body into dust?

Where might someone like him spend eternity? I didn't know. Some things were a mystery, even to someone who had lived as long as I had. I hoped for the Elysian Fields. But I could not be certain that his illegal turning of Allison would grant him from the afterlife most Creatures wished for. I could not be certain that it would not, either. So I tried to have hope.

I did not even know any more if Fabian had done the wrong thing. It had felt so clear before—the line between good and evil, between right and wrong. No, that wasn't really true. The grayness between had been growing for some time. It was only Fabian's death that solidified it for me. After all, I had made decisions well in the gray area. My own decision to allow Allison to live with the knowledge of Creatures was certainly gray. And there it was—I had played some role in Fabian's death, through my unwillingness to adhere to my duty as a Fury.

My own decisions had led to the death of my friend. I claimed to be so sick of secrets, so tired of playing the silly games The Twelve seemed to constantly trifle with, and yet my secrets had caused this.

The guilt and the grief combined in a way that I thought might kill me. I think I wanted it to. Whatever tethered my soul to this reality had my permission to wither away. The heavy weight of sadness and knowledge of my role in Fabian's demise pulled me down into the depths of darkness I had thought I escaped long ago. But the darkness welcomed me. I folded myself into its embrace. I did not have shadows like Gabrielle, but I could wrap misery around me just the same.

Not wanting her to share in my sense of responsibility for Fabian, I pulled away from Allison. She deserved so much better than someone like me. Her life shouldn't be tainted by my anguish. I pulled away from my sisters and my Guardian, too. I laid there in anguish, letting my melancholy seep into everything.

I held onto my duty. Even in despair, I could not walk away from it. I patrolled into the pink-orange dawn and then again once the green-gray dusk of night settled over the city. I hunted those whose names appeared in my amulet without feeling much of anything. In that, I returned to who I had been just such a short time before.

———

"Yuri Oneida, you have broken the laws of your brethren, and so you must pay your debt in full."

The delicate features of the vampire twisted with fear. The bright lights of billboards and flashing signs and skyscrapers of Beijing were all around us. The nearness of the ever-present crowds didn't faze me. Yuri's fear barely registered. As she looked up at me, the scent of sage drifted from her. It was the only thing about her I'd deigned to notice. I had no sense of how old she was. I did not care.

"I, the Alekto, release your spirit to be guided to Tartarus, where you will be judged for your rebellion and disregard. The truth of your nature will be revealed," I said as I pulled my witchblade across the vampire's throat.

I let the body fall, but I did not watch as it crumbled to dust. I had more Creatures to escort, and I could not bear to have my very fears about Fabian come to life before me. I would never watch a Creature turn to dust again.

———

The wolven fought me with all the strength of his will, which was vast. His canines snapped at my throat as he pinned me against the outside of the Brooklyn townhouse I'd located him in. Hot breaths brushed against my face. I twisted beneath his arms and caught him off-guard. Soon enough, he was on his knees with his arms behind his back and held with the Hephaestian chain I carried. I pulled his long, blonde hair back to force his face to look up at me so I could begin the ritual.

"You have broken the laws of your brethren, Samuel Mills, and so you must pay your debt in full."

"I owe no debts!" Samuel roared.

The drama. The yelling. The fighting. I was sick of it. I was sick of their lies. I held the witchblade against his throat to prevent him from speaking further. A cold nothingness rushed through me as his eyes closed and his lips silently formed prayers that would not be answered.

"I, the Alekto, release your spirit to be guided to Tartarus, where you will be judged for your rebellion and disregard. The truth of your nature will be revealed."

The witchblade did its work of releasing his soul from his body, and I twisted away from the scene in the wind.

———

I found the lone fae hidden amongst the debris in an abandoned alley. I lifted a pallet from where it leaned against a pile of stinking plastic bags near a rusted dumpster. His too-long arms wrapped around knees of his too-long legs, and the dark green of his leaf-like hair trembled. I chose to believe it was because of the winter wind that whipped through the narrow walkway between brick buildings. I could not stomach his fear, though the sour scent of it burned my nostrils. It was not fair for him to be afraid and to show such fear to me—I, who was just trying to fulfill my duty. He had broken the laws. He had no right to be afraid of the consequences of his own actions.

"You have broken the laws of your brethren, and so you must pay your debt in full. I, the Alekto, release your spirit to be guided to Tartarus, where you will be judged for your rebellion and disregard. The truth of your nature will be revealed," I said.

I grasped the arm of the fae and dragged him onto his knees. His soft whimpers did nothing. I would not let them. I simply held my witchblade to his throat and sliced.

FORTY-TWO

I lost count of the number of Creatures I sent to Tartarus. I moved from location to location in the wind, embracing all that I was and needed to be to perform my duties. I did not listen, I did not feel, I did not pause. I simply did what I was made to do.

I scented other beings nearby, at times, but I knew they were no match for me. I did not allow concern for them to shape my actions in any way. Not even when a familiar scent wound its way into my consciousness near the dwelling of another unruly wolven.

I carried out my duty, wiped the witchblade clean on my black jeans, and strode back out and into the wailing winter wind. I reached for it and caught just enough to twist myself into it when a hand grabbed my arm and pulled me back.

I stared up into eyes I had never wished to see again.

"Olivia," Alex rasped.

He was covered in tight-fitting black gear from the tips of his heavy black boots all the way up to the knitted mask over his face. He tore it free and, breathing heavily and exhaling swaths of steam into the night air, stood before me.

"I was hoping I'd come across you," he said quietly.

I did not speak.

"Olivia, please," he said. "Speak to me."

So I did.

"You're too late for this one, Fiagai," I said, gesturing at the home I'd just left.

"That seems to be happening a lot lately," Alex replied.

His eyes burned into mine, but I refused to bring down the walls and let him in. He wanted the familiarity of what we had, but I did not. I could not forget what had been said already and could not forget what had been done.

"Perhaps you are too human for such a task," I said with a shrug. "But I will be grateful that at least your lot isn't killing indiscriminately, as you are so inclined to do."

Alex scoffed.

"That would be your conclusion, wouldn't it?" he asked.

I did not grant him a response. His human emotions were rising, and no doubt my ability to keep mine in check would only anger him further. *Good.*

"We're hearing things about a ringleader," Alex said finally after long moments of silence.

He had exhaled thirteen times.

"Ah, yes. The Creature who is not a Creature. The Twelve are aware," I said in a brusque tone, waving his words away.

He smelled like cedar and cinnamon.

"We could work together to find it," Alex suggested.

His face was haggard.

"We could, but I do not require assistance to fulfill my duties."

"It's for the good of all," Alex said.

"You do not know the meaning of that particular ideal," I hissed at him. "You murder at will simply because of a Creature's existence and not due to their actions. I want no part of your belief system."

"And you are so certain of their actions?" Alex asked, swinging one arm wide toward the house. "At least I know who and what I'm killing. I have a mission. You have a bunch of monsters giving you orders."

I didn't say anything. I didn't need to defend myself—not to him.

"Do you know who you're killing, Olivia?" he sneered.

He didn't know that I sifted through the memories of every Creature whose name appeared to me in my amulet. I had not shared with him the ritual we were pledged to perform. That he assumed I was so monstrous as to blindly follow orders made me want to scrape my nails down that handsome, too tired face. I may not have agreed with the judgments, but each one of the Creatures I escorted had committed crimes. I saw them. I could have screamed into the night if I'd allowed myself to feel an ounce of the pain he meant to inflict.

"I would ask you the same. You kill these Creatures because of what they are. You say you know who you're killing? I would argue the opposite. You and your brethren are just as monstrous as we are."

I saw my words hit him, but I did not pause to see if they sank in beneath that glorious, tanned skin. I told myself it was because I didn't care, but in truth, I didn't want to know if he refused to hear what I'd said. I pulled at the wind and escaped.

———

I entered Tully's with the blood of Creatures on the soles of my boots and likely splattered across my dark clothes. No doubt everyone around me could scent it. I didn't care. I was still seething from my run-in with Alex. The rage felt nice. Hot. I wanted the burn of alcohol and perhaps the company of someone, anyone who might draw me out of my melancholy.

A curvy blonde stood behind the bar, her heavy-lidded eyes telling me without words that she'd get me anything I needed as her mouth asked what I wanted to drink. Whiskey, but I'd certainly keep her in mind for entertainment once I was good and drunk. Gaia knew that was going to be a task in and of itself. Ancient beings like me didn't get drunk easily. It was going to take a lot of alcohol at a rapid pace.

I tossed back the contents of the glass Serena (thank Gaia for name tags) brought me and motioned for another. The burn of the drink did nothing to soothe me, but the flames of my rage couldn't burn any hotter, either, so at least there was that. I downed the second glass and gave the girl a fanged smile when she brought a third without me having to ask. I saw her pupils dilate at the sight of my fangs and knew she was no stranger to being bitten. Something about that lessened my interest.

"Stop it," Gabrielle said from my right.

I turned to look at her. I hadn't been paying attention to anyone or anything as I'd come into the bar, so I couldn't be sure whether she'd followed me in or had already been inside. Dressed head to toe in black, I knew she'd spent her evening in a similar fashion as I had. She looked much better than I probably did, though. That almost brought a smile to my face.

"Stop what?" I asked.

"Flirting with the poor thing," she said with an eye roll.

I rolled my eyes, too.

"Bring us the bottle," Gabrielle said over her shoulder to the bartender.

She'd already grabbed my hand and pulled me back toward one of the booths. Rowdy cheers from the tables we passed had me wanting to see just who else was on the premises, but Gabrielle's grip remained tight.

"Fuck, since when are you the uptight one?" I muttered as she pushed me down into the pleather seat.

"Since you came in looking like a gods-damned Fury," my sister snapped.

She sat across from me and glared. I laughed. The bottle of whiskey was put between us, as well as a couple of clean glasses. I tried to pull Serena down into my lap, but Gabrielle tossed money at her and waved her away.

"What is your deal tonight?" She snapped.

"My deal, sister dearest, is I just ran into fucking Alex."

I poured myself a few fingers of whiskey, relished in its smoky scent, and leaned back against the wooden frame of the booth.

"So fucking what. You let that Fiagai get to you?"

I wasn't really in the mood to tiptoe around the subject, though, and with as quickly as I put the whiskey away, I soon wouldn't be able to keep secrets.

But Gabrielle has her own secrets, doesn't she?

I narrowed my eyes at my sister and drank down the alcohol. I poured some into the second glass and pushed it across the table at her.

She held it in her hand, looked at it, and then looked at me. I poured some into my own glass and raised it.

"To family," I said with a laugh, before I downed the entire contents of the glass.

"To family," Gabrielle said with a sigh and drank down her own glass.

She held it out for more.

Well, well, well. The little Fury came to play.

FORTY-THREE

"What brings you to this fine establishment?" I asked my sister.

She sipped at her second glass.

"Finished my list. Didn't feel like going home quite yet."

"And which home would that be?" I asked sweetly. She rolled her eyes. "No friends to visit?"

"No," she said, with a confused look on her face. "You know I don't really do 'friends.'"

I laughed. *Isn't that the gods-damned truth.* But it was also the very thing that made my little sister look so guilty.

"Glad it amuses you," Gabrielle muttered.

"As a matter of fact, it does amuse me. And you know what I find even more amusing?"

"What is that?"

"That you, out of all of us, the one who holds so tightly to this godforsaken duty we've been given, are the very one working against it."

In a blur, Gabrielle had me out of my seat and against the back wall of the bar. We barely drew a glance from any of the other patrons. One of them might separate us if we actually got into a fight, but even that was pretty rare. Tully decided when it was time to intervene. Everyone else in the bar was content to watch the melee.

"What do you know?" she demanded.

"What do I know?" I laughed.

The speed at which I'd consumed the alcohol had caught up to me a bit.

"I know that you've been disguising yourself and meeting with factions," I spat at her. "Leslie and I have followed you. We know you're somehow involved with the waking of the Old Ones."

Gabrielle fell away from me with a gasp. Her eyes were large. If I didn't know better—*and I did, didn't I?*—I'd say my sister had no idea the Old Ones were being awakened, accidentally or on purpose.

"Liv, what the fuck are you talking about?"

I stared into my sister's too-wide blue eyes. We had known one another for centuries and yet there were so many mysterious parts of her that I didn't know or understand. I had seen her beguile, mislead, and outright deceive. But I also knew that she favored the more forthcoming side of her nature, and it was that I counted on.

"I want to believe you truly don't know," I said.

"Let's talk, then."

My sister gestured to our seats just mere feet away, but it felt so much further. We watched one another warily for long moments. The silence wrapped around us. Finally, Gabrielle reached for the bottle of whiskey and took a long pull from it, not even bothering with a glass. I recalled, fuzzily, what the Fates had to say to me about trust and love, and I knew I needed to play this carefully. Gabrielle wordlessly handed the bottle to me. I took a drink. Whether for fortification or out of shock, I wasn't sure, but it could have easily been either.

"I have been disguising myself and meeting with various factions of Creatures," Gabrielle admitted when I set the bottle back down on the table.

"That much I knew," I said.

"Yes, well, it seems that you thought you knew a hell of a lot more than you do, so shut your trap and listen."

Gaia, I had missed talking with her. Not that I'd admit it.

"I met with the factions because Demetrius asked me to," she continued.

Now that was a surprise. It probably shouldn't have been. Demetrius and I had never been close. He and Gabrielle were far more alike in their thinking. It wasn't farfetched to consider he might have wanted a spy of his own. In fact, it was logical. The question was, did Sunee, Atara, or Ramiel suspect? And did they involve me in their plans because of Demetrius' involvement of my sister?

"He needed someone who wasn't aligned with a particular unit, and as you damn well know, there aren't a lot of us," Gabrielle said.

I nodded and waved her on.

"There were rumblings about some kind of Creature meeting in secret. With no reports of what the Creature looked like, though, Demetrius wanted me to see if I could gather intel from those he had confirmed to have met with whomever it was."

"It's not a Creature," I said as I leaned forward.

"What?"

"It's some sort of myth, based on my own intel."

"Well, I guess I can see how you connected the dots," Gabrielle said. "A mythical non-Creature."

"Exactly."

Gabrielle's lips pursed as she thought. "But what in the world does that have to do with the Old Ones?" she asked after a moment.

I really had put my foot in it. I'd said way too much, clearly, and I was going to have to say more to get myself out of this without the revealing of all my secrets. I did not relish the thought of trying to explain this to Sunee.

"The Old Ones are waking," I said quietly. "The unrest, the riots—it's causing them to wake from their sleep."

"After all this time?" Gabrielle breathed.

She looked as horrified as I remembered feeling when I'd first found out. Her breathing quickened. She wasn't afraid—Gabrielle never really was—but I knew she felt uneasy. Her quick grab of the liquor and the several fingers she poured were clear signs. If she started drinking straight from the bottle, we were both in trouble.

"All I know is that Demetrius asked me to investigate some of the more well-known houses, just to see if they'd tell me anything. They didn't, really. One stranger showing up and promising them freedom is intriguing; two strangers is odd," Gabrielle said.

"That seems obvious," I replied.

Gabrielle narrowed her eyes at me.

"So why were you following me?" she asked. "And why was Leslie doing it, too?"

"You were the only Creature-like thing we ever saw with the factions. There aren't any other leads."

"So, Leslie and you, you're some kind of team?"

I wasn't sure Gabrielle's feelings could ever truly be hurt, but if they could, it looked as if we'd neared that moment. She crossed her arms over her chest and leveled her gaze at me. Maybe she was as mistrusting of the moment as I was attempting to be. I doubted, though, that she had the words of the Fates running through her mind and robbing her of peace. *Lucky bitch.*

"We happened to discover that we'd both seen you in some fairly compromising positions."

Gabrielle laughed, but in an awful, scratchy sort of way.

"At the behest of the Steward. What's your excuse for creeping about?"

I stayed quiet. The light burning in my sister's eyes turned into a blaze as her anger rose in the silence that stretched between us. She stood from her seat. Before she stepped too far, she paused next to me long enough to say a few words.

"Keep your secrets. Gaia knows I'll be keeping mine, as well."

She stalked away, and I lost myself in the bottle of whiskey. I didn't want to feel anything, and if I drank it all down fast enough, there was a good chance I could get almost an hour of alcohol-induced fuzziness before my body burned through the liquor.

FORTY-FOUR

In the days after, I tried avoiding the entirety of my household except for Allison, whose presence in the house strangely invited stability. Stability wasn't foreign to us. After all, we were Creatures of a sort whose life was dictated by duty. We fell into these new patterns easily. With Allison being such a new vampire, keeping her on schedule with her blood intake was important. It became a sort of congregational event our mealtimes had not resembled in ages. We didn't bother with having a dining table in the house, but we often used the more formal parlor for the gatherings.

My own hunger was increased. My sisters', too. The lists of names had grown again, and our hours of hunting were long. We traveled far and wide across the globe in search of Creatures whose behavior had triggered a response from The Twelve. I tried not to dwell in my thoughts. Irritation would so easily spill over into frustration, which always built into rage. For Allison's sake, I tried my best. I could not bear to do anything that might get me sent to Tartarus—not when she was seemingly thriving surrounded by her new and admittedly strange family.

My sisters and I, sometimes alongside our Guardians, found ourselves in the early hours of dawn and at dusk meeting for "breakfast" and "dinner" as Allison referred to them. I could not recall the last time I had considered mealtimes. I couldn't remember the last time we'd all spent so much time together in the same place. It was a pleasant thing to revisit, all in all. We mellowed a bit in the afterglow of shared memories. It provided an enjoyable respite, even if we knew it couldn't last.

One evening, as the stars once again showed in the earth realm, I rose from my bed with the kind of single-minded focus I'd grasped onto for survival. Unfortunately, I needed to loosen my grip just a little and deviate from what had so quickly become my normal routine. I showered and dressed and then admitted I couldn't delay any longer. I grasped my amulet and traveled to Bellanca.

I gave myself a full week to think over all that had been said between Gabrielle and I, but Sunee needed to be made aware of the developments. I had hoped other information might come to light—something that might aid me in clearing my sister off the board of potential enemies—but it hadn't. Everything had grown murkier. Since I could not sort it out myself, it made sense to present it to Sunee and possibly other members of The Twelve and allow them to deal with it.

I walked slowly through the stone hallways of the realm, lost in thought. I found myself standing before Sunee's door much sooner than I wanted to be, hesitating before I knocked. In that moment, I realized I could hear voices inside. Raised voices. I doubted anyone else would have been able to hear with such clarity, except for wolven or a vampire, but those weren't typically wandering the halls. There certainly wasn't anyone else around I could scent. Instinct told me to listen. I knelt and did just that.

"She suspects Gabrielle, trust me."

Leslie?

I knew that voice. Even as my brain wanted to toss away the possibility of hearing my sister, I had to acknowledge I would recognize her voice anywhere.

Why would Leslie be meeting with Sunee? She had seemed so surprised when I'd told her about Sunee's requests. A vast pit opened up in my stomach. I almost hoped it swallowed my heart. I wasn't sure I could withstand more secrets. Worse yet, betrayal loomed as a possibility, as my sister spoke of framing our other sister—a framing I had so easily fallen for. Had I truly been so eager to find fault within my sisters? Had my resentment over their need to disperse and find separate lives no longer so connected to my own built to such a degree? I swallowed hard and continued to listen, but I was afraid of what else I would hear.

I heard Sunee respond in her more dulcet tones, and I then heard my sister—the very one I thought I understood best but apparently did not truly know at all—confirm she had encouraged my distrust of Gabrielle. I wanted to rise, weapons in hand, and prepare for battle. I wanted the calm that settled over me before a fight. But I also wanted to throw the door open and demand explanation.

My pride smarted, and my rage burgeoned to life in the wake of that initial, sharp twinge of pain. *How dare they use me like some kind of tool?* But I forced myself to remain crouched. I forced silence. I forced my pulse to slow and my breath to even. Come what may, I would have answers. This was likely the easiest way to get them. I had to remain logical and just as calculating as it seemed my sister had been.

"I thought, for a moment, you know, that we might be able to persuade her," Sunee said.

"She'd never side with us."

"But the power."

"It's not what drives her, and you know that."

"Tragic. The Old Ones—they wielded you with such finesse. They gave you the freedom to be yourselves. With them awake, you will become all you were supposed to be when you were created."

I had heard enough. I stood and backed away from the door as silently as I could.

"Oh!"

I whirled around and found Allura, Demetrius' secretary of sorts. She stared at me quizzically.

"Alekto, my sincerest apologies. I thought you heard me."

"No, no. I didn't. I'm so sorry."

I looked at her carefully and tried not to let the whirlwind of emotions within me show on my face. Allura looked between me and Sunee's door.

"Did you need to meet with the councilwoman?" she asked. "I can see if she's available."

"No!" I exclaimed, much louder than I needed to. "I mean, thank you, but no. I was just lost in thought and found myself wandering around over here."

"Ah," Allura said, nodding.

I said my goodbyes and quickly left the realm, desperate to be away.

The next few days were lost in a maelstrom of dark emotions. I pulled away from everyone, even Allison. It was rare I allowed myself to be swept into such a state, but everything the Fates warned me about had come to pass.

"You are going to want to trust the ones you love,
And love the ones you trust,
But love and trust are not worth the price you'll pay for them."

I had not thought such a sense of loss could rock me. My relationships with my sisters had waned over the centuries. The loss of that closeness—of my small, little family—had been the worst thing I could have imagined. But there had been more. All I could lose hadn't added up to much in mind. I was so very wrong. In a matter of a single moon cycle, I lost all sense of whom I had loved and whom I had trusted. It all went upside down and sideways in a way I knew, even with the Fates' warning, I never could have predicted.

"A point of no return is coming,
And power is the prize,
"Find a way to move ahead with neither your heart or eyes."

It was the same question over and over again: how was I to do such a thing? Turning to either of my sisters was out of the question, and Evangeline was sure to act if she learned even a hint of all that brewed underneath her very nose. Allison had more than enough to deal with. The fear she might feel compelled to assist me was also very real. I remained silent and holed up inside my room.

Until I remembered that I had a potential someone who might understand exactly what I was going through. *Sabri.*

FORTY-FIVE

The house stood silent and foreboding. I wasn't sure what I'd expected. Had I imagined Blythe and Istvan had worn the far more serious Sabri down and painted the manor pink or some other wild color? How silly.

I strode to the front door and knocked, using the familiar ouroboros knocker. I waited for a few long moments before I knocked again. Nothing. Silence. Evening had fallen, its darkness vast and void-like there on the edge of the city. I listened again. My ears met with the absolute silence of an empty house—an empty tomb. I wrenched on the handle of the door and broke it open. Nothing. The kind of nothing that skittered up a person's spine and raised their hackles. The manor was utterly devoid of any kind of fresh scent. That in and of itself would have been odd, but combined with the absolute silence was almost maddeningly strange. I ran inside and whipped through, seeking anything that could tell me what had happened. The nest was gone, that much was clear. Whether their disappearance was through death was what I sought to discover.

And then I found a dust pile at the top of the stairs with jewelry that reminded me of Blythe's. Istvan's watch was covered in dust in the room we'd watched television in. They were gone. True deaths for Creatures I had known. My head hung as I whispered a blessing for their souls.

Who had done this? Leslie? The Fiagai? There were too many options, and none of them were good. To the best of my knowledge, Blythe and Istvan hadn't been involved in Gregory's exploits. And though Sabri certainly thought little of them as vampires, even she didn't think they'd taken up with the cause after their leader's death. That the Fiagai had entered and wiped out the nest made the most sense, but the possibility that one of my sisters could have done this was too logical to ignore.

Where was Sabri?

Istvan had told me Gregory kept a few coffins down in in the basement for safekeeping and safeguarding. *I wonder...*

"Sabri?" I called into the darkness before descending the staircase.

Dimmed sconces provided minimal light down the cinderblock hallway. I listened carefully and hoped for a whisper of anything that might lead me to answers. I checked each room, but each coffin I located was empty. I paused before the final room.

Slowly, I walked in and whispered Sabri's name. I swore I heard a shuffle of some kind, but before I could even bother to investigate, a Creature launched itself at my throat. Whatever it was, I was stronger. I blocked my throat with my forearm and felt the sharp bite of fangs. I shook the Creature off, but it only flew at me again. With a cry, I pushed it off and heard a crunch as it hit either the floor or wall. I threw myself over to where I thought it had landed. A musty smell rose from the Creature. I recognized it as the scent of a starving vampire.

"Sabri?!" I cried.

She was emaciated to a horrifying degree. Her body, soft and curvy and beautiful, was barely more than skin stretched over a skeleton. Her previously lush, dark hair hung in lank ropes of sorts, knotted and tangled. Her skin which had been such a warm brown, like honey, was pale and sallow. Sabri hissed at me, fangs bared, and I knew she wouldn't recognize me. Though she was strong with the bloodlust pushing at her, I was able to hold her arms behind her and drag her to the hallway and up the staircase. I didn't even bother warming the blood bags before I tossed them in front of her.

Sabri, or at least the corpselike Creature who barely resembled her, tore into the bags with a voracity that shocked even me. I had seen Allison grow "a bit peckish" as Evangeline explained it, but it was nothing like the scene before me. Blood gushed out of the bag and mostly down Sabri's throat, but a portion of it trailed down her neck in rivulets that were stark against the paleness of her skin. She moved from one bag straight to the next. I stepped away only to grab more bags but kept my eyes on her the whole time. She was a ravenous thing—barely a Creature. I could not trust her. Not yet.

After five bags, Sabri's skin had filled out, but the hollows beneath her eyes remained. She was nowhere near as beautiful as she had been when I'd first met her. She brushed the dark, rope-like strands of hair behind her ears. Her ebony eyes pierced through me, but at least I saw recognition in them at last.

"Sabri?" I inquired.

She nodded, her eyes lowering in embarrassment.

"I—I'm sorry," she rasped.

Not only were her vocal cords shredded from the starvation she'd endured, but it was clear some of the hoarseness was from disuse. She coughed and sipped at the sixth blood bag I'd tossed onto the counter.

"I'm sorry," she repeated in a stronger voice.

I waved the words away. She behaved as any starving Creature might. I was far more interested in what caused her deterioration.

"What happened?" I asked.

The dark circles beneath her eyes already gave her features a haunted look, but as she worked to recall what happened, the darkness seemed more prominent.

"A Creature of some kind. She came. She tore through them," Sabri said.

Her eyes were not capable yet of forming tears, but it sounded as though she would be crying if physically able. I knew she hadn't been that close to Istvan or Blythe. But loss is loss. She had experienced a lot of it.

"I thought she was you, at first," Sabri continued. "She looked like you. Dark hair and eyes of an unnatural blue."

It was too easy to think of Gabrielle. My insides shrank and churned. I felt a bone-deep chill wash over my skin.

"Did she say anything?"

Sabri looked thoughtful.

"This is important," I said quietly.

"She performed some kind of ritual as she cut their throats," Sabri said.

Her eyes had grown unfocused, as if reliving the memory.

"I don't know if she knew I was there. I ran and hid in that coffin— it was Roland's. It locks from the inside and spelled, as well."

Roland had been a bit paranoid. It was easy to believe he had secured a safe place for himself where the only person who would be able to unlock it would be the person inside.

"How long ago?"

"I'm—I'm not sure?"

Sabri looked around, as if seeking a calendar, but there was nothing in the kitchen. I pulled a phone from my pocket and told her the date.

"It's been at least a week, I think," Sabri said.

At least a week. My indecision over my sister may have cost these Creatures—and they were innocent, too, as far as I could see.

Sabri had no interest in remaining at the manor. I certainly didn't blame her. For all either of us knew, Gabrielle could come back and finish the job. We still didn't know if she was aware there had been three Creatures in the house when she went there. The spelled coffin may have thrown her off the scent.

I made sure Sabri was packed and on her way before I allowed myself to truly react to what I had learned. It was official. I could not trust either of my sisters. Evangeline might have been in on it all, as well, for all I knew. I felt dreadfully alone, standing on the sidewalk outside the manor. The wind was icy, and it whipped around hard enough that I almost wished it would slice me right down to my core. Physical wounds to match the emotional ones.

The grief for Alex and what we had been and perhaps could have had was something I had not allowed myself to feel. I couldn't hold it back anymore. It loosened itself, and a scream tore from my throat as an overwhelming sadness took me to my knees. In the midst of a cold winter's night, I curled on my side in the snow and cried.

FORTY-SIX

I must have lain there for hours. Brief, cloudy moments of consciousness granted me visions of the stars shining overhead in the sky. The snow continued to fall and build until the crisp scent of it was all around me. Hazy, far-off noises of sirens and trains met my ears. I continued to lay there, buried underneath the fallen snow.

The tears stopped after a long while, but I hadn't tried to move. I hadn't wanted to. There was a distinct part of me that wanted to drift away like the snowflakes floating in the air above me. What I would have given to not be myself. Guilt over Fabian, guilt over Istvan and Blythe, and even guilt over who my sisters had become hung over me. Things had grown beyond complicated. Everything felt impossible. The weight on my shoulders dragged me down into an abyss of darkness I would have been perfectly content to remain in. It seemed more likely than ever that the Old Ones would awaken, and I did not want to live in that world. It was all too much.

A pair of strong arms wrapped around me and lifted me out of the deepening snow. I came to somewhere amid the movement. It was still dark, but the hours of cold and exposure to the elements had affected me. It felt like my limbs cracked in the icy cold as I was shuffled into position. I heard voices but did not recognize any. I saw the haziness of hot breath exhaled into winter air. I felt the beat of a human heart.

A human heart?

The steadiness of it captured my attention, and I slowly gained awareness over my other senses. There was warmth in the solid body that held me tightly. I heard murmurings as the wind carried the voices up and away. I felt leather against my cheek, smelled cinnamon and nutmeg and... *cranberry?* The scent of bergamot rose around me, finally, and I knew whose arms held me. I considered pushing Alex away, but I felt weak, and his strength was a comfort I didn't want to refuse.

Sleep claimed me again, and I did not open my eyes until I felt the rumbling of Alex's voice underneath me. I was still in his arms, but he was sliding into a vehicle.

"Just put her in the seat," I heard someone say in a deep voice.

Leather and metallic scents filled my nostrils. Other smells, too, that were familiar to weaponry and things I had often associated with Leslie. I couldn't think about that. I didn't want to think about that. I kept my eyes closed and focused on the steady thumping of Alex's heart.

"I've got her," Alex said to whomever was with us.

Voices raised, hissed, argued. Alex stopped it all with a word, and silence fell. I buried my face in his neck and slept once more. I woke again when Alex slid out of the vehicle and carried me into some sort of building. The warmth of its interior hit me like a wall. Up an elevator and down a hallway where a mixture of food smells lingered. I realized we were headed for Alex's apartment.

I heard him speak to someone behind us. There was an order to remain outside. Again, there was an argument, albeit brief. Alex didn't raise his voice, but the implication of his words were clear. Those around us—and they had to be Fiagai—were quickly admonished by Alex's tone, and the arguments ceased. He moved quickly. The front door was shut behind us, leaving whomever else was with us outside, and then we were through the black and white of the kitchen and down the white hallway.

A kiss was pressed to my forehead. I did not ask any of the questions that rose within me. I couldn't comprehend what it had meant for Alex to carry me past his brethren, maybe even his father. Too much to consider. The weight of it all too heavy. Everything felt too heavy. I buried my face back in his neck and inhaled again. The scent of him was delicious and inviting, and I wanted his presence to mean something—and something much more than it probably should have.

"I'm going to draw you a bath, babe," Alex murmured.

He put me down on the slate tiles of his bathroom floor. He turned the handles of the freestanding tub near the floor-to-ceiling window. The blinds were down half-way already, but I could still see the lights of the city shimmering for miles. I let Alex remove my boots and socks and then tug at my jeans, sliding them over my chilled skin. My jacket and sweater went into the pile next, leaving me in just underwear and a lace bralette. I felt Alex pause as he stood before me. I finally met his eyes, and what I saw there was a whirlwind of emotions. It occurred to me then what may have caused Alex to pause in his undressing of me.

Fabian's ring hung chilled and heavy around my neck on its own chain just below my amulet.

"I'll leave you to it," he said in a gruff whisper.

It felt like he was escaping, like once he had me in his apartment and mostly naked he wasn't quite sure what to do with me. I didn't know what to do with him, either. The reminder of Fabian—the distinct chill of it—had broken me somewhat out of my stupor. I stripped off the remaining clothing and slid beneath the hot water to luxuriate in the vanilla scent of the bubbles Alex had added.

I don't know how much time passed before Alex worked up the courage to return. But when he did, he came bearing gifts: a thick, fluffy towel and a dark blue robe. He stood for a breath and looked me over. I brazenly met his gaze. I invited whatever he had to give, be it grief or hatred or something else altogether. But Alex surprised me. He wordlessly scooped up my clothing and left the room. He did not return.

———

The water cooled eventually, and I pulled the stopper from the tub. I dried off with the towel and looked at myself in the mirror. My hair hung in a damp sheet, tangled from the snow and the bath. I ran my fingers through it. I didn't feel like searching through the bathroom cabinets for a brush. I took one more look and noted the dark circles under my eyes. I would need to feed at some point but didn't dare ask. Not here. I could not ask Alex. I shook my head to clear it and went to retrieve the robe he had hung on the hook of the bathroom door.

The robe was far too large. It was warm and soft, however, and just what I needed. It was also the only thing I could wear, since Alex took my clothing, probably to launder it. I couldn't very well parade around Alex's house nude, could I? I didn't know where we stood. What was more difficult was I didn't even know where I wanted to stand. Too many thoughts. Too much to dig through. And I was still tired.

I padded softly out of the bathroom. If I turned right, I would find Alex's bedroom, but the other living spaces were to the left. I turned left. I had only been in Alex's apartment a few times, and I guess I had expected more to change in the time we'd been apart. Everything else had changed so much that it felt odd to see everything exactly where it had been the last time I was here.

Alex lay sprawled on the sofa in his living room, long legs outstretched and encased in gray sweats. A black tee-shirt covered his upper half. His feet were bare. I knew he would have heard me leave the bathroom and walk down the hallway, but his eyes were focused on the television as I entered the room. I stood in the archway for just a breath, and then I strode forward. His eyes flicked to me and remained steady on my face.

"Why?" I asked.

I stood before him. His eyes raked over me, drinking in the sight. His breathing quickened. He did not move. It seemed very careful, the not moving.

There were so many other things I could have asked him. There were too many other things I wanted to ask him. But our last moments together had been fraught and heavy. I believed he hated me. But his actions were not those of a man with hatred in him.

"I was in the area," he finally said.

I raised a brow skeptically, and it earned me a heavy sigh.

"There was a vampire in the area," he explained. "I followed the trail but found you."

For a long moment, the only sounds in the room were of us breathing.

"So, you were hunting." Silence. "The vampires in that house," I began, but my throat grew thick.

"They're dead."

I nodded.

"But you knew them?" he asked.

I nodded again. I quickly brushed away a tear.

"I—I didn't have anything to do with it," Alex said.

"I know."

"How...?"

"One of them was left alive. She told me who killed her nest-mates." Silence.

"I... I think it was my sister."

"They were marked?" Alex asked.

He moved, then, and leaned forward, elbow on knees.

"I don't know," I whispered.

Alex's eyes widened. He leaned back against the sofa, hands in his hair. He loosed a long breath. I watched him calculate the new information.

"That was Roland Gregory's house. What were you doing there?" he asked, finally.

"It's a long story." Silence. "You could have left me there," I pointed out.

"No, I couldn't have," he said with a shake of his head.

"I wouldn't have died," I argued.

"I don't care. I couldn't... I couldn't leave you there like that."

His eyes were sad. I took a step forward, then another. I placed one knee on one side of his hips, and moved so that I straddled him. His arms lowered. He paused before he put his hands on my waist. There was caution, but I watched Alex's throat move as he swallowed hard. I heard the beating of his heart increase. I liked the rhythm of it. I liked that it reminded me I was alive. For better or worse, we were alive, and there had been so much death. I wanted Alex. I didn't want to think about the rightness or the wrongness of it. I just wanted him.

"I want to kiss you," I said softly.

Alex nodded. I put my arms on either side of his head, palms flat on the back of the sofa, and slowly leaned forward until my breaths mingled with Alex's. We both waited there, as if we thought a lightning strike might come from Zeus himself to tear us apart. But Zeus had been asleep for centuries, and there was no one to make this choice for us except us.

Our lips met and our tongues tangled. Hands glided over flesh and fabric. We soon divested one another of clothing. The air around us was cool, but the heat of our skin was enough, and I needed, desperately, to be pressed against him. Hadn't we made vows to one another, once upon a time? Hadn't we been happy, for at least awhile? Hadn't we loved, for those brief moments?

I knew it was more nuanced than that and infinitely more complicated, but I was willing to set my darker thoughts aside for whatever time I could have with my lover. There would be time later for talking and fighting.

We fell asleep wrapped around one another on the floor near the fireplace. Just before we drifted off, Alex pulled a blanket down from the sofa down and covered us. Sleep claimed me soon after, and thankfully it did not bring dreams.

FORTY-SEVEN

When consciousness found me next, it was clear Alex was just as confused as I. Neither of us spoke. It was as if we silently agreed that no peace could be found within words. Instead, we settled into the silence and chose a more physical route. Sex was simpler.

And I had missed him. Gaia knew I had. I couldn't explain the depth of feelings that burst forth within me. There was no logical explanation for what I felt for him. I wasn't ready to explore those feelings, though. They were too tangled up in the mess of everything else.

My sisters.

I pushed those thoughts away. It was too much. I wasn't ready. Would I ever be?

Hesitant, probing kisses became more and more insistent. Hands that had been gentle in their exploration of skin grabbed and pulled. Perhaps we both wanted to lose ourselves for just a while longer. I know I did. I was not ready to think. I wanted only to feel. I dragged my nails down his back and relished in the sharp intake of breath it resulted in from Alex. His mouth slid from my own and down my jaw and neck. Where my pulse beat a rhythm, he pressed an open-mouthed kiss before sliding his mouth down to where my neck and shoulder met. He bit down, causing me to cry out. There was no kiss to soothe the bite, no pleasant meandering of a mouth over skin. It was all urgency, pumping blood, and tastes of battle.

I dug nails into his shoulder blades. I felt one of Alex's hands wrap itself in my hair, and then he pulled it back. Sharp tears sprang to my eyes. Our coming together became an angry thing with teeth and nails. He shoved himself inside of me with a ferocity I desperately craved. I wanted his rage and maybe even his hatred. Or maybe I just wanted it so we were a matching pair of killers on the edge.

———

I felt Alex shift beneath me in his early state of waking. My eyes opened to find his staring down at me, as if he was certain I'd be gone when he woke. I probably should have been, but I didn't know where else to go. If both my sisters were working against me, how safe was I? I couldn't be certain. Until I had at least some semblance of certainty, I was loathe to move away from Alex and begin the work of thinking through my next set of options. I tucked my head under his chin and snuggled in. We couldn't ignore the world for much longer, not in the state it was in. It was time for words.

"I'm sorry, Liv," Alex said, breaking the silence before I could.

I felt his fingers rest on a bite mark I knew had been left on my right breast.

"I liked it."

Alex sat up, and then we were sitting naked in front of the fireplace, facing one another. *I'm not ready for this. I'm not ready for this. I'm not ready.*

"I'm sorry for more than these," Alex said, gesturing to the other bite marks on my neck, shoulder, and hip.

I cocked my head to the side. I had not expected an apology. I didn't want to have that conversation. It would have been so much easier to return to heated, angry sex. I knew how to do that. I had little experience in navigating emotions, and these were far and beyond anything I'd ever felt.

"Don't apologize," I said.

My voice came out more sullen and tempestuous than expected.

"For these or for anything?" Alex asked, his own voice a growl.

"For these, at the very least."

"And the other?"

"Are you truly sorry?" I demanded.

"I... don't know."

"Then don't say the words. Not if you can't mean them."

"I am sorry for hurting you."

"It wouldn't have changed anything."

"No," he admitted.

Silence.

"I'm not ready to hate you again. Not yet," I whispered. "I... I should have told you about Fabian."

"No. This—we... you didn't owe me that."

"I should have told you why he changed her."

"I wish I knew if it would have mattered."

"But it could have. It could have changed everything."

More silence.

"If it wasn't me who found him, it would have been someone else. Another Fiagai."

I hated that he was right. Fabian had all but signed his death warrant the moment he turned Allison.

"Something happened," he deduced.

"I can't."

"Liv."

I met his eyes and crumbled. Hot tears fell. Alex's eyes widened, but he grasped at me, and I wrapped myself around the lifeline.

"My sisters," I said quietly. "They're... not who I thought they were. I don't know who to trust anymore. I'm so tired, Alex. I'm so fucking tired."

"And me? Do you trust me?"

I pulled back to look at him.

"I... don't know. I want to, but..."

"I killed Fabian," he acknowledged.

Alex reached out slowly and examined the ring on its chain. He studied it carefully before he set it back against my skin.

"Logically, I know you were doing your duty," I admitted.

"I truly didn't know he was anything to you."

"Would it have mattered?"

Alex sighed.

"I want it to have mattered," he said.

That was probably the best I could hope for. We were victims of broken systems. Alex's viewed all Creatures as enemies and mine repressed and punished in ways that, lately, seemed archaic.

"And your sister?" I asked.

Our daughter.

"I don't know how to be around her," Alex said quietly. "Everything in me senses her as an enemy. But in my heart, I see the little sister I've spent my life protecting and loving."

A tear slid down his face, and I brushed it away with my thumb. I held his face in my hands and looked at him like I was memorizing his features.

"We will find a way," I vowed.

"Please," he whispered.

I held him for a long time after that. Slowly, softly, silently we came together once more, pressing gentle kisses to the wounds we'd inflicted on one another hours prior. And I think somewhere in that I felt the beginnings of hope begin to stir.

FORTY-EIGHT

H ope is a fragile, delicate thing. The merest of winds could break it apart and send the pieces scattering to the four corners of the earth.

And we were in a maelstrom.

FORTY-NINE

The dreams found me. Everything was smoke and ash and blood. Unsurprisingly, I woke with vengeance on my mind and the scent of violence in my nostrils. The lure of Alex's warm bed was strong, as was the abandon I knew I could find there again with such little effort, but I forced myself to rise and dress. I was grateful Alex remained asleep. Had he woken, it would have made my exit that much more difficult. I already needed to get past the Fiagai stationed outside his door. I wasn't sure what my reception would be, and frankly, I wasn't that interested in finding out. The Fiagai were not my priority. As I pulled my jacket on and considered my options, I noticed the fire escape. *Perfect.*

I pulled the windowpane up and was grateful it made only the barest of noises. I carefully, silently crept out, one leg at a time, until I stood over the city. The lights were bright, chasing away the darkness I wanted to hide away in so I could take my leave. There were things that needed handling and problems that would only continue to carve away at me, bit by bit, until they were dealt with. It was time.

The night air was brutally cold as it whipped around the buildings, but I took a moment to breathe in its crisp freshness. I glanced back through the window and saw Alex's sleeping form beneath the sheets, blankets strewn across the bed. *No. Focus.*

I climbed over the railing, the metal like ice beneath my hands, and jumped. The fall through the air was nothing, and I landed on my feet with barely a sound. There was the merest of clicks as the heels of my boots hit the pavement. I felt eyes on me, and I whirled around looking for the source. *Who could be awake at this hour?* Then I glanced up.

Alex watched me through the window, his face a mixture of things that settled into confusion. I didn't quite know where we stood with one another, but it felt like we were at least on a pathway to something with the potential of being beautiful. I could so easily ruin it, I knew that. It was important to me that he be aware of my intentions. So, while I knew it was foolish and knew it likely damned me in the worst of ways, I blew him a kiss.

He smiled softly and returned it. It was as much of a blessing as I might get from him to handle things the way I needed to. If anyone could understand duty, after all, it was Alex. With one more glance upward to where my heart most wanted to be, I turned away. For awhile longer, I needed to listen to my head. I forgot I wasn't supposed to be listening to either of them.

———

I stepped out of the ice-cold wind and strode into the house. I followed the oh-so-familiar scents of gardenia and peony as I stalked through the first floor. Evangeline sat in the parlor, embroidery hoop in hand, making neat stitches in probably yet another tablecloth or napkin. Near her sat the sister I was looking for. With a growl, I pinned Gabrielle against the sofa with my hand around her throat.

I heard Evangeline rise, and I heard the soft click of the embroidery hoop as it was placed neatly on the table beside her chair. I stared into the blue eyes of my sister and allowed all the grief I'd felt not long before to show in my face.

"Why?" I ground out.

I hated the burn of tears I felt, but I let it all show as I refused to look away from my sister or wipe away the signs of my sadness.

Gabrielle's eyes widened with surprise, and she stopped kicking her feet and attempting to pry my hand from her neck. I held her tightly, and there would be no escape for her. Not even my grief could allow that. Not until I had some answers about what occurred at the Gregory Estate. I needed answers. More than that, I wanted them. I pushed just a bit harder on her neck, and Gabrielle's eyes grew even wider. Her breath was barely more than a wheeze.

"What is the meaning of this, Alekto?" Evangeline asked.

Her voice was deadly quiet. I spared her the briefest of glances over my shoulder.

"I'll be happy to explain once the Megaera has."

I looked back at my sister. There was a witchblade at my neck before I could take a breath. Evangeline's dainty hand held it steadily.

"Umm... I can come back," Allison said from the doorway. "I'm sorry. I just heard you come home—"

"It's fine," said Evangeline, with the infinite patience of a mother utterly exasperated with her wayward children. "We're all going to take a seat."

I released a ragged sigh, nodded, and let go of my sister. She remained against the back of the sofa, gasping for breath. I rolled my eyes, pivoted off the sofa, stalked to a chair, and took a seat. I crossed my legs dramatically and studied my nails as we waited for Gabrielle to recover herself.

"You, too, my dear," Evangeline said to Allison, gesturing at the sofa.

Allison hurriedly took a seat, though not too close to Gabrielle.

"What is it you are accusing her of?" Evangeline asked me.

She was primly seated back in her chair, legs crossed, with the witchblade hidden once more. She had not, though, picked up her embroidery again. Her eyes met mine, and she tilted her chin in the direction of Gabrielle, who stared at her feet. I clenched my jaw stubbornly. Allison's eyes watched us all, her brow furrowed in concern.

"I'll wait," Evangeline said.

I watched her for a moment, and I knew what she said was true. She truly was infinitely patient. I was not. I knew that she knew that I was not.

"I found the remains of several vampires at the Gregory Estate," I finally said.

I watched Gabrielle carefully as I said the words. She did not look surprised, nor did she look saddened or full of regret. I think I wanted her to be. I felt the anger rise once again in my chest. Allison fidgeted in her seat.

"Blythe Baker and Istvan Narkovic. Were they marked?" I asked.

One succinct nod.

"When?"

"Last night, just before."

"Why?"

"What kind of question is that?" she asked.

Her blue eyes met my own, filled with the kind of aching frustration I knew too well. It was something, at least. And, frustratingly, she was right. We never had cause to ask why.

"You missed one," I pointed out.

"Sabri Elam," she said. Gabrielle tilted her necklace so I could see the name in the stone.

"I found her," I said.

"Ah," was all Gabrielle replied with.

"What are they to you?" Evangeline inquired.

"I was asked to find out who is prompting the Creature riots," I said. "I went there for answers. They had them, and they willingly gave them up."

"And they probably died for it," Gabrielle said dryly.

Both Evangeline and I stared at Gabrielle. Allison's eyes moved quickly between the three of us.

"What do you mean?" I asked.

"Yes, what do you mean?" asked Evangeline.

"I know you were following me, watching me. I was investigating, just like you," Gabrielle said to me.

I nodded. No use in lying when I had already admitted that to her at the bar. But I knew it was time to share what I hadn't before.

"I looked into who was visiting the factions. Given some of what Roland said the night I escorted him to Tartarus, it made sense to start with his nest mates," I explained.

"Demetrius asked me to do the same," Gabrielle said. "Only I think we were being pitted against one another."

Evangeline tittered in now-obvious exasperation. I, however, was intrigued.

"You think the names we're receiving—they're due to someone clearing the board?" I asked.

What a deadly game we were playing.

"Signs point to it, yes. It's clear that the Old Ones are being awoken on purpose. Everything else that's happening? I think it's just a distraction."

"It can't be Demetrius. Sunee doesn't trust him, and they're calling the shots with whatever the hell Leslie is up to," I said.

"You silly little fools," Leslie said from the doorway.

FIFTY

Gabrielle moved closer to Allison. I was grateful. I was too far away from my daughter.

My daughter. It was the first time, really, I'd thought of her that way, without hesitation. *My daughter.*

Leslie paced around the room, hair messy and unkempt, clothing askew, and eyes wild with various emotions. She smelled of weaponry and the oil we used to clean our blades. A faint hint of electricity in the air around her. A witchblade was held loosely in her hand, and she gestured with it as she spoke, which prevented us from rushing her.

I did my best to turn my confusion into nonchalance. I settled back into the chair and waited.

"Don't you see?" Leslie asked. "There is no place for us here unless the Old Ones wake and rule."

Her voice held the surety that is present only when one believes the words they're saying. I shuddered.

"You've lost your godsdamned mind," I said quietly.

Leslie cocked her head, her eyes burning with a strange eccentricity. The secrets she must have kept hidden for all this time were aflame. She looked inhuman, more Creature than anything else. She was hunting, and I didn't want to be prey. Leslie turned her attention to our sister.

"Gabrielle, surely you see reason, don't you? Olivia's been blinded by the fragility of the humans and their tragic plights, but you—you have always kept yourself away from their weakness."

Her voice was gentle, pleading, and there was a slight echo of magic in its allure. I wonder just how much power Sunee had been willing to share. Gabrielle shook her head in an attempt to rid her mind of the magical tendrils that reached out in thread-like patterns from Leslie.

"I want no part of this," Gabrielle said.

"So weak," Leslie spat. "Too weak to separate yourself from the group, as if you're the runt who will be snatched up by the nearest predator."

Then Leslie threw her head back and laughed. Allison cringed at the sound. Gabrielle stood and pulled Allison up with her, shoving the vampire behind her body and away from Leslie.

Evangeline stood nearest to our third, and she held her arms gingerly at her sides, non-confrontational and weaponless. But we'd known one another too long, and Leslie surely knew that Evangeline had at least one knife hidden somewhere on her person. The Guardian always did.

"Leslie, you are undoing everything you were created to stand for," Evangeline said sadly.

"And what was that exactly?" Leslie sneered.

"Justice."

Leslie threw her head back and laughed again, the sound of it harsh and grating. Gabrielle looked away from her as if she couldn't bear to see her. I felt similarly. I kept my gaze even and steady, though. I would not shy away.

"What a riot," Leslie giggled. "We meted out punishments for Creatures who wanted a better world, and we called it justice."

"We could change things," I prompted.

Leslie's gaze leveled with my own. She twirled the witchblade in her hand by its handle. I tried to keep my eyes both on it and her.

"You have had opportunities to change. They've had opportunities to change. Instead, we cowed to their rule, and The Twelve made us puppets for their whims."

"And what do you think Sunee has been doing to you?" I cried.

"She's clearly been pulling at your strings and controlling every action you've taken!"

"Ah ah ah," Leslie said, waggling her index finger at me. "Sunee is a visionary. She sees the power we could have if only we were freed from the shackles the Twelve have bound us in."

"She's one of them!" I said.

"She's seen the error of her ways. She's tried for so long to get the rest of the council to understand and agree, but matters had to be taken into our own hands."

"You've gone mad."

"If I have, it was at your hands."

"Leslie," Evangeline gasped.

Leslie's head whipped around to look at Evangeline.

"You all just stood there and let her die."

Vallerie. It all came back to Vallerie and our unwillingness to involve ourselves. Allison's eyes met mine in confusion. There was no time to explain. My stomach dropped.

"Vallerie?" Gabrielle asked. "You're doing this because of Vallerie?"

"I loved her!" Leslie screamed. "And you let her die!"

"We were not to intervene!" Gabrielle said.

"Why? Because she was a known witch to the pathetic humans who sought out her spells and charms? Because she catered to the whims of those little worms?"

"It was her fate," Evangeline said quietly.

"All this power, and we bow to them? Three supernatural beings who keep themselves separate from everyone and everything?" Leslie raged.

"Everyone bows to the Fates! Even the Old Ones did!" I reminded her.

"Things change. Things need to change," Leslie said.

"I don't disagree. You know I don't."

I fell silent and watched my sister, her chest heaving.

"I loved her," Leslie repeated, her voice low.

"It is not for us to know why she was to be sacrificed," Evangeline replied in her even, quiet tone.

"We had already sacrificed so much," Leslie said, her voice a deep well of sadness. "I wanted one thing. Just one thing. One small thing to be my own. I had her. I had her and I loved her, and she loved me. She loved me! And you let her be taken."

"We couldn't intervene," Evangeline said, her voice full of pleading for Leslie to understand.

"Wouldn't."

Leslie glared at us all, the blade twirling madly in her hand.

"And that was the day I swore that this rage, this vengeance that keeps us all going—for better or worse—would someday be your undoing. And your day, sweet Alekto, has come," she said.

"What are you talking about?" I asked.

Allison. Alex. No. No! Gabrielle moved backward, forcing Allison even further back into the room. I met Allison's gaze and willed her not to make any sudden movements.

"Oh, you'll soon discover the depths of grief that I myself have drowned in," Leslie said in an off-beat, sing-song type of way.

She pointed the witchblade at me.

"What have you done?" I demanded to know.

"Nothing... yet. But you will soon wish for death, as I did so long ago as they dragged Vallerie from me and I was forced to let her burn. I'll never forget the scent of her flesh... the screams that fire tore from her throat," Leslie said, ending in a ragged whisper.

Her eyes were unfocused as she so obviously relived the memories. I don't know that any of us had known just how deeply the loss of Vallerie had affected her, but it had clearly unhinged her in a way we had never understood.

"Tisiphone," Evangeline said.

She used Leslie's title, as if hoping it would break through the crazed stupor my sister appeared to be in. And Leslie's eyes did indeed refocus. They sleepily traveled over to Evangeline, and a smirk lifted one side of her mouth.

"Yes. I am the Tisiphone, one of the Furies. I was given my powers by the Old Ones themselves, and I don't listen to you—not anymore!"

Leslie threw the witchblade with her perfect aim, and Gabrielle and I watched in horror as it embedded itself in Evangeline's heart. Leslie vanished by the time Evangeline's body hit the floor.

FIFTY-ONE

We were on our knees on the hard wooden floor beside the body. I didn't want to think of it as Evangeline's, especially when there was seemingly nothing to be done. The blade had struck true, as Leslie's always did. Darkness swept outward from the wound, dark tracings of the veins beneath the skin, which hinted at some kind of poison. One of the two may not have done Evangeline in, but both surely did. I left the witchblade where it was. I detested the sight of its beautifully etched silver handle protruding from my Guardian's chest. I wanted to rip it out and toss it away, yet I was afraid that it might cause us to lose her faster. Gaia, how much pain must she have been in? Should I have removed the blade? I could not make the decision. My eyes found Gabrielle. She was in no shape to make the decision, either. Tears streamed down Allison's shocked face.

I hated that hopelessness that filled me and weighed down my limbs. I hated the soft sniffles of Gabrielle's that I could hear. I wanted to hate Leslie for what she had done... but she was still my sister. I thought about Sabri and how she must have felt when she learned of Roland's death.

There was so much to be angry about. There were so many questions. More than anything, I wanted answers. Why had Leslie thrown the blade at Evangeline? Had she meant to kill the Guardian, or had her anger simply gotten the best of her? I held Evangeline's left hand between both of my own as tears welled up in my eyes. Evangeline's dark eyes fluttered before they found me, and I could see the effort she put in trying to focus. She swallowed a few times before she was able to speak.

"Demetrius," she gasped.

"Shh... save your breath," Gabrielle said.

She held Evangeline's head in her lap. Her gentle hands brushed Evangeline's dark hair away from her features. One of our Guardian's hands reached for me, the other for Allison. Allison grasped her fingers as if she could hold Evangeline within her body.

"You must trust him."

"We will," I vowed.

The smallest of nods told me she heard the vow and understood it for what it was. Gabrielle continued to gently smooth Evangeline's hair, as if she just needed something to do with her hands. It spoke volumes that she chose a gentle action. I wanted violence, but I quietly held Evangeline's hand. For now, I could be still. It was what was needed. Allison continued crying, whispering prayers in Greek.

Our Guardian took her last breaths mere moments after the blade was thrown. For a long time, Allison's sobs echoed throughout the house.

———

Lightning flashed, too bright in the darkness that had descended over the house in more ways than one, and thunder clapped soon after. I braced myself, grasping at Gabrielle's hand as a sharp wind blew through the house. In its wake, the three Fates stood. They were dressed strangely in long, black gowns that twisted around their limbs in the wind. Lexi's eyes were already filled with unshed tears, and Chloe threw herself to her knees beside Gabrielle and put her arms around her. I was grateful the embrace seemed to quiet my sister's sobs. Atlanta, stoic as ever, simply looked at me and indicated with a movement of her head that she wanted to talk away from the others.

I gently folded Evangeline's hands over her abdomen, well beneath the blade, and stood.

"Please," I said to Lexi, who immediately moved in beside Allison and held her sobbing form. Before I left the room, I dropped a kiss on Gabrielle's forehead and murmured words of thanks to both Lexi and Chloe. I took a step out into the hallway, inhaled a deep breath, and looked to where Atlanta stood beside the staircase railing, arms crossed over her chest.

"I'm sorry, Olivia," she said, her voice low and quiet.

I nodded. It took me a moment to gather myself. Then I cleared my throat and spoke.

"What's going on?" I asked.

"We didn't see this. Leslie made a very sudden, drastic change to her path, and we.... Well, then we saw this. We got here as soon as we could."

"It wasn't premeditated?"

"It was not."

That was comforting, in some small way. I said as much.

"I just wanted you to know that we didn't See this."

"Thank you—but it's not like you could have intervened, anyway, right?"

Atlanta nodded, sadness in her eyes. It struck me for the first time how difficult it may have been for them to exist as they did, forever seeing tragedies play out before them with absolutely no course of action. So much unfairness. Leslie's experience with it had broken something within her. How close to that edge were the rest of us, and we just didn't know?

"Are you able to See Leslie now? Do you know where she is?" I asked.

"Even if I could—and I'm not saying that I can or cannot See her right now—would you really want to know where she is?" Atlanta asked.

She had a point. Knowing Leslie's location wouldn't do me any good until I knew what I was going to do about her. Since I didn't, having the knowledge was useless. First things first, the Steward needed to know.

"Someone needs to get Demetrius," I said.

Atlanta nodded, paused to place a hand on my shoulder and squeeze, and then she disappeared back into the room. There was another crack of thunder that signaled at least one of the Fates leaving the realm. Atlanta returned in just a moment.

"Demetrius and Allura will be here soon. They will make the proper arrangements. You and your sister, unfortunately, are going to have your hands full."

I heard the warning for what it was. Whether I could muster up the energy to care was something else entirely. We had lost our Guardian. And worse, the loss was due to cold-blooded murder committed by one of our own. We weren't even three in number, anymore. We had never been otherwise. Could we stand against our own sister? And could we stand against her with the power of at least a few members of The Twelve? I didn't know. I hated that I didn't know.

———

Another crack of thunder alerted me to the return of one of the triplets —I wasn't sure which one Atlanta had sent to the other realm as a messenger. I went back into the parlor to see Demetrius standing several steps away from the body. His face was drawn, and he clasped his hands in front of him like he wasn't sure what to do. I noticed it took him more than a mere moment to gather himself enough to speak. He and Evangeline had known each other for a few decades, and they had worked closely together when he took over from the previous Steward.

That one had been a demon. Before that, the Steward had been fae. And the first one? The first Steward had been a witch, like Demetrius. Her name was Leda.

"To be honest, Evangeline, I think The Twelve are scared of them," Leda said in a hushed voice, with a gesture at the three of us.

Evangeline smiled in the way she did before a battle. She wanted us to be feared, had trained us to be deadly. The more careful The Twelve was with us, the better chance we had of surviving in a new world that was still being assembled.

"I know the demons and wolven are resistant for governance, so they will see the girls for what they are: weapons," Evangeline acknowledged.

Leda nodded gravely.

"It would be a mistake for anyone to underestimate their power," Evangeline noted.

"But surely you want them to be seen as just a facet of the new regime?" the Steward asked. "They will work at the behest of The Twelve and no other."

"They exact justice, Leda. It should not be minimized."

"But they can no longer mete it out as they see fit!" Leda exclaimed.

"Perhaps," Evangeline said, "but the more they are feared, the better off they will be. It is not only for the sakes of the Creatures that I say these things. It is for their own."

Leda raised an eyebrow in question.

"If they are feared, they will remain separate from the world of Creatures. If they are to continue to be the weapons of justice and escort the souls of our miscreants to Tartarus, they are better off to remain as they are."

"Alone? Separated from the factions?"

"Indeed. Forming relationships will only harm them."

My sisters and I stood before them as they spoke of us. We did not move from our battle stances, but they knew we were no danger to either of them. Evangeline was practically our mother—she had been there when we awoke as Furies. She had been the one to hone our vengeance and sense of justice into something we could wield. It was only with her assistance that we had stepped away from our cold savagery. She was our savior, our guardian. Before the Old Ones slept, Athena had named her Guardian, and so she was made immortal as we were. Our lives were forever entwined.

"Casimir and Valentin are sure that you will ensure the witches remain powerful," Leda said.

Evangeline had been a witch, but she had given up her status when she became a Guardian. As a Guardian, she was expected to maintain a kind of neutrality that, previously, only certain gods had been able to achieve. Gaia knew most of them tended to have their favorites.

"The witches are powerful enough without my assistance," Evangeline scoffed.

"But you were not asked to give up your powers."

"Athena believed I would need them."

"But Athena is asleep, and there are too many who are ready to forget about the gods all together."

"That is their decision and their right. I will not wield the Furies. I will guide them. And it will have to be enough."

Leda left after that, and we returned to training.

It was too easy to wonder if Evangeline had, in solidarity with us, her charges, abandoned that part of her life. As far as we knew, she had lived a quiet life. Some of The Twelve wondered within range of our hearing if something more went on between our Guardian and the current Steward, but Evangeline did not seem to prioritize anything romantic. She had a few friends, of course. There was Yasmina the healer. Evangeline sometimes had tea with Razalia, one of the fae members of The Twelve. And she had spent quite a bit of time with Leda, especially in those early days when The Twelve were deciding how best to rely upon us. Our amulets had been Evangeline's own little bit of genius, in fact. She had spelled them herself. The blessings on our witch-blades were done by her, too. Her life was anchored in so many parts of our own. What would we do without her?

"This is a grave loss," Demetrius said, looking meaningfully at my sister and me.

Gabrielle opened her mouth to say something, but her tears got the best of her, and she shut her mouth, waving a hand in front of her, telling us without words that she was unable to speak. I thanked Demetrius quietly.

"If you wish," Allura said as she stepped out from behind Demetrius, "I will take her body to our realm and prepare her for her final rites."

I went over and helped Allura gather Evangeline's body into her arms. Gabrielle's soft sobs began all over again as Allura stood and flashed away.

"How did this happen?" Demetrius asked.

I had hoped that perhaps whichever one of the Fates had gone to get Demetrius would have been able to fill him in, but alas, they had not. I motioned for Demetrius to follow me, and we left the room and went to the rear of the house to our other sitting room. I heard Chloe and Lexi take Gabrielle and Allison into the kitchen, which was good. No one needed to spend any more time in that parlor where the blood still puddled on the floor.

"It was Leslie," I managed to say to him.

We took seats in the black velvet chairs near the fireplace. Atlanta strode in, but she didn't say a word as she seated herself on the sofa.

"Leslie did this?" Demetrius asked.

Clearly, he was shocked. It seemed we were not the only ones who had not expected this from our sister.

"The Fury has been working with certain members of The Twelve, Steward," said Atlanta.

Demetrius turned to look at her and motioned for her to continue.

"Sunee," I supplied. "Probably Ramiel and Atara. Maybe a few others."

Demetrius nodded thoughtfully as he held his chin in his hand. I told him with as much detail as I could about how Sunee approached me and asked me to investigate the unrest amongst the various factions of Creatures. His reaction was one of unhappiness and sorrow.

"I'm sorry that I did not inform you," I said to him.

"You did not know. And, for all intents and purposes, you do work for them," he said with a shrug.

He had said those words for centuries in various ways, letting us know, always, that we worked at the whim of the council. What that council's future was, I could not have guessed. With certain members working to bring back the Old Ones right under the noses of the other members, I could not see a peaceful path forward.

"You did not set the council down this path, Fury," Atlanta said.

"She is correct. You are not to blame yourself for any of this," Demetrius added.

"My own sister did this. She has been steadily working against us all!"

"We did our best to warn you," Atlanta said sadly. "But what you must know is that there was never a way to avoid this. Even if you had not trusted your sister, she still would have worked with Sunee and the others."

"I don't think we can best her," I admitted to both Demetrius and Atlanta.

"I don't think you should try. At least, not yet," Demetrius said.

Leslie's work with weapons was renowned. Though either Gabrielle or myself might be able to take her in hand-to-hand combat, the chances of us ridding Leslie of her various weapons was minimal at best. And with at least one witch on her side and us without a Guardian to rival those powers, I was admittedly skeptical of our chances.

Chloe and Lexi came into the room, then, closely followed by Gabrielle and then, finally, Allison. My sister looked wrung out and exhausted. Allison didn't look much better. I did appreciate, though, the goblets of blood the Fates carried. Many of us needed the nourishment. I took long drinks from my glass, and I noted that Gabrielle did the same. It appeared all hope was not lost. If I still had one sister, I was willing to try and fight, as long as we had a plan.

"We should return to the other realm," Demetrius said. "All of us."

Atlanta nodded.

"The Steward is right. Your presence will be required there soon, anyway, I'm afraid. We will arrive when it is time, but not before. Be well, Olivia, Gabrielle. Be well, Steward," the Fate said.

Chloe and Lexi gave us impossible-to-interpret looks before they took Atlanta's outstretched hands and disappeared with another significant clap of thunder. Demetrius sat back and waited as my sister and I finished our goblets.

FIFTY-TWO

We arrived in Bellanca and found it disturbingly normal. I suppose I wanted things to feel as if they were upended, as my own life had been. I wanted to see the evidence of the chaos that I felt inside. But instead, various faction members strolled through the cavern entrance as they did any other day. Gabrielle looked around at everyone, as well, as if she had similar thoughts to my own. Allison gazed around wordlessly.

"You're going to need weapons," Demetrius said as we followed him out and into a stone hallway.

We'd been to the weapons cadre many, many times before. It was strange, however, being there without Leslie and her unabashed excitement. She loved anything new the blacksmiths forged, and she liked to consider what we needed to best suit our battle styles. I tended to select daggers, but Leslie pushed me to become just as comfortable with a bladed fighting stick. For Gabrielle, our sister had specific bows made for her slight frame. She had even convinced one of the fae to make Gabrielle a special bow and a quiver of arrows out of the lightest of the elven woods. That bow, of course, was at home in our own weapons area.

Chances were that we'd face Leslie in a smaller space, anyway, which meant we needed daggers—lots of them—and swords. I grabbed Gabrielle a fighting stick before I chose one for myself. Gabrielle wasn't as comfortable as I was with it, but she had been my sparring partner often enough that I knew she could hold her own. I handed Allison a knife and a thigh holster to put it in, as well as a bow and quiver of arrows. She strapped them on as if she was born using them, no doubt remembering, as I did, when Leslie had first showed her how to wear the weapons. Now she may very well have to use them against her.

We left the weapons room as the stone around us began to tremble. Gray-brown dust fell around us. Gabrielle's wide eyes met my own. Allison ducked down and pulled us with her. We knelt on the stones, covering our heads.

"What's happening?" I yelled to Demetrius over the rumble.

"Nothing good!" he called back.

Just a moment later, though, the trembling stopped. We'd been able to remain on our feet, and it looked like the stones around us had held. I shuddered at the idea of being buried beneath any of it. I might be able to whirlwind out if I could get ahold of a breeze. I still had my amulet, as well. I caught Gabrielle sheepishly feeling for her own necklace.

"Meet me near the entrance," Demetrius said. "I need to find Allura."

We watched him go.

"How could she?" Gabrielle finally asked.

"I don't know."

I reached for her hand and squeezed it.

"I want to kill her, but I don't know if I can," Gabrielle admitted.

I sighed. I wished I didn't feel the same, but I did. I was so angry, but I also understood that Leslie had done what she did because she thought it was the right thing to do. And hadn't I been doing that? I had made choice after choice that complicated my life—our lives, even, to some degree—because I thought they were the right choices to make.

I too easily remembered the look on Leslie's face as she talked about Vallerie. I hadn't known then what it was like to love someone so deeply. I hadn't understood loving someone and accepting the difficulties that came with it. But I had begun to understand it, because if I was honest with myself, I loved Alex. I loved his smile. I loved his sense of duty, even when it put us at odds. And I loved that he was willing to keep trying, even when things looked impossible. He was a good man. And I only hoped I would have a chance to tell him all of that.

"I remember being so angry with her about Vallerie," Gabrielle said.

I looked up in surprise.

"What?" I asked.

"She wouldn't walk away. Even though we knew what was going to happen, she just wouldn't walk away from Vallerie, and I was so angry with her about that. She was obviously hurting, but I could not, for the life of me, understand why she couldn't just be done with it."

"You weren't the only one who didn't understand. I don't think any of us did."

I thought of Evangeline again. I remembered how we had wondered about her and Demetrius. I wondered if she regretted walking away from everything. Maybe that had been why her last thoughts were of Demetrius.

"I want to hate her," Gabrielle said.

"I know. I do, too."

"But I can't."

"No," I agreed.

"What are we doing to do?"

"I don't know," I admitted.

"Things are never going to be the same."

I shook my head. She was right. We would never be the same. I didn't know what that meant for our futures as Furies. Worse, I didn't know what it meant for our futures as sisters.

As we entered the main cavern once more, the stones trembled. I crouched down. Gabrielle and Allison did, too. The few Creatures around us ran to the various hallways open to them. The trembling stopped much more quickly this time, and we were on our feet again.

———

Out of sheer habit, I checked my weapons. I had small twin daggers in sheaths at my wrists. There was a witchblade strapped to each thigh and a blade tucked into my right boot. If I was at home, I'd have donned my spine sheath, but spine sheaths weren't used often enough for them to be in the armory. The good news was that I still had everything I'd walked out of the weaponry with. What I couldn't be sure of was whether any of the weaponry I'd collected would do me any good. I wasn't even certain of what or whom I faced. Sunee had done well to keep their allies a secret beyond Ramiel and Atara, and we had always known the atlanteans favored the ways of the Old Ones. They were their descendants, after all, and as a whole were a bunch of demi-gods and demi-goddesses bitter at their power being limited to that of the other Creatures.

Ramiel and Atara likely had powers born in nature--water and wind were most common amongst the atlanteans. Sunee, I knew, was one of the most powerful witches to walk the Earth realm. I hadn't been able to confirm if her counterpart on the council, Veradis, was allied to her. If they were bound together in their schemes, it would be near impossible to combat their powers. Sunee was known for fire magic, while Veradis wielded earth magic. Last I knew, Veradis dabbled in darker magics, too, like necromancy. His presence could mean total chaos.

"I don't like this," Gabrielle said.

She'd completed checking over her weapons.

"I don't, either," I agreed.

I glanced at Allison, whose face was devoid of emotion. It was good for battle, but I hated it, anyway.

We both pulled witchblades and held them at the ready, but Gaia only knew if they'd aid us in whatever fight we found ourselves in. It seemed farfetched to believe that Sunee or my sister could have anything to do with this, but I'd underestimated them both before, and it had resulted in consequences the likes of which I had never dreamed.

Demetrius and Allura came toward us, cloaks billowing behind them. Their steps were quick and sure, the only sign of anything being amiss was the lightest dusting of stone on Allura's braids. I ran a hand through my own hair to confirm that my strands, too, were dust-covered.

Just as they reached us, the earth that encased us resumed its shaking. It was the sort of movement that triggered thoughts of the end of the world. The entirety of the realm flashed several times, from lightning bright to midnight dark. A primal screaming echoed off the cavern walls as everything continued to shake. The screaming grew louder and more intense by the second. Unable to maintain the strength it took to stand, my knees hit the hard rock of the floor. I saw Demetrius throw his hands out and attempt to create some sort of shield around us with the air, but it must have been difficult. His muscles trembled with the effort, and the shield flashed around us for one second before it was gone. He cried out in frustration. Allura's magic was in potions, which were of no use to us—at least, until we knew what we were fighting.

I felt blood drip from my nose, and I saw the evidence of other drips in the dust near my feet. I tried to look over at Allison, but the pressure in my head built too quickly. I dropped my witchblade and put both hands over my ears, murmuring old prayers in the hopes that someone might hear them and end the Gaia-forsaken shaking. Just when I thought my mind might shatter beneath the weight of it all, the world went dark.

FIFTY-THREE

I came to on the dusty cavern floor. The shaking had ceased, but we could feel the slight aftershocks in the stone below us. Allison stirred beside me. Blood was dried underneath her nose, and one swipe at my face with the back of my hand showed the dark, tell-tale signs of my own damage. I grabbed at the witchblade I'd dropped and looked around at the devastation.

Some of the witchlights in the cavern had gone out, so it was much darker than it usually was. I could just make out a few of the more familiar things, like the large table in the middle which usually held some kind of floral arrangement. The flowers were husks of what they had been. They stood dried out and scattered amongst the pieces of the glass vase they had been held in. Various stone tables were cracked or shattered. Many of the pillars remained standing, but I noted a few cracks that might be worrisome later on.

I helped Allura to her feet as Gabrielle assisted Demetrius. Allison already stood on her own two feet, looking around at the various Creatures shuffling through the cavernous space. Voices echoed as they crawled from hiding places.

"What was that?" Gabrielle asked.

"An Old One has woken," Demetrius said gravely.

"What?" Gabrielle croaked.

"An old god? The ones who are supposed to be sleeping?" Allison asked.

"Yes."

"That's not great," she surmised.

"Not at all," Gabrielle muttered.

"Chloe told me to watch for these signs," Allura said.

Damn the Fates and their secrecy. Atlanta could have told us what we were walking into. Allura went to assist some of the other Creatures who'd been in the main cavern with us. Most of the damage, I was pleased to see, was small bumps and bruises. A few cuts here and there required some bandaging, but it looked like those were the worst of the injuries. Demetrius began to shout orders as Allison made a sort of triage area for the wounded.

Gabrielle and I assisted where we could, but we were soon put to better use flashing back to the Earth realm for healers. I was grateful one of the first we were asked to get was Yasmina, but that joy soon turned as we had to fill her in on what happened. Gabrielle's soft voice told the story of Leslie's betrayal. Though Yasmina's lip quivered as she heard of Evangeline's death, she was soon patting our hands and trying to comfort us. We delivered her to Allura.

"I cannot find Sunee, Ramiel, or Atara," Demetrius told us as soon as we'd found him.

"Damn it," Gabrielle said.

"Is there any way to sense if they are in this realm?" I asked.

Demetrius shook his head sadly.

"How can we find out which of the Old Ones are awake?" I inquired, attempting to pivot.

Demetrius looked thoughtful for a moment.

"Until they present themselves, we won't. But it is likely they would go to parts of the realm we don't use anymore."

"We moved to this part of the cave system after they went to sleep," Gabrielle recalled.

"Let's go."

"Wait! I'm coming with you," Allison said, holding onto her bow as she ran in our direction.

I wanted to say no, but the idea of being separated from her filled me with such dread that all I could do was agree and gesture for her to follow us.

———

Gabrielle led us through various winding hallways. It was difficult to know whether the dusty state of them was wholly due to the quaking, but the spiderwebs in some of the corners made me believe the space was truly abandoned. Demetrius caught me looking around as we squeezed through one of the nearly blocked doorways.

"We've had no use for these paths, I guess," he admitted.

We kept moving. We must have gone at least a mile through the twisting stonework before coming into the space that had been used for those who traveled in from outside the realm. Water flowed in a fountain against the wall, though some of the fish that had been carved were chipped in places.

Flecks of gold shone beneath the layers of dust on the floor. I brushed away at it with the toe of my boot to reveal the gold and white tiling I knew I'd find there. The walls around us were much fancier than the newer landing place I was used to. The stone had been left its natural color, but the carvings along the walls told the stories of the gods and gold paint had been used to highlight. Even through the dust and grime, it was beautiful.

"I remember this place," Gabrielle breathed.

We spun in slow circles, taking it all in. Allison murmured sounds of amazement.

"I was told there were those who wanted to move on from the Old Ones, start anew," Demetrius explained. "I am glad you have not completely forgotten it."

But I only vaguely remembered using this room. It had been so long ago, and only the barest of memories of it remained. It was odd, having a kind of sensory memory tied to something of the Old Ones that didn't bring fear or pain to mind. As if Demetrius had similar thoughts, he began to ask questions.

"Did Leslie mention which of the gods they were trying to awaken?"

"No, I'm sorry."

"Was there more than one?"

"I'm not sure."

I could tell Demetrius was growing frustrated, but I had shared all I knew. Before he could open his mouth to ask more questions I was certain I didn't have answers for, thunder rumbled. The Fates.

They stood, suddenly, in front of us. Dressed similarly, as usual, and in all black, looking chilling and ruthless. Chloe looked around the cavern, disgust obvious on her face, while Lexi brushed away at dust already accumulating on one of her heeled boots. Atlanta sought me out.

"A decision has been made."

Her face was unreadable, as usual, but there was a tightness around her eyes that wasn't so typical.

"It would be nice, Atlanta, if we saw each other because good things were happening."

She smiled wryly at me.

"There are worse paths than the one we're on," she said.

That was good news, I suppose. It was the best news we were likely to get aside from someone shaking me awake and telling me it was all a dream. Atlanta motioned for me to follow her into one of the nearby, smaller caverns.

"You were told secrets," she said.

"Such as...?" I responded.

"Secrets of reincarnated souls."

"I was," I admitted, glancing at Allison.

Atlanta held up a finger for silence. A faint rumbling in the distance could just barely be heard. The main cavern was quaking again. Interesting that this place wasn't.

"The Old Ones empowered this place," she said quietly.

"It's safe from their power?" I asked.

She nodded in response. Well, that certainly made sense. It also meant Demetrius was probably right in that whoever had been awakened would make their presence known here instead of in the parts of the cave system we used currently. The rumbling rolled to a stop.

"You were told of Iason and Eleni," Atlanta said.

I let out a breath.

"So it's true? I really had a husband and a daughter?" I asked.

I had started to question everything I had known once Sunee's scheming had been brought to light. It had been devastating to consider that it might just have been a tale I was told.

"You did, Olivia. But—" Atlanta paused.

"But what? What is it?" I demanded.

"They were not reincarnated."

"You're lying."

Atlanta shook her head sadly.

"Their souls are still in the Elysian Fields, Olivia."

"Lies!" I cried.

"Who better to know than a Fate?" she asked.

I didn't remember falling to my knees and grasping at my abdomen. Until later, I didn't recall placing one hand over the heart that had so easily drawn Allison and Alex inside. It had been so easy to care for them, to love them, and to worry about them. And they were my family, so why should I not have let it be so easy?

But this?

This heartache ricocheted through my body, and I screamed.

FIFTY-FOUR

"Shhh," Allison said.

She had her arms around me and gently rocked me back and forth. I had no idea how much time had passed. I saw Atlanta holding Gabrielle back. I had held this secret from her. I had kept this monumental piece of our story from my sister... and for what? It was a lie.

It was all a lie.

No, no, no, no, no.

I must have chanted the words out loud because Allison resumed her quiet shushing. I continued to rock back and forth, clutching at my chest and my stomach, the pain inside me unbearable. I couldn't remember what it was like to lose them—my husband and my child—but this grief felt like it would destroy me. I thought I had them. I never did.

Was everything with Alex a lie?

"I know this hurts," Atlanta said.

How would you know? You keep yourself separate from humanity. I should have. I should have maintained the distance I was taught to. Damn all of you.

"Olivia, they may not be your long-lost family, but they are a family of sorts. Look at her."

I looked up into Allison's face, full of concern. It was too difficult. I lowered my head and let the tears fall.

"Why?" I asked. "Why would they tell me this?"

"I have to assume it was a distraction."

Well, Gaia knew it worked. I remembered the mourning I had done when I'd first learned of Alex and Allison and their supposed connections to me. It paled in comparison to the tidal wave of grief that swept through me.

"I know that what you are going through feels impossible, Olivia, but I need you to get up. An Old One has woken. Sunee and Leslie have made decisions about their final plans, and you are crucial to stopping them."

I wasn't sure I cared.

"You have to do this," Allison said softly in my ear. "You can rage about this later."

"I can't," I said.

I felt lower than I ever had. I felt more lost than I ever had. There were too many secrets and, somehow, too many truths. A light was being shone on everything, and I wanted nothing more than to sink into the darkness that beckoned so beautifully.

"We can't let her win," Allison said.

It felt like she already had.

"Do you love him?" Atlanta asked.

I pulled back and stared at her. She'd let go of Gabrielle.

"What?" I finally said.

"Do. You. Love. Him."

"Yes," I whispered.

"Then get off your ass. If the world ends, you won't get to tell him. And, frankly, I'm sort of betting on the two of you weirdos figuring it out and doing that whole happily ever after thing."

I stared. Allison squeezed my hands in hers.

Then Atlanta's eyes went white.

"Olivia. Leslie is coming. She cannot see you like this. Get up."

———

I pulled myself to my feet and wiped the tears from my face with dust-covered hands just before Leslie blinked into existence in front of us.

"Bitch," Gabrielle snarled. "Murderer."

Leslie laughed a high twinkling sort of laugh that immediately made me want to slit her throat just to stop the gods-awful noise. I saw Allison's hand reach for her knife. *Like mother, like...* The pain began anew.

"Ah, ah, ah," Leslie said, wagging her finger at Atlanta. "You don't involve yourselves, as I recall. Just bystanders, right? There to see the fates of everyone but not doing anything about them?"

Atlanta took a step backward from me.

"That's much better," Leslie purred.

"What could you possibly want?" I demanded.

I was almost surprised to see I held a witchblade out in front of me, but I suppose my body was far more used to my sense of vengeance than I realized.

"You're too late, you know," said Leslie.

Whereas Gabrielle and I stood dust-covered and bloody, Leslie was practically pristine. Her clothes had the tiniest amount of dust on them, but it certainly looked like she'd been able to avoid the worst of it. Our sister stood there, one hip cocked out, happily and calmly twirling a witchblade around in her hand.

"Not to kill you," Allison said.

She took a step forward and brandished her own blade.

"Killing me wouldn't do a Gaia-damned thing. An Old One has awoken!"

"Killing you might make me feel better," I said.

Leslie rolled her eyes.

"You killed a Guardian!" Allison cried.

"So I did," she said with a shrug. "We don't need our Guardians."

"We haven't *needed* them in centuries!" Gabrielle yelled. "But they are ours. Evangeline was ours. She cared about us."

Leslie cackled.

"You little mouse of a Creature. She didn't care about you. She cared about the mission. And our mission will change now that the Old Ones are awake."

"She didn't have to die," Gabrielle said.

Leslie shrugged again.

"You're right. She didn't have to. But she deserved it."

"Then so do we. We all let Vallerie die," I said.

"True. But, someday, I might be able to forgive you for that. Maybe. The cold, hard truth is that I'm stronger as long as you're both alive, so I'm rather hesitant to kill you."

"Then we'll kill you," Gabrielle growled.

"You can try," Leslie called as she turned and sauntered away.

FIFTY-FIVE

It was clearly a game of chase, but we followed, anyway. We were drawn even deeper into the caverns within the older part of the stronghold. Whatever magic held up most of the hallways and main areas of use had clearly not been as strong there. Rocks and dust covered the floor. Once-tall, sandstone pillars were crumbled or broken into pieces that we were forced to climb over. Carvings done long ago on the walls had been all but brushed away, with just the barest of ridges showing the shapes that must have once been sharp and clear. I did not recall this part of the realm. There had been little reason to wander, and based on all I could see, many others must have felt that way. Demetrius remained near the entrance to the large room, but Gabrielle and I darted forward. In the center of the large, open space, Alex was chained to a rock, like Prometheus had been. Leslie stood nearby, waving her knives around like she might tear into his body at any second.

And the laughter as she did it grated on me. She twirled away from Alex's body and danced around the cavern, witchblades in both hands, whirling about like a madwoman. I watched her in disgust. How could she have hidden this madness from us for so long? Or was it the impending appearance of the Old Ones which made her so gleeful? I noticed that Gabrielle's eyes followed her, as well, but there was more sadness on her face than anger. Allison was all fury and righteous anger.

I needed to be the same. As long as Alex was in some kind of danger, I needed to hold tight to my sense of vengeance. I'd once done it so easily. I found that slipping back into the habit was not as easy as I'd thought it might be. It fit oddly, as if I'd outgrown its tight wrappings. Maybe I had.

"He has no part in this," I called to Leslie.

"Oh, but doesn't he? I can't very well allow you to keep your love when you took away mine, can I?" Leslie asked.

"I didn't take Vallerie from you!" I cried.

"You may not have done the taking, but you allowed it all the same," Leslie replied in a low voice as she stopped twirling directly in front of me.

"You said you weren't going to kill us," Gabrielle said.

"She's not chained to a rock, is she?" Leslie asked, gesturing with her knife at me.

"If you're not going to kill us, what do you want?" I asked.

"For you to make a choice," Leslie said. "Now, of course, I can't let you have him. No, no, no. There will be none of that. But you can let him die and live with the knowledge that it was your choice."

"And the other option?" I asked quietly.

Leslie laughed softly.

"You can turn him and live out the rest of your miserable eternity in Tartarus."

"I can't turn him," I said. "We don't have that kind of power."

"We do," Leslie said as a smile stretched over her face. "You see, I was the one who turned Allison."

"But—" Allison started.

"You didn't," I said at the same time.

Demetrius made a choking sound from behind me. It made me believe the otherwise-insane words that were coming out of her mouth.

"Oh, and then I used a spell to make Fabian think he did it," she laughed. "After that, it was a piece of cake to lure the stupid Fiagai into hunting him."

Leslie's smile widened. She knew what the loss of Fabian had done to me, and she had twisted the knife even further in her madness.

"And you—you thought you were so smart," Leslie laughed. "You kept the Fiagai away from us, thinking we'd never figure out what the two of you were up to."

"What is she talking about?" Gabrielle asked.

"Our dearest sister—our center—has taken a human lover," Leslie answered.

Gabrielle stared at me. I could see the surprise, but the hurt was even more stark. She frowned and looked away.

"I'm sorry," I whispered. "I didn't mean for it to happen. It just did. And telling you—it put you in danger."

Leslie cackled louder.

"Oh, of course you did it for *us*," she practically purred. "It had nothing to do with your own desire to have something of your own, something not connected to being a Fury."

She was right. I had enjoyed having something that was just mine, something I had built for myself. Everything, for so very long, had been about the three of us. But Alex was mine. He was just mine, and I had liked not sharing him with anyone.

"Your silence speaks volumes, *sister*," Leslie said.

Gabrielle continued to stare at me accusingly, and her eyes were filled with hurt.

"I'm sorry. I am. I should have told you."

"Yes, you should have."

"I'm sorry," I repeated.

"Even now, she won't tell you her secrets," Leslie crooned.

"There's more?" Gabrielle asked.

"Oh, yes. You see, her attraction to the Fiagai wasn't random. He is the reincarnated soul of her husband, Iason."

Gabrielle's jaw dropped and her eyes went wide. Allison, too, looked shocked before rage filled her features once more.

"Y-you.... You had a husband?" Gabrielle gasped.

There was no point in telling her that Alex was not Iason. Because the truth was that I had learned we had human lives—perhaps we had all had human partners—and I hadn't told her. It didn't matter, not in this moment, that Alex and Iason were not one.

"Oh, she had a husband," Leslie informed her. "And they had a baby. She had a whole fucking *life* that she didn't tell us about."

Gabrielle's eyes filled with tears.

"Did w-we have human lives?" she asked quietly.

"I don't know," I said. "But it's possible."

"You knew there was a possibility that we had human lives—our own loved ones that could be reincarnated—and you didn't say a damn word?" she asked.

All I could do was nod. Gabrielle turned her face away from me. It felt worse, knowing that I'd never even realized that Gabrielle might want something like that. It had never occurred to me that she might desire a family. I had assumed she was so content. But, then again, I had assumed Leslie had gotten over Vallerie, and we had found ourselves in this mess.

"Oh, Gabby, baby, it gets so much worse!" Leslie crowed.

Gabrielle slowly turned to face Leslie and lifted her chin, waiting defiantly for what our sister had to say.

"She brought the reincarnated daughter into our lives. It's Allison."

Gabrielle stared at the vampire. Allison's eyes moved between us all, unsure of who to look at. I didn't blame her. I wasn't even sure where the threat was truly coming from anymore.

"I've heard enough."

"Gabrielle, I'm so sorry," I whispered.

And I was. I was overwhelmingly sorry that I had played my role in all of the secret-keeping. Our triad had never been as strong as I thought it had been, and my secrets were certainly part of that.

"I said I've heard enough."

"Oh, Gaia!" Leslie laughed. "This is just as much fun as I'd thought it was going to be!"

I tore my gaze from Gabrielle and looked back to Alex. I took one step forward, but Leslie was immediately in front of me, witchblades flashing.

"What's your choice going to be, huh, Liv? You gonna watch him die?"

"I don't know what to do," I admitted, staring into Alex's eyes.

"I bet she's gonna let you die," Leslie said to Alex.

She dropped a kiss to his face, and though he tried to flinch away from her, he couldn't really move. A blade *snicked*, and blood dripped from a wound near his collarbone. I stepped forward, and again, there was Leslie and her moving witchblades. Allison growled nearby. The hum of his blood was so close, but I couldn't get anywhere near him.

"I know you don't want this kind of life. You'd lose everyone... everything," I said to Alex.

He didn't say anything for a moment.

"Everything in me is raging against the idea of becoming a Creature," he admitted.

I nodded. Of course it was. It was in his blood. I looked down at my dust-and-blood-covered boots. I didn't want to watch him die and know I could have saved him.

"But—" he said.

I looked back up and stared at him. I wanted him to say anything that would let me turn him. I couldn't let him die. I couldn't.

"I could be with my sister," he said.

I nodded. Leslie rolled her eyes. I watched Alex's pulse beat lightly, hammering a cadence under the smooth skin of his neck. The rhythm was nervous, at odds with the words he was saying to me.

"What do you want me to do?" I whispered.

"Turn me," he said.

"What?" Leslie and I both said.

"You don't really know what you're asking for," I added.

"Just do it, Liv," Alex whispered, fervent and urgent.

I felt the burning pain inside me and its desire to rush me, as well. The sinful scent of his blood was too much, and there was a sharp twinge of fear that I might ravage him. I'd never had to have any type of control. Again, I smelled his blood, and I stumbled backward.

"She can't do it," Leslie giggled. "Or maybe she will and she'll tear him to pieces."

Alex angled his head, his neck bared to the light. His blood called to me, whispering in a language that felt far away and long forgotten. I stood in front of him in the ruins, in the midst of so much destruction, and kissed his lips. That, too, seemed familiar.

"Olivia," Alex whispered again.

We had to hurry. I knew it. I didn't have time to contemplate. This wasn't where I would have chosen to do this, and now I'd been robbed of the choice. I leaned my forehead against his, closing my eyes.

"Forgive me," I whispered back.

Before either of us could change our minds, I pressed my mouth to the side of Alex's neck and slid my fangs into the pulsing warmth of his life force.

FIFTY-SIX

The blood drummed a rhythm through me, and it felt just as I thought it would when I first heard it calling to me from beneath Alex's tanned skin. Strong hands grabbed at my arms and pulled me backwards. The warmth, though, like liquid sunshine, was pouring into my mouth. I fought, nails clawing at anything they could find purchase in, to stay where I was. The hands were too strong, though, and I was yanked backward and away from the blood. A sharp slap brought me back to myself.

In horror, I looked at Alex. His head drooped, as if he'd gone unconscious. I could still taste his blood in my mouth.

"Oh, Gaia," I whispered.

Allison roared, her anger a palpable thing.

Gabrielle and I could do nothing but watch the vampire scream. It held us in a thrall of sorts before light blinded us. We fell to our knees. Screams ricocheted.

Power pulsed through the cavern. Its heaviness weighed down my limbs. I couldn't move. I tried to lift my head, to look at Allison, but it was all too much. It was too bright and too loud.

And then it was silent.

Allison knelt, head down, the earth scorched around her. When she raised her head and her eyes met mine, they were a brilliant, unnatural green. I didn't know what it meant.

"You need to complete the ritual," Gabrielle reminded me.

I scrambled to Alex's side, used my own fangs to break open the thin skin at my wrist, and I thrust the bleeding appendage in front of him. He did not wake.

"Fuck," I whimpered.

Gabrielle grabbed my wrist and held it to Alex's mouth, tilting his head back to let the blood roll down his throat. It felt like time stopped, as tears poured down my face and I hoped he would drink from me. Finally, his throat convulsed once, then twice, and he drank greedily until my sister tore my wrist from him.

"You've had enough to make the change," she bit out.

Alex's eyes blinked once before they closed, and he fell unconscious again. Gabrielle ripped a section of her shirt off and wrapped my wrist, even though we both knew the wound would soon close.

When we looked up, Allison hadn't moved. Leslie stood staring at the scene as if in shock. I couldn't think about what I'd done for too long, so perhaps I was also in shock. I looked behind me and found Demetrius, his eyes pinched tight and jaw clenched.

"I'm sorry," I whispered.

I wasn't sure who I was apologizing to. I wasn't even certain if I was sorry. Alex had asked me to turn him, and so I did. It might mean damnation, but he would be alive, and that was more important to me than anything. Was I sorry at all?

"You did what you had to," Gabrielle said matter-of-factly.

Demetrius' jaw worked as sadness filled his features. Of course, it would probably be up to him to sentence me. And since he'd watched me commit the crime, I would, of course, soon be on my way to Tartarus.

I heard the metallic *clunk* of chains hitting the ground. Gabrielle stood with Alex leaning heavily against her.

"Help?" she asked.

I raced forward. Allison stared without seeing, still kneeling in the burned circle.

"Alex?" I said quietly.

He didn't answer. But Demetrius was finally shaken from his stupor.

"Olivia.... Alekto. You have committed the gravest of crimes, and thus you will be—"

There was a sharp crack, like thunder but not. It felt as though electricity filled the air for just a breath, and everything around me crackled.

"Alekto," a golden voice intoned.

I sank to my knees. That voice, in all its richness and its haughtiness, could only belong to an Old One. Everyone around me hit their knees, as well, including Leslie. Gabrielle struggled a bit with Alex's weight, but she, too, went to her knees in obeisance.

"Rise," the voice said.

I stood, but the sight when I raised my head was not at all what I thought I would face. It was not any of the Old Ones I recognized. But her long, light brown hair and bright blue eyes were not all together foreign, either.

"Aphrodite," Demetrius breathed.

"It is I," she said with a gentle smile.

"My lady," said Leslie.

Aphrodite glanced down at her still-bowed form but then looked around at the rest of us.

"I believe I may have arrived just in time," she said. "You were about to sentence Alekto?"

"I was, your highness."

"Oh, good. I'll take things from here."

Here it was, the moment of judgment. I bowed my head once more.

"Alekto?" Aphrodite asked.

I looked up.

"Why did you turn him?"

I looked over at Alex, whose body was still being held up by Gabrielle. I took in the planes of his face and was sad that his beautiful eyes were closed. As I looked at him, I was even more certain of my choice.

"Because I love him."

Demetrius let out a heavy breath. Gabrielle closed her eyes and inhaled. Leslie looked over and smirked. The Old Ones were not known for their interest in "love."

"Do you love him because you believe him to be your reincarnated husband?" she asked.

I shook my head.

"I think—" I began, "I think I would have loved him, anyway."

As I said the words, I knew they were accurate. Alex's sense of duty, his understanding of what it was like to serve—those were the things that had brought me to him, again and again. He was pretty, there was no doubt about that, but it was the way his life's patterns had echoed my own in so many ways that had intrigued me, as nothing else had intrigued me in centuries. I loved him. *I loved him.*

Aphrodite nodded thoughtfully.

"What if he had made a different choice?" the goddess inquired.

"I would have let him go."

And, though it probably would have nearly killed me to do it, I would have. If Alex had preferred death to being made into a Creature, I would have respected that. I loved him enough to do that.

"Steward, what is the sentence deemed appropriate for the turning of a human?"

Demetrius cleared his throat.

"Tartarus."

"For how long?"

"Eternity," he responded.

Aphrodite looked at me, then. Her blue eyes didn't miss anything. I let her see my understanding and even my willingness to accept my punishment. I would not cower. I was a Fury.

"Well, there will be no need for that," Aphrodite said succinctly.

Leslie stared, mouth agape, at the goddess. Even Demetrius looked shocked. I barely had the energy to stand, let alone experience such surprise, so I merely stood there. I looked back over to Gabrielle, who, to my shock, had tears streaming down her face.

"But... your highness," Leslie started.

Aphrodite held up a finger for silence.

"You awakened a goddess, did you not?" she asked.

Leslie nodded.

"Then you will live with the consequences."

I felt that too-familiar, telltale warmth at my throat. I looked down and immediately closed my eyes against what I saw. The amulet's heat did not abate, though, and when I opened my eyes, the name I had seen before was still present and clear as day.

Leslie, the Tisiphone.

———

Leslie, Gaia bless her, did not even attempt to run. She stood still as I moved behind her under the gaze of Aphrodite. Gabrielle stood next to me. The Tisiphone knelt without being asked on the dust-covered stone of the cavern. We had not yet abandoned the place where she had meant for me to be doomed to an eternity in Tartarus. There we were, amongst the ruins still, and about to take a step forward into a future neither of us had ever envisioned.

Leslie had so thoroughly believed that the awakening of the Old Ones would bring about a life she wanted. And, perhaps, she had not considered what she really wanted, which was to be reunited with Vallerie. Only death might give her that chance. And she would wish for death long before it would be granted to her.

"Tisiphone of the Furies, you have broken the laws of your brethren and so you must pay your debt in full. I, Alekto, release your spirit to be guided to Tartarus, where you will be judged for your rebellion and disregard. The truth of your nature will be revealed. In Tartarus so it shall be."

But when I went to drag my witchblade across my sister's throat, the goddess held up her hand.

"The newest Fury must fulfill the old one's sentence, I think."

"What?" Gabrielle said.

I was just as surprised.

"It is what should be," Aphrodite said gently.

She looked back to where Allison knelt.

"It is your duty," she said.

Allison said nothing, only stared at her for a long moment. There was a single, quick nod before the former vampire rose to her feet. She stalked across the cavern, took the knife from hand, and pulled it across Leslie's throat. No hesitation.

As blood gushed, she smiled.

FIFTY-SEVEN

O nce again, I clung to my sense of duty as emotions flooded through me. I dropped to the dust-covered floor. Silence. I could not even hear breathing from the still-living around me. I wanted to reach for Gabrielle, but how could I, with the blood of our sister in a pool around us?

I closed my eyes against the sight of my dead sister, but I could see her face swimming behind my eyelids. Had I ever truly known her? It seemed I might never know. I wanted to feel something, but there was a great maw of emptiness where I thought grief should have been. So much loss in such a short time. I had not been prepared. Could one have prepared for such events? I didn't know. I suppose it didn't matter, but my thoughts continued to meander in those patterns.

A gentle hand fell upon my shoulder. I looked up into Aphrodite's eyes. It was odd that they were so like my own. The blue of them bright and strange and glowing. Understanding was present in their depths, and I would have sworn a saw a bit of grief, as well.

"Come. There is much to tell you," she said softly. "All of you," she amended as Allison watched us.

Her face turned toward Demetrius. The chiton whirled around her. It was like she traveled with her own breeze. It wafted the long tendrils of her hair away from her face and caused the edges of the skirts to flutter. Demetrius swallowed hard and lowered his eyes.

"Steward?"

"Yes?" Demetrius said as he looked up at her through dark lashes.

"Please take the Creature to safe quarters. I must speak with the Furies."

I opened my mouth to speak, to stop Demetrius from taking Alex away, but Aphrodite silenced me with a look.

"He will be unconscious yet for several hours. We have time."

Her voice was gentle but with a rigidity underneath. It would be best not to argue. Demetrius lifted Alex's body easily from where Gabrielle stood with him. In this large space with so few of us, she looked even smaller. I had never thought of her as delicate, but she looked it. Her heart-shaped face was pale between curtains of dark hair.

"Steward?" Aphrodite said.

Demetrius turned and waited.

"Tell no one what you have seen here. I will reveal my presence soon enough."

Demetrius nodded sharply, just once, and turned away to disappear into one of the hallways. He did not struggle under the weight of my lover. I could only assume he would take Alex to one of the areas more recently used to await our return. I felt, though, a strange tug as he went out of sight. I could have sworn I saw them travel as if through a veil.

Aphrodite began to move, though, and I didn't have more time to ponder the strange pulling sensation. Gabrielle, Allison, and I followed her, silently, back into the main landing area. We did not stop there, however. The goddess, her pale pink chiton trailing behind her through the dust of the abandoned halls, went through a narrow bit of stone and out into a much wider space, much more like where Leslie first drew us into.

As we entered the cavern, it transformed before our eyes. The grime seemed to float away, and white walls revealed. Stone pillars with large bases stood tall, unmarred. Various lounging surfaces revealed themselves, bright washes of colors stark against the otherwise white space. Long-dead plants were rejuvenated, their leaves transformed from the brittle, dry existence and into a lush green that almost overwhelmed. It was beautiful.

I grasped Gabrielle's hand and squeezed. I was met with a tentative look, but she squeezed my hand in return. I hoped we could repair what I had done.

Aphrodite gestured for us to be seated. She posed upon a chaise lounge with pillows in white and gold. I sat in a pile of various pillows upon the soft, woven rug. Allison kept herself at a distance. Gabrielle sat next to me. I was grateful for her nearness. Though Aphrodite did not seem to be of the same ilk of Old One I had, for so long, remembered, she was still a goddess. She was not to be trusted. Not yet.

"I'm going to tell you a story," Aphrodite began.

And we listened.

————

Alekto stood in the sand between her sisters, Tisiphone and Megaera, as waves crashed around their feet. Aquamarine waters of the vast ocean sparkled in the warm sunlight that shone down on them. Their black hair glinted blue. Though they had left their home that morning with hair in braided crowns, each had loosed their hair as they sat upon the sands. They would return to their mother with tangled tresses, but they were not worried. Their mother was long used to their wildness.

The loss of Alekto's husband and daughter had been grave, indeed. A toppled boat during a storm. Iason and Eleni had been lost. And so Alekto herself was lost. She felt murmurings of their presence with her as she stood in the waters. The grief that had threatened to sweep Alekto away lessened ever so slightly near the ocean. Her sisters, her lifelong companions, accompanied her to the beach each day, grateful for the bit of their sister's soul they saw return to her.

Their mother, Electra, had been concerned she might drown herself in the ocean if unaccompanied, so deep was Alekto's sadness. Tisiphone and Megaera had not left their sister's side since. Tisiphone's wife, Callandria, stayed behind to mind their farm, and Megaera had not yet left home.

Screams pierced the air. Alekto grasped at Tisiphone and Megaera, their hands gripping each other's tightly. Almost as one, they turned and raced back to their mother's home.

They raced through the open archway of the front of the sandstone dwelling and through the lavender curtains billowing in the oceanside winds. Alekto, Tisiphone, and Megaera took in the scene. Electra and her brother Estes stood over the body of Nestra, their mother. Blood soaked Nestra's green chiton. Her dark eyes had already glazed over.

"What have you done?" Megaera cried.

Electra and Estes whipped around, their faces masks of fury and vengeance. Tears ran down Electra's face, but her mouth was set in a firm, grim line.

"Away with you, daughters!" she said.

Estes took a step forward and brandished the dagger that still dripped his mother's blood upon the stone floor. Alekto pushed Tisiphone and Megaera behind her. She stood straight, though her height could never have matched that of Estes.

Lightning flashed and thunder cracked so loudly that Alekto felt it in her teeth. She immediately felt for the hands of her sisters and grasped them tightly.

A woman stood where no one had stood before.

Athena.

The goddess' black curls glistened in a halo around her head. A gold circlet sat upon her brow, indicating her status, as if anyone could have mistaken her for anything other than what she was. A bow was strapped to a leather holster against her back. The royal blue chiton floated around her ebony legs, and the slit allowed the quiver of arrows strapped to her right thigh to be visible. Alekto swallowed hard. She and her sisters hit their knees in obeisance. Electra and Estes soon followed.

"Electra, daughter of Clytemnestra and Agamemnon. Estes, son of Clytemnestra and Agamemnon. You have committed the gravest of sins," Athena intoned in a voice like velvet.

"My mother," Electra cried, "was a murderer!"

Tisiphone gasped. The sisters had known their grandmother to be an angry woman, but to call someone a murderer was a serious claim. They had certainly not seen evidence of anything.

"Your mother killed your father, 'tis true. But you have, in turn,

committed matricide, and such a sin cannot be overlooked or ignored. You must pay your debt," Athena replied.

Electra cried out, and Estes moved as if he would swipe at Athena with the dagger. With one move of a finger, though, the knife ripped from Estes' hand and was sent flying across the stones. He fell back on his knees. Tears fell from his eyes.

"Electra, you have broken the laws of your brethren and so you must pay your debt in full. I, Athena, will carry out your judgment and release your spirit to be guided to Tartarus. The truth of your nature will be revealed. In Tartarus so it shall be," Athena said.

Alekto gripped her sisters' hands more tightly, willing them to stay where they were.

The Fates stood before them all, faces empty of emotion. Clotho held up a thin, shining, golden string as Atropos wielded a pair of golden scissors with ivy leaves upon the handles. Lachesis' eyes were opaque white and illuminated from within. They were Seeing. Alekto, Tisiphone, and Megaera were pulled to their feet. They each stood, alone and with wide eyes, staring at the goddess.

"No!" Electra cried, stretching her hands out.

"You have committed the gravest of sins," Lachesis said in a strange, airy voice.

"You have betrayed your family," Atropos added.

"You have killed one whom you should hold dearest," Clotho said.

"You may not have wielded the weapon," Atropos spoke.

"But you are responsible just the same," murmured Clotho.

"The punishment will endure for the rest of time," cried Lachesis, eyes shining brighter even than before.

Instead of cutting the string, the golden thread held by Clotho burst into flame as they all watched.

"Your daughters three shall forevermore be Justice, carrying out the sentences for those who commit crimes such as yours," Athena continued.

A furious wind blew through the dwelling. Alekto felt as if her entire being was on fire. Her muscles went rigid, and she threw her head back to scream into the whipping storm. Lightning crashed around them, and the thunder bellowed its deep tones. To Alekto, Tisiphone, and Megaera, it felt *as if the thunder shook their very souls. The world was nothing but pain for several moments.*

When the wind stopped, the three sisters stood with ebony wings and electric eyes.

"You will be known as Furies, vengeful and the punishers of evil," Athena said to them.

The sisters nodded in unison as Electra screamed. The scream died, though, as Athena shot her arrows into both Electra and Estes. Their bodies fell to the floor and lay there.

Alekto, Tisiphone, and Megaera dispassionately took in the scene before them. Justice had been served. They turned and faced Athena, who smiled warmly at them.

"Come. We have much to do and many souls to avenge."

And so it was that Alekto, Tisiphone, and Megaera, three daughters of Electra and Thaumas, became Furies. Under Athena's tutelage, they were vengeful and judicious, and they clung to their sense of Justice like a treasured weapon.

Unknown, though, to the sisters and to Athena, was that Electra had been visited by a god. The blood beneath Electra's body slowly began to solidify and morph in the abandoned dwelling. When Thaumas returned later as the sun set beneath the ocean, he discovered a baby.

He named the baby Aphrodite, and it was many years before he realized he was raising a goddess.

FIFTY-EIGHT

"Oh, Gaia," Gabrielle breathed.

We clung together in the wake of the memory dissipating from our minds. Aphrodite sat before us, still and watchful. The knowledge of who and what we were was heavy, and I did not yet know if I had the strength to hold onto it. It was like I could feel the confines of my mind threatening to break under the strain. I reached up and felt for the chain at my neck.

We had been given the amulets so long ago. There was no catch, even, to remove it. I pulled with all the strength I had left in my body, and the chain snapped. The amulet tumbled to the floor near my knees. I did not reach for it.

I felt a sharp pain in each of my shoulder blades. For just a few seconds, my body felt enflamed, as if it was burning away the residual magic of the amulet. I wrenched away from Gabrielle and fell to the floor. I crouched there like a Creature as my wings burst forth. Pain wracked my body, and a heavy sob tore from my throat. It took me a long while to find the strength to fight against the burning pain in my back to stand. When I did, I couldn't help but look down at the bottom parts of my raven-colored wings. They nearly met the floor.

I was unbalanced by them. Their presence felt simultaneously wrong and right. I was meant for wings, but I had forgotten what it was like to have them. But they were mine, and I wanted them.

Gabrielle cried out as her own wings unfurled from her back and the pain took her to her knees, as well. Her amulet, cracked and broken, was near mine on the stone floor. Gabrielle stared up at me, and I pulled her to her feet. Our matching sets of blue eyes taking in all that had been stolen from us as we looked one another over.

"Your truths revealed," Aphrodite said after a few moments.

"Why?" Gabrielle asked.

But memories were spilling forth in my mind.

Most of the Old Gods were asleep. Many Creatures I recognized as former council members stared at us across one of the caverns. My sisters and I held our ground, daggers out. No witchblades. Finely made knives were in our hands, points sharp and blades well-oiled. But too many spells came at us all at once. The Twelve had worked together to subdue us. Atlanteans stared down at us and laughed at the chains that held us to stone slabs. One of my wings felt broken, and I screamed in rage at being held on my back.

More spells. More whispers.

Darkness.

When we woke, we wore the amulets, and our wings were gone. They had been hidden away by the bewitched necklaces. Blessed blades, witchblades, were handed to us. The new rules were given. We did not question. We did not remember.

The Twelve wielded us as their own.

Aphrodite had been watching us with her now-too-familiar blue eyes, our sister. The knowledge pulsed in my mind as I stared back at her. She looked away and swallowed hard.

"What was done to you was unforgivable," she said.

We said nothing in response. The amulets turned to dust before our eyes. When we looked back up at the goddess, our half-sister, rage filled her face.

"You will no longer be wielded," she intoned. "None of you."

Allison stepped forward, her own dark wings billowing at her back, and her eyes glowing. Gabrielle reached out and took my hand, then Allison's.

"There must be three," was all Aphrodite said.

I nodded, though there was still so much I did not understand.

"I am sorry we did not have a chance to meet," Aphrodite continued.

"I am glad to meet you now," Gabrielle replied.

Aphrodite smiled, and it was like sunlight lit her from within. It was almost difficult to look at her, but Gaia, she was beautiful. In some ways, she did resemble our mother, but her mouth was unfamiliar, and I wondered just what God had visited Electra.

"I still do not know," Aphrodite said.

I gaped at her.

"I'm sorry. I did not mean to intrude upon your thoughts," she replied sheepishly.

She was young, so young. And she was so very unlike the gods and goddesses I had once known. But before my mind could continue down that path, I felt that tugging sensation from deep within once more.

"You feel something?" she asked.

It was clear she knew I did but was attempting to be polite. I nodded. I felt my brow furrow as the tugging commenced. It was so light—like the brush of a sparrow's wing—but so present all the same.

"It is Alexander," she said.

"What?" Allison said.

It was the first thing she'd uttered. Her voice was harsh and gritty, no doubt painful in her damaged throat.

"He is alive. Well, in a way," the goddess answered. "Alekto turned him, and therefore she will be connected to him for the rest of eternity."

I let a long breath out.

"You did not realize?" she asked, tilting her head in a very other-worldly way.

I had two new sisters this day, and both were off-putting.

"What Leslie said about him... is it true? Is he Iason?" Gabrielle asked as she placed a gentle hand on my arm.

I shook my head again. Tears welled in my eyes. I could feel the burn of them.

"A trick," I whispered.

"Sunee's crimes were vast," Aphrodite acknowledged. "She will be sentenced accordingly."

Gabrielle and I looked at one another and then back to the goddess —our sister.

"She was in my tomb—some kind of apparition formed of her power—when I woke."

"We will hunt her," Allison said savagely.

I nodded my agreement. It was no more and no less than she deserved. I repeated that to myself. It was clear that once I had felt the fire of Justice within me, but if any was left, it was only in embers. Gabrielle put a hand on my shoulder and tapped lightly.

"But you love him?" Gabrielle asked me.

"I do."

"I am happy for you."

"Are you?" I whispered.

"Truly, I am. I only wish you had told me."

"We weren't... you know how it was. We were not meant to have those kinds of lives."

"No, you were not," Aphrodite said sadly. "Athena meant to rob you of your futures to punish your mother."

"How is that fair?" Gabrielle asked.

"It isn't. But fairness isn't something I would often equate with my brethren," Aphrodite admitted.

She was right.

"However," Aphrodite continued. "I have returned. I think it is only a matter of time until more of my brothers and sisters awaken. There is no need for The Twelve to rule in our stead any longer. I also see no need for you to live these sheltered lives."

Gabrielle looked hopeful. It was not a look I typically associated with her, but it gave life to her features and brightened her eyes.

"Until Athena awakens, my sisters, you are free."

FIFTY-NINE

Aphrodite, with the softest of touches, was able to restore our strength. It was time for us to hunt.

Gabrielle, Allison, and I, like the Creatures we were, tracked Sunee by scent. She cowered in a cave, covered in dust and debris, and surrounded by wreckage caused by the rebirth of a goddess.

"I only meant to free you from your chains," the witch pleaded.

"We will hear no more from you," Gabrielle intoned.

My sister's shadows swirled around her like dark magick. For a moment, I was sure she was preparing to deal with Sunee in the way we had dealt with the former Tisiphone, but the Megaera had other plans.

"This is for Evangeline," she purred.

Her witchblade plunged into the depths of Sunee's chest, straight into her heart. Blackness spread out from the wound immediately. Poison.

"I hope it's painful," Allison whispered gleefully.

She would fit right in.

I took my sisters by the hands, and we watched, stone-faced, as the witch struggled toward the death of her body. Her soul would be on its way to Tartarus when she finally succumbed, and the torture her physical body faced would be a thousand times worse for her soul.

I felt peaceful, and judging by the look on Gabrielle's face, she felt the same.

When Sunee's body was nothing more than a husk, we turned and walked away. We did not perform rites. We did not whisper blessings. Justice had been delivered.

———

We managed to retrieve Alex's unconscious form from Demetrius' rooms and take him back to the earth realm before he woke. When he did, though, it was to his new existence as a Creature. What kind of Creature, unfortunately, was still unclear.

"We don't know what we're dealing with quite yet," Demetrius explained to us.

Allison had gone for him the moment her brother had awoken. It was amusing to watch her test out the new Fury powers that had come to her in that rage-filled moment in the cavern.

"What does that mean?" Alex said, worry filling his features.

"You were turned by a Fury. Not a vampire or a wolves. You're exhibiting traits of at least a few different species. We'll monitor the situation."

Gabrielle had rolled her eyes while Allison smirked. She, I think, relished the idea of being able to teach her brother something about being a vampire, even if her time as one had been cut short.

I, of course, had been worried about how he might react once he realized the ramifications of his decision. I worried he would resent me for wanting him to live in what he had before seen as a lesser existence. And I had wanted him to live. But I expected the sadness that came in waves, too, and I held him through the worst of it. It would take more than the few weeks that had passed for him to truly come to terms with his new life. I was so grateful for Allison and her forgiveness of her brother. I don't know that I could have so readily offered grace as she did.

Communications were sent to the Fiagai to alert them of Alex's death. That's how he wanted it. He thought it best that his father and the brotherhood not commit their lives to avenging him. The message that was sent also included information about Allison's vampire death —Alex's attempt to protect his younger sister.

"You're stuck with me," Allison had murmured against his shoulder. "Forever."

He'd only smiled at her. None of us wanted to be apart any more than we had to. There had been so much loss. We packed up our manor, though in truth we wanted very little of what was still there. It was a bit early for us to move away from a city and alter our identities, but too much had happened, and Allison and Alex needed to be far away from Detroit. No one mentioned that they'd be able to return in just a few decades when their parents were gone. It was too melancholy and, perhaps, a bit too much to think about so early on in their long-lived existence. The reality of it would soon come to them soon enough, Gaia knew.

Aphrodite tried to convince us to live in her palatial rooms in Bellanca. When we declined, she offered us our own rooms, and we were forced to give our regrets a second time. The Creature riots had not ceased, and we knew that Aphrodite's re-entrance into our world could only be delayed for so long. Once she was known to be awakened, more chaos would ensue. There were plans to mitigate it, of course, but Demetrius could only do so much as he attempted to balance out the needs of The Twelve in the wake of so much betrayal from the atlanteans and the witches.

We had not yet found Ramiel and Atara. Gabrielle, though, was on the hunt. She wanted the heads of anyone who'd had anything to do with the death of Evangeline. Allison was just as invested. The two of them were terrifying and beautiful. *My sisters.*

With so many changes, it had been difficult for Alex and I to establish anything beyond our knowledge of our feelings for one another. I loved him as much as I had before. It truly did not matter to me that he was not Iason.

"I love you," I whispered to him each evening when we awoke in my bed.

"I know," he answered with a smile.

After all, I'd risked everything for him. The weight of that, for a while, could be ignored. For now, at our darkest and our lightest, we held tightly to the love between us. It was what I needed. I did not want to think about the future.

Gabrielle and I were working to be more communicative with one another. It helped to have Allison there, too, in our building of a new and different relationship. Our triad existed once more, and we were all determined that it be a healthier one.

A quiet memorial of sorts was held for our Guardian. Demetrius spoke the ancient blessings over the body, shrouded in thin white fabric. Flowers covered the base of the stone she had been laid upon. Additional blessings were said by some of the witches, as was custom, for Evangeline. For although Guardians had to forsake their birthright status as Creatures, it was seen as a true sacrifice by the various factions. It was one of the few things they managed to agree on. It was a solemn, quiet service.

Evangeline was entombed near other Guardians, most of whom had fallen in battle during the early Creature wars. It was almost unheard of for a Guardian to fall in modern times. A new Guardian had not been called forth in centuries. We knew, though, the call would soon go out, and another young Creature would be given to the Guardians for training.

For my sister and I, the pain was unimaginable. Evangeline was our earliest confidante, friend, and maternal figure. She had trained us night and day. We were taught the rules that protected us and kept us safe by her with a quiet, firm voice. We would never hear that voice again. And we mourned it. We mourned her. We were able to tell Aphrodite stories of her, though, and keep Evangeline's memory bright in unanticipated ways. So even in our sadness over the loss of our Guardian, we were able to find joy in getting to know our half-sister.

And we waited for the other gods to awaken. Because when they did, the realm of Creatures could not remain what it was.

ACKNOWLEDGMENTS

It will shock no one (who knows me, anyway) that I am crying while I'm writing this. But there is an entire community to thank for their support of me and this work. My village is such a cool one, and I am so grateful.

B, first and foremost, thank you. Thank you for giving me grace when I was so enveloped in this world of my own making that I barely functioned. Thank you for supporting me, for going to the library with me (to do what seemed like endless amounts of research), for cheering with me, and for doing your best to understand the highs and lows of this writer life. The balancing act is not an easy one, and if I have any modicum of success, it must be because of this little team of ours. I wouldn't trade our years together for anything. You are my best friend, my home, and my anchor.

Weston, you are a dream come true in so many ways. I love you. Thank you for being so understanding when Mommy needed writing and editing time. Thank you for asking questions and for cheering me on. You deserve many, many beach days.

To my parents, Marvin and Carla: you told me I could be anything I wanted, and I believed you. Thank you, and I love you.

To my siblings and their partners—Michael, Yuan, Katie, and Trevor: watching you go after your dreams has been so inspirational. I am so proud of each of you, and I can't believe I am lucky enough to be a big sister to you all. I love you so much, you weirdos.

To Brittany, the best editor a writer could have, but also a friend, a cheerleader, and a voice of reason when I need it: you were the one who saw what this story could be, and you are the reason it's in the world.

You bring out the best of my writing in a way that seems like pure magic. You are incredible. I remain, as always, in utter awe of you.

Nicole, you are light and joy in human form. I have never met anyone so thoughtful and generous. Your love and support have been instrumental and you, boo, are the rarest of gems. I love you so very much.

Desiree, Javier, Carey, Brittany, and Lindsay, my phenomenal writing group: you gave me the confidence to see this through. Your love for this world and its cast of characters helped me keep hold of my own, even when loving this story was so very, very hard. You are some of the best people I have ever met, and I am grateful for your wisdom, your kindness, and your creativity.

Readers, thank you for reading my story. I hope that you love these characters and this story as much as I do. This work is nearly 15 years in the making, and if that's not a sign that you should manifest your dreams, I don't know what is. You have something special; I know it. Don't hide it away. Don't let it sit on a shelf. Show your light to the world—we need it more than ever.

THE CHANGELING

SHAELYNN LONG

Excerpt from The Changeling: "The Witch in the Woods"

The fumes of Titian's latest concoction bloomed large and hazy purple like a terrible, overgrown violet. It was akin to something the overtasked gardeners of the Fae palace would magic into existence, or so Titian thought. She could too easily imagine a rose the size of a fully-grown Fae male towering over what had once been a lovely garden path of stone. Their pride was sometimes too much for sense to outweigh it, in her opinion. She'd seen it all firsthand, even if it had been decades since. There was little chance they'd changed.

Titian could too well recall the heady scent of violet that had been so thick in the air of Sansevieria, the capital, though it never quite permeated the musky perfume of magic which hung low like heavy clouds throughout the city.

A moment of admiration for her work burgeoned within her before the smell, noxious and as in want of avoidance as a skunk's rear end, overwhelmed everything. Throwing open dirty kitchen windows, Titian gagged and coughed into the cool, autumn air. She tried to ignore the nausea, focusing on the expanse of dark evergreens, with tall maple, oak, and walnut trees scattered amongst them. Despite her love for the quiet, isolated darkness of her forest cottage, the beauty was not enough to settle her stomach. It roiled with the sickness brought on by the awful smell of her potion and the anger that she still hadn't quite gotten the mixture correct.

She didn't care that she'd been self-taught, not having the benefit of potion masters in Faerie, nor the alchemical knowledge of wizards in Ostaria or any of the surrounding islands. Neither were open to someone like her. It still rankled, after all these years.

As she was clearing her nostrils and throat of the moon-forsaken smell with the clean air of the surrounding forest, she made the mistake of breathing in too deeply again and realized she'd been wrong. It was more like a skunk had bathed in sulfur and then waved its rear end around the entirety of the small cottage. Gagging again, her stomach nearly brought up the dinner of roasted vegetables eaten just an hour prior. Swallowing hard, Titian sagged on the dusty sill, gulping down air tinged with the scent of pine.

"Are ye all right?" a timid voice squeaked.

Titian's gray eyes shot up, roving the meager yard. Two scrawny human children stood a few yards away, skin and clothes nearly as dirty as the cottage's windows. Their eyes were wide, staring at Titian out of heart-shaped faces. Their features were carved into sharp distinction, likely by the starvation that plagued most of the surrounding villages. They were rather pale, more like the northern Ostarians instead of the citizens of the southern provinces where Titian had settled herself.

"I'm not interested in whatever it is you're selling," Titian called to them, already pulling the window closed against the dusky sky.

But the foul air closed around her again, finding its way down her throat, and once more she found herself gagging and spitting. Titian lay over the windowsill again, ultimately losing her dinner. The two children drew closer, caution in their slow, almost silent steps. That caution should have sent them running in the opposite direction if they had any sense at all.

Titian held up one finger as she finished retching. Then she turned the hand slowly, pointing the long, thin finger at them.

Titian was known to be Fae to those in the surrounding area, even if the truth was more complicated than that. The rumor prevented anyone from getting too friendly with her, even if they sought out her talents. She'd lived too long--one hundred and three years to be exact. Long enough to be untrusting of the Fae; long enough to be wary of the humans. Even if the ones that stood in front of her were not even into their adulthood, they were still a threat.

She would not allow herself to be tricked by any hooligans hoping to find something valuable enough to sell for a pint or a meal. She absolutely wasn't foolish enough to care for their survival, either. Some other poor sap could take the young ones in, perhaps allow them to bathe, give them food, earn whatever gratitude they were capable of. Titian knew enough of the world to know any kindness granted today wouldn't mean a thing in the days to come. They'd simply have to find more food and another safe place to sleep as time went on. It would be better to aid them in hastening the end instead.

"Do not come closer," Titian warned, throat hoarse from the retching.

The children stopped. They looked at one another, though, as if they thought it still might be worth their while to stick around. A silent sort of conversation seemed to pass between them, and Titian let loose a growl.

"Off with you," came the words.

Desperation must have made them stupid. Neither moved a muscle, not even so much as a twitch.

"Only need a bit o' somethin' to eat, if ye please," the young male said, his voice deep but scratchy with disuse... or overuse.

But Titian wouldn't think about that. She couldn't. One particular memory slashed its way into her consciousness, but even as she shut her eyes against it, the feeling of her throat, the way she would have sworn it had been shredded, was too easily recalled. The hurt. The blood. The pain that went deeper than skin--the kind that left a mark on a soul. Things that had to be done to survive were not unknown to her--not in the slightest. She would not relive her worst days and nights.

Not all of them had been in Ostaria. Faerie was just as cruel.

Moon damn them all, Titian thought.

No. She would not welcome these children and their problems in. They could find some other foolish Fae or mortal to fleece.

"Whatever she's cooking smells awful ripe, Kip," said the female.

The little imp didn't even try to whisper.

"And yet the moon-forsaken smell hasn't run you off yet, has it?" Titian snarled.

The horrid, little female had the gall to smirk!

"Haven't you heard the rumors about toying with the witch in the woods?" Titian asked, letting her inhuman eyes flash like a storm on the sea.

"So you are the witch," the girl said, hand on one hip. "Kip thought so, but I thought a witch's cottage might, I don't know, smell like freshly baked bread? Or pie? Who are you tryin' to catch with smells like that?"

Titian snarled again, her lip curling. The girl only eyed her a bit more closely. Out of her periphery, Titian saw the way the male one, Kip, was eyeing the pile of sick.

That was the final straw.

That he was so hungry he'd even consider something so foul was too much, even for Titian's cold, dark heart. She reached into the bowl of apples kept near the window and tossed four of them over.

Kip's lips moved to form words of gratitude, but Titian spoke first.

"Off with you!"

The young ones had the good sense to listen, and Titian sagged over the windowsill. She hated visitors. She didn't care if they were the humans who came seeking potions or poisons, Changelings needing shelter, or Fae wanting whatever their vast power hadn't already allowed them to take. Not one of them would have cared about Titian when she was without.

Fools and cowards, all of them.

———

To finish reading Titian's story, please check out *The Changeling* by Shaelynn Long, published by Conquest Publishing.

ABOUT THE AUTHOR

Shaelynn Long (she/they) is a writer and teacher from Michigan. They've previously published urban fantasy, as well as other poetry. Shaelynn has a fantasy romance novel, *The Changeling*, coming out in December 2025.

instagram.com/shaelynnlong

threads.com/shaelynnlong